JUAN IN AMERICA

JUAN IN AMERICA

BY

ERIC LINKLATER

MACDONALD PUBLISHERS · EDINBURGH

Other Linklater novels published
by Macdonald Publishers:

White Maa's Saga
Magnus Merriman
Laxdale Hall
Position at Noon

Publication subsidised by the
Scottish Arts Council

Published by
Macdonald Publishers
Edgefield Road
Loanhead
Midlothian EH20 9SY

ISBN 0 86334 015 6

Printed in Scotland by
Macdonald Printers (Edinburgh) Limited
Edgefield Road, Loanhead, Midlothian EH20 9SY

CONTENTS

TO
PHOEBE AND HAMILTON
GILKYSON
IN THEIR HOUSE
NEAR
VALLEY FORGE

PROLOGUE

This prologue forms a link in time between Byron's Don Juan and his Anglo-American descendant. Only readers with a rigid historical sense should start the book at page 15. *All others should begin at page* 63, *where the account of* JUAN IN AMERICA *really opens. Then, having completed the story, any academic curiosity about the hero's antecedents and youth may be satisfied by returning to these preliminary chapters.*

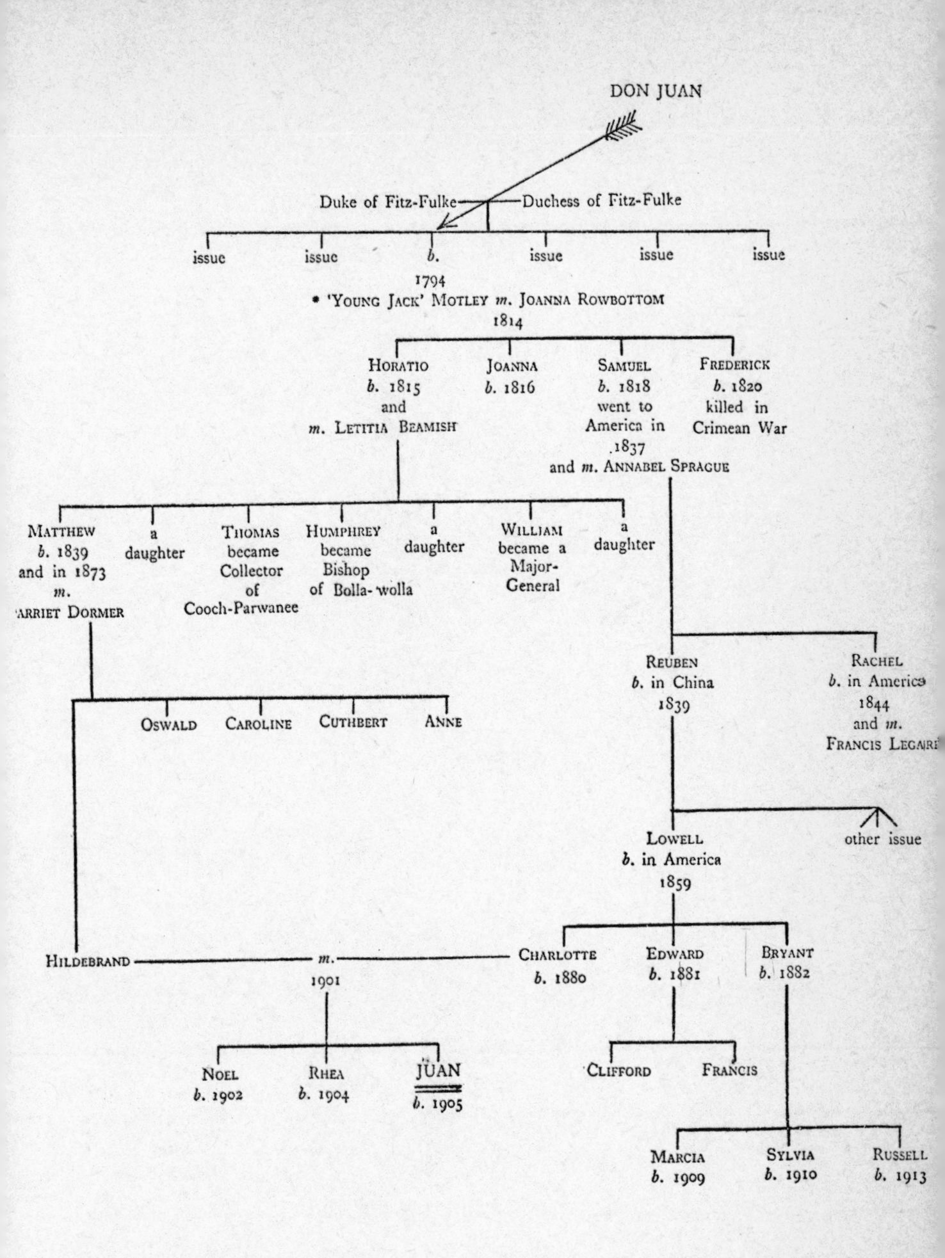

* Brought up in the household of the Rev. ABEL MOTLEY, he assumed his guardian's name.

THE FAMILY TREE

I

When the Duchess first had cause to suspect that all was not well with her she frowned, bit her nether lip, and tapped the floor with her simple low-heeled shoe. A frown on that bland forehead was like the wind-flaw on a saucer of milk that some petulant child has blown across. Her lip, when those gleaming teeth compressed it, blanched momentarily and filled with deeper red. And her shoe reiterated *tat-tat*, *tat-tat* on the responsive floor. After a few minutes, however, she controlled her emotion and decided calmly to wait until rumour – as it were – should be confirmed or happily denied. As people wait to-day when they hear the first of the three bells that warn them of a ship's going to sea, so the Duchess put aside alarm and resolved to wait awhile. For the first bell is not really dangerous.

A new moon came into the sky, a fragile cedar-shaving, very pale in the afternoon sunlight. Then the shaving strengthened and grew clear-cut and strong, a silver sickle that nightly waited for darker skies. And the sickle broadened perceptibly so that presently it became one of those curved Eastern knives whose shape is so much more dangerous than the simple harvest-hook, since they are meant to cut down men instead of grass. The Duchess remained calm until one night the kukri became a gourd, and quite evidently a gourd that was bent on swelling. Then her breathing quickened and she wished that it would hurry and die, so that she might know whether the first bell had been a false alarm or not. But the moon swelled and swelled in the most significant way and grew darker in hue, turning from the virgin pallor of the sickle to a ripe-looking yellow, and not content even with perfect rotundity it became swag-bellied and overladen as though some night it might burst and bring forth a thin new recruit for the choragium of the stars. But the Duchess only looked at it once when it was gibbous (she went early to bed that month), and saw nothing of the way it shrivelled and grew thin like an old, old lady in a low chair. Nor was she awake when finally it slipped out of the sky so unobtrusively whilst the east grew rosy-red and a cock ruffled its neck-feathers and crew lustily to its old master the sun.

But that morning the Duchess bit her lip again and spoke sharply to her maid; for the second bell had rung, and it seemed certain that by-and-by another little ship would put out into the curious, cold, dull, stormy, sometimes spice-island-studded, but ultimately unpredictable sea that is called life.

For a week she was frightened, avoided her friends, wept frequently, and prayed in great confusion. She had double cause for weeping in that hitherto she had been both virtuous and fortunate: virtue, that is, had been her normal companion, and on holidays (when virtue happened to fall asleep before she did) good fortune had protected her; and to lose in one short night luck and virtue too was a heavy blow. Nor could she find a proper god to take her sorrow to. All the Holy Virgins so patently believed in the merits of maternity; Jehovah thundered his blessings on a prolific stock and constantly bade his people wax fat and multiply and fill the earth with the teeming pledges of their affection and unabated vigour; even the Saints, ascetic in themselves, beamed softly at others' children. To whom could she pray for relief from what was obviously, in the opinion of Jehovah and the Saints, a precious gift? – for naturally she did not care to admit in her prayers that the blessing had not been begotten by the Duke. But pray she did, illogical and undirected and quite unpunctuated prayers, in the nebulous expectation that her petitions might find their way to some anonymous and amoral Beneficence unaccountably seated in the Kingdom of Heaven.

This week of tears and petitioning was followed by reaction and seven days' vivacious exasperation during which she entertained her friends with unusual gaiety and wit. Then came a week of grave and gradually happy contemplation. She avoided the world again and thought, with a kind of luxurious simplicity, of motherhood untroubled by subsequent responsibility or the previous acquiescence of society; of country lanes – she would go down to Gloucestershire – and sheep in a meadow; of children's laughter and the serenity of love untrammelled by convention; of the new world that seemed imminent, and of lofty ideals curiously swaddled in a soft homespun blanket; of the Rights of Woman – an appendix to *The Rights of Man* which Tom Paine had published not long before – and, in brief, of herself enjoying these rights, those lofty but simple ideals, that motherhood, and the sight of sheep in a Gloucestershire field.

The season was suitable for such contemplation. The Eighteenth Century was dying, and Time was already busy with a nursery for the Nineteenth: a plain and spacious room, for freedom and simplicity were essential to the coming child of Chronos. Young men no longer wore perruques and hair went unpowdered – partly because powder was taxed and flour scarce, but more because the revolutionists over in France had proved to the world that men could live freer, better lives if their hair grew shaggy and natural and their shirts were a little soiled. Ladies' dressmakers cast inspired eyes on the flowing lines of classical attire, or modelled their creations on a peasant's smock. All through the week of her new-found serenity the Duchess wore her hair in long ringlets *à la guillotine*, and a muslin wrapper which fell loosely from her shoulders to her heels. It had no waist, but a ribbon sash confined it slackly below her shoulders. Sometimes she even wore sandals. Probably this robe was partly responsible for the freedom of her mind, and undoubtedly, she thought, it would be increasingly useful as the blessing grew.

Allied with philosophy was a memory that she could not regret. The Duchess was, of course, English, aristocratic, and worldly. But a frolic strain hid in her heart that the House of Lords had seldom satisfied. For years she had whetted a secret appetite with dreams of something – of someone – at once wild and graceful, gallant but *en règle*, virile but not *farouche*. These qualities she had found, miraculously it seemed, in the handsome Spaniard who had been her fellow-guest at Norman Towers.*

How she loved him! His grave and handsome youth, his sweet singing-voice, his dancing, and the passion that slumbered lightly beneath a calm exterior. His carriage in a resplendent Russian uniform, his feats in war, of which he never spoke, but which Rumour had told with an excited voice. His riding to hounds which he, though a foreigner, did as prettily as an Englishman. The English admitted it – peers, Guardsmen, and hard-riding farmers – and swore approvingly. Nor after hunting did he fall asleep over his wine, but sat and talked of this and that, of fashion in Madrid and Petersburg, or deftly danced and looked at beauty with admiring eyes. Oh, a paragon! And to her eternal credit she had gone laughing to the love which she desired; not importunate, though thirsting; not jealous of her rivals, but contemptuous.

It is true that she would have been satisfied by love without so vital a pledge of it. She had already borne two children to the Duke, suffering considerable pain and great inconvenience, and really they were not worth it. But Juan's child might be different. She was lonely too, since Juan had been compelled to leave England in a hurry after running his sword through Lord Henry Amundeville's left lung – a foolish quarrel which helped no one. And the Duke was in Italy or Athens. Or

* A detailed account of Don Juan's entertainment in England can be found in the last three or four cantos of Byron's poem.

perhaps Constantinople. Somewhere on the rim of the Cradle of Civilisation. With luck he would stay there until another cradle had been filled and emptied again. . . .

The Duke, however, a whimsical gentleman, arrived home unannounced at the most inopportune moment, which happened to be early in June – the year was 1794. Finding his London house deserted he posted immediately into Gloucestershire, where he had large estates and a commodious mansion. The lodge, which he approached with a suitable ostentation of horns and sweating horse-flesh, was empty as his London house had been. More quietly, being somewhat perturbed, he drove up the long avenue which led to Fulke Court, and there the main door stood open though not a footman or maid, butler or boy in buttons, was to be seen. Greatly astonished he looked into one room and another, salon and library and the breakfast-room with the south exposure. Dust lay so thickly that even he could see it, and yet the rooms all looked as though people had recently moved in and about them. A book lay on a chair, some fruit on a table, and a white Persian cat rubbed its arched back against an open door. The Duke went upstairs.

He hesitated a moment before turning into the corridor which led to his wife's bedroom, and round the corner encountered a little man in wrinkled black, a nervous little man with a Bible in his hand and two days' beard on his face.

'Why, Motley,' said the Duke, 'what's the meaning of this strange unceremony?'

The Reverend Mr. Motley, who was the Duke's private chaplain, turned very pale and dropped his Bible with a crash.

'Oh, your Grace,' he stammered, 'your Grace has returned. The fig-tree putteth forth her green figs, but this is no place for your Grace, in the clefts of the rock and the secret places of the stairs.'

'Never mind the green figs,' said the Duke. 'Where is my wife, and where have all the servants gone to?'

Before Mr. Motley could reply – and the question was a

difficult one for him to answer – the door of the Duchess's room opened and Mrs. Motley emerged with a white bundle in her arms. She also turned pale, seeing who was there, and endeavouring to throw up her hands – her habitual reaction to surprise of any kind – let fall the bundle as Mr. Motley had let his Bible fall. This time, however, instead of a crash there was a little thud, and immediately following that a thin but piercing wail.

'My God,' exclaimed the Duke. 'Whose is that?'

But Mrs. Motley and Mr. Motley were both on their knees beside the small, salmon-coloured, feebly-moving object which had escaped from the roll of shawls and wrappers and now cried dismally for its first encounter with life. Moaning incoherent endearments Mrs. Motley gathered it up while her husband, tears suddenly streaming down his cheeks, babbled, 'Oh, so small and unwelcome in this house! Take not his garment for a surety. Be merciful, your Grace, and make me not to eat the bread of deceit lest afterward my mouth be filled with gravel!'

'Sweetums, sweetums,' crooned Mrs. Motley, 'Oh, hush, my lambkin, hush!'

'Whose child is that?' repeated the Duke in an agitated voice, but before anyone could answer a faint noise attracted their attention, a faint voice said 'Charles!' and in the doorway to which they turned stood swaying a tall figure in white. With a scream of apprehension Mrs. Motley thrust the infant into the Duke's arms – he all unwilling – and sprang to her mistress's side. She, making a gesture of weary magnificence, stretched a pale hand to the Duke; her bare arm was ivory, her golden hair in disarray; 'Charles!' she said again; and suffered Mrs. Motley to lead her back to bed.

There she lay still as death while the good Motley, whispering distracted blandishment, examined the whimpering child for injuries and the Duke, choking a little, looked with eyes that indignantly bulged towards the Duchess who lay so still in bed.

There was a marmoreal quality, as of the tomb, in her blanched and massive beauty. Expostulation froze at such a sight. The Duke thrust open a window to let out the sick-room air, but Mrs. Motley with an exclamation of dismay and one sweeping movement pulled it to and then threw a quilt across the child.

''Twill catch cold, your Grace,' she cried, and the Duke was abashed.

The Duchess returned to life. 'I have wronged you, Charles,' she murmured, and lay so still and impersonal in her exhausted beauty that no man could blame or even contradict her. The Duke cleared his throat, and in the succeeding silence a heavy sound of breathing was heard from the corridor outside.

'God damn his asthma!' roared the Duke in a sudden temper, and flung open the door. The chaplain, who had not dared enter without invitation, came hurriedly in.

'Death and life are in the power of the tongue,' he said, his voice all tremulous. 'By mercy and truth iniquity is purged. Oh, make her not the reproach of the foolish, your Grace!'

'Be quiet, Abel,' his wife reproved him.

'I am a silly dove,' he replied meekly. 'I am Ephraim, I am a cake not turned.' And humbly, his Bible in his hands, he fell to his knees at the foot of the Duchess's bed; a position – for its structure was lofty – in which he was quite lost to view.

'Who is the father of this child?' asked the Duke.

His voice, though loud, had a hollow tone, for he was uncomfortable in this stuffy keep of womanhood; a little frightened, faintly disgusted at the smell of human affairs and lavender water. Neither jealousy nor indignation could grow to proper dimensions in this unexpected air. And now the Duchess opened her eyes – slowly, for the lids were heavy with long lashes, and under the white lids were wet sapphires; her lips trembled apart and a filament of moisture stretched between them as they opened, like a silver string for Love's bow; and in a word she answered the Duke's question. Sweetly and simply, 'Love,' she said.

Thereupon the Duke retired, for it embarrassed him, and seemed slightly indecent, that a woman could talk of love in such circumstances. And in cooler air, walking on the fine smooth turf of an immense and meticulously gardened lawn, he tried to simplify the chaos in his mind.

He was a man of wayward enthusiasms and little balance. He was perpetually travelling, but whether in Paris, Naples, Rome, or Cairo, constantly protested that no country in the world was one tenth so fair or fine as England. He was a Whig and yet for the moment a whole-hearted adherent of the war party. Immediately after arriving in London he had looked into Brooks' and found Lord Grey and Mr. Fox all by themselves, so that his heart warmed to their loneliness. But outside the mob was singing lustily and giving three hundred and three huzzas for Lord Howe, the news of whose victory over the French on the Glorious First of June had just reached town; and the Duke, in the scandalised silence of Brooks', cheered too, and even danced a jig in front of Mr. Fox, whose buff waistcoat shook with anger. And yet never in his life had the Duke felt so affectionately disposed to Mr. Fox. They had the same Christian name. 'Charles,' he said, 'damn my immortal soul, Charles, if he hasn't sunk a dozen ships of the line!' And he rushed out to join the mob, though even in his excitement he detested the smell of a crowd.

His mind had been further upset by reading a novel called *Caleb Williams* while posting down to Gloucestershire. Its author, Mr. Godwin, was some kind of a philosopher, and the Duke regarded philosophy of any sort with superstitious reverence. To find Godwin, then, mocking the sacrament of marriage, thrusting the whole moral code into a pillory, not only shocked him profoundly but seriously shook his faith in conventional standards. Perhaps Godwin was right, and sin was not what ordinary people imagined it to be? Perhaps he had no business to feel his wife's infidelity like a spear in his side, and anger against her crowding his brain?

Suddenly he felt unhappy, crushed between rival creeds, and sick of the apparent necessity for reproaches. He only wanted to talk to her, not to scold her, but to discuss Caleb Williams's adventures with her, and – he grew more cheerful at the thought – to tell her about Howe storming through the narrow seas and smashing the damned Frenchmen to smithereens; and of poor Charles James Fox, all fat and lonely in his blue coat and big dusty boots. Oh, a great world it was, with English topsails proudly on the horizon, and redcoats rampaging (so he had heard in London) through the West Indies, and philosophers teaching freedom – if only duchesses would enjoy it more discreetly.

And then little Motley came out to him, his black coat green and dusty in the sunlight, and said that he had brought up a bottle or two of port from the old bin in the smaller cellar.

'Wine on the lees, well refined, your Grace,' he said, buttressing his timid soul with Isaiah and breathing hoarsely.

Awakened from his reverie the Duke remembered the strange absence of servants. 'Where are they?' he asked.

Mr. Motley looked imploringly at his patron, and nervously twisting his hands said, 'Her Grace sent them all away, your Grace, trusting herself in the hour of darkness to me, though I am not worthy, and to Mrs. Motley who worketh willingly with her hands and whose candle goeth not out by night. They will return in a week, or two weeks, and Mrs. Motley and I will care for the child.'

'Here?' asked the Duke.

'The living of Belfry is vacant.' Mr. Motley looked modestly at the grass, which he patted softly with one foot.

'It is yours,' said the Duke moodily.

'Oh, your Grace!' cried Mr. Motley, his face suddenly so radiant that it made his shabby old coat look greasier and greener than ever. 'Oh, your Grace, Our Father which seeth in secret rewardeth openly!'

'Don't talk to me about fathers,' said the Duke.

But as he had never seen or heard of Don Juan, he had nothing tangible that he could tack jealousy on to, and he felt no particularised animosity towards the child. The shock that he had experienced drew his attention very strongly to the Duchess, however, who in consequence submitted to more babies for three successive years. The cuckoo in this growing brood was put out to board with the Motleys in the vicarage of Belfry, where he thrived indifferently. The lower part of his spine had suffered damage of some kind when Mrs. Motley dropped him, and his legs grew weak and spindly. True, he seemed to be a bright child, but all the Motley children and all the village children – perhaps all the children in Gloucestershire – had thick, strong, straight legs that carried them tirelessly wherever they might go, and so young Jack – thus unremarkably he was called – suffered in comparison until the year 1800 when a serious epidemic of smallpox swept the country.

In the nearby village of Berkeley lived Dr. Edward Jenner, whose experiments in vaccination had for some years been the talk of the countryside. The Duke had succumbed almost at once to the novelty of Dr. Jenner's theory, and was indeed one of the first to be scratched. But the Duchess, who disliked cows and Dr. Jenner with an equal mind, would have none of it, nor would she suffer her children to go near the odious man. The Motleys were in the same mind as the Duchess – because of an obscure verse which Mr. Motley had found in Leviticus or Deuteronomy – and none of their children had been vaccinated either. And yet all had so far escaped the pocking which was their due, and Dr. Jenner was not too well pleased.

But in 1800, when the disease re-appeared, the Duke – who happened to be at Fulke Court – rode over to the vicarage of Belfry and boldly kidnapped young Jack, whom he took straight to Dr. Jenner's house in Berkeley. And there the boy was vaccinated in several places.

By-and-by the smallpox came into Gloucestershire and spread with awful speed. Cottage and manor, tavern and farm, vainly closed their windows against it; vainly the villagers avoided their neighbours; vainly burnt stinking weeds and drank the water of sour-smelling herbs. Into every house the red scourge came creeping. At the Belfry vicarage Mr. Motley fell first, and one by one the eight young Motleys felt cheeks grow hot, eyes sore, and tongues dry. Two or three of them died. And when Mrs. Motley had nursed the rest to recovery, she too fell sick.

At Fulke Court the servants got it first and in a drove took to their garrets and attics. Then the children fell sick: that lubberly little boy, the Earl of Spoon, his sisters Caroline, Theodosia, and Fanny, and the infant William Edward. The Duchess, panic-stricken, sent imperatively for Dr. Jenner, but before he arrived she too was in bed, flaming hot of skin and anguished in mind.

Only the Duke and young Jack escaped infection. They only, of all at Fulke Court and the Belfry vicarage, had smooth cheeks when finally smallpox died out of the stricken country. The lubberly little Earl of Spoon was left with a face like a colander, and his mother, poor lady, was no better. All his brothers and sisters were hideously scarred, and the infant William Edward survived with no eyebrows and very little nose. Mr. Motley lost an eye and round the vacant orbit clustered a number of lesser foramina. Pitted and perforated like honeycomb was the row of faces that gathered at last in the vicarage pew to give thanks for their delivery. As tunelessly they sang their hymns it seemed that the pious sound escaped from a score of orifices in each pock-marked visage.

But young Jack grew richer by the epidemic. The Duke was so pleased by his foresight in having had him vaccinated that he considered himself – as doubtless he was – young Jack's preserver, if not his creator. The boy had guineas slipped into his pocket, and was presently sent to Eton, where he was very unhappy, for his legs were quite unreliable, and Eton considered well-shaped calves and a sturdy thigh to be matters of importance.

While Jack grew up England became poor at home and powerful abroad. Six dukes – but not the Duke of Fitz-Fulke – joined Mr. Wilberforce's Association for the Better Observance of the Sabbath, and the Archbishop of Canterbury let it become known that he was deeply and unfavourably impressed by the 'torrent of profaneness' with which men outfaced the tribulations of their time. Nelson, after sinking a prodigious number of French and Spanish ships of war, exchanged his mutilated body for the perfection of immortality. As if to allay the anxiety caused by Mr. Malthus's theories, war seemed indissolubly wedded to the life of the world. The teeming wombs and regrettably fruitful loins of humanity that threatened to eat the earth bare of crops and cattle were themselves more seriously threatened by muskets and bayonets in India and North America, in all the more important parts of Europe, in islands of the sea and the dubiously-christened Cape of Good Hope. And soldiers, with all their wounds in front, still bled copiously behind, for Wellington's colonels believed in the cat-o'-nine-tails, and indeed made a very useful army with its help. Wheat rose to a fantastic price and Britain's national debt became a fabulous figure, something like Napoleon. And then came Waterloo, after which all the sailors and soldiers were unemployed and discovered – what they had not guessed for years – that peace on a pension of fourpence a week, or so, was not worth fighting for.

But young Jack Motley was not concerned with war. His legs were scarcely fit to carry him into a battle and certainly would have been unable to fetch him out of one, which is often a more hurried matter. Instead he lived very comfortably – once he had finished with Eton – on a generous allowance from the Duke. The latter, in the early years of the century, had gradually concentrated all his errant enthusiasms on agriculture, and with the constant rise in wheat prices had become enormously wealthy. His pock-marked family were but a small expense to him – the Duchess died of a cancer in 1818 – and so young Jack, who looked handsome enough on a sofa, was exceedingly well provided for. And when at the age of twenty he proposed to marry the penniless eldest daughter of a half-pay naval captain, the Duke very handsomely bestowed on him the small but agreeable estate of Mallieu and a sum of £10,000 in the Funds.

Joanna Rowbottom, who thus became young Jack's wife, took her father with her when she married and Mallieu proved a charming anchorage for his old age – he lived to ninety-eight. Captain Rowbottom had lost his right eye at the battle of the Nile and his left arm at Trafalgar. The company of this disabled hero prevented young Jack from becoming too satisfied with life, and his gruff voice, his tales of war and political injustice and the havoc which both had evidently wrought upon him, were valuable factors in the education of Jack's children. For it cannot be denied that the latter was a feeble parent, and Joanna, a placid creature with a pretty complexion and fond of cream, was no better. Young Jack read poetry and philosophy: the poetry of Mr. Wordsworth and Mr. Coleridge, the philosophy of Mr. Godwin – to whose philosophy, indeed, he partly owed his present comfort. He read the disturbing new poetry of Keats and Shelley, and was properly astonished. Somehow or other, between *Endimion* and *Cenci*, his brood was begot and born: Horatio in the year of Waterloo, Joanna some fifteen months later, Samuel in 1818, and Frederick in 1820. And thereafter young Jack sank into a premature decline.

He lay long abed, his physical strength diminished rapidly, and he avoided his wife.

Perhaps it was poetry that confused his mind and sapped his manhood; perhaps the injury to his spine grew worse; perhaps he brooded over his bastardy, about which he had always been sensitive. Whatever was the cause he fell ill, and his wasted legs were soon matched by hollow face and bony hands. Poor Joanna's pink and white cheeks were beslubbered with constant tears and her father strove piously to moderate his quarterdeck voice. The children went tiptoe and servants spoke hoarsely in whispers. Oh his thirtieth birthday young Jack slept long. At nine o'clock in the morning he slept, at ten he slumbered still, and at noon he was past rousing.

There was little more than his name to put on his tombstone – and even the name was not his own. He had helped to prove Dr. Jenner's theory; he had provided an old sailor with a good home; and he had begotten four children, three of whom were sturdy youngsters. Such was the brief and uneventful life of one conceived in the Gothic darkness of true romance.

II

Within a year or two of young Jack's death Mallieu became a happier place. The children, though none of them promised the disreputable vitality of their Spanish grandfather, were strong – except Joanna – and Captain Rowbottom made for their instruction working models of a sloop, a frigate, and even a seventy-four. Sometimes he would show them the round glossy stump of his arm and carefully explain where the rest of it had gone. Old Mr. Motley came over once or twice a year from Belfry and offered advice on education. He lived long enough to confirm all four children, with whom he was a great favourite – like their grandfather, whom they adored, he was short of one eye, and so had Lord Nelson been, after whom Horatio was named.

Only one incident marred the serene growth of young Jack's family. Their mother took them to Brighton for a brief holiday, and there they chanced to see at close quarters the

Duke of Cumberland. The encounter had an unhappy consequence, for Joanna, a nervous and delicate child, went into hysterics at the sight of his plum-coloured awful face. Her shrieks attracted the attention of the Duke, who visibly snarled. Joanna's pitiable excitation was aggravated, her shrieks grew even louder, and a crowd assembled. A doctor, fortunately among the spectators, bled her on the spot, but her condition scarcely improved. Hurriedly the Motleys returned to Gloucestershire, but for many weeks Joanna was plagued with nightmares and her mental development was completely arrested. She grew, however, into the handsomest of the family and in due course married a neighbouring squire whose own intellectual capacity was equally negligible.

Horatio became a thoughtful and ambitious young man, and circumstances turned his attention to politics. In 1837 he lost some money by speculating in one of the many bubble companies of that year, and in 1839 he happened to be visiting friends in Monmouthshire when the Chartists rioted in Newport. He was justly incensed at the state of affairs which let a man lose more than a thousand pounds in a few weeks, and his anger rose alarmingly when he discovered that the Chartists demanded such things as universal suffrage, a secret ballot, and abolition of the property qualification for Members of Parliament.

In order to stop the rot he determined to enter Parliament himself.

Unfortunately for Horatio's ambition there was no immediate opportunity for him to acquire a seat. The Whigs were in power, and for two years more they did their best to drive the country to the devil while Horatio fretted impotently in Gloucestershire. But perhaps impotent is not the word to describe him, for he occupied this period of political inactivity by marrying Letitia Beamish, the daughter of a neighbouring magnate, and becoming, without waste of time, a father. And then in the General Election of 1841 Peel led his party into power and Horatio was magnificently one of them.

In the House he early established himself as an energetic speaker interested in whatever was being discussed, and in his own county he was well thought of as a model landlord and a liberal friend to all who voted for him, so that for thirty years without interruption he retained his seat and wondered more and more that his virtue went unrewarded by his party chiefs. But not till Lord Beaconsfield's ministry in '74 was Horatio rewarded, when he was given the Mastership in Lunacy. The office gratified him immensely, with its gift of precedence over Companions of the Bath and the eldest sons of younger sons of Earls. Without a sigh he abandoned the hopes of Cabinet rank that he had cherished for many years and devoted his stipend of £2,000 to improving Mallieu Hall.

The alterations and additions were the work of his eldest son Matthew, who was already known as one of the most promising architects of the day. Where his artistic talents came from no one knew, but if mystery surrounded the vital source of his inspiration, the expression of it became yearly more visible. He built banks, churches, country mansions, museums, libraries, memorial fountains, family vaults, barracks, prisons, railway hotels, and hostels for fallen women. In astonishing profusion they rose over England, and no one was ever in doubt as to who had designed a Motley bank or a Motley hotel, for his personality was carved upon the rock. Not that he adhered rigidly to one style, as some of his contemporaries did. He was master of all, and in that was he most clearly the son of his father who had all his life been willing, and was still, to address the House on social reform or the Schleswig-Holstein question, on Free Trade and the Church in Ireland, on topics so widely disparate as penny postage and side-wheels versus propellers for battleships. And with kindred universality his son Matthew built after the fashion of the Italian Renascence, in the manner of Gothic art, or according to the current ideas of Scots baronial architecture.

To see him was to believe in his genius. A tall man, burly,

side-whiskered, bowed and a little paunchy even at thirty-five, he was remarkable chiefly for his eyes. They were large, brown, and calm in their expression. Under a broad white forehead and straight brows they looked out so clear, so mild, so full of moral assurance, that one immediately recognised the power of the soul to which unquestionably they were windows. His mouth too, under a long and righteous lip, was set in calm and heavy lines. His chin was powerful and smoothly shaved. A man, one felt, who could build pyramids with a pious look about them. And that was his secret. Everything he built was an argument for morality. That there are sermons in stones is part of our creed, but they are generally mute. Different were the ashlars Matthew cut. Under his eye they became eloquent, and bricks grew positively evangelical.

Horatio's younger children were also successful, though none achieved so monumental a fame as Matthew. Thomas joined the East India Company and became Collector of Cooch-Parwanee. Humphrey went into the church and was made, after long service, Bishop of Bolla-wolla in Australia. William, though as a junior officer he incurred the dislike of his superiors, died a Major-general; he was one of the first to suggest dry canteens for the Army, he deprecated blasphemy as an aid to instruction, and was affectionately known to the Royal Artillery as Piles on Parade. Horatio's daughters – he had several – gave him no anxiety, for they all married worthy men to whom they had been introduced by their brothers. The family indeed conducted itself admirably, having been taught from youth that life was real, earnest, and a good field for the investment of natural or acquired talents.

But it is Matthew with whom we are concerned. In 1873 he married a Miss Harriet Dormer, by whom he had issue Hildebrand, Oswald, Caroline, Cuthbert, and Anne. They, with their father's ever increasing wealth, were brought up in surroundings of righteous prosperity. As children they were patted on the head by Lord Salisbury, Lord Tennyson, Lord Lytton, Lord Wolseley, Lord Rowton, and many worthy commoners. In adolescence and young manhood their eyes grew used to the massive splendour of those magnificent years between the Queen's two jubilees. They were indisputably the heirs of all the ages, and when grandfather Horatio died in 1886 he was surrounded by grandchildren who seemed destined to perpetuate, and even to exalt, the tradition of honourable service to England – if not to lunacy – which he had so worthily established. But, in spite of their environment of success, they never became so successful as the previous generation of Motleys. Even in their mother's eyes – for the Dormers, too, had their traditions – they were not to be wholly satisfactory. Caroline, for instance, became a dreamer; Oswald played baccarat with unfortunate results; Anne, at seventeen, demanded a career for herself; Cuthbert, enlisting in a Yeomanry regiment, was to get killed in dispute about one of South Africa's less important kopjes; and even Hildebrand, to whom, as the eldest, his parents' hopes were most obviously pinned, gave some cause for anxiety by his reluctance to study and the apparent difficulty he found in dealing with even the simplest of abstract ideas.

In 1890 their father became Sir Matthew Motley. This was another disappointment, for he had expected a peerage and often murmured an anticipatory 'Lord Mallieu' to his shaving mirror; tasting the syllables, the *aw* in Lord said slowly, the *a* in Mallieu – pronounced Mally – very short and given a bell-like clarity by attention to the liquid *l's* behind it. Lawd Mally. Even the final *y* had a distinctive quasi-aspirate sound when Matthew ennobled the image in his shaving glass. His brown eyes, lambent and clear, had the exquisite quality of eyes painted by Vandyke. His nose was dignified and pure in colour. Slowly he soaped his chin. Lawd Mally. The razor made an elfin harshness on his healthy skin. Lawd and Lady Mally. The new asylum at Chippenhurst was almost finished and rarely had he looked on any concept of his brain with such pride. Because of his father, Matthew had been given a free hand with the Chippenhurst institution, and with singular light-heartedness he had added to a utilitarian Georgian basis some Turkish features, of which a large blue dome and four minarets were the first to catch a traveller's eye. Minarets, perchance, from which unhappy lunatics might hear the muezzin of returning sanity, a dome like that inverted bowl we call the sky – for not wantonly – though with unusualgeniality – had Matthew wedded these heathen novelties to a Georgian frame. Lawd Mally, he repeated, and dried his face with a Turkish towel – curious, was it not, how all unmeant the Islamic motif returned? He smiled beneath the obscuring napkin.

When the postman came, and he discovered that he was not Lord Mallieu after all, but only Sir Matthew Motley, his anger was terrible.

Then with an effort he controlled himself, and regarding his family, silent round the breakfast table, said harshly: 'Let this morning's news be a lesson to you. Ingratitude, whether to parents or to other benefactors, is the lowest sin of all. It springs from a warped and jealous heart, unable through vice or the faults of nature to entertain fine feelings and generous thoughts. Beware of ingratitude in yourselves, but learn, as I have learnt, to encounter the manifestation of it in others with Christian fortitude and the unshaken calm of one who is the master, thank God, of his own soul.'

With heavy steps Sir Matthew left the room and spent the morning designing mausoleums for his enemies.

III

Two of young Jack's family have remained so far almost unnoticed: Sam, who went to America, and Frederick, the youngest of the family. Frederick joined the Navy and his grandfather Rowbottom's lack of influence got him sent to the West African station. He saw many ports and finally died of wounds, unmarried, beneath the guns of Sebastopol. His brother Horatio was horrified at the news, and with all the eloquence at his command urged the House of Commons to prosecute the war in the Crimea with unceasing energy and sternest determination. The children, who had rarely met their uncle, were not upset by his death, but old Captain Rowbottom was heart-broken. He refused to speak and lived thereafter almost entirely in one of the attics of Mallieu Hall. For eight years – a tottery old man with rheumy eyes – his chief occupation was peeping at the fields of Gloucestershire through a spy-glass, waiting for French or Spanish sails to show above the hedges. At last he saw them – they were white cows going slowly to be milked – and piping in a cracked voice, 'Nelson expects you all to do your duty!' dropped dead of heart-failure.

Sam, in America, flourished exceedingly. With an introduction from Baring Brothers he joined the firm of Russell, Sturgis and Company, merchants of Boston. From his stool in their warehouse he looked out at sailing ships. The harbour was full of them. Every day they came in, exquisitely limned against the oyster-pale sky. Every day they sailed out to trade with amazing cities: Calcutta and the ports of China, and all the spice islands in between. Every day as he wrote in his calf-bound letter-book Sam snuffed the fragrance of foreign cargoes, the smell of tar, and the pungent odour of rope. He became enthusiastic over his new estate, and indeed it was a brave sight to watch commerce moving under white wings, as though sea-birds should bring gold to men. The agreeable appearance of the merchants was also remarkable. To see them on 'Change at one o'clock was to see the law-givers and soldiers of Rome; wisdom and not cunning gave life to their features, their whiskers framed a manly beauty, they stood erect, and their jutting eyebrows threw the shadow of a lofty destiny. And if the merchants were handsome their sea-captains were superb. Storm and sleet had thrashed their New England bone to something imperial, wearing away all that was soft and unworthy and leaving, as if carved in bronze or marble, the grave contours of beauty. The habit of command sat easily upon them, and their lips that fitted comelily to psalms ashore became at sea the rim of a terrible trumpet whose voice divided the hurricane and wrought obedience on the fore-topsail yard.

With such a one, Captain Jonathan Sprague, Sam presently sailed to Canton, China, in a Medford-built Indiaman of five hundred tons burthen. His object, in which his employers concurred, was to gain experience by personal contact with the firm's consignors in foreign parts. But the divine energy of America, which had inspired him from the moment he landed, would not let him idle away so many weeks as a passenger, and he very soon set about learning the ancient craft of the sea. Before they rounded the Horn Sam could hand, reef, and steer, and set a topgallant sail. But one day, going aloft to send down a royal yard he came down with it, quite unintentionally, and was fortunate to escape with a broken collar-bone, some bruises, and the tip knocked off the olecranon process of his ulna. While physically inert, following this accident, his unconquerable spirit found fresh occupation courting the captain's daughter Annabel.

Now Captain Sprague had no cause to love the English – for he had spent some trying months in Chesapeake Bay during the war of 1812 – but Sam's instinct for seamanship had made a favourable impression on him, and Annabel, a lovely creature with no political animus whatsoever, was so clearly in love with young Motley, that he did not seriously oppose their wedding, which took place following the ship's arrival in Canton.

After three years in China, during which he learned a lot about the commercial possibilities of tea, silk, and opium, Sam and his wife returned to Boston, taking with them some native servants, furniture, tea-sets, paintings, screens, and so forth.

He had prospered during his sojourn in Canton and presently bought a ship of his own. Captain Sprague joined him in a mutually profitable alliance; they bought more ships; two were in the China trade, two went round the Horn for Californian hides, and two brought coffee from Brazil. These were good ships of their kind, but presently a new sort of craft appeared on American waters, something narrow and deep with cutaway bows and the lines of a thoroughbred. This was the clipper, the ultimate perfection of her kind. Motley, Sprague and Company bought clippers. Donald Mackay himself designed them – that Phidias of the sea – and when Sam Motley saw the first of his new ships he wept openly to think such loveliness was his. But on her return from California he had no time for tears, being too busy computing the profits on potatoes that had sold at sixteen dollars a bushel. A handsome profit, he felt, on such humble vegetables; but the 'Forty-niners were ravenous men and seldom lived long enough to regret extravagance. And ten dollars a dozen for eggs. Well, they were good eggs originally and the voyage had only taken a day or two over three months – that was the advantage of a clipper ship, for eggs carried in an ordinary bottom would be six months old at least before they reached the voracious gold-diggers.

Though in other ways he accomplished far more than his brothers, Sam's family was a small one. The lovely Annabel bore him two children only, Reuben and Rachel. Rachel became a big disappointment and – so many thought – a traitor, but Reuben was an astonishingly precocious boy – he had been suckled by a Chinese nurse – and at the age of sixteen or seventeen persuaded his father to sell the clippers and keep his money ashore. Sam, though loth to do it, consented and got rid of them all before the Indian Mutiny brought freights tumbling down to nothing. With new capital he enlarged his investments in real estate between Salem and East Point. That interesting coast was becoming fashionable, and sea-side farms on it were soon to be as valuable as Californian goldfields. With the assistance of Reuben sensible and attractive buildings were erected, communications improved, and profits reaped that exceeded the forty dollars a ton of China voyages. But Sam never got the pleasure out of brick and shingles and stone that ships had given him, and the white bellying of great sails. He and his Annabel, growing old, talked more and more of that first voyage of theirs, and rehearsed by firelight the many sails of a tall ship, from mainsail to little moonsails and the outflung frippery of skysails and stu'nsails. They grew tender over memories of lobscouse and dandyfunk, and technical about such obscure arts as splicing, seizing, graffing, and pointing; or boasted of trade-winds and day after day with the lee-rail buried in a singing smother of windy sea.

But there was no sentiment about Reuben. Reuben married well at nineteen and made millions during the Civil War by selling boots and brandy to the Federal Government. Not only boots and brandy, but shirts, biscuits, bandages, blankets, tombstones, and everything else he could think of. And as these commodities brought in handsome returns he invested the proceeds in railroads; and when the war was over added banking to his interests, and while still in command of all his faculties became exceedingly rich.

At forty he found himself a grandfather, for his son Lowell had also married soon after learning to shave, and promptly begotten a daughter upon the compliant person of his wife – a pleasant girl. And old Sam was still alive. Indeed old Sam was only sixty-three when his great-grand-daughter Charlotte was cutting her first tooth. The thought of his family branching and budding with this alarming rapidity made Reuben unusually serious, for he saw it suddenly as only a single strand in the vast network of America. And every strand in that colossal net was similarly engaged in thrusting out fibres that promptly forked and split into still propagating filaments. And thousands upon thousands of strange fish from overseas were coming into the net: Swedes and Slavs and philogenitive Sicilians. . . . As if in the hold of a fisherman's boat Reuben looked up and saw the hatch above him dark with creatures of the sea that were being cast in on top of him: haddock and cod and flatfish and eels, thumping and writhing and filling the hold without order or plan. . . . 'We must educate them,' said Reuben, and became in that moment a patriot, a philanthropist, and the founder of what was to become the eighth largest university in the United States.

All the energy that had characterised his commercial career he now concentrated on the education, humanisation – or if not these at least graduation – of Americans yet unborn; of Americans so far existing only in the spermaries of Bulgaria and Norway, in the ovular content of Bavaria and Portugal and the Chersonese. He bought land, architects, politicians, engineers, landscape gardeners, bricklayers, contractors, bankers, artists in stained glass, woodcarvers, and finally some professors. Father Sam Motley shared son Reuben's enthusiasm. The passion of building fell on them, the joy of creating some enduring thing in this young and empty giantland. Grandson Lowell, realising the social increment of large-scale philanthropy, more coldly allied himself with their enthusiasm. And in the western hill-fastnesses of the state of New York, Motley College slowly came into being. In the freshness of spring, birds hushed their singing at the noise of hammers on wood or stone. For succeeding summers masons and carpenters wrought according to their skill, and in the bright red autumn and the smooth white winter building went on till Motley College was ready for its first students.

Its development as a cultural force fell more and more into the hands of grandson Lowell, who kept abreast of modern thought – not always strictly academic – and in time added to the original foundation such departments as accountancy, hotel-management, bee-keeping, journalism, and psychiatry.

These deviations from the classical route were welcomed by enlightened opinion, and in due course the college was styled a university.

As it grew so did Lowell's first-born, Charlotte. She became beautiful, graceful, good-humoured, accomplished, charming, and in some respects sensible. She had light brown hair, a clear skin, grey eyes, and walked with an air of frank assurance, carrying her head high. But she did not keep up with modern thought so completely as the college. In certain matters she retained all her life a romantic outlook, and it was she who decided that contact should be re-established with the Motleys in England. Occasional correspondence had crossed between the families, but neither was greatly interested in the activities of the other. What were a Master in Lunacy and Victorian architecture to the masters of the sea and the great builders of New England? And how could the raw brightness and noisy assertion of America attract people sitting in the old brick-walled garden of Mallieu Hall, enjoying their tea and strawberries, half-hearing the bees, and mildly cognisant of flowers, tempered sunlight, smooth turf, and the ordered security of their lives? The infrequent letters that dared the Atlantic were polite but not affectionate.

And then Charlotte spoke. England to her – before she had seen it – was Kenilworth Castle with Sam Weller at the gate. It was Canterbury and the Cheshire Cheese. It was a mixture of Vanity Fair, the Last of the Barons, and Zuleika Dobson, with a dash of Shakespeare, a charm that refused analysis, and a damned stupid air of self-satisfaction. She did not, however, condescend to this particularity when she told her parents that she felt inclined to pay England a visit.

She merely said, 'I should like to be presented, and the Queen is old. . . .'

Old she was, in a white imperial caducity, but the awful power of sovranty was in those plump hands, and her aged majesty was incontestably splendid. . . . And presently

Charlotte was taken to a cricket match to see Hildebrand Motley make eighty-two runs for the Gentlemen.

IV

Charlotte became an Anglophile, and was not quite happy in her love. She wanted rather more than England seemed ready to give her. Day after day she woke with an excited apprehension that something splendid was going to happen, and day after day she was disappointed.

Cousin Hildebrand, though handsome enough to win anyone's favour, was an imperfect complement to some of her moods. At times he would listen to conversation with an almost stupid stare. His slightly protruding blue eyes looked at such moments like glass eyes, and his smoothly brushed hair and fair moustache also assumed an artificial appearance, as though they had been hired from some very good theatrical costumier. But no really dull man could score, as Hildebrand did, off Hearne's bowling, and hit Rhodes all round the wicket. Nor would a fool be likely to have such charming manners as Hildebrand's. And yet. . . .

Oh, somewhere lying snug must be the things one wanted! Somewhere in ambush, or disguised, was surely that last little bit of wildness or glamour, that elusive ferment which would bring all the cask to life. . . . With a freakish twist of her mind Charlotte thought suddenly of Hildebrand's young brother Cuthbert, who had left home to get killed in South Africa. A pimply youngster with a sullen mouth, gone off to fight in his country's war. . . . Surely Hildebrand, so splendid to look at, would have been a better champion! And Hildebrand, all unperturbed and without a blemish on his face, continued to play cricket. It was very curious.

The American Motleys had cherished their family tree, in spite of its bastard graffing, with a great deal more pride than their English cousins had, and there probably survived in Charlotte some quality of the Duchess of Fitz-Fulke; whose portrait by Sir Thomas Lawrence she had recently admired at Burlington House. Like the Duchess she was gay and independent; she had a frolic strain in her; and under the double curtain of assurance and high spirits lay a tiny moonlit well of excitement, like that which faintly bubbled in the hearts of Icenian girls when the Romans camped at their forest-edge. And whose lips would first find that antique spring? Whose tongue would be refreshed by its swift and secret waters?

Hildebrand playing cricket at Lords was a magnificent sight. Opening his shoulders to hit expansive sixes, running between the wickets, fielding perilously at cover-point: these were pictures of athletic perfection. Only when caught in some alien tide of artistic or scientific conversation did Hildebrand become incomplete and appear to have glass eyes and wear a flaxen wig. And when he fell in love he wooed as the cricketer Hildebrand, not as the wax-faced auditor of poets or biologists. His love-making was graceful and accomplished, whole-hearted and expressed with a bright energy. Charlotte protested in vain. He treated her opposition like loose bowling and eventually carried her to church with pride and aplomb, as he had many a time carried his bat to the pavilion. And Charlotte was temporarily satisfied, for the England she had dreamed of and passionately desired was, it seemed, no more than England animated by an Englishman in love.

The American Motleys crossed for the wedding – which had to be postponed because of the Queen's death – but the family reunion was only indifferently successful. Father Sam Motley and his Annabel were both dead by this time –

> 'He first deceas'd, she for a little tried
> To live without him, liked it not, and died' –

but Reuben and Mrs. Reuben came, with two sons and their wives, a daughter and her husband, Mrs. Lowell's two sisters and their husbands, Charlotte's young brother and sister and some cousins for bridesmaids, and one or two aged aunts with their companions. The English exhibited a cold curiosity, the Americans a warm amazement that was alternately respectful and hilarious. Mallieu Hall impressed them, and the familiarity of its owners with titled and otherwise famous people made them openly reverent; but Sir Matthew's righteous pomposity roused the demon of Yankee laughter and one day two of the bridesmaid-cousins were found shaking with mirth over an album of Motley architecture.

Hildebrand had a simple position in the War Office, so he and Charlotte lived in London and were happy. Charlotte acquired a portrait of the Duchess of Fitz-Fulke – a Romney, more artful than the Lawrence she had seen at Burlington House – and was pleased to think that her sons would be the descendants of that great-hearted and fantastic aristocrat. As Romney painted her the Duchess had a languorous bedroom-look which did not always please Charlotte, who was clean-cut and lovely on a windy day. But sometimes she yielded to soft and luxurious thoughts, and then the Duchess was a good companion. And when she dreamed about the children she would have – children whose father and mother both traced their life back to that romantic womb and the alien seed of Spain – then the Duchess became of absorbing interest.

Presently she stopped going out to dinners and the theatre, and with proper regard for a serious occasion prepared herself to suffer the birth of a Motley heir. All through the slowly growing excitement, the increasing bustle of preliminary dispositions, Charlotte maintained an admirable calm, and her son was born after a model labour. In a very few months it became evident that he was going to resemble his mother; and when in another eighteen months or so a girl baby was born she as speedily took after her father. The boy was christened Noel and the girl Rhea, and to all observers but one they were children to be proud of. Their grandfather was extremely pleased with them and repeatedly pressed their mother to bring them down to Mallieu Hall. Charlotte generally accepted his invitations, feeling sorry for the old man – his wife had died some years earlier – and being sometimes oppressed by Hildebrand's new manner of responsibility. Paternity had been quick to have its effects on him. He had given up cricket, transferred his services from the War Office to the Treasury, and now devoted himself to grave and patriotic endeavours for the welfare of his country's government.

Sir Matthew had weakened with age. His powers of artistic invention had left him and his pride dwindled to a solemn iteration of platitudes. He liked to walk in the woods picking flowers with young matrons or his neighbours' daughters.

It was on an afternoon in the spring of 1905 that Charlotte suddenly shrieked and ran away from these circumstances of safety and comfort. She had left Hildebrand in London. By her side, where she sat on the terrace at Mallieu, Sir Matthew droned of life and art and human obligations. She could see little Noel playing on the warm grass and in a perambulator near him the baby Rhea lay. An efficient nurse watched over them. Asleep the baby was alarmingly like a doll, and in Noel Charlotte saw nearly a replica of her own childhood. . . . This repetition, she thought, is as dull as my father-in-law's discourse. Was that all the coming together of the right and left arms, the disparate nationalities, of Motleys could do? Had they not two drops between them of the dark Spanish virtue, to create something more coloured, more live at heart, than these blond Anglo-American dullards? A pang of remorse shot into her heart.

'No, no, I didn't mean that,' she cried, and disregarding Sir Matthew's amazement ran on to the lawn, and dropped to her knees beside Noel, and hugged him to her.

Noel had found a bird's feather on the grass.

'I've found a red fevver,' he said proudly.

It was no brighter than brown, but Charlotte was pleased to

find some imagination in Hildebrand's son, and picking him up carried him shoulder-high to the terrace.

'Mother's boy,' she said.

'I've found a red fevver,' he told his grandfather.

Sir Matthew adjusted his spectacles. 'I should call it brown, Noel.'

'It's red,' said Noel.

Sir Matthew addressed his daughter-in-law. 'The faculty of accurate observation,' he said, 'cannot be inculcated too early. I myself, largely by my own endeavours, learnt while still a mere child to distinguish not only the primary colours in natural objects, but also many of the intermediate shades and gradations. This, I suppose, was an instinctive preparation for the noble vocation of art to which I dedicated the best years of my life. And so when I admonish error or warn against inaccuracy it is because my ample experience of life in all its phases has taught me the value of scrupulous exactitude.'

'Run along, Noel,' said Charlotte. 'Yes, you can have another biscuit if you promise to go straight back to Nanny.'

'I admit, of course,' Sir Matthew continued, 'that exact observation may be carried too far; or perhaps I should say that the expression of it may become excessive and immodest. A French biography that I read some years ago showed just such a fault. We must exercise restraint, and I believe that no Englishman with the proper chivalrous instinct of his kind would be capable of writing such a biography as that to which I referred. My own aim has always been to avoid malice and uncharitableness, or even idle gossip.'

Charlotte pressed her hand to her side. Her heart, for some reason, was beating faster than its ordinary rate. She was going to have another baby in September.

'Fair play,' Sir Matthew said, 'is no bad standard for a life in any profession or even trade. By cherishing such an ideal we exclude anything un-English from our actions – yes, and from our thoughts. You should encourage your children to play manly games. I myself, when young, entered with zest into whatever games and honourable forms of sport my father approved of. Such sport often took me far afield, and it was while shooting grouse on Lord Muchalls's moors that I first became aware of a certain kinship with nature of which I grew more assured as the years rolled on. Nature, Music, Architectural Beauty, and Things Consecrated by Time are, as it were, sacred guiding lights to a just and worthy life. We should, of course, endeavour to suppress, or at least to disregard, the less attractive features of Nature, which is sometimes – how shall I describe it? Would it be too harsh a criticism if I were to say that Nature is sometimes un-English?'

Hush, beating heart, thought Charlotte. He is an old man and he has lovely white hair, now that he has stopped dyeing it. But will my baby be like him? Hildebrand is getting like him. . . .

Sir Matthew talked on, smacking his lips a little over an occasional phrase, clearing his throat with a fleamy rattle between sentences. There were flecks of yellow in his once handsome eyes, and his cheeks drooped loosely to the jaw-line. For some minutes – so intent did her heart seem on escaping from its prison of ribs and corset-bones – Charlotte scarcely heard what he said. But the sound of his voice became intolerable, like the Chinese torment of dripping water, and the endless petty *thud-thud* of falling syllables on her ear-drums made her tremble all over. 'Mr. Gladstone,' he said. Charlotte felt as if she were drowning. . . .

'Though I never sympathised with his political views, which were sometimes scarcely those of a gentleman, I remember being greatly impressed by his pious assurance. Some scoffed at a Liberal leader who could say and believe – as Mr. Gladstone did – that "The Almighty seems to sustain and spare me for some purpose of his own," but I myself have always freely admitted that an Opposition party is essential to the English political system. . . .'

'No, no, no, no,' said Charlotte in a voice fierce and low, striving to forbid the growing forces of rebellion in her breast.

It seemed to Sir Matthew that she was objecting to his broad-minded views, and he smiled tolerantly. 'Perhaps it is different in America,' he said, 'but free speech and fearless criticism are our birthright here. An Englishman's home is his castle. . . .'

Charlotte sprang to her feet and screamed like a peacock. Her throat was dry. Her heart pounded violently and her eyes felt hot, as though she had been driving on dusty roads. Sir Matthew sat back in his chair, frightened and aghast at this exhibition. Charlotte's screams continued. Sir Matthew's face was a sagging mask of amazement and his knees shook. Only his carefully brushed white hair remained smooth and untouched by emotion. On the lawn, fifty yards away, Noel and his nurse stared in bewilderment at the harsh peacock cries, and the baby sat up in her perambulator and crowed excitedly. The butler came on to the terrace, white-faced, and dared not speak.

Presently Charlotte's voice lost its strength and she began astonishingly to laugh. But her laughter was not mirthful. It was hoarse and punctuated unpleasantly by hiccups. And then she ran from the terrace, ran upstairs with her head bent down and her elbows far out from her sides, put on a hat, ran out of the house, and did her best to run to the railway station, which was half a mile away.

But her legs, hampered by a long and heavy skirt, soon grew tired, and her pace slowed to a hurried walk. Sir Matthew had sent servants to follow her. They shuffled at her heels, deferentially attempted to expostulate with her, timidly begged her to return. She ignored their unconvincing pleas. Still they followed her down the hedge-guarded lane. The butler panted, a housemaid whimpered, the children's nurse laid a restraining hand on Charlotte's arm, and burst into tears when her mistress terrifyingly bade her 'Let me alone!'

There happened to be a train in the station, so Charlotte

was able to continue her flight without any abatement of its initial impetus. But where she was to go she had no idea.

London first, of course, but where after that? I want freedom and I want colour, she thought. If only some translucent star-fragment would slide between the sun and England and, like a burning-glass, throw piercing rays through the mist-umbrella that shelters it! Or a gipsy Christ come to redeem it from respectability! Or a Carmen to enslave the Primate! She began to sing the Habañera from *Carmen*.

At Paddington she took a cab to drive to Sloane Square. A thin fog abetted the darkness and street-lights shone like yellow oranges. London was as full of oranges as Seville. Fantastic woolly oranges that grew under the damp leaves of the fog. She would talk to her portrait of the Duchess when she got home. Through the fog loomed a succession of grotesque figures like cartoons by Goya. A newspaper placard caught her eye: the Queen of Spain had given birth to another child. Spain again. . . . Spain of course! It called to her in everything she saw. That was where she must go. The Spain of Don Juan and golden oranges and irrepressibly fertile monarchs and Goya and the glamour of the Moors and the lawless Habañera. Spain. . . .

V

Somehow or other the Motleys managed to avoid a scandal. The story of Charlotte's escapade never became public, and in later years she herself seldom referred to it. Hildebrand spent an anxious summer tracking her from the Pyrenees to Algeciras, and from Madrid to Barcelona. She had plenty of money and a will o' the wisp imagination that baffled pursuit, so that it was by the merest accident he at last found his wife in a hotel at Barcelona. She was wearing a Spanish shawl and her beauty had somehow burgeoned with a new and strange luxuriance. Hildebrand on the contrary was thin and haggard with worry. When they returned to England it was he who appeared the runaway – now worn and penitent – while Charlotte concealed her shame under a bloom of splendid indifference.

Her child was born in September and Charlotte insisted on its being christened Juan. Nobody dared to object – though everybody disliked the name – lest Charlotte should again run away. Neither Hildebrand nor his father had ever dreamt that young mothers were so unstable, such wilful and flyaway creatures. They treated Charlotte with infinite circumspection, never reproached her, laughed warmly at her jokes, let her buy a new house, and anxiously approved her lesser fancies. Charlotte soon acquired an air of indolent authority and an enigmatic smile. When Juan was six she engaged a tutor for him, a pleasant young man with long eyelashes.

Almost from birth Juan was utterly unlike the other children. They were fair and he was dark. They were chubby and he grew lean. They were frank and open as daylight; Juan had a secret which ever and anon peeped like a star from his infant eyes. He was naughty, and knew it, and laughed at punishment. His mother loved him more than she loved Noel and Rhea, and Juan, even at three years old, recognised this and traded on it; but with his father he was wary. His nurse was devoted to him. When he was a tiny child and she slept in his nursery he had wakened once while she was undressing; the girl turned and saw two dark eyes fixed intently on her; she blushed, quite absurdly, and covered her bare breast with her hands; then, still red-faced, picked him from his crib and crooned sweet nonsense to him. Baby Juan shook with laughter. Thereafter she was his slave. But Watson, the elder children's nurse, pressed her lips together and frowned at Juan's wickedness.

For the children's sake the Motleys lived much of the year at Mallieu. Sir Matthew had had a stroke and disturbed them little; his shrunken body, in clothes too big for it, was clumsier than he could manage without assistance; he amiably doddered and his lower lip became increasingly pendulous. Noel and

Rhea disliked being with him, but Juan would listen to his grandfather's senile chattering with an interest that none could fathom. The old man sat in his chair and talked of this and that over his drooping lip. His words dragged like a shot balloon. But Juan squatted cross-legged at his feet and listened with a dark and dancing light in his eyes. Then, growing tired of sitting still, he would run off to look for his brother and sister. A hidden space, dry and dusty, among the rhododendrons was their favourite retreat, and there, while they were entertaining each other with mild romances, out of the dark green bushes would come a hoot of treble laughter and Juan's face, a dark lock of hair tumbling down his forehead, mocked them with faun-like lifted eyebrows and a gamin-glimpse of tongue. Horribly disconcerted they would flee to their sympathetic nurse.

He was even naughtier than that. Rhea was a modest child, and Juan would climb over roofs to the bathroom window and look in while she was being bathed. Rhea would scream with rage and shame. Noel too could be tormented almost as easily. Juan played whenever he could with the village children, from whom he learnt two or three lewd words and a morsel of blasphemy. These he would rehearse to Noel in the early morning, and when the elder boy grew childishly indignant – which he invariably did – up went Juan's eyebrows, and teeth and tongue would show in impish ecstasy of mirth. Into the cool white morning slid the ripple of laughter, and tossed in it were dirty little words like black pebbles. Noel would sit up in bed and cry 'Stop it, Ju! Stop it, I say!' And Juan would laugh again and again.

The tutor, who arrived soon after his sixth birthday, was not unneeded then. Noel went off to a preparatory school and Juan began to learn a whole host of things from Mr. Wickham. In addition to his attractive appearance Mr. Wickham had an acute and sympathetic mind. He was not a scholar, though he had many scholarly interests, and in spite of an athletic figure he was not an athlete. Mr. Wickham, indeed, was incurably lazy and constitutionally without ambition. His duties at Mallieu suited him very well, for Charlotte had formulated for her youngest child's benefit a theory of education which eliminated much of the usual drudgery of teaching.

She talked to Mr. Wickham over the tea-cups about this theory. 'It's absurd, don't you think,' she said, 'to hammer nonsense about the cat sitting on the mat into a child's head? And to insist that three times two is six? For such results as those a child is going to hate having to use his brain, and most of us are incurably stupid because we decided, somewhere about the age of ten, that learning was just waste of time. Now I want you to give Juan a general idea of things. I don't much care if he knows how to spell or how to count, but I want him to grow up with the consciousness that there are sensible countries beyond England, that human beings are alive, that it is amusing to know things, and that all knowledge is incomplete and relative. Tell him about Greece and the moon and Cortez and rabbits; though as a matter of fact I think he knows quite a lot about rabbits already.'

'I was very interested in them myself when I was a small boy,' said Mr. Wickham.

'I'm sure you were,' said Charlotte, 'but Noel gets much more heated about stump-cricket. A conventional English education will suit him admirably. Juan, though, is a proper subject for experiment, I think.'

Two years passed pleasantly. Juan's curiosity was readily diverted from bathroom windows to the subjects which Mr. Wickham chose for discussion, and since Mr. Wickham had enjoyed, while at Oxford, a reputation for knowing less about his own subject – which was History – than almost any other one could mention, and yet had taken a very good degree in History, Juan's education proceeded on catholic lines.

Had it not been for the war it might so have continued, sensibly, and without hypocrisy. But the war upset everything and everybody. Charlotte immediately became fantastically patriotic. She wrote cheques for every soldiers' charity organisation as soon as it was announced, and letters that contained nothing but Allied propaganda to her friends in America. She was in a mood to beat a laggard lover to the wars and welcome him bleeding home with arms of infinite tenderness and a breast that could scarce contain its adoring passion. But unhappily she had no lover to lend the King, no son tall enough to give to England.

Hildebrand at forty was far too important a person to go to war. He wished quite sincerely that he was ten years younger. 'But,' he added wisely, 'wishing won't help the Allies. Those who may not fight must work. Work as they have never worked before. Work to avenge an intolerable insult to England, an intolerable outrage on Belgium!' He grew excited as he talked, his face flushed, and Juan watched him in utter amazement. His father had always been calm and dignified as befitted – what he was now – a Companion of the Most Noble Order of the Bath and Deputy-Comptroller of the Acquests and Dispersals Department of H.M. Treasury.

Strangest of all, perhaps, was Mr. Wickham's behaviour. He, so detached and even cynical in his views, he who by rights of culture and intellect had all Europe for his country, he who was too lazy to work, now wanted feverishly to fight. His philosophy rocked as if to an earthquake, crumbled and fell, and out of its dust rose a proud and passionate love for England. He felt as all the stupid young men from the Universities felt, as all the stupid young men from farms and factories felt, that there was nothing in life so golden-proud and fiercely fine as to wear the King's khaki and fight for an invisible England of their hearts. On August 10th Mr. Wickham left Mallieu for London, en route, as he hoped, for the front; and his expression was half that of a Crusader and half that of a schoolboy going home for the holidays.

For the first time in his young life Juan was seriously perturbed. The cataclysm which shook the world shattered too his tiny calm. He became unimportant even to his mother. He saw the standards by which he had been taught rooted up by his own teachers, and in their place a Union Jack was planted. He felt puzzled and lost, for he alone at Mallieu was unexcited by the war, and he could not understand his loneliness. Then, in a couple of weeks' time, Mr. Wickham returned and Juan was further bewildered.

It seemed that Mr. Wickham's eyes were not too good and his kidneys little better, so that no regiment in all the British Army wanted him, and he was forced to remain a civilian at the only period in his life when he had wanted to be anything but a civilian. His new-found patriotism, however, burgeoned tremendously after it was prohibited from practical expression, and Juan's fine rational education went all to pigs and whistles. Mr. Wickham began to teach him so-called practical things – sums and the date of the battle of Agincourt – because everybody else was doing such practical things as forming fours and rolling bandages and making T.N.T. Not unnaturally Juan rebelled against this unnatural discipline and took to running away from Mr. Wickham.

But one hot September afternoon – the third or fourth occasion on which he had escaped – while he was sitting on a stile beside the high road, understanding came to him between music and a cloud of dust. Why, he was thinking, had all his elders so suddenly lost their wits? Why, instead of being cool and good-humoured, were they hot and angry and excited and prone to tears? He knew that his grandfather was a silly old man, that Rhea was a silly little girl, and that the village children were incurably stupid; it was fun to recognise such things, and his secret soul had fed happily on these and similar perceptions. But to see all the world go mad was terrifying. He couldn't laugh at that. . . .

Two soldiers rode past on bicycles. Then half a dozen more. Their bicycles were heavily laden with rifles and khaki packs.

By-and-by a sound of music blew down the road, sweet in the distance but growing harsh and thrilling as it approached. A regimental band came into sight. The men were red-faced and little clouds of dust blew up as their boots struck the road. Their legs swung stiffly in time to the music, and the music as they passed was an intoxicating brazen clamour. Behind the band rode two mounted officers. One of them, Juan thought, was like his father. The other was young, hawk-faced and brown. And behind the officers came an endless stream of men. Hundreds and hundreds of legs, thick and stiff in their khaki puttees, swinging tirelessly to the splendid beat of the music. The road shook to the thudding rhythm of their march. Some of the men laughed and made jokes. Others stared straight ahead. Most of them were quite young, but some had V-shaped stripes on their sleeves and looked fierce and masterful. Every now and then came a mounted officer riding high above the khaki stream of men. And the stream was endless.

Juan had not known that there were so many soldiers in the world as now marched past, singing about Tipperary, on the white high road between familiar dusty hedges. But the noise of the march was changing. Perhaps it was coming to an end? Not yet. The thud, thud of marching boots indeed grew thinner, but a rumble-rattle, rumble-rattle took its place, and guns came round the corner, and the acrid smell of horses, and soldiers who sat their horses with a swagger, and more soldiers laughing on the limbers. Rumble-rattle went the guns, and the gunners sitting easy, and the drivers with their caps thrust back and cigarettes between their lips. And there was an officer handsome as Apollo, and a young one looking fleet as Mercury on a thin chestnut mare, and a hard-faced man with a crown on his sleeve who turned his head and shouted villainously. . . . Now more soldiers marching. Juan grew dizzy as they swung past. His eyes were tired with the ceaseless swinging of legs and the swagger of swinging arms, and the upthrust muzzles of another thousand rifles. His heart beat quicker and quicker. Another band came, daunting the sky with its brazen din, and it too faded into silence, and still the soldiers came, red-faced, singing a song that rose deafeningly till it became a shout of gigantic laughter. Their boots thudded on the road with little wings of dust about them, their mouths were open and the sweat ran down their ruddy cheeks as the song swelled to this vast nonsensical mirth. Ten thousand Englishmen roaring with laughter as they went to war. . . .

'Oh, go on, go on!' cried Juan suddenly. His voice was hard and shrill and he stamped on the ground as he called to the marching soldiers. 'Go on, I say! Beat the old Kaiser! Beat him! You will! I know you will!'

He threw himself down on to the grass behind the hedge, out of the soldiers' sight, and lay there sobbing. . . . Still the soldiers marched; jingle of harness, rattle of wheels, the thudding of boots; roll of drums and fifes calling sweet and high; men singing again with hoarse and lovely voices; the smell of sweat and khaki and boot-leather; dust like wings about their feet, and horses astrain at the limbers. . . .

In the shadow of the hedge Juan lay sobbing, his heart full of love and hatred that he could not understand.

He had joined the war party.

VI

The effect of this submission to romance was profound. At eight years old Juan was a singularly clear-sighted youngster with a keen perception for the grotesque and ridiculous; mentally robust, and very well-made and wiry as to his body. He was, perhaps, just a little frightening. His vitality was remarkable and his faun-like laughter frequently unnerved old ladies. And then came romance. Its first effect was to dull the edge of his perceptions, to mute a little the clear timbre of his laughter. He became more ordinary, less critical, anxious for company and though his range of interests was probably extended, his judgment was curtailed.

The romantic attitude lasted rather more than four years. During this time all sorts of things happened and the romantics had many moods. Frequently they were bitter. Sometimes they grew desperate. Now and then their spirits rose wildly. Often they wept. But they never despaired, they never doubted their romantic assurance that ultimately Britain would win, and never did the sight of their soldiers marching fail to fill them with pride and affection. In many ways, of course, all this was admirable, but it was the worst possible atmosphere in which to educate an intelligent boy like Juan. For everybody was so busy loving and hating and weeping and working and giving three cheers that nobody had any time to think. Neither the generals – though perhaps it made little difference to them – nor the politicians; and of course the common people, who know what they want, have never troubled about thinking. But people like Charlotte and Mr. Wickham, intelligent people, biologists, lawyers, historians, even Jews – all these people stopped thinking and merely believed: they believed in Kitchener and French, the Grand Duke Nicholas and Lloyd George, Beatty and Townshend and Northcliffe; in the invincibility of Australians, Scottish Highlanders, and tanks; they believed that the Turks crucified their prisoners, that German spies could signal with bicycle lamps from Scarborough to Kiel, and that munition workers earned the wages they got. They believed whatever they were told to believe until the very end, when their new American allies told them who had won the war; and that they flatly declined to accept. This was the first bit of incredulity in England for nearly four and a half years.

And so the excellent beginning of Juan's education was obscured by a long period of emotionalism from which he never quite recovered. It forced a dual nature on him, and the intelligent pagan – which his infancy had promised – was coupled with an irrelevant romantic. The combination proved unruly and troublesome.

At seventeen, for instance, he was forced to leave one of the very best of public schools because of an intolerable invasion of his housemaster's privilege. It was rather a romantic curiosity than any faunish pricking of the flesh that led him astray. The housemaster's wife was much younger than the housemaster, pretty, adventurous, and bored by school society. Juan was handsome, attractive, and nearly free from the customary gawkishness of seventeen. He preferred the lady to cricket – though he was an accomplished bat and, like his father, fielded boldly at cover-point; and she found him more comforting than cards – though she played very good bridge indeed. But if both were talented neither was careful, and one night – a sweet-smelling restless night with a hint of rain in it – the housemaster caught them in his garden.

Juan bolted at once and dropping into the road on the far side of the high garden wall unfortunately twisted an ankle. He limped a little way and then sat down to think. He decided to go home, for his mother, he knew, would forgive him anything. His father – Sir Hildebrand now – would raise a storm, but his mother had a way of reducing alien fulguration to something no more dangerous than painted flames on a firebrick. He would go home. But now the rain was falling, his ankle had swollen horribly, and it was two miles to arailway station. And so when he reached home he looked disarmingly like a penitent, baptism and all, and very soon took to his bed with pneumonia, which was still more disarming.

Sir Hildebrand Motley was by this time a figure of large importance. A K.B.E. and a C.M.G. had been added unto him, and for the last five years he had been Comptroller and virtual head of the post-war Ministry of Rebuttals. Somehow or other he pacified the poor horned housemaster – Juan, delirious, had a look of woodland suffering in his eyes and was like to die – and comforted his own distressed fatherhood by deciding that his son had been seduced only after long and pious resistance. *Mutatis mutandis*, the housemaster's wife told just such another lie to her husband, and used certain private and illogical arguments of her own which she very well knew would satisfy him. Eventually, therefore, the only sufferers were Truth and Juan himself; and Juan recovered and was sent on a long convalescent holiday to Hyères in the south of France.

Three years later, while an undergraduate, he became involved in another romantic scandal, in which the poor girl found herself in trouble and didn't know what to do about it. She was the daughter of the chapel clerk at Merlin College, a blue-eyed frailty called Dora, whom Juan had first seen in chapel and later met at the Annual Ball of the Cambridge Licensed Victuallers' Association – where he had no business to be.

Had Dora been a porter's child or a bedmaker's daughter some discreet arrangement might have been possible. But her father was the Chapel clerk, and to debauch a girl whose father served not only Merlin but God, was to profane the mysteries. It was – the Chapel clerk said so himself – dangerously near to blasphemy. He took his tale to the Master and Juan was sent down.

This was more than Sir Hildebrand could stomach. He disliked even hearing of immorality – an unusual trait – and to be brought into actual contact with it roused him to a passion of anger and disgust. There was a dreadful scene at Mallieu and a worse one at Cambridge. At Mallieu Sir Hildebrand thundered denunciation and looked, with his red face and flaxen hair, like an evangelical Viking. Even Charlotte stood mute before his anger, while Noel – a model young man in the Rifle Brigade – and Rhea – a gentle, narrow-minded girl – took their distress on long miserable walks through the woods. Then Sir Hildebrand insisted on taking Juan back to

Cambridge, and in the shining neat sitting-room of the Chapel clerk's invaded house made such reparation as he could. He was indeed so generous as to freeze with a kind of hoar amazement the lamentation of Dora's parents. But Dora herself still cried and clutched her chubby hands, and looked so soft and piteously at Juan that he determined to make her happy at least once more before going to Australia.

For that was to be his punishment.

The late Bishop of Bolla-wolla (the Right Reverend Humphrey Motley, son of Horatio who was Master in Lunacy) had many years before done a little real estate speculation in Queensland, and left to his heirs – he deprecated celibacy – a very fine sheep station. The present Australian Motleys were handsome, hearty people, between six and seven feet high, who cared nothing for an odd peccadillo and readily agreed to find work for Juan. He sailed from Tilbury under a cloud and for two years rode horses and tended sheep in the bright sunlight of the Antipodes.

These two years passed without scandal, and then Charlotte grew unhappy for her youngest child, an exile far away, living roughly in a new land. He was, she felt, too intelligent to spend all his life among tups and gimmers and drinkers of strong tea. Untimely ripped from the arms of his Alma Mater he was still only half-educated, and Charlotte (this was her American blood) thought highly of university education.

'Give the boy another chance,' she said one morning from her pillow.

Sir Hildebrand stood at the bed-end dressed in sable formality – silk hat in hand, crape armlet, black gloves, a Stygian ensemble – for his father's funeral.

'I am uncomfortable about him,' he answered.

The blackness of Juan's hair was so unlike this funeral black.

Charlotte's nose was pink. She had a heavy cold. 'Let him finish his education,' she pleaded.

'I must go,' Sir Hildebrand answered.

While the concourse of ebon-draped mourners stood round the grass-lipped raw brown grave of his father, and while the heavy earth thudded down to cover the poor old dotard – whose brain had ten years predeceased his body – Sir Hildebrand felt his heart soften; but still he was uneasy at the idea of Juan's return, and scandal perhaps attaching itself to the immaculate Ministry of Rebuttals.

He resumed the discussion with his wife. 'Have you thought of a profession for him? Has he thought of one for himself?'

'Business,' said Charlotte. 'The Stock Exchange. He has a personality. Now listen.' She sat up in bed, vehement in spite of catarrh. 'There are colleges in America that make a scientific study of business methods; of finance, that sort of thing. Collateral securities, operating on a margin – everything in fact. There's one at Motley – my father endowed it – which is among the very best of them. Let Juan go there. In three years he will get his degree – B.C.T., I think they call it; Bachelor of Commercial Technology – and then, with an American business education behind him, let him make his career in England, instead of among bushrangers and kangaroos in Bolla-wolla.'

Charlotte opened her mouth and sprayed her throat with a germicide solution.

'Send him to Motley!' Sir Hildebrand discreetly coughed. A little amused smile hid behind his fair moustache. Even just after his father's funeral he could not help being tickled by the thought of an American university; pole-jumping and cheer-leaders. He knew all about them. But to have Juan safely occupied in America for three years was an inducement. And there might, after all, be something in this notion of a business training. The boy ought to have a profession. . . .

'Yes,' he pronounced, 'it might be a good idea. Perhaps you should write to Juan and see what he thinks about it.'

'I have,' said Lady Motley, and rubbed a little eau-de-cologne on her forehead. 'Here is his answer.'

BOOK TWO

THE LAND OF INFINITE POSSIBILITY

I

Clamour and arc-lights surrounded the embarkation of the many passengers who joined the ship at Le Havre. Motor cars – olive-grey, silver, gleaming under the lamps – lurched through the air, hung motionless from the stiff forefinger of a derrick, slid through the forward hatch. Far off, on a dark hill, were quiet unwinking lights. Liquid gleams like mercury on black velvet slipped and shone in the black dock-water. Tumult of passengers and porters echoed in the hollow white-lit sheds. Laughing, still animated in their conversation at near midnight of their last day in France, the Americans came aboard.

'He hung a lullaby on the Frog's chin – socko!'

'Did he fall?'

'I'll say he fell!'

Here deep laughter, girlish laughter, then manly again, and a confusion of voices: 'Hank was tickled pink by the Gioconda – He's still pie-eyed – It was real smooth Scotch – I got quite a kick outa Roma – Aw, be your age! – No kidding? – Sister's just crazy to see Peoria again – Well, she won't be long now!'

Spectacled, fat, benign, alert, young, gay, hard-faced, handsome, tidy, slovenly, smart, stalwart, slim – three hundred holiday-makers going home, stepping aboard the ship with casual Yankee unconcern as though it were a foot-plank crossing a creek. The heirs of Time and applied Science, they used a forty-thousand ton liner like a rowboat or a penny ferry. Children of immensity, they were unabashed by immensity.

Juan stood at the rail and watched them.

Girls with small hats pushed back off their foreheads; young men with parti-coloured shoes and loose trousers; faces behind heavy spectacles of tortoise-shell or horn; thick-set women with puffy cheeks and bad-tempered eyes; knees that thrust flimsy skirts away and came boldly into sight; pretty cosmeticked girls; burly young men and corpulent middle-aged men – out of the yellow-white brightness of the quay, the shed that looked like an incandescent beehive in the purple darkness, out of starlit alien Europe came the holiday-makers.

Presently the gangway was empty.

Then the last of the passengers, a group of five persons, came aboard. Their appearance was remarkable.

In front walked a tall man with a slender girl on his arm; then a waddling, panting, short-legged old woman with bright eyes; then two men of whom one looked plump and mournful, the other middle-aged, stout, and so hard that knives might blunt themselves on his saurian, muscle-packed hide. None of them spoke. The girl was dressed in black. The way she walked made Juan feel alert, almost excited, and a glimpse of her face as it came from the shadow into the glare of a light evoked his liveliest admiration. But the face of the tall man at her side was revealed at the same moment, and seeing it Juan felt as uncomfortable as if a cold pebble had stuck in his throat. The stranger had heavy eyebrows, a thick Roman nose, and a skin like a yellow glove. But these features were not shocking. It was the newcomer's right eye that horrified. At some time, apparently, he had been stabbed in the corner between nose and frontal ridge. The lower eyelid was everted and the inner canthus curved downward beside his nose in a red liquid gleam. When he looked to that side it seemed that he stared over a trickle of fresh arterial blood.

Close behind the red-eyed man was the short-legged woman. She had a sprinkling of purple powder on her fat grey face.

And behind her, like a bodyguard, the plump melancholy man and the stout ugly man who looked knife-and-bullet proof.

They crossed the strip of bright-lit deck. The fat woman walked noisily on her heels, but the men moved silently, and suddenly, with a kind of compact and dramatic disappearance, the group was gone and the deck was bare again.

Presently the *Corybantic* put to sea and Juan, walking about with a great curiosity in his mind, scarcely noticed the splash of the last rope that bound him to Europe. He was practically in America already. The ship was full of the ebbing tide of summer tourists. The wave that had just come bustling aboard, so loud and bright, was purely American. And the last quintet – black, as when wind ruffles the sleek hide of a wave and shows the underlying darkness – that also was probably American, for all manner of things could happen in Oklahoma that would be incredible in Kent. The life of America was spread over so vast an area, and was everywhere so vigorous, that any number of strange and sinister interludes could be enacted without upsetting the national equilibrium. Those miraculously united states with their wild harmonious names – Utah, Wisconsin, Oregon, Kentucky – were the home not only of Republicans and Democrats but of peacocks and mandrills. Gold and ivory were in their houses as well as rocking-chairs and motor cars. Fantasy lived there, satyrs walked in the woods, and millionaires built with the large and unstudied imagination of Haroun al-Raschid. America was the last home of romance and anything could happen there. . . .

The deck was deserted. The sea-wind blew colder and Juan went below.

But he could not sleep. The rough-lipped sea was too loudly caressing the vibrant ship, and the image of the black-clad girl was vivid in his mind – the exciting rhythm of her walk, the red-eyed man to whose arm she held. Now on one side, now on the other, Juan sought sleep in his narrow bunk, but sleep was not there. Instead he entertained a vision of his father, who had been cold and uncomfortable in his son's presence during the month that Juan had just spent at Mallieu. But Lady Motley had been very happy. All the month long her eyes had danced, and several times she had taken Juan's hand and led him to the Romney portrait of her Grace of Fitz-Fulke, to look from one to the other and at last to say in a voice no mother should use to her son, 'I really think, Juan, that you're a throw-back to your very-great-grandfather. Would you have fallen to Fitz-Fulke?'

'She's not a patch on you,' he had answered.

'I'm beginning to feel old,' she had said.

'High time, too,' he agreed.

And Lady Motley had laughed, pleased enough, for in her son's refusal to flatter her more she read the realisation that she was still worth flattering. . . .

Now Juan slept, having been wooed to peace by the thought of his mother who had rescued him from the wilds of Bollawolla and given him – a queenly gift – three years to taste and explore the rich civilisation of the West.

But – all England and a strip of sea between them – Lady Motley herself was still awake, playing bridge in a shooting-box in Perthshire whither she had gone immediately after saying good-bye to Juan. And her thoughts were of him. She was delighted with herself for having borne such a son. Vivid, darkly handsome, capable of irreverent laughter. This was the wildness she had longed for when Edwardian England, with its comfort and complacence, had weighed too heavily upon her. This was the lively darkness she had desired when Hildebrand's blond moustache, glass eyes, and yellow hair had exasperated her. This was the life she had sought in Spain during the fantastic months of her third pregnancy. His hair was black and unruly. Two years in Australia had strengthened his body and tanned his skin to a very agreeable brown. His eyes were brilliant, his features regular and full of character. When he laughed his eyebrows rose at the outer corners, so that he had an antique sylvan look, and he showed his teeth, all gleaming white.

'Double three hearts,' said Lady Motley in a well-pleased voice.

II

The following morning at breakfast Juan saw two of the strange quintet. The men whom he had thought of as a body-guard were seated at a nearby table eating one of those cereal foods peculiar to the American breakfast table – a mess of husks in milk and sugar – and while such a meal appeared suitable enough for one of them, a trickle of milk on the razor-blue chin of the other looked comical indeed. For the melancholy-seeming one had a little wet pursy mouth, and staring eyes, and a great convex forehead that gave him so mild and embryonic a look that milk might well have been his proper food; but the face of his bullet-proof companion was brick-red where it was not razor-blue, his hair was close-cropped, and his ears and nose and cheek-bones had a thickened look as though they had been battered and banged into toughness. He seemed a carnivore from birth, and no milk-drinker unless from a tigress's udder.

During that day and on following days these two became a familiar spectacle. They were always together and they made no friends. One night on the boat-deck Juan saw them sitting side by side, and while the hard-looking one smoked a cigar the soft-looking one cried in the vagrant moonlight. His face was glistening wet with tears. The corners of his pursy mouth drooped darkly and his chin quivered with emotion. He made no effort to conceal his sorrow – his hands were buried in his trouser-pockets – but shook and sniffed and whimpered without embarrassment or restraint.

His companion spoke to him in a harsh *faubourien* voice.

'Snap out of it, hophead,' he said, and puffed a pale cloud of cigar-smoke that flew swiftly astern to join the huge black streamer – moon-dappled, rolling in sooty volutes – that issued from the liner's funnels.

Discreetly, and somewhat astonished, Juan retreated from so intimate a scene. He had no clue to the nature or language of such men as these. And to his intense disappointment he had not seen again the red-eyed man, the slim girl, or the stout woman. They did not eat in the saloon, nor with the majority of passengers did they lie on deck-chairs, rug-wrapped, staring at a heaving empty horizon. Round every deck, morning and afternoon, Juan searched among sea-drugged travellers for the girl who had swayed in her walk; and searched in vain. She and the red-eyed man took no part in the life of the ship. They had either vanished or retired to a private suite.

Juan's cabin companion was an associate-professor of American History in the University of Minnetonka. He was an enthusiastic young man who had just spent two months in the art galleries, museums, and cathedrals of Europe. He knew a great deal about them and was ready to share his knowledge with Juan. But Juan was pre-occupied. There was a large number of comely young women aboard, and they did not arouse him. He saw their smart red lips, their blanched noses, their bright enquiring eyes. But he felt no more interest in them than in such names as Uffizi, Chartres, and Luxembourg, that he heard every day from Professor Timson, his travelling companion. For his mind was occupied with the face of the girl in black, a white profile so lovely as to be memorable for years though it was seen only for seconds.

The grey-green sea slid past under a whitish sky. In an ever-vanishing but ever-persistent trail the black streamer from the ship's funnels sped eastward, and America came nearer and nearer. Juan felt his curiosity quicken. No more than twenty-four hours beneath that level horizon lay hidden the precipitous sky-line of New York.

'A land of amazing opportunity,' said Professor Timson.

'A land where there are no barriers to achievement. The janitor of to-day may be the millionaire executive of to-morrow. You'll find it a stimulating country, Mr. Motley. It's a country where anything can happen. Yes, anything. Men make millions overnight. And it's a friendly country. You're friendly with the man who shines your shoes, with the barber who cuts your hair, with the waiter who brings you your glass of iced water. Why? Because you know that these men may some day be prominent citizens. And even if they don't make that much money it's a very pleasant thing to establish contacts with your fellow-men.'

Then, on their last night at sea, when the smoking-room was crowded and stewards ran faster and faster with ever more glasses on their trays, Juan saw her again. Framed in the window of a cabin on the promenade deck she looked out at the darkness. Her lips were parted as if to taste the black salt air. With a quickening pulse Juan walked a little way farther, turned about, went back to her window, and said 'I saw you come aboard at Le Havre.'

'Yes?' she answered doubtfully. 'But it was late at night.'

'There were lights above the gangway.'

'I suppose so.'

She was not helpful, and during the trivial conversation which Juan made seemed to be listening for something else. When he suggested that she come on deck and walk awhile she smiled, but before she could answer an angry exclamation and a torrent of expostulation interrupted her. The short-legged woman had come unnoticed into the cabin. She screeched first to the girl, then to Juan, then to the girl again, in Italian or Neapolitan. The girl replied in the same language, angry too, but controlling her anger. Then the old woman pushed her away and thrust her own purple-powdered face through the embrasure to spit some quite unintelligible reproof at Juan. After which she pulled a curtain across the window.

In the smoking-room stewards dashed to and fro carrying

trays heavy with glasses of whisky, bottles of soda-water, liqueurs, beer tumblers, small ports and large ports, Courvoisier brandy and Guinness's stout. Every passenger on board – except the considerable number making love in quiet cabins or dark corners of the deck – was busy drinking as much as he or she could hold while the *Corybantic* still enjoyed the freedom of the seas – for the bar would be padlocked as soon as they got into American waters. It was a lively scene. Louder and louder grew the voices. Bottles clinked and trays clashed. With a *glug-glug-guggle-ug* another bottle of beer was poured out for the gentleman from Iowa, and his wife took her seventh Benedictine gratefully, knowing how difficult it was to get Benedictine in Iowa, and three large ports went smack! into the inflamed stomachs of three school-marms from Kansas. 'Whoopee!' shouted the college boys, and swigged off their highballs like gentlemen. 'Stooard, stooard!' Cognac for the Senator and his lady and the large red realtor from Pasadena, Calif., and a cherry-brandy for the Senator's daughter before she starts her freshman year at Vassar – she'll get nothing but bootleg rye and bath-tub gin for long enough after this, poor girl. Soda squirts, and the man from Chicago tells the man from Yonkers, N.Y., precisely where to get off. 'And how!' says the little lady from Milwaukee as she pours her brother's whisky into what's left of her lager. 'Over there – Over there! Oh, the Yanks are coming, the Yanks are coming!' – 'I'll say we're coming!' And there's nothing left over there but effete Europe full of empty bottles and ten-dollar bills. 'Ta-ra, ta-ra-rah, ta-ra-rah!' 'Bring the goddam cask, stooard!' 'We've had the heck of a time but there's nothing like little old N'York after all!' 'I'll tell the cock-eyed world there's nothing like it. . . .'

After having a drink or two with Professor Timson Juan went out to walk up and down on the boat-deck. There were few people there, for the wind blew cold, and Juan considered without distraction the imminence of America. He was conscious of a vague dismay at the thought of its territorial vastness and the strident energy of its hundred million people.

I feel like a tadpole swimming into a salmon-river, he admitted. And at that moment, going round the corner of a deckhouse, he saw three men standing in the shelter of a canvas dodger. He recognised them immediately as the red-eyed man and his two followers. They were on the weather side of the ship and it happened that a backward gleam from the starboard light shone directly into their faces, turning them a sinister villain's green. Disconcerted by this unexpected and hardly pleasant sight, Juan stood for a moment to stare at the grass-tinted trio. They, immediately aware of observation, stared back. The bloody streak on the tall man's face was black in the viridian glare, and the melancholy man, with his convex embryonic forehead dyed green, looked strangely like something in a biologist's bottle. There was silence except for the hiss and surge of the cloven sea and the distant *Hoo-hoo* of the wind. Juan called his wits to order and walked hurriedly away.

III

Under the night stood New York.

Racing the ship by some hours the busy sun stripped from its topless towers the clinging darkness, swept the shadows from gloomy far-sunk pavements, and touched with bright fingers its myriad windows.

Passengers ran to the rail.

They looked once more at the statue to Liberty. They stared, worshipful, at the mortal Andes of Manhattan. Its smooth walls reared above them, square-cut, serrated. To one high pinnacle a cloud hung like a pennant to a flagpole. Towers thrust back the arch of heaven. The sky was their province, and to these Babel was a mudpie in the hands of children, and the multitude who worked in Babel would here be lost in a single street, and all the tongues of Babel might find neighbours at the street-corner.

'We certainly do lead the world in architecture,' said Professor Timson. 'Architecture, I take it, is the natural artistic expression of a young nation. Youth wants to build, and Manhattan Island kind of looks as though we've done what we wanted.'

'It's magnificent,' said Juan.

'Quite a city,' agreed the Professor.

Youth wants to build, thought Juan. But what kind of youth could build like this? Some Titan's brood, or nurslings of Brobdingnag. Was blind Polyphemus sent to stud, and did he cover Irish giantesses? Else how came this race that built forty storeys high to show it had done with teething? Either there were giants in the land or they had genies at command. And genies would get their fill of work from a nursery. 'Build me a church five hundred feet high,' the nursery might say. 'Bismillah,' the genie would answer. Timber and sandstone were no good for that kind of job, of course. Concrete and steel were what this nursery played with, and out of them the genie would build their church. The nursery would look at it and remark, 'That's fine. Now what about an insurance office *six* hundred feet high?' And the genie would shift its quid and get to work again, thinking no doubt, 'Youth has to build.' So Manhattan grew, like the Rocky Mountains in bulk and inconstant as a fashion-plate.

But Juan was not giving all his thoughts to New York. More than once he turned away from its tremendous façade and searched among the mass of passengers for a last sight of the girl in black. Even in the Customs Shed – where for half a mile on every side people stood with their luggage, group by group, like villages on a stony prairie – even there Juan looked hopefully about him, though he would have needed a spy-glass to recognise anyone halfway across.

Slightly depressed, he drove to the Hotel Connecticut. None

of his American relations was in New York, as it happened, for they were all holiday-making in Maine and Canada and Europe. But the Hotel Connecticut did its best to comfort lonely travellers.

Two thousand nine hundred and eighty rooms, two thousand nine hundred and eighty baths – this was its professional boast and official capacity. Many a hotel would have yielded to a fulsome pride in round numbers and proclaimed its possession of three thousand rooms and three thousand baths. But not the Hotel Connecticut, for the two favourite remarks of Mr. Ginsberg, its proprietor, were: 'Tell a lie and lose a customer,' and 'Honesty pays dividends.'

And perhaps he was right. Certainly the main floor was more populous than many a market town in England, and infinitely busier with its elegant shops and offices and the intricate threading of messengers through the ceaseless crowd. But Mr. Ginsberg also recognised the shyness of the human soul that bids it seek recurrent privacy, and its weakness for domestic ease. Every one of the two thousand nine hundred and eighty rooms, therefore, was furnished in such a way as to suggest Home to its transitory occupant. Not Mr. Ginsberg's home, nor Juan's, but an abstract generalised home; or perhaps the Lowest Common Denominator of Home. On every bedside table lay a Bible and an anthology of American poetry entitled *Heart Throbs*. A small cabinet contained a wireless apparatus which, on being carelessly handled, would reproduce the sound of a jazz-band. And beside every radiator (that is, in front of every window) stood a brightly polished cuspidor.

A little embarrassed by these furnishings Juan left his room as soon as possible, and after lunching very well on shad roe and bacon and canteloupe, he went to walk in Fifth Avenue and adjacent thoroughfares and adapt himself to the use of superlatives.

In many ways, he thought, photography has done us disservice. By showing us pictures of everything it has robbed us of surprise. I am all admiration for what I see – these commercial palaces, these bronze gates, jewels, and plumes, and sables; the sharp straight lines, the height and the smartness of things; but I can't feel astonishment, for I have seen it all before at the cinema and in the illustrated papers. And I should be astonished, I should be amazed, for the like of this was never seen on earth till now. When desert dwellers rode to Babylon or Gaulish captives saw Rome they threw up their hands and were dumb with surprise. Pilgrims fell on their knees at the first far glimpse of Jerusalem. Travellers have a right to be astonished. I deserve amazement; but the cinema has robbed me of my capacity for amazement. I yearn for surprise, I should welcome consternation. But what can surprise us to-day, when we have seen pictures of everything? Nothing.

At this moment Juan saw, no more than ten yards in front of him, a body tumbling through the air. It went into many shapes in its rapid descent, and fell on the outer edge of the pavement with a loud horrible noise like the bursting of a very large paper-bag. Immediately a crowd collected with cries of terror and interest. A policeman who had been standing nearby, playing idly with the baton which depended from his wrist by a leather thong, now ran up, and rudely parting the people who formed a tight ring round the dead girl, forced his way to the centre. The increasing crowd hemmed Juan in. He was aware of white faces close to his, horrified, all alive with eagerness to see what could be seen. A man fainted. Reluctantly the spectators gave way so that he could be dragged out. Through the momentary avenue Juan caught sight of a crumpled heap in a thin green dress, blood-splashed.

A little Jew, jerking up and down on his toes beside Juan, remarked, 'I bet she's pretty too. It's only pretty ones that throw themselves outa windows.'

His voice was thick and husky. Between black-rimmed spectacles and an unshaven chin his face had a friendly look. As the crowd swayed this way and that he and Juan were

thrown to its periphery, and attracted by their common experience they walked on together.

'I suppose it was suicide,' said Juan.

'Suicide?' echoed the little Jew. 'Sure. Sure it was suicide. They're always doing it. Their boy-friend goes out for a walk and forgets to come back, see? And the jane, she hasn't got any dough – he's borrowed all she had – and there's sixty or seventy bucks owing for the room, and she can't write home because the old folks won't have nothing more to do with her. She's in dutch all round, see? And maybe she's got a pretty fierce hangover from the night before. So she opens the window and looks out, and there's all the people going up and down, hurrying from one place to another as though John D. Rockefeller had sent for them. And she's got nowhere to go. She isn't like anybody else, and that makes her feel lost. And she's got nobody to talk to except the bell-boy, and he's a Swede. See? And all the noise in the street goes to her head and she gets kinda dizzy, and she thinks she's going bug-house, and that scares her more. And then she thinks, "I'll fix the dirty bum that framed me! I'll do him dirt! I'll put his name in the papers!" But she won't, because he gave her a phony name, and the hotel's in cahoots with the reporters so's they won't say nothing about it anyway. But she don't know that, see? So then she climbs outa the window and gives a scream. But nobody hears that because of the traffic. And there's the blonde standing on the window-ledge, and she looks up and there's ten storeys above her, and she looks down and there's thirty below, and the avenue all moving and spotted with people. See? And she's feeling sick and scared, and she can't hold on no longer, and she lets go. And that's all, see?'

As many people were walking in the contrary direction to that taken by Juan and his new acquaintance, this recital lasted a long time. Often the little Jew was driven to the extreme inside of the pavement, Juan to the very kerb. Sometimes the story was shouted over the heads of intervening pedestrians and its more dramatic points made evident by gesture. So rhetorical were the Jew's hands, indeed, that a boy who passed too close got slapped on the face and several people escaped a like punishment only by clever ducking and side-stepping. Juan listened as attentively as he could.

By the time the story was done they had returned to Fifth Avenue and were at that point where, with histrionic suddenness in a landscape perpendicular and staccato, Central Park greets the eye with verdant undulation.

'Do you like seeing animals?' said the Jew.

'Very much indeed,' replied Juan.

'They've got some cages here. The regular zoo's out in the Bronnix. It's the biggest zoo in the world. But they keep some coyotes and wolves in the Park just to let folk think about nature, see?'

A remarkable sight awaited them. After regarding depressed Virginia deer, a few rather shabby bears, and so forth, they came to an enclosure large enough to give some degree of freedom to a pair of yaks. These handsome animals had already attracted some eight or ten children and two elderly men of the type commonly seen frequenting public parks. Paying no attention to this unworthy audience the yaks were engaged in amorous exchanges. Slavering affectionately, the male nuzzled the shaggy hide of his companion and amicably licked her quarters with a thick purplish tongue. Saliva dripped sympathetically from her mouth. Her bovine eyes were soft and moonish. They stood side by side, she facing the spectators, he with his stern to them. She was patient, expectant. He was fidgety. He pawed the ground. Only a little distance away the motor cars and the motor buses raced up and down Fifth Avenue, and like a cloud in the air was the hum of further traffic.

Suddenly with a grunt the male yak moved. Wheeling round he reared his hairy mass into the air and, like a falling cliff, concluded his addresses. His mate was unshaken by the mountainous occursion.

With awe in their faces Juan and his Hebrew acquaintance watched this Himalayan consummation. The younger spectators chattered excitedly and the nondescript old men sniggered and licked their lips.

'Now,' said Juan, 'is that utterly incongruous or is it typical of America? Those shaggy brutes were born in Tibet, in mountain silences broken perhaps by the thin sound of bells from a neighbouring lamasery. In appearance they are prehistoric. And yet we see them mating in New York, untroubled by sky-scrapers, the subway, night-clubs, five (or it may be ten) million inhabitants, and other aspects of a life utterly unlike their own. It strikes me as incongruous, but perhaps it is symbolical of America the World Refuge, the international Home from Home. What do you think, Mr. ——?'

'Cohen,' said the little Jew, 'Isadore Cohen.'

'And I am Juan Motley.'

'Pleased to meet you,' said Mr. Cohen. He blew his nose that the pungent odour of captive animals had titillated.

'I think it's all right,' said Mr. Cohen. 'I don't think it's anything to be surprised at. It's nature, see? Suppose you took a young man and a young lady from Brooklyn, for instance, and sent them to Tibet and put them in a cage, don't you think they'd do the same?'

'Even with a dozen lamas looking on?'

'Sure,' said Mr. Cohen, 'if there was no other way, and they'd got used to the lamas being there and knew they didn't mean any harm. Sure they would.'

Mr. Cohen's conception of nature, and his lack of surprise at its implications, seemed to Juan the characteristics of a sound man, and as they continued their walk he remarked that this was his first day in New York and he had no plans for the evening's amusement.

'You go and see *Black Bread*,' said Mr. Cohen immediately. 'It's the best show in town. It lasts four and a half hours, counting the intermissions. You won't get better value for your money anywhere. And if you want to go and have a drink when it's over I'll meet you outside and take you to a good place where the liquor's good and you know it's good. See?'

'You mean that you're going to *Black Bread* yourself to-night'?

'Sure,' said Mr. Cohen. 'I go every night. You look at the orchestra when you get there. That's where I sit.'

IV

Returning to his hotel with an hour to spare before dinner Juan bought several newspapers and prepared to interest himself in the day's news. It seemed that he had landed during an epidemic of violence. Florida had apparently been laid waste by a hurricane and its population – or such part as had escaped destruction – was being kept alive by Red Cross relief trains. A series of fires had consumed half-a-billion dollars' worth of timber in Washington and Oregon, and there had been an earthquake in Southern California. A lady in South Bend, Illinois, had killed her husband's paramour with a hammer, and a Pennsylvania salesman was attracting wide attention by the novel revenge – chiefly a matter of gasoline – which he had taken on his wife and her lover. 'Holocaust in Love-nest' was the title given to this tragedy. Apart from climatic and domestic disturbance, however, there was nothing that deserved headlines except a crisis in the national baseball competition.

Then, on the front page of one of the liveliest journals, Juan was amazed to find a photograph of three of his late fellow-passengers on the *Corybantic* – the man with the wounded eye and his followers. Even more arresting than the picture was the caption, which announced: 'Red-eye Rod Gehenna and his bodyguard homeward-bound. "European trip was just holiday," declares Beer Baron.'

With growing wonder Juan read on:

'"There's no beer-racket in Paris or Rome, and even if there had been I wouldn't of tried to muscle in on it."

'This was the admission made by Chicago's Underworld Tycoon when he received reporters in his private suite on the *Corybantic* this morning. With Rod were his two most trusted lieutenants, Rocco and Wonny the Weeper. Rod wouldn't spill anything about his trip to Europe. "Just a holiday," was his story, and he stuck to it, so rumors of a Chianti racket or a corner in *vin rouge* are obviously premature. A sad duty waits for Rod in his adopted empire of Chicago. Cola Coloni, who always drove his armoured car, was shot to death Saturday by rival gangsters, and his funeral has been postponed so that Rod can attend.'

Examining the other papers more closely Juan found similar stories in most of them. Red-eye Rod Gehenna – a forceful name – was important enough to have his arrival chronicled as thoroughly as that of a cinema actress or a foreign prince. And of his two lieutenants – Rocco and Wonny the Weeper – Rocco was the tough-looking one and Wonny, quite obviously, he who had blubbered so sadly in the moonlight. A strange couple. Juan remembered the sound of Rocco's voice as he bade his weeping friend, 'Snap out of it, hophead!'

So much was clear, but Juan was not yet sufficiently acquainted with America to understand 'racket' and 'beer baron.' The conjoint phenomena of organisation by violence and feudal chieftains to control such organisations no longer existed in England, and Juan had not realised the extent to which these characteristics of a healthy mediaevalism still flourished in America. Moreover, certain journalistic mannerisms – such, for instance, as a rash juxtaposition of *oratio recta* and *oratio obliqua* – made some of the reports unduly obscure. But in spite of difficulties this was evident: that Gehenna and his friends were figures of importance in the American underworld. In other words, they were famous criminals. And yet their movements, apparently, were not a matter for police supervision, but merely a source of interest to newspaper-readers. . . .

I am a prig and a pharisee, said Juan to himself in some disgust, having thought so far. Britannic righteousness is an uncomely trait, and these reporters are better men than I. They don't condemn Red-eye for being a citizen of the underworld; they clap him on the back because he is a king of the underworld. Nor do they make a text out of his sins against society, whatever they have been. Instead they take pains to tell us that he is warm-hearted, capable of sorrow, and grateful – that he is even now on his way to Chicago to stand bareheaded, wet-cheeked (or perhaps Wonny will do all the weeping that's necessary) by the grave of his fighting chauffeur, Cola Coloni.

But why, thought Juan, are they silent about the girl in black and the old woman with short legs? There's not a word about them anywhere. Did the reporters ever see them? Or had Red-eye kept them hidden?

Excited by his recent contact – however fleeting and unrealised at the time – with such stirring personalities as these, Juan went down to dinner. More keenly than ever he regretted his failure to make friends with the girl in black, and keenly he desired another opportunity. It was, perhaps, absurd to think of her now that he knew the nature of her travelling companions, but though he disapproved of the men, the girl, he found, shone more vividly in his memory by reason of her lawless *entourage*. The huge improbability of ever seeing her again, of discovering who or what she was, daunted but did not quite dismay him.

He felt alert and expectant, then, as he walked to the New Artists' Theatre, where *Black Bread* was being played.

Black Bread was the sensation of New York. Its author, Knut Blennem, was recognised to be the leader in histrionic innovation and the adaptation of stage practice to modern theory. It was he who had said: 'Psychology is our generation's gift to the world. Psychology has revolutionised philosophy, art, science, and society. Psychology has made men like gods. It was psychology that taught me to write plays.'

Ecstatically the critics had lauded his play. Their columns had been stuffed to bursting-point with superlatives and semi-naïve confessions of the emotional havoc which it had wrought in their semi-naïve but critical minds; for emotional havoc is much sought after in America. 'Here is a play to tear your heart out,' said one. 'Pity caught at my throat and choked me,' said another. This one's soul was slashed with anguish, that one's wrung with terror, and still another's turned in his breast like a babe in torment. When this was its effect on critical hearts and souls, what was the reaction of ordinary people likely to be? Juan asked the girl who sold cigarettes on the mezzanine floor of the Hotel Connecticut.

'Say,' she answered, 'it's a panic, it's a wow!'

And so wherever it was mentioned Mr. Blennem's name went up like a balloon on shrill blasts of adulation. For this play was to-day's asseveration of its powers, and before such powers as these it was clear that the so-called Immortals of yesterday were nothing but flops, four-flushers, and false alarms. For one and all they had died without ever hearing of psychology.

Black Bread was the story of the woman Kathleen and her three lovers, Sidney Bush, Walter Hood, and Gerald Tomkins. A secondary plot dealt with the affection entertained by Livia (Kathleen's sister) for Walter Hood; a vain affection. There was not very much action in the play. Every half-hour the scene shifted. Kathleen was introduced on the verandah of her home in the Adirondacks. She was talking to Sidney and Gerald. Then she was shown in bed, talking to Walter. Then in the living room, the dining room, on board a train, in an art gallery (some enlightened observations were offered here), a corridor, a garden, and a bathroom. But wherever she was she talked, and Walter, Gerald, and Sidney very often replied to her. But more often they wrote in their diaries. For this was the revolutionary device invented by Mr. Knut Blennem for discovering to the audience the true and secret thoughts of his *dramatis personae*.

It is notorious that we speak no more than half-truths in our ordinary conversation, and even a soliloquy is likely to be affected by the apprehension that walls have ears. Only to our diaries do we tell the whole truth and nothing but the truth, and by writing a play whose characters were all habitual jotters-down of errant thought, Mr. Blennem was able to show in the fullest detail his masterly psychological insight.

No less admirable than the original concept of dramatic diary-makers was Mr. Blennem's device for revealing to the audience, piecemeal and as they were written, the endless confessions of his characters. A frame of white screens surrounded the stage, each one clearly marked by a name, as Walter, Sidney, or Kathleen. And as each character wrote in his diary, what was written appeared on the appropriate screen, flashed on to it by a projector of the kind used in cinemas.

For example, Kathleen would say to Walter: 'I am weary to-day. I feel the life under my heart.' (For she was pregnant.)

And Walter would answer: 'The weather is growing sultry. There are more and more clouds in the sky.'

But in his diary he would scribble this, and this would flash on to the screen: 'The woman frightens me. I feel the dark power of her soul, and my soul struggles feebly in the whirlpool of her *ens*. She has engulfed me. Will she never tell me if I am the father of her child, or if Sidney begot it; or perhaps Gerald?'

For all three men were Kathleen's lovers, and all three knew that she was pregnant, but none (perhaps not even Kathleen herself) could say who was the father of the coming child.

In sharp contrast to Kathleen was Livia, who had no lovers, and her diary revealed with great sincerity her sex-starved – indeed famine-stricken – soul. She was in love with Walter, but he was frightened of her and always, when he was staying in Kathleen's house, slept with his door locked. This offended Livia who wrote in her diary: 'An open door is God's blessing to a wall. He who bolts a door will deny his Master. Dear heart, and his bed so broad!'

After several acts in which Kathleen grew more and more mystical and her lovers wrote quicker and quicker, the baby was born, unexpectedly, in a florist's –'In the beauty of roses did I labour. Between white roses and dark roses was my baby born. In the scent of many flowers he first smelt life'– so the mother-triumphant, some time later, described her ordeal. But not before a scene almost too dramatic, and very harrowing to conservative opinion in the audience.

The baby was black.

Sidney, Gerald, and Walter were all quite white. They had hereditary taints to prove their impeccable ancestry. And there was only one other male character in the cast – Kathleen's negro chauffeur, Ham.

Ham, the gigantic Nubian, was the baby's father.

Their feelings intolerably wounded, Sidney, Gerald, and Walter make ready for a lynching, and Ham is apparently willing to submit. But before removing his collar he sings a few verses of 'Swing low, sweet chariot,' and the noise brings Kathleen to his defence.

She is wearing a dressing-gown which Gerald at once declares (through his diary) to be symbolic. It has a black and white chequer-board design. With Ham crouched at her feet, shapeless, inhuman, looking indeed rather like an outcrop of black basalt, Kathleen declares: 'I sing the song of miscegenation. Black shall mate with white, negro with northerner, and the strength of Africa run hot in Nordic veins. Zion shall lie down with the Lap and the pledge of their love be fertile over the earth. In my heart are many mansions, and every nation is my guest – Eskimo, Teuton and Gael; Slav, Polynesian, Trinobant. . . .'

There was a majority of women in the audience. The spectacle of Kathleen with her court of four men exalted them, for they had no more than one man apiece (if that) and he, perhaps, was tongue-tied, and gravel-blind to their deserts, and weak in the back, and given unduly to sleep. But there, on the visible stage, was a woman with a man at every point of the compass, a man in every corner of the room, so that wheresoever she might turn there was one to cosset and comfort her, and foment the unhealing wound of Eve. So should all women be accommodated, thought the esurient ladies in the audience, and loudly clapped their hands; and such husbands, lovers, and male dinner-partners as were present clapped too, without enjoyment indeed, but realising – as good Americans – that when it comes to culture women know best.

'Well, how d'you like it?' said Mr. Cohen, hurrying round the corner of the building and finding Juan on the edge of the emergent crowd. Juan told him.

'Don't speak so loud,' said Mr. Cohen. 'Not here, with all these ladies round us. They think it's swell, see? and after all, if you got nothing to do all night you can park your fanny here for four and a half hours – instead of two and a half at any other theatre – so you ought to be more careful what you say, Mr. Motley.'

The speakeasy to which they went was rather more than a hundred yards from the theatre. There were several nearer than that, but Mr. Cohen thought their exertions in going so far would be repaid by better liquor and more attractive surroundings. A slight formality preceded their admission: a knocking at doors and being considered, through a shutter, by pale and globous eyes. Then they found themselves in a room occupied by twenty or thirty people who sat at little tables or stood at a small but useful bar. Some glass aquarium tanks gave the place a certain character of its own. Brightly coloured stupid-looking fish swam mildly to and fro in the greenish water, and reflected from their iridescent scales odd gleams of light. Because of the heat there were little beads of moisture on the glass walls. The other furnishings were unremarkable, though dim lighting fashioned them into a semblance of comfort, and the variety of bottles behind the bar made specious promises. The whisky had a slight flavour of burnt sugar, but was very powerful. The customers were of several kinds. Some were hearty robust men with brightly painted ladies. Others were pale young men with equally blanched companions. Several by their bluff but maladroit assertion were obviously provincial visitors. Tobacco smoke and a subdued babble of talk disputed for possession of the air with a smell of spirits and the several odours – of powders, perfumes, and essences – emanating from the women. An argument, animated but monotonous, was in progress at a table near to that occupied by Juan and Mr. Cohen.

'Oh yeah?' said a man.

'Yeah,' replied the woman with him.

The first *yeah* had a rising inflexion, and the man's voice was exaggeratedly bitter, sarcastic, and incredulous. The responsive female *yeah* declined and deepened in tone, and the woman spoke harshly, combatively, and doggedly.

'Is zat so?' enquired the man, and seemed marvellously sceptical.

'Yeah, that's so,' replied the woman.

'Well, that's too bad,' said the man. 'That's just too bad.' His sarcasm sharpened to an almost metallic edge.

'Oh yeah?' said the woman, in her turn incredulous.

'Yeah,' replied the man, and his voice was harsh and dogged.

'Is zat so?' enquired the woman. . . .

Exchanging their simple weapons in this way they continued the debate without embarrassing each other by introducing new arguments, and only interrupted their sequence of enquiry and denial to order more drinks.

'Cosy little place, eh?' said Mr. Cohen.

'Very interesting indeed,' said Juan, and looked over his

shoulder at the other half of the room. At a table beneath a tank in which swam globular, grossly pouting and silver-glistening fish, sat four men engaged in earnest conversation. Two of them Juan instantly recognised as Rocco and Wonny the Weeper. Mildly astonished at the coincidence he shifted the position of his chair so that he could watch them out of the corner of his eye.

'And what d'you think of America?' demanded Mr. Cohen.

Juan explained that his preconception of it had been something like the sound of a carnival or large circus in progress. . . .

'Yeah,' said the woman at a nearby table.

'Is zat so?' enquired the man.

'Yeah, that's so,' re-affirmed the woman. . . .

'You see,' said Juan, 'when we're unfamiliar with a place we seldom realise its more serious activities. That is a human failing, Mr. Cohen –'

'Call me Isadore,' said Mr. Cohen.

Juan attempted to elaborate his first impressions of New York. It was, he said, very large and noisy, and it appeared to have remarkable powers of assimilation. It could naturalise marvels. Strange and horrific events seemed in the turbulent flux of Manhattan no more than feathers on the Amazon.

Isadore listened politely. The whisky, with its curiously artificial flavour, was undeniably strong, and Juan began to find entertainment in the sound of his own voice. The heat of the room and the propulsive force of the whisky were speeding his blood on its tortuous somatic voyage. Many other voices jostled for air in the busy room, but Juan heard his own much more distinctly than anyone else's, and he enjoyed the obedient way in which clause fitted into clause, and his sentences slid to their appointed periods.

'Like feathers on the Amazon,' he repeated. 'Above all, the traveller must be impressed by your gift for domesticating the outrageous and patronising miracles. That's it. You patronise miracles and domesticate the outrageous.'

Isadore made little deprecatory noises with his lips. 'I'll tell you what America's like,' he said. 'It's dull.'

'Dull!' Juan expostulated.

Isadore nodded his head. 'That's what wrong with America,' he said. 'It's dull.'

The argumentative man and his controversial companion had relapsed into a sullen silence. From a further group came a voice, heavy with emotion, asserting with singular intensity, 'He's a swell guy when you get to know him,' and someone else, lauding a hero equally anonymous, shrilly declared, 'Well, he just kicked the pants off him. Yes, sir. Just kicked the goddam pants off him.'

Under the tank that held globular silver fishes Rocco and Wonny the Weeper were apparently at odds with their neighbours. Three of them sat with their elbows on the table bending forward, heads thrusting to a centre, and argued with muted violence. Wonny sat upright, looking mournfully at nothing. Immediately above him one of the silver fishes stared in the same direction, opening and closing its small thick-lipped mouth with mechanical regularity. Bony ridges above its eyes gave it a worried look. Its mouth gaped. So did Wonny's. And Wonny's protruding embryonic forehead shone mildly in an aqueous light.

Juan heard Rocco saying, 'He's goin' to-morrow on the Broadway Limited.'

'It's dull,' said Isadore, and showed the red cavern of his mouth in a wide yawn. 'There's too much noise, for one thing, and too much noise makes you thick-headed so as not to hear it, and when everybody's thick-headed you got to shout like hell to *make* 'em hear. And that's more noise. When a cop pulls his gun on you he doesn't shoot once, he shoots all he's got. Nobody's going to pay attention to one shot, see? Not in Chicago or N'York, and they set the fashion. And nobody's going to pay attention to a guy that plays the violin just well, or a guy that paints a picture that's just good, or writes a book that's just good. Everybody wants big time stuff, something *de luxe*, so these guys claim they are *de luxe*, and their pictures and books the smartest things you ever seen. And that's dull, because they aren't, and by-and-by you get to know they aren't and don't even expect them to be.'

The man and woman who sat nearby were again arguing, and at Rocco's table a quarrel seemed imminent.

Under the silver fish Wonny, wide-eyed, stared sorrowfully into space. But the two strangers stared at Rocco and Rocco's eyes were busy with them. Their slouching attitude had subtly changed. Anger had made their muscles tense and so the slouch had become a crouch. They growled across the table. One man's chin stuck out fiercely and a snarl had contorted Rocco's mouth into a curious triangular shape. People at neighbouring tables, aware of the brewing storm, forgot their own topics of conversation and looked nervously over their shoulders, and craned to hear the mutter of voices which might at any moment discover itself as the prelude to violent action.

It was the man opposite Wonny who started the fight. With dexterity that a conjuror might have envied he produced an automatic pistol and fired one shot. He had no time to fire more. For if he had been quick as a conjuror Wonny was a veritable magician. His pistol simply appeared from nowhere, and before the sound of the first man's shot was complete two bullets sped from Wonny's gun in nimble twin assault and the Weeper's rash opponent sank foolishly into his chair and, like a horrid drunkard, fell sideways to the floor.

The first bullet, rising high, had missed Wonny altogether and smashed the aquarium tank above his head. It hit, indeed, the globular gaping fish that had so long and stupidly stared into the smoky room. Wonny disappeared under the deluge of water and broken glass and the unexpected draught of fishes, and the bullet-struck fish, its silver skin laced with its golden blood, lay on the floor unseen. Its shining plump companions flopped and wriggled beside it, drowning in the hot air of the speakeasy, trampled on by the panic-feet of the men they had seen so often and so uncomprehendingly. Their fishy eyes stiffened into dead jelly, and their silver mail was broken on the floor where customers had thrown the butts of their cigarettes. So, killed astonishingly by a gangster, one by one the silver fishes died, far from the cold native silence of their sea, and the jungle softness of waving weed, and the white labyrinthine shelter of coral reefs. And by-and-by a policeman spoke their epitaph in blasphemy as he trod on one, and slipped, and fell bluntly to the wet floor. . . .

But long before the police arrived, before the fish had gasped twice or their glistening scales were bruised at all, Juan and Mr. Cohen had left the scene of disorder and were hurrying downstairs to the peaceful tumult of the streets. While their ears still rang with the noise of the pistol shots, and while everybody else stood foolishly, and shouted or screamed with excitement, the quick-witted Isadore grabbed Juan by the arm and dragged him to the door, and through the outer door, and away from all the disintegrated fragments of a once-respectable speakeasy.

'You see what I mean?' he said excitedly. 'Always your conversations are interrupted in America. By a fire, by a murder, by an automobile accident. There's no peace, no time to think, and if you can't think you're dull, see?'

They walked towards Broadway. The street was dark and there were few people about. Isadore was angry at the way in which their discussion had been cut short, and Juan contended with several conflicting emotions. Inclined to be frightened by a world in which revolvers were hidden under a veil of amiability – and when that veil was torn leapt out, barking – he also felt disposed to cultivate a tough hard-boiled attitude, a swaggering pose in which he should pretend that gun-play was quite *à la mode de chez lui*. This unnatural reaction was due to the bad whisky that he had drunk, however. A more native emotion was amusement at Isadore's conception of dullness. It was, he reflected, the ultimate stage of sophistication to be bored by murder – and then his leaning to laugh at Mr. Cohen changed to respect.

The street lost its narrow darkness in the noisy brilliance of Broadway.

Juan remembered something. 'What is the Broadway Limited? Is it a train?' he asked.

'Sure it's a train,' said Isadore. 'The fastest train in the world. It goes to Chicago three o'clock every afternoon.'

The lower sky was daubed with dazzling clusters of lights. Incandescent banners flared on every roof. Now this one paled and that one flushed. A livid eruption leapt from the darkness to laud a play; a scarlet rash proclaimed a motor car; emerald coruscations announced a dentifrice; and like some dreadful acne of the night a rosy itch of gigantic letters formed the catchpenny name of a cigarette. The crowd surged this way and that, and traffic passed, and as though tidal waters met and contended between the alpine walls here were the ceaseless roar of a whirlpool, the ground-bass of distant storm, the angry shrieking of gulls, and the blare of present tempest. Lit brightly as by searchlights the faces of the people who crowded the pavements looked vivid and unreal. Ten thousand faces animated with little flickering emotions. Not real emotions like hunger and love, but skin-deep sensations and the pin-prick of a joke. White faces like masks, and faces that were only a soft cover for the thick fantastic bone that underlay them. It was no wonder that women who had to meet such lights as these should paint their cheeks and plaster their lips till they looked like red india-rubber. Rouge, perhaps, could hide their mortality from the searchlights. And many of them had pretty faces too, faces as pretty as magazine covers, and very like them to look at. A parade of magazine-cover faces. And the men were smoothly shaven, and looked self-assured, and not unlike the magazine photographs that advertise collars and ties and safety razors. A parade of collar advertisements. Except that there were too many Jews in the crowd, and advertising experts never use photographs of Israelitish customers to recommend their goods – but the Jews faced the arc-lights better than the Gentiles, for their eyes were darker and the bony substructure of their faces came from an antique mould.

A saffron effulgence tinted all within its radius. The source of the light was a booth selling fruit drinks. On snow-white counter and shelves were golden pyramids of oranges. White-coated servers jerked at a gilded cistern and drew from it cups of orange-juice which many of the magazine-covers and collar-advertisements stopped to buy. These midnight New Yorkers had, it seemed, individual impulses. They obeyed at least one of the laws of physiology. They might even be human? – White masks, masks with carmine lips and darkly shadowed eyes, masks with smooth and lovely contours, and masks of men with thin hard lines between nose and mouth, eyes like a pebble, and fleshy jowls. They probably were human, in spite of the noise which filled the air and seemed like the noise of a great clockwork engine to keep them running. They drank orange-juice. That was a human habit. No, gentler than a human habit – a nursery taste. And equally it was a nursery game to wear masks, and coloured lights were the trappings of a nursery.

Then the meaning of the gorgeous sky-signs became clear to Juan, and he saw that they were nothing like fever-rash or pock spots or acne. He had been stupid beyond measure to think of such unpleasant similitudes. They were playthings, birthday toys, carnival lanterns, Christmas-tree candles, nursery night-lights – a million night-lights to frighten away ghosts and bogeys and things that go bump in the night. Manhattan was a nursery, a superb and opulent and spacious nursery where the children could stay up all night. That's what they meant by the Statue of Liberty – there was no one to come and put them to bed. And of course when one looked at them carefully the buildings were fashioned with astonishing accuracy on nursery models that one used to construct with wooden blocks. They were square-cornered, straight up and down, gradually recessed, and the real point in erecting them was to see how high one could go without toppling over. . . .

'Let's go somewhere and have another drink,' said Juan.

'Sure,' said Isadore, 'but we'll go to a safe place this time.'

They took a taxi and drove to Fifth Avenue and northwards along Fifth Avenue past the silent gloom of Central Park, till they came to streets midway between the eightieth and ninetieth parallels, and there turned east again, and finally came to a thoroughfare that looked and somehow felt very different indeed from the gaudy turbulence of Broadway and the deep darkness of the tributary theatre-streets. Here was a middle state, neither lit too gaily nor lost in Cimmerian night. Here was a good broad street, not crowded and not deserted. Here people neither rushed to and fro nor with sinister intent waited stilly in doorways, but went leisurely about their business. And here, plainly to be smelt, was an English or German smell, very pleasant, and charged with the power of evoking memories that ranged from amiability to the most jovial excesses.

'All these places sell beer,' said Isadore. 'D'you like drinking beer?'

Without unnecessary discussion they knocked at a door and were admitted by way of some stairs and a long passage to a scene of stimulating geniality. In a spacious cellar people were drinking at their ease. There were fat men and fatter women, their flaxen-fair daughters and broadly backed, broadly smiling sons. On every table stood handsome tumblers full or half-full of beer, and even where no more than an inch remained it was instructive to see how lovingly a gleam of light would linger in the amber shallowness, while full glasses shone like burnished copper under their cool heads of foam. Nor was drinking the only amusement offered, for song added its graces. Waiters humorously clad in Tyrolean costumes put down their trays and gave stout baritone voices to Germanic praise of love and wine. A pianist played tirelessly. Between songs he would improvise a little, very quietly, and then glide or dash into a chorus that set everyone singing and clapping on the tables. Red and rotund fathers pushed back their chairs so that their bellies might have room to swell as they searched for sweeter notes, and pot-modelled matrons shrilled breathlessly, found they had no wind for singing, and took to beating their hands on table-tops – and then, such bounty was in their bosoms, their arms seemed all too short for clapping, and so they gave it up and very good-naturedly laughed instead, at themselves and their yodelling bed-mates, and shook as they laughed till their chairs (which they all overlapped) creaked and creaked again.

Juan, delighted with such a spectacle, drank glass after glass of beer and joined in all the choruses though he knew none of them, nor indeed more than a dozen German words all told. But in the hearty mood induced by drinking there seems to be an intuitive understanding of foreign tongues: not, of course, Hottentot or Hamitic tongues or the chirping bird noises of Tongkinese; but the *bel canto* of Italian and the throaty ballad-mongering of German, to an Englishman lightly in his cups, need no interpreter, for they are kindred growths of the humus from which his own sweet wordage nobly grew.

Isadore, however, was not so moved. He still thought that America was dull.

'Now you come from England,' he said, 'and in England you've got lords. And a lord's interesting, I should think, though I've never seen one. Anyway they're lords, and different from ordinary people. Well, we got lords here too – guys that's rich enough to be lords and maybe even kings. But they aren't interesting. And why? Because they aren't any different from you and me. They may lose their money any day, and then where would they be? Jerking soda or pressing pants. The same with engineers and college professors and Baptist ministers – they may be selling real estate to-morrow. There's no real trades or professions left in America. There's just different ways of making money, see? And so nobody's really any different from anybody else. They just say they are, see?'

But as if purposely to contradict Mr. Cohen the waiter at that moment singing was quite obviously different from the common run of mankind. He was a Siegfried of a waiter, whose voice was like thunder in a honey-dripping cave. His Tyrolean costume made evident that even his knees were comely – strong, round, and rosy under their brief leather trews – while so vast an expanse of chest as strained to view between his green braces had rarely been exhibited since the days when heroes lodged on earth. His close-cropped hair was bright gold and so was the moustache that grew upwards and outwards in Hohenzollern fashion. His nose was magnificent, his teeth white and even, and his eyes recited eclogues. They were marvellous eyes. Madrigals and triolets hid in their lyric depths, and when they rolled – as they often did – it was in no common roll, but a barcarolle.

The waiter's name was Alto, and he was deservedly popular.

Following Alto came a singer so amazingly stout that his Tyrolean small-clothes were scarcely visible. His body swelled cumbrously above them. His belly, balanced on those inadequate garments, looked like an acorn on its shallow capsule or like an Easter egg served on a liqueur glass. To exaggerate his ovoid appearance he was quite bald, and his tiny eyes were scarcely visible in the huge expanse of a face that extended in homogeneous pink from cranium to the ultimate convexity of his lowest chin.

His preparations for a song were warmly applauded. He hung a scroll upon an easel. On the scroll were pictures of simple objects such as a ring, a rose, and a book. The pianist played a dashing prelude and with a baton the egg-shaped man pointed to one of the diagrams and chanted to the audience: '*Ist das nicht ein' Schnitzelbank?*'

Immediately the audience banged their fists upon convenient tables and roared the unanimous affirmative, '*Ja, es ist ein' Schnitzelbank!*'

Then the egg-like man (whose name was Eitel) swung his baton widely and gathered them into a rolling chorus: '*Eine schöne, eine schöne, eine schöne Schnitzelbank!*'

There were some twenty-four pictures on the scroll and they were all employed in the catechism.

'*Ist das nicht ein golden Ring?*' he would ask, and promptly the audience reassured him, '*Ja, es ist ein golden Ring*!'

Then from one object to another – '*golden Ring, schönes Ding*' – dancing here and there across the chart, the point of his baton hopping nimbly as a flea from picture to picture, and the choir breathlessly keeping pace – '*Blaue Rose, redliche Dose, Heiliges Buch, warmes Tuch*' – till at last he brought them back to the declamatory and melodious chorus:

'*Eine schöne, eine schöne, eine schöne Schnitzelbank!*'

In a stricken solitude of insusceptibility to choral heartiness, Isadore had relapsed into melancholy spectatorship.

'I guess I've been here too often,' he said when Juan expressed surprise at his indifference. 'I go to lots of places. This is a pretty good joint, but they don't change their songs more than once in a lifetime.'

Everybody else was sweating freely, and fat Eitel looked as wet as Thames valley in flood. Sweat rolled off his hairless head, down the pink dome of his forehead and the smooth expanse from ear to eyebrow, and ran steadily over wet cheeks into the gully between his true and first adventitious chins. This in time it filled and like a waterfall flowed over to the second gully, and so to the third, and presently down his neck where some half a gallon was absorbed by his shirt and the rest meandered down his deluged chest, the flood being constantly reinforced by rivulets from his shoulders and springs that gushed up everywhere. And all this sweat that ran downwards, ultimately to make pools about his feet, was in addition to fountains that flew sideways whenever Eitel, with impatient hands, dashed half a pint from his forehead and a gill or so from dewlap and jowl.

For some minutes after the song was finished the whole audience clapped and cheered, and innumerable glasses of beer were handed to Eitel, who drained them so quickly that the beer seemed to evaporate at the mere sight of his face.

V

Forty storeys high, five hundred feet above the pavement, Juan slowly undressed. His window stared coldly at the mountain tops. He looked out and down at the distant street. It grew narrow and receded still farther. Very gently the towering hotel began to sway from side to side like a lily nodding heavily in the breeze. Across the street rose another gigantic wall, pierced with a multitude of casements, square black holes, entrances to a thousand caves. Presently the window-riddled wall, very slowly and with a kind of magnificent hesitancy, started to sway backwards and forwards like a scuttle opening and closing to the long roll of a ship. Juan hurriedly drew in his head.

He had said good-night to Isadore. Behind his thick spectacles the Jew's eyes had been blurred with tears. 'It's dull,' he had muttered. 'Everything's very, very dull. No, I'm not talking about New York now. Just life. You ever been married? Well, you don't know nothing yet. I've been married six months. She looks like a million dollars, but she only knows a hundred and twenty words and she's only got two ideas in her head. The other one's hats. And I got to go home. I got to go right home. I got to go right home this very minute. And there's nothing new about it now. It's just dull. Everything you got to do over and over again is dull. And life is just doing things over and over again. It's dull, see? Awful dull.'

Staggering a little he had walked away, and turned to wave his hand, and slowlier walked on again.

Now Juan reviewed as well as he was able his first day in America, and found it a puzzle-picture of German waiters, and speakeasies, and girls tumbling horribly through the air, and ponderously loving yaks, and pistol shots, and a great din of traffic, and ten thousand faces flaring whitely in a cruel glare, and cliff-dwellings, vast and man-made, and a Bible on every bedside table in the land. . . .

In the Hotel Connecticut were two thousand nine hundred and eighty rooms, of which a third were doubly occupied. Here then, in this one building, in this steel and concrete cliff, in their tiny caves in the cliff, slept four thousand mortal souls. Extra-territorial troglodytes, the new cliff-dwellers. Row upon row, layer on layer, the sleepers sprawled secure in the contiguity of their Bibles, their radios, and their shining cuspidors. Forty deep. Men and women from all the provincial states of America, gaping and unguarded in slumber, lying forty deep in a giant external catacomb. . . . Juan moved uneasily to think of the solid three-dimensional mass of stertorous humanity, the ranks and piles of sleepers, the multitude of bodies generating excrement and dreaming their Freudian dreams. . . . The sanitary arrangements of the catacomb were, of course, magnificent; nothing more perfect than the American bathroom – save perhaps the Ionic column – has been given to the world of men. . . . But dreams! Ay, there was the rub. For in that myriad-minded sleep what volitions out of quod might not fill the incorporeal air? Or, lying as they did in beds alike, in like rooms; their stomachs filled alike with chicken *à la* king and pie *à la mode;* their flesh tickled by the same lush details of the current boudoir crime; their brains filled with the moist pabulum of the same moving-picture theatre; their eardrums still aquiver with oozy jazz and the whine of the same radio-minstrel – uniform in so many ways, perhaps even their dreams were uniform? Perhaps one huge and hazy-purple vision hung over the entire hotel, seeping and drifting into room after room; a democratic same-for-all dream, efficient and mindful as a department-store catalogue of the five senses that it had to gratify – and so to the four thousand sleepers would be given the sight of thousand-dollar bills, and the sound of a broadcasting supernal *minnesinger*, and the touch of silk or flesh as smooth, and the odour of French perfumes, and the taste – why, of the fine liquor they had drunk before Prohibition, or to the virtuous tenth the delectable flavour of a chocolate soda.

Made restless by these fancies Juan turned again to the window and looked out, but was careful not to look down. . . . Towers rose, night-grey, square and strong. And other towers, not grey but brilliantly illuminated by concealed flood-lights, that were not content with strength alone, but flowered consciously into beauty. Having climbed so high and reached free air their architects had drawn flourishes and scrolls instead of straight-edge lines, and added to the harsh utility of concrete blocks a cupola and spires, pinnacles and minarets and a fretted balcony. Here was a golden dome in a daffodil field. There, faintly blue, was a stone lantern prinkt with jewels; topazes and blood-red rubies and a hoop of jade. And over the way, as pink as ever desert sunrise painted one or rosy dreams of Isfahan could dye it, stood an apparent mosque – minarets and marble dome in a flush of peach-bloom light – with two-score storeys between it and the reality of the street.

A curious phenomenon, thought Juan, was this sky-high romanticism of New York. Why should steel and concrete put forth these white irrational petals and golden buds? Why did life insurance offices lift a carved stone lantern to the stars?

Why? So that New York could play at fairies on the house-tops; and keep a rendezvous with the genies and black Masrur of the Arabian Nights; and live with Prester John in castles of the air.

Why? Because the incurable adolescence of Ireland, the sentimental heart of Germany, and the lively passion of Italy had all taken out naturalisation papers and turned American, and New York, unhampered by the wealth of Midas, was become the last capital of Romance. . . .

So thinking, at any rate, Juan went to bed and, but a minute later, to sleep.

VI

'It is, I'm afraid, a romantic thing to do,' said Juan; 'and when I say romance I mean a certain kind of unreason which is superficially attractive; I mean a daedal optimism; I mean a leaning towards beauty without any settled notion what beauty should be; I mean a rather blood-shot sentimentalism; I mean a restless inclination to escape from reality and look for a brightly coloured nothing-in-particular; I mean a childish belief in the value of tasting everything that's likely to taste sour or sweet or rancid or spicy or triple-*sec* – anything that isn't just plain and wholesome.'

He was addressing the image in his shaving mirror.

'When I say romance,' he continued, 'I mean a certain kind of silliness on a large and pleasant scale; I mean a denial of tasteless common sense for the sake of pungent nonsense. I mean that although there are a million girls in New York my present impulse is to look for a girl in Chicago; or one about to be in Chicago. A girl dressed in black, of whom I know these things: that she has a beautiful face, a voice that can make very ordinary words sound attractive, and a manner in walking of which even the memory is exciting; and of whom I infer this, that she is a relation – either by blood or subsequent exchanges – of Red-eye Rod Gehenna, who is a criminal.'

Juan wiped some fringes of soap from his neck an l cheeks. His eyes were a little hot, his skin a thought too dry, his head slightly sore, and his stomach inclined to be queasy. But the night had been worth such small discomfort, and his malaise was actually inciting him to further action. The scrap of conversation that he had overheard in the speakeasy, when Rocco spoke of the Broadway Limited, referred in all probability to Red-eye's plans. And if Red-eye were going to Chicago was it not likely that the girl would be going with him? At any rate Red-eye was the only connexion with her, the only means of rediscovering her, of which Juan knew. The nervous irritation which commonly follows excessive drinking can often be allayed by action. Frequently it demands action. And so Juan, at first only idly contemplating a journey to Chicago, found himself urged to undertake it by a physical disquiet arising from alcoholic dehydration of his tissues.

Having packed a suitcase he arranged for the rest of his luggage to be sent on to Carthage (the small town adjacent to, and largely dependent on, Motley University) and drove to the Pennsylvania Railroad Station, the appearance of which very nearly sent him back to his hotel, for its size was an embarrassing circumstance to an errand so foolish as his. Apparently it had been designed for the inception of a Crusade, for while it was large enough to accommodate a World Fair and several circuses it also contrived to carry an episcopal manner, and one looked vainly for a cardinal, or at least a bishop with crozier and mitre and a pail of holy water, to bless the engines ere they thundered out to girdle their demi-earth with smoke. But there was no bishop. And so huge was the vista and so high the roofs that even the vastest, most arrogant engines were dwarfed, and their thunder seemed almost an impertinent thunder, and probably they were very glad to be away from such an overgrown cathedral of a station, and out into the fields where they could snort in honest pride and feel sure of their importance. . . .

Just before the train started Juan caught sight of Wonny, bare-headed, on the platform. This reassured him to some extent, though he had not yet discovered whether Red-eye was aboard. But there were many so-called drawing-room compartments on the train, whose occupants, if they chose, could maintain complete privacy. Red-eye and the girl in black were probably in a drawing-room.

Wonny's peculiar forehead loomed larger and rounder than ever owing to a cut, swollen at the edges, and a greenish bruise that he had apparently suffered when the shattered fish-tank fell on him. It was a little odd to associate a man so mild, indeed so foolish in appearance, with murder performed so expertly – sitting so quiet and abstracted at one moment, and the next, without hesitation and without a flourish, shooting swiftly and accurately. There had been half a second between the other man's threat and the waterfall from the broken aquarium tank – and in that half-second Wonny had produced, aimed, and twice fired his pistol. Had he been a man of stern expression and handsome features Juan would have found this nimble feat much more credible, but to find military virtues in a man who looked like an imbecile was rather shocking. He was also a little curious to know why Wonny had not been arrested; for his ideas of police methods, being founded on English procedure, were still limited.

In a short time, by diligently searching up and down the train, Juan discovered Red-eye in one of the private compartments. The door was half-open as he passed, so that he could see Red-eye and Wonny sitting together. There was no sign of Rocco or the girl.

Juan returned to his seat in an ordinary Pullman car. He began to suspect the insufficiency of his plan, to which he had not given much serious consideration. He had assumed that the girl would still be travelling with Red-eye, and if she had not – she had perhaps gone on ahead – then he could follow the kenspeckle Gehenna, discover where he lived, and there – walking in the garden, looking out of a window, returning from a ride – there would be the girl. Now it occurred to him that perhaps a King of the Underworld did not live as other men live. Strange ceremonies might await his arrival in Chicago. Juan had imagined the homecoming of an ordinary citizen: a wife and daughter, or perhaps a son and daughter, meeting the train – a little group walking up and down the platform, chattering, laughing, looking round to see that their several porters still followed – a chauffeur respectfully saluting, holding open the door of a large glossy dark-blue motor car – its orderly progress to some residential district where streets were broad, and trees grew, and houses stood away from each other in a satisfied and portly way. If Red-eye's reception were like that it would be an easy matter to follow him. But it might be very different indeed. He might be met with pomp and ceremony, a brass band, a red carpet, a mounted escort, an address of welcome – or he might be smuggled away under a cloak of sinister precaution. And to make the future even more speculative, there was this matter of a funeral: Cola Coloni's obsequies, the chauffeur who should have respectfully opened the door of the glossy dark-blue limousine – but Cola Coloni had driven not an ordinary limousine but an armour-plated one, and that, of course, was the reason for his demise.

It seemed to Juan that things might be more difficult than he had anticipated. But he was not dismayed at the prospect. Indeed, having once decided that his course of action would have to depend entirely on the circumstances of Red-eye's reception in Chicago, he thought no more about it, but looked out of the window at the unfamiliar landscape.

Curiosity was still a major influence in Juan's life. It no longer took him to bathroom windows, as in the uninhibited days of his childhood, but it invested all he saw with interest and compelled him to live very much in the present. His actual environment generally occupied his attention to the exclusion of both past and future. The experience of the past was somewhere in his brain, neatly stored and ready for reference; but he did not care to dream about a reference library. And as to the future, why, that was doubtless a charming prospect, but it was still round the corner and it was foolish to speculate much on coming views when one's neighbours even now were a handsome hill, a pleasant river, and a large red barn of an unusually jocose appearance.

This satisfaction with immediate surroundings had kept Juan from giving more than the most cursory thought to his coming occupation with Motley University. To his mother's first suggestion of it he had replied without any eagerness whatsoever. Then he had thought better of it. It would at any rate mean escape from sheep-farming, and sheep had brought him nearer to boredom than any other form of life with which he was familiar. Sheep were things that you counted when you wanted to fall asleep. They were superfluous creatures in the morning and a weariness to the flesh at afternoon. But according to all reports life ran briskly at an American college. Juan became enthusiastic; wrote once more to his mother; readily agreed to study Business Administration, Industrial Management, Applied Accountancy, Corporation Finance, or any other of the arts and sciences recently invented by the indefatigable New World. He was even willing to become a financier if the professors of these subjects could teach him an easy road to affluence. His attitude was ingenuous. He felt that it would be a pleasant experience to own a million pounds – or even a million dollars – and he found it easy to believe that the Americans had reduced the acquisition of such a sum to an exact science and were ready, in the spirit of true democracy, to explain their methods to all who could pay the necessary fees. *Ex America semper aliquid novi.* He was, then, quite ready to spend a couple of years with the lively young people at Motley, and incidentally pick up the secrets which told in what dark cave or on what topmost shelf lay hid a million pounds – or, not to be greedy, a million dollars.

Once or twice he had felt a little itch of doubt. A course in Business Ethics (which Motley advertised among other attractions) obviously meant a course in which one was taught how to make a fortune in three years; that was the simple ethic of all business. And yet if the Googleheim professor of B.E. (as it was commonly called) really knew how to make a million in so short a time, why did he not make one for himself and go to live in Capri? . . .

The term at Motley would not begin for another week or two. This digressive journey to Chicago need not hinder the commencement of his studies unless something quite unforeseen occurred; and Juan did not bother to canvass destiny for possible mishaps but let the hours pass easily till bed-time came. Then, when the negro conductor had transformed the coach into a dark green-curtained aisle, with ship-board bunks two-deep on either side, then, in the midst of these strange and clumsy preparations for night, then came gusts of foreboding, and Juan was moved by something between fear and antic laughter.

The train roared loudly through the darkness. Eyes accustomed to the brightness of the coach could see nothing through a window. The outer blackness was solid, as though the train were in a coal-mine. The thunder of its passing was like the roar of falling roofs in a gallery in a coal-mine. Then, as the green curtains came down, the lights were dimmed. In the end compartment, which was a combined lavatory and smoking-room, fat men took off their coats, washed their faces, brushed their teeth, gargled and spat. There was a mingling smell of tooth-paste and cigar-smoke. The mirrors in the smoking-lavatory reflected its occupants from three sides, so that there appeared to be a multitude of fat men whose shirts escaped in untidy flounces above their belts, whose chins were streaked with little dribbles of tooth-paste and saliva, and the napes of whose necks all went into thick rolls of fat as they bent back to swill out their mouths.

Then, with the healthy taste of carbolic or peppermint fighting the stale hot tobacco-flavour on their tongues, the fat men went ponderously bedwards, swaying from side to side of the rocking coach till each found his own dark bunk. Now as they swayed there came from the mystery behind the green purdah little shrieks of pain and fear, for there, already in their cells, women were undressing. The curtains bulged outwards. The train rocked round a curve. The fat men put forth fat hands to steady themselves, aiming instinctively for those solid-seeming bulges. Then came the shrieks. For every bulge was a female head or shoulder or perhaps (for some were very large) a female buttock, as some stout traveller knelt and desperately twisted her body out of tight garments – and what might be the meaning of a stranger's hand clapt suddenly on a woman's haunch in the midst of disrobing? Rape at the very least. Shriek then, you Sabines, and in the greenish dusk of your retreat clutch your poor shift about you and pray – if you chance to recall a prayer or two – pray that your virtue be respected or your ravisher be handsome. . . . And now be at ease (for it was a false alarm, as you knew from the beginning) and as best you may tug off your stockings, your corsets or whatever you wear, and find a night-gown – and that's no easy thing to wriggle into in a bunk the size of a biggish coffin – and then put out your light, listen awhile to the iron lullaby of the wheels, and sleep if you can. . . .

But the fat men are still undressing, pulling off trousers and drawers and shirts in the minute privacy of their cells. *In privacy*. That's the secret of it all. We must be private in these matters of dressing and undressing, no matter how uncomfortable we make ourselves, how stupid the contortions that are necessary in a Pullman bunk before trousers and shirt will part company with their poor comrade the body. Privacy's the thing. For some of us look respectable when we're fully clad, and a few bear studying naked, but none, man or woman, looks anything but pitiable half-way between bare skin and broadcloth. Shirt-tails, sock-suspenders, armour-plating for ruined belly-walls, bandages to support this and that, moulds that a pair of breasts may be stuffed into and empty cups for no breasts at all; long drawers wrinkling down the scrawny legs of old men, and short drawers on the fat thighs of middle-aged men; ringlets of red crushed flesh above women's knees where their garters clipt; vests that stick slightly to a man's hot chest and coyly repeat his umbilical dimple – these may not be shown. These are shameful things. These are the deformities of our wardrobes and conspirators with our corporeal frailty. These are ludicrous, these wake laughter, and laughter is destructive. Keep them hidden, then. Wriggle in your bunks, dislocate your joints and break your backs, but take off your trousers in secret, you travellers – protruding through your green serge curtains the strange shapes of kobolds and gnomes – for your trousers hide not only your nakedness but your kinship to the clown. . . .

VII

At ten o'clock in the morning Chicago looked brisk and clean. Over half the sky were little round clouds in long straight lines, not close together but with space between, as if some heavenly drill-sergeant had but lately taken them in hand, barking in the way that sergeants use: 'Clouds, 'tshun! Open ranks, *march!*' And turning smartly on his heel saluted his commanding officer (who was well above the horizon in spite of a heavy night with the Marines in China) and indicated that all was ready for inspection.

Little round clouds, then, filled one half of the sky and the other half was bright blue. The lake glittered under the sun and a pleasant wind sent the waves chasing after gleams of light that constantly mocked them and rode sparkling on their unsuspecting backs. The water stretched to a horizon of its own, and that was no boundary either, for the lake went far beyond its first skyline, and the wind blowing off it had the keenness that comes from so vast and lonely a playground.

The beach was like no other beach in the world. Well out

of harm's way – for in winter the lake would throw mountainous waves ashore – stood a magnificent row of perpendicular castles. They soared into blue space, elegant, spectacular, and immensely strong. From a distance they looked like marble; but actually marble was too frail for their stupendous weight. And yet they had no appearance of weight, but the look of haughty elegance, an air of assured and calculated sublimity. The water-front of many towns is a squalid province of Barbary, but Chicago's lake-front is a splendid façade before the fat prosperity of the Middle West. . . .

When Juan arrived he had no time to look at all this breezy magnificence, for he was immediately occupied with the necessity of keeping Mr. Gehenna in sight. At first this was not difficult.

About five hundred people were waiting to welcome him with shouts of '*Evviva* Red-eye!' Most of them were Italians of robust appearance who chattered loudly and pressed forward to greet their ruler. Several photographers claimed his attention, for whom Mr. Gehenna obligingly posed, and some reporters talked with him in an animated way. They laughed loudly at his several jokes and told him one or two of their own, whereat the King guffawed in the pleasantest manner. There were also half a dozen policemen present, with whom Mr. Gehenna shook hands and to whom he made remarks as witty as those which had entertained the reporters; and on the outskirts of the crowd were a dozen or so more officers, some of whom stood with their thumbs tucked into their belts, looking conscientiously pugnacious and quietly ready for anything, and others leaned forward with ears greedy for the quips that made their superiors so merry, and eyes that looked enviously at all who were admitted intimates of the King. The only man unmoved by the reception was Wonny the Weeper. He stood by Red-eye's side, hands in pockets, his hat (because of the lump on his forehead) several sizes too small, and his spaniel eyes looking past all the vivacious Latin faces into some melancholy region of his own seeing.

Presently there was a murmur of new interest, and the crowd parted before a man who had the smooth and burly look which municipal politicians frequently acquire. He wore a rather wide-brimmed felt hat, and his jowl shone pink above a bright cravat. His coat was open to give his stomach air, and he walked through the crowd with a manner that effectively displayed his importance. Even Red-eye's attitude underwent a subtle change when the burly man greeted him by name.

'Well, Rod,' he said in a loud and juicy voice, 'How's tricks?'

The King, though not unduly flattered, showed that he appreciated the compliment of the other's appearance.

'Fine,' he answered, 'just fine. How's yourself?'

The crowd made sibilant noises of respect and admiration as these two figures of importance – tall men, both of them – stood hand-clasped and smiling; and the photographers, once more insistent, took several photographs of the handshake and the warm smile that each man maintained *in situ* for some time. Then there was a general move.

Outside the station a commission of two or three hundred school-children waited for the King: little girls in white dresses and little boys with button eyes and wetly brushed black hair. Their voices rose shrill as macaws and cockatoos and wildly they waved the Italian and American flags which they carried – American in the right hand, Italian in the left. Red-eye walked smiling between the childish ranks, pausing here to pat a little head, there to chuck a little chin, and even to distribute occasional largesse of quarters and dimes. While he was so engaged Juan found a taxi-cab and told the driver that he wanted to follow Mr. Gehenna when the latter drove away.

'Follow Red-eye?' said the taxi-driver, and made a sucking noise with one half of his mouth. 'He'll be going to Cola Coloni's funeral, I guess.'

'Then we'll go there as well,' said Juan.

'Five bucks down and the fare when we get there,' said the driver.

'That seems extravagant.'

'Tain't always good for your health, followin' Red-eye,' explained the driver.

Juan paid him five dollars and got into the taxi, though not without some misgivings. He had not been very surprised at the demonstration made by Red-eye's adherents. It was, of course, interesting to see a criminal treated so amiably and welcomed by the very people one would, in normal circumstances, imagine to be his enemies. But his experience in New York had warned him against too much astonishment at such a spectacle, for travel quickly broadens the mind. And, indeed, Juan had expected a brass band, so that the presence of the school children, which otherwise he would have admitted to be a pretty gesture, now seemed a puny one. They might at least have carried larger flags, he thought.

Red-eye got into a waiting motor car. The little girls and boys cheered him shrilly. The man who looked like a municipal politician waved him good-bye. Red-eye drove off. Several other cars, full of his friends and supporters, followed closely. After them went Juan's taxi.

They had a long way to go. Once the turmoil of the business quarter had been left behind, the streets were not impressive. They were rather shabby, and it seemed to Juan that the city sprawled in a vast and aimless way. But towns nearly always look aimless to a stranger, though to their inhabitants they are not only full of purpose but full of the most important purpose in the world.

The surface of the road was bad and the procession of motor cars all jarred their springs as they passed the same points. There were a lot of negroes on the streets, and many southern Europeans. Had the sun not been shining everything would have looked very grey and depressing, but the sky was blue, or blue and white with little clouds, and the wind came merrily round corners and picked up odd bits of paper and shreds of rubbish, and threw them about like an urchin playing football with a bundle of rags.

Progress became slower. Traffic was holding them up. The street was crowded with people. Taking advantage of a halt the taxi-driver removed his cap and combed his hair with a small comb that he kept in his breast-pocket. Then he replaced his cap. After another hundred yards he turned and said, 'I can't get any farther this way, but the Rigoletto Funeral Parlor's just round the block. That's where the body's lying. They're not letting traffic through because of the crowd. Only Red-eye and his lot. You'll have to walk if you want to go farther.'

Red-eye's car had disappeared, waved on by a stout Irish policeman whose pistol-holster stuck out at a tangent from his round belly.

'What can I do with my suit-case?'

The driver shrugged his shoulders, not being interested.

Juan remembered the name of a hotel near the railway station. 'Take it there,' he said. 'Give them my card and say that I'll arrive later.' He took a note of the taxi-man's number, paid him what he asked, and then, hurrying, walked into the crowd.

This, he imagined, was not the neighbourhood in which Red-eye lived. The most notable characteristic of the street was a smell that emanated in separate gushes from the small restaurants that half-filled it, and joined with more odours pouring from upper windows, behind which lived many large families. It was a warm and clinging smell, and a king would not want to live always in its midst. Red-eye's business here was the funeral. The *cortège*, moving slowly at first, would be easy to follow, till somewhere on its route one could pick up a taxi. From the cemetery Red-eye would surely go home, and there the girl in black would be waiting for him. So Juan thought.

He had to push his way round the corner. Cola Coloni, the fighting chauffeur, had been a popular figure and his obsequies were attracting a great deal of attention. The crowd, however, was not compact, and Juan was able to squeeze and insinuate himself among the other sight-seers until he came very near to the front row and could observe the segment of open street opposite the Rigoletto Funeral Parlor. A hearse stood there and in a line neatly behind it were the motor cars in which Red-eye and his friends had driven. On the far boundary of the open space was another crowd of spectators.

The hearse was already half-covered with flowers. Superb white blossoms grew on its roof and on the pavement outside the Funeral Parlor were banks of lilies. Except for the unfashionable neighbourhood it might have been a queen's funeral instead of a gangster's.

This, thought Juan, more than compensates for the inadequacy of Red-eye's reception. I wonder if they will have choir-boys?

The people crowded about him carried on lively conversations, but unfortunately he could understand nothing that was said, for they spoke mostly in the argot of Naples, with here and there a little Czech, Finnish, Gullah, and Yiddish.

Suddenly a hush fell on the multitude and from the Funeral Parlor stepped Red-eye himself, carrying a great faggot of Easter lilies. Behind him, covered with purple silk and snowy cyclamen, came the coffin borne by six men. Reverently they carried it out into the middle of the road so that a press photographer could take a picture of it, and silence lay so heavily on the street that beneath its weight the spectators stood staring and still.

Doubly, trebly astonishing then, was the shot that split that ponderous quiet. It was fired from an upper window and smashed into the flower-covered coffin, whose bearers dropped it with a crash to the road while they fled for shelter. Two more shots followed the first ear-splitting detonation in the stony chasm of the street, and from the crowd of sightseers rose a harsh and multi-lingual yell of fear. Turning from the battle centre they fled outwards, like cattle in a panic, like a storm-driven wave, like jungle trees bent before the fierce monsoon.

In half a minute the street was empty for fifty yards in each direction – except for Juan, who stood like an innocent (but vastly interested) in the very middle, and Red-eye and Wonny, lying under cover of the coffin to fire through a parapet of lilies at the enemies who had taken them by surprise.

The battle was now in full swing. Several bullets struck the road no more than a few inches from Juan's feet, and realising, almost too late, that he was in grave danger, he ran to one of the motor cars that stood in line behind the hearse and leapt inside. By this time he was very sensibly afraid and still intensely curious, for this (except the minor episode in the New York speakeasy) was the first time that he had ever been under fire. Half a dozen bullets ripped through the roof of the motor car in which he hid, and the *tat-tat-tat* of machine-guns came from several directions. But in spite of the danger Juan raised his head to peer cautiously over the back of the seat.

Cola Coloni's coffin had burst open in its fall and Cola Coloni, very stiff and ungainly in his best suit, lay half out of it, half on a snow-white heap of cyclamen and odorous white violets and lilies of the valley. Over the edge of the coffin, between green leaves and white flowers, there thrust into sight the muzzle of a rifle and a hand that held an automatic pistol. The intrepid Red-eye and Wonny the marksman still held the fort. By now their followers had penetrated to the rooms above the Funeral Parlor, and bringing shot-guns out of their trousers, pistols from under their arms, and machine-guns out of a bed where they had been concealed for such an emergency as this, they crowded to the windows and engaged the rival gangsters entrenched in the house opposite.

The magnificent plate-glass sides of the hearse had early disappeared, shot starrily to pieces, and very soon all the windows in the vicinity were full of prickle-edged holes or had become mere frames that held a few jagged splinters. A burst of machine-gun fire, ill-aimed, ripped into a pile of wreaths and sent white rose petals dancing into the air. A gangster, wounded in a tender place, howled with anguish. Several bullets lodged in motor car tyres which added their harmless explosions to the battle. A man tried to run across the street, but, mortally wounded in mid-passage, his knees sagged, his arms shot out, and his fingers just touched the farther pavement as if in a clumsy dive. He lay still.

And now Juan suddenly felt a violent blow on his left shoulder. From his kneeling position he fell to a sitting posture on the floor of the car, while a spasm of pain spread rapidly into his neck, and over his chest, and down his arm. With a feeling of mingled surprise and alarm it occurred to him that he was wounded. There was actually a hole in his coat, shoulder-high and close to the left lapel. When gingerly he thrust his right forefinger into it another wave of pain spread this way and that, and carefully unbuttoning his waistcoat he was concerned to find that his shirt was already bloodstained.

A feeling of intense indignation followed his initial sensation of alarm, and succeeding the indignation came mere unhappiness. With a handkerchief he tried to staunch the bleeding, and with all his heart he wished that he had never seen Red-eye. There were still bullets thudding against walls and making the wickedest noise imaginable as they flicked over into a ricochet. But the fight grew more leisurely with the increasing scarcity of ammunition. The very last bullet, however – so Juan reflected, and crouched lower to think of it – could hurt as much as the first.

Then approaching with great speed, there came a fresh noise, a clangour of bells and sirens, a stormaway Anvil Chorus, and more shooting. The police were coming. They had open cars with machine-guns mounted in them, and they had borrowed a fire-engine to which twenty officers hung, holding strongly with one hand and shooting desperately with the other at every tempting window as their crimson juggernaut roared up the street. All the cowboys between Laramie and

Las Vegas, galloping together, could scarcely have made so impressive an entrance.

The fire-engine stopped abruptly. The policemen leapt down, darted into doorways, and ran up strange stairways shooting as they went. The gangsters fled.

There were, it seemed, ways of escape from these houses, for with enviable ease the combatants simply disappeared before the breathless police. At the first sound of their sirens Red-eye and Wonny had slipped away. The King had already compromised himself by taking part in open warfare, and to find him still there when they arrived would have grossly embarrassed every policeman on the force. But Red-eye was a tactful man and fled in time. And so after all the shooting there was no one to arrest except the corpse on the road and two corpses in a house whose walls were well holed with bullets – and one of the latter had patently been lifeless for several days.

With this small reward for their exertions the policemen welcomed the sight of Juan who, acutely sorry for himself and anticipating the generous sympathy of others, now emerged from his bullet-spattered car.

'Well, look who's here!' exclaimed a sergeant in a jocose and brutal voice; and immediately Juan found himself covered by six or seven revolvers and menaced with a large array of handcuffs.

'Take those things away,' he said irritably. 'I had nothing to do with all this tomfoolery. I'm wounded and I want to see a doctor.'

The strange intonation of an English voice attracted more attention.

'For Christ's sake!' said one of the policemen. 'Boys, it's the Prince of Wales himself.'

'Who in hell are you, and how did you get here?' asked the sergeant.

Juan explained that he had been an innocent bystander and, caught between two fires, had taken the first refuge he noticed, which unfortunately had not been a secure one.

The sergeant listened attentively, conferred with a superior, and then sent for an ambulance, leaving Juan in charge of a stout red-faced officer.

'So you're an Englishman, are yez,' said the latter. 'Well, glory be to God!'

He looked lovingly at Juan and patted his arm, and then unable to control his emotion longer threw back his head and laughed with the utmost merriment, so that he almost split his red face in two.

The ambulance arrived and the Irish policeman, after helping Juan in, followed and sat beside him.

'An Englishman,' he marvelled, 'the first limey I ever saw shot in Chicago. Praise God I've lived to see the day. There's more sense in those gangsters than you'd be after thinking.'

And once again his head jerked back, his mouth sprang open, and he laughed as noisily as a quire of cornets, while the ambulance raced through the streets and Juan wore an expression as near disdainful indifference as he could contrive.

VIII

The battle over Cola Coloni's funeral provided Chicago with conversation for several days, and Juan, in hospital, was treated with distinguished consideration as soon as he had established the innocence of his participation. His photograph appeared in several newspapers and his account of the conflict, carefully edited, was printed beneath it. All the nurses were interested in his experience and whenever they had time came to entertain him with their conversation. Even the policeman who had been his companion in the ambulance visited him and talked in the friendliest way, but could not help laughing at the coincidence of a stray shot in a Chicago gangsters' conflict finding its billet in the only Englishman present. Once he brought some flowers that his wife had sent, and almost blew their heads off with the great wind of his mirth as he set them on the table.

Juan's wound was not serious. The bullet which struck him had evidently ricochetted off some part of the motor car, for it entered sideways and lodged against his collar-bone, which suffered a greenstick fracture. Some fragments of clothing had been carried in with the bullet, but as soon as these were removed the wound healed rapidly, and his initial unhappiness was replaced by a mild satisfaction in having added to his tale of life an experience that many go to their graves – even in Chicago – without acquiring. It did him no good, of course. On the contrary it caused him great inconvenience. But mortal man is avid of sensation and counts all that he survives as gain; though indeed it may teach him nothing.

The policeman's laughter, however, impersonal as it was, continued to be irksome, and Juan decided that the Irishman's sense of humour was warped.

A bullet in one's own shoulder is so much more important than the fate of other people that he almost forgot Red-eye and felt no anxiety for Wonny the Weeper. (Neither of them suffered any molestation from the police, the other gang having clearly been the aggressors.) Even his failure to track Red-eye home seemed unimportant, and his disappointment over the vanishment of the girl in black, that now seemed irremediable, for he was not inclined to look for her farther, was tempered in the heat of his wound. When he was released from hospital and stood ready to leave Chicago he felt a pang, an emptiness of heart, at having to forsake the hope he had entertained so briskly and to no avail – but (and this he realised) the pang was not so acute as it might have been, and to be shot, he concluded, was either an antidote to affectionate aspirations or a substitute for them.

His suitcase had been safely delivered to the hotel, and that was another comfort. He bought a ticket to Carthage and wondered, with a suitable degree of interest, what would happen there.

IX

The state of New York is an enormous triangle pointing downwards and outwards to its apex in the city of New York; the Hudson River and Lake Champlain make a perpendicular side; the northern boundaries of New Jersey and Pennsylvania a horizontal one; and the St. Lawrence, Lake Ontario, and part of Lake Erie combine to form its remarkably elongated base. In so great an area there is naturally a large variety of scenery, and the irregular harshness of wide areas is in whimsical contrast to the elegant rectangularity of the metropolis.

Along the base line there are many lakes, deep and long and narrow, and in this region, as in some others, the towns are distinguished by classical names. The little cities, half as old as time, that were heroic memories when London was a Roman camp have brash young namesakes here. Here are Troy and Ithaca. And the great men of antiquity are honoured here. Here are Cicero and Homer. And old enemies live in peace here – here are Rome and Carthage. They have no past, save in their names, and though all claim to have a future the greatness they anticipate is merely swelling of population, a multiplication of bank-balances; no such future of beauty and flames as waited for older Troy when Paris turned home with Helen at his side; no braggart grandeur such as old Rome demanded –

> *Hae tibi erunt artes, pacisque imponere morem,*
> *Parcere subjectis et debellare superbos* –

but a good slap-up future of new motor cars and louder radios and brighter lights and larger jazz-bands and stronger gin and sweeter banana-splits. . . .

And yet they have natural beauties thick about them, that should turn men's thoughts to splendour instead of belly loves. There is beauty in the hills, beauty in the lakes, that could breed new beauty in the brain and beget greater thoughts than the thought of a new motor car. In summer the lakes are as blue as ever the Aegean was. In winter the hills are white as ever the cloud-capped top of Olympus was. And between summer and winter the trees flare red as the spears of the Spartans at Thermopylae.

But what of that? Beauty is unaccountably akin to bitterness and death, and this is the age of peace. Let us, then, banish considerations of beauty except for advertising purposes, for which it is invaluable. But as a serious concern, why, no. It has been an obsession in man's brain ever since the later palaeolithic age, when the Cro-magnards wasted so much time prawing reindeer on their walls; and from Solutré through the ages to Versailles men have been killing each other in the intervals of considering beauty. So away with beauty and the murderous heat it breeds, for this is a cool age, and likely to be colder yet as we sit and wait for the new glaciation of universal peace. . . .

In the not unpleasing melancholy that comes with solitude and darkness Juan lay abed and considered such things as these. His first sight of Motley University had made him think well of his American grandfathers, who clearly had been men with an eye for country. The buildings, some of which were better than others, stood irregularly about a large plateau with hill rising behind them, hill rushing down in front to the lakeside, and tall trees that grew in such a way as to give the less handsome structures a compensatory appearance of ease and being-at-home. To the north and the south the campus was bounded by deep ravines, bristling with trees to the very foot, where streams ran headlong to leap successive waterfalls. And so the appearance of his new dwelling-place was all that Juan might have asked.

But the spirit of it was strange and remote indeed from that of Merlin College, where he had enjoyed himself so well until he came a cropper with poor little Dora. It was remote in so many ways that it was difficult to enumerate them. There was, however, a large supply of Doras, for the university was co-educational and there seemed to be as many female under-graduates as males. That was distressing on two counts.

In the first place Juan had a very reasonable dislike for the constant and unavoidable presence of women – a dislike which was counterbalanced by a certain enthusiasm for their individual and selected company. And in the second place he had just been relieved – unhappily relieved – of an illusion which he had long indulged in common with many other people who live outside America: that is, that all American girls, and especially all American girls who go to college, are extremely pretty and mate as freely as the birds. The first part of this belief was due to American moving-pictures, which falsely indicate a female population wholly composed of houris, peris, Hebes, snow-maidens, sylphs, and undines; and the second to the mass of writing – fictive and pseudo-social – with which America advertises its national features.

Within a few days Juan had been disillusioned. He had stood at cross-roads on the campus watching all who passed – not vulgarly, not viciously quizzing, but as a keen and sympathetic tourist watches fakirs in India, gondolas on the Grand Canal, ski-jumpers in Norway, or any other national exhibit. And to his growing dismay he found that the girls who passed were no prettier than those who might be seen on any street in the Old World. Many, because of a lavish and indiscriminate use of cosmetics on an undistinguished uniformity of features, were actually less attractive than girls elsewhere. And very many were handicapped by a lack of calves.

It was their own affair, of course, and no business of any-body else's. Juan did not rush about and upbraid them. That, he felt, would have been an impertinence – though American tourists would probably complain if the gondolas on the Grand Canal were replaced by punts. But he was none the less dis-appointed, and he began to suspect that the bird-like freedom in mating might also be a myth, in spite of the prominence that American writers had given it. For such freedom is often connected with a bird-like beauty of appearance – unless it were a conscientious social experiment? Juan's spirits sank lower and lower at such a thought and he was on the point of turning away, thoroughly depressed, when he saw a girl approaching so exceptionally lovely by any civilised standards that his heart leapt up with instant gratitude.

He followed her for some little distance, admiring the springing lines that opened like a calyx to hold the deep bud of her calf, and several times exchanged a glance with her: when she looked round once to see who was behind her, twice to discover if he were as handsome as her first glance had led her to suspect, and thrice out of pure good nature. And then unfortunately she met a little group of friends. But the mere sight of her had been enough to restore Juan's spirits.

After that he had a great number of formalities to attend to; papers to sign, fees to pay, and a hundred and one irrelevant questions to answer before he was allowed to enrol as a student in the college of Business Technology. American efficiency, he discovered, was responsible for a vast multitude of printed forms all over the country, which all manner of people were required to fill with suitable answers on all kinds of occasions. The issuing of questionnaires had become a national habit, and work was provided for many people, who might otherwise never have found employment, in dealing with such returns: that is, in docketing them, tabulating, copying, indexing, cross-indexing, re-arranging them according to ethnic, religious, social, geographic and other factors, and eventually composing a monograph on them for the Library of Congress. . . .

Among the other formalities – dwarfing most of them by its portentous circumstance – was a medical examination. No student, it seemed, might sip the Pierian spring of Motley until he had revealed his nakedness to those who guarded it, and so Juan became one of a long procession of self-exhibitors. In turn he submitted to examination by an oculist, a dentist, and an ear-nose-and-throat specialist; to stethoscope and enquiring fingers; to the attentions of an underling who weighed him, measured his chest, and whispering hoarse instructions thrust a little bottle into his hand.

Nor were the examiners content with examining. They also chronicled. Juan's height was five feet ten inches and his weight one hundred and sixty-three pounds. They wrote this upon a card. He had had chicken-pox at the age of four, measles when he was six, his tonsils removed a year later, a collar-bone broken when he was twelve – and half-broken quite recently, a tooth extracted the day after his fourteenth birthday and a boil evacuated in October of the same year – all this was solemnly recorded. He had never suffered from gout, epilepsy, rheumatic fever, gall-stones, or neurasthenia; nor from botts, blains, gapes, itch, scab, or scurvy – these evasions were noted approvingly. For three minutes he hopped on one foot; his pulse returned to a normal rate after half a minute; this information was given a prominent position on the card. His normal blood pressure, the location of three metallic stoppings in his back teeth, and his ability to distinguish between red wool and green were also remarked. Then a gentleman with a confidential manner enquired as tactfully as possible whether Juan's immediate relations (if indeed they were still alive) suffered much from mental and pulmonary diseases. Regretfully he noted, on a distant corner of the card, that they were apparently untouched by insanity or the bacillus of tubercle. . . .

'Turn the tap on, that helps sometimes,' said the underling in a kindly way as Juan endeavoured to fulfil the last request. . . .

Clothed again at last – and seldom had clothes seemed so necessary – he had walked a little way apart from men, and thought with a kind of awe that he had now a place in the archives of America. He and every other student at Motley were secure, immortally card-indexed, pigeon-holed in some desk vast as eternity. The million students who attended the several hundred colleges of America were all safe, for this docketing of individual myopias, chronic rheums, or gladiatorial perfections was a national institution. Now at last had the People a place and a name on the scroll of their country. Now at last were their qualities and characteristics – such as hammer-toes – classified and recorded with those of generals and statesmen and builders of cathedrals. The future was being made safe for biography. No longer would men be misrepresented when their biographers could search the national files and see for themselves what the youth of Admiral Dish had been; how Senator Slop had hopped mightily on one foot; and that Bishop Blurb, even in childhood, had passed a little sugar in his water.

Juan had asked one of the doctors the reason for all this examining, and particularly what purpose such elaborate records could serve.

'Well,' said the doctor a little vaguely, 'it helps us keep a check on people.'

Perhaps some inhuman colossal Mendel was preparing the data for future generations of scientists, so that in 2000 A.D. all the mutations of democracy could be traced home to their great-grand-parental sources, and America would be the biggest biological laboratory in the world. It might even be that the foundations were laid for a national eugenics campaign. After all, that would only require some propaganda, another amendment to the constitution, a little more prohibition, and ultimately bootlegging of a more lively commodity. . . .

While Juan was musing thus, lying abed and waiting for sleep to come, he thought of the girl he had seen, the lovely creature with darkly gleaming hair, a brow of alabaster, and eyes that had looked so bright in their three enquiries. . . . He could, if he cared to, search the archives and discover the state of her kidneys. Not that he wanted to. But there the information was, preserved for all time by this national paternalism. Perhaps, in a certain system of filing, the report on his cardiac condition might lie side by side with a description of hers. 'Under our new tabulation-scheme, Miss Jones, all those with an aortic index of eight will go in this compartment.' So there they might be, lying heart to heart in a filing-cabinet, wedded by a bureaucratic whimsy. Well, they might be. . . .

X

With some dismay Juan discovered that the school of Commercial Technology expected him to work very hard indeed. He was supposed to attend lectures on Accounting Principles, Finance, Commercial Statistics, Industrial Management, and Business Ethics. All these courses were introduced with portentous phrases about 'the confidence of your employers,' 'opportunities for executive responsibility,' 'the fundamental facts of industry,' 'the ethical problems of corporation policies,' and so on. Not one appeared to offer suggestions for floating private loans or discovering short cuts to affluence. There was no secret revelation of 'How I made a Million in a Month.' There were no plain statements: Do *This* and Money Will Accrue. There was, instead, dull instruction on the difference between Capital and Revenue, the Sale of Commercial Paper, and the Analysis of Estimates.

To the other students these matters seemed not only interesting but exciting. When they heard such terms as Index Numbers, Over-investment, or Fiduciary Relations their lips parted and their muscles grew taut, as if they were the beleaguered garrison of Lucknow when the noise of Havelock's pipers blew in upon the hot wind of Oudh. But Juan's attention wavered from the start.

The undergraduates he found hearty people. They wore slovenly clothes, cleared their throats *hawk-a-toosh* as they walked, and spat lavishly in all directions. They were well-inclined to be friendly, but there was an unfortunate barrier to friendship in the many differences which existed between their background and his. It was surprising that with the same language there should be such disparity. In many cases the idiom of their thought was foreign, though their words were not, and more than once Juan suspected that he would have more in common with Frenchmen or Germans than with these young Americans. This distressed him somewhat, for in certain ways he admired them: this large university was theirs, built where, a hundred years ago, there had been a half-tamed wilderness; they were frank to the point of *naïveté*, and willingly amused; they were ready to endure many discomforts to acquire an education, for large numbers worked their way through college by undertaking duties of a menial kind.

America, he supposed, was so very large that it tended to obscure, for Americans, the reality of all countries that failed to compete with it in territorial magnitude. Smaller countries were merely curiosities, the focus of a faint sentimental regard, the vague birthplace of Goethe. . . . And yet had not the navel-string of America been tied to those smaller lands? Was there not an essential one-ness in their thought?

But the first thing a doctor does is to cut the cord, said Juan to himself; and though children must suffer the sins of their fathers they need not endure all their gods. And he went to the Library to see what there was to read.

The several hundred thousand volumes in the library were arranged in metal stacks that reached from floor to ceiling in a building several storeys high. A quiet gloom filled the narrow alleys between the cases, lit here and there in small areas as some student or attendant switched on a light to find a book. Some floors were lonely places and twilight seemed a native thing between the long rows of dusty volumes that were no longer read, or read by only a few out of the thousands at Motley.

On one of the less frequented floors, where books devoted to historical travel stood, Juan was startled to see, not two feet from him, a pair of familiar eyes and some small part of their owner's face. The books on the fifth shelf from the ground did not reach to the top of their compartment, and it was between them and the shelf above that the eyes so strangely shone. There were tears in them. The first time that he had seen them, when they had looked round once, twice, and again to see who walked behind, it had not occurred to Juan to wonder how they would seem when half-dim with weeping. For then they had been merry eyes. And still, as he looked into them over the top of so many dull books, it seemed that the dew lay in them lightly, not hurting but only bathing them; and they did not readily turn away from his.

Many men would have been abashed and gone quietly away, ashamed to be a partner to sorrow. But without more than three seconds' hesitation Juan walked round the stack and found to his satisfaction that the face he had so admired was in no way distorted with grief, but merely softened a little, the eyes made wider, the lips a little full and tremulous. So, he felt, should womanhood always present her sorrow.

'What's the matter?' he asked. 'Can I help you?'

'No,' she answered, making a sad little note of the word. 'Nobody can help me.'

Juan was sympathetic.

'I saw you a few days ago. You looked so happy then.'

'Did I? I guess I was, too. But we never know how long happiness is going to last, do we?'

'Nor unhappiness. I was rather depressed myself the other day, but I felt much better after seeing you.'

'Oh! wasn't that funny?'

She looked floorwards at her foot, that was tracing little marks in the dust.

'I remember seeing you too,' she admitted, and by now the tears were gone and her voice was definitely more cheerful.

'Not really?' said Juan with mendacious humility.

'Yes. I thought you looked cute.'

This engaging *naïveté* took Juan by surprise and he had no answer ready.

'You're English, aren't you? My girl-friend had an English beau once. He dressed well but he'd no senses of humour, so she gave him the air.'

'I'm sure he deserved it. My name is Juan Motley.'

'Oh, isn't that a cute name! The same as the college?'

Juan smiled affirmatively.

'Mine is Leonie Ramper.'

Miss Ramper looked expectant, as if the mention of her name should evoke some instant and specific response. And then, as Juan evidently found it no more remarkable than any other name, she explained, 'My father's the football coach here.'

Again Juan showed nothing more than polite interest, and Miss Ramper, a trifle condescendingly, added to her information.

'I suppose that doesn't mean anything to you, but in America a football coach is a mighty important person. My dad has a bigger salary than the President – he only gets fifteen thousand. The President of Motley, I mean, not of the United States of course. You don't play football in England, do you? Well, not proper football. How much do you pay your football coaches?'

'I'm afraid we haven't any,' said Juan.

'Well then, you can't play *proper* football, can you? That's just what I said.'

'Rugby is a magnificent game,' said Juan.

'You wait till you see Motley playing Princeton. Oh boy! You'll just go wild with excitement. I *know* you will. Everybody does. All the cheer-leaders, and the band, and big Becker crashing through off tackle, and Merejkowski throwing forward passes! The way *he* throws a ball is nobody's business. Oh, it's the berries. Honestly it is!'

Miss Ramper's vivacity added no little grace to her remarkable good looks, but Juan found her meaning occasionally obscure – he was not yet at home with America slang, nor did he know anything about American football – and he was curious to discover the cause of her grief that had so swiftly vanished.

'Why were you crying?' he asked.

At once she grew sad again. Reminded of her sorrow, vivacity fled, and her eyes, like violets under gossamer, gently clouded.

'I had a quarrel with my boy-friend,' she confessed.

'Tell me about it.'

Miss Ramper was willing to expound her sorrow.

'It was last night,' she said. 'I had a date with him. We were going out to dinner and then to the movies to see Phryne Fuller in *Painted Sinners* – she's hot, isn't she? Well, but I had another date for lunch with Ed Kieffer – he's another boy I know – and after lunch we went for a ride, so I was late getting home, and when I got there Red Roper – that's my boy-friend – Red was waiting for me with an *awful* expression on his face. There was no one else in, because mother and dad were out visiting with some friends. So Red got up and said "Where have you been?" in the roughest sort of voice. Well, that kind of thing just rolls off my knife, naturally, and I laughed at him. I was wearing a great big corsage of the loveliest roses that Ed had given me; he always buys me flowers when I go out with him; and Red shouted, absolutely shouted, "Who gave you those dam' flowers?" So I just said, "Please don't be vulgar, Red," and sort of smiled at him. Then he snatched the roses out of my dress with one hand, simply ruining them, and smacked my face with the other, and said, "Laugh that off!" Then he stalked out and I haven't seen him since. . . . So I got thinking about it when I was here all by myself, and that's how I was crying a little when you came in.'

Having offered consolation of a simple but apparently acceptable nature, Juan suggested that he should take the place of the irascible Red and entertain Miss Ramper to dinner; evening was fast approaching, and one must eat, he said;

and perhaps they could see *Painted Sinners* afterwards.

'No, it's *Dancing Fools* to-night,' said Miss Ramper. 'I'd love to see it, and I think it's sweet of you to take pity on me like this.'

For a moment she looked pensive again; she even sighed; and then a smile, doubly brilliant because of the reverie it displaced, enchantingly re-animated her face and she patted Juan's arm with a little hand whose trust and gratitude he could feel plainly through his sleeve.

Well, well, he thought; and they went to Miss Ramper's car (which waited conveniently outside the Library) and drove first to Miss Ramper's home so that she might put on a dress more suitable for dinner and the motion pictures.

Mr. Ramper had the figure of a heavyweight wrestler and the expression of an evangelical gladiator. His voice rose from the depths of a cavernous chest or pealed in lordly head-tones at will. Umbrageous eyebrows threw their shadows over eyes in which burnt quenchless flames. His nose was short and straight, with generous nostrils that expanded under emotional stress. A ponderous and combative lower jaw was controlled by frontal and masseteric muscles of unusual strength, for they bulged prominently whenever he closed his mouth on the tail of a noble hortative such as he loved.

When Juan was introduced Mr. Ramper shook hands warmly, looked him up and down, walked round him, prodded his thighs and chest, felt his biceps and shoulders, and finally pulled up his trousers to inspect his calves.

Then he said, 'Have you ever played football?'

'Both at school and at Cambridge,' said Juan

'Ah!' said Mr. Ramper, 'but not as we play football here.'

'Rugby,' said Juan, 'is a magnificent game.'

'But unorganised! Merely a pastime. An excuse for running about. An exercise. In America football commands the attention of millions, and not only the attention but the purses of millions. The production of football players – which is *my* business – has become one of the great industries of America. Football is an inspiration to every young man and boy in the country. A first-rate quarter-back is worth his weight in platinum. I consider Merejkowski, our present quarter-back, as God's greatest gift to Motley!'

Touched with emotion at the thought of the superlative Merejkowski, Mr. Ramper brushed his eyes, which had become a little moist, with the back of one large hand and stared moodily at the radio cabinet.

Juan was a little astonished at his concern, as he had been slightly perturbed by the impromptu physical examination to which he had submitted. He had already observed the large amount of space devoted by every newspaper to discussion of the approaching football season, but he was not aware of the real significance of the game to modern America. Gladiators in ancient Rome, bull-fighters in Spain of yesterday, cricketers in England, and operatic tenors in Italy have all enjoyed in their degree popular acclaim beside which the reputation of Prime Ministers and Field Marshals is but a little thing. And yet no gladiator, no bull-fighter, cricketer or tenor singer was ever taken so seriously as football players in the United States, where every natural enthusiasm is properly encouraged by the agents of general welfare and publicity.

Mrs. Ramper, a lean lady with thin lips and eye-glasses, remarked, 'I think you had better sit down, Mr. Motley. Leonie will probably take some time to change her dress. How do you like America?'

Mr. Ramper turned once more to Juan.

'Your physique seems excellent,' he said. 'Have you done any hammer-throwing, shot-putting, boxing, pole-vaulting, broad-jumping, or wrestling?'

'All of them,' said Juan, lying stoutly for the honour of England.

Mr. Ramper appeared to be impressed.

'We might make a player of you,' he said. 'Each of the sports I have named provides some part of the technique of modern football. I should like you to turn out with my training squad. It will make a man of you! The sort of man who brings tears of pride to his mother's eyes, and weaves an imperishable garland of glory about the topmost fane of his dear old Alma Mater! You will learn to disregard pain and selfish ease, and at the word of command – *my* word of command – summon every ounce of your strength and charge like a wounded elephant battling in defence of its mate. That is what football means. And in return for what you give to football, football will give you courage, fire, and dogged persistence in the face of insuperable odds. It will put red blood in every vein of your body and grow hair on your chest, my boy!'

'Here's Leonie now, Mr. Motley,' said Mrs. Ramper pleasantly, and Leonie came into the room, kissed her father – his face was hot with the ardour of rhetoric, but it showed that she knew how to do such things – and led Juan prettily away.

Some time later, having recovered from his slight stupor, he said, 'Your father wants me to play football.'

'Juan,' exclaimed Leonie. 'You'd like me to call you Juan wouldn't you? I hoped you would. Oh Juan, that's just splendid! I *am* glad. You've no idea what a difference it will make to you at Motley, socially and in every way. It means that you'll be asked to join one of the best Fraternities now, Phi Phi perhaps, or Delta Tau, or Mu Chi.'

'Mu Chi?' enquired Juan.

Leonie told him some things about Fraternities, those semi-secret organisations of supreme social importance, that are mysteriously known by letters of the Greek alphabet.

Juan ate his chicken salad and decided that he would have little opportunity to study Business Ethics with so many avocations as now confronted him. After dinner they went to a cinema and saw *Dancing Fools*.

Mr. and Mrs. Ramper had gone to bed when they returned. Leonie turned on a light that threw downwards a tactful flush and sat beneath it.

'No, no, no!' she protested as Juan bent to kiss her. 'No-no-no-no-no!' And in the pronunciation of these pretty sounds her lips pouted in the most inviting way possible, and she retreated only to the end of the sofa, where she exclaimed 'Oh!' instead of No' and permitted herself to be kissed with every appearance of enjoyment.

XI

Mr. Ramper was exercising his footballers.

Pickets guarded the field in which they worked. Mr. Ramper was one of the three or four really great coaches in the country, and the spies of lesser men were constantly endeavouring to discover his training secrets. Every day then, before he led out his teams, a thorough search was made of the surroundings and a defensive screen thrown out to keep off hostile agents.

At one end of the field stood a large wooden platform loaded with twenty or thirty tons of rock. It was mounted on little wheels. A dozen men with their shoulders down to it were slowly pushing about this artificial mountain to develop the strength necessary for success in a scrimmage.

Elsewhere large gallows had been erected from which hung sacks full of sawdust. At the word of command – there were several subordinate coaches present, besides Mr. Ramper himself – men charged desperately at these heavy dummies. A successful charge was one which ended in a flying leap, so that the man's feet were off the ground before his arms embraced the sack. This exercise encouraged robust tackling.

In other parts of the field instruction was given in sprinting, kicking, wrestling, leap-frogging, and the use of the straight arm.

After an hour or two of this, teams were lined up and charged each other instead of sacks. A man was carried off unconscious. The weaklings had to be eliminated.

Juan often felt a little weary when the day's practice was over, for these exercises, strenuous enough in themselves, were carried out in complete football uniform, which comprised a stuffed leather helmet, leather pads for shoulders and chest, and breeches stiffened with cowhide at all tactical points. But, he discovered, there were compensations. As a member of the football squad he was not expected to do very much work of any other kind. His class-fellows in the school of Commercial Technology now regarded him with open admiration and his professors were gratified if he ever attended a lecture. Mr. Ramper's lectures, they knew, were more important than theirs.

Mr. Ramper addressed his men two or three times a week.

'Boys,' he would say in a very earnest tone, 'I don't know what's wrong with you, but you're not working as you ought to. You're not putting your hearts into the game. Perhaps your arms and legs are all right, but your hearts aren't with them. And it's a man's heart that makes him win battles. What's the matter, boys? Am I getting old? Are you getting tired of me at Motley?'

And there Mr. Ramper would stand, with his arms flung out and a great appeal in his eyes, till some weak-minded giant replied, 'Aw, you know we're not, Chief. You know we'd do anything for you.'

Instantly Mr. Ramper's manner changed. He grew fierce. His index finger pointed accusingly. His voice bit like a cold chisel.

'Then why don't you?' he demanded. 'Why aren't you like the men I used to have here? Like Fleischhacker and Stomp and Sokolovitch? They would crash through a stone wall if I told them to. They'd tear down concrete. Iron bars couldn't hold them. I taught them tackling against oak trees till there were no oak trees left for miles around. But you, you paper heroes, you fish-gutted false alarms, you couldn't bend a lily on its stem!'

Then, as the hundred or so men who listened to him grew pale with anger, and bit their lips, and plucked at their shirts, then the Chief's voice would change again and rise into a battlecry.

'When I send you out for your first game,' he cried, 'I'm sending you on to a battlefield. My orders will be to fight. To fight! That's all. When that other team comes out I want you to see red. I want you to give them hell. I want you to *want* to give them hell! Jump on them from the whistle. Bam! You've got to go through that other team like a herd of buffaloes thundering through the wind. And how are you going to do that? By fighting!'

Through this companionship of the tented field, as it were, Juan was invited to join the Mu Chis, and dined at their Fraternity house on several occasions. All the Fraternities had houses of their own, frequently large and handsome buildings, which served as clubs to non-resident members and to residents as centres for a remarkable communistic existence characterised by a great deal of noise and elaborate codes of behaviour.

To become a full member of a Fraternity it was necessary to submit to an initiation ceremony, the nature of which was kept a profound secret; outsiders, however, whispered that novices of the Mu Chis were branded before being admitted to all the privileges of the order. Juan listened to such rumours with unconcealed alarm, and failed to see the advantage of so much mystery. He went so far as to say that he thought it childish. He then learnt that many millions of American citizens, men in middle life and past it, belonged to organisations quite as secret as Fraternities, though not enjoying the social esteem of the latter: organisations such as the Ku Klux Klan, the Knights of Columbus, the Knights of Pythias, Shriners, Elks, Buffaloes, Oaks, Woodmen, Kiwanis, and Cedars of Lebanon, whose members not only performed secret rites but dressed up as Turks, Cannibals, Crusaders and such, in order to improve the occasion. And how could a custom be childish that attracted several million men in the fullness of adult life?

'Now be broad-minded,' said his companion of the moment, 'and admit you're wrong.'

Juan came into contact with another side of American university life in the house where he lodged. Half a dozen men lived there who were all graduates working for a higher degree. Such was the competition, they had found, that one degree was of very little assistance to anyone contemplating an academic career. For a young lecturer the orthodox number was three. The attitude of these men was very different from that of undergraduates. They pursued their chosen ends with amazing industry, and sometimes the ends were also amazing.

There was, for instance, a historian interested in British Colonial Administration. His advisers had instructed him to begin at the beginning, and he had therefore commenced a study of the duties of the Officers of the Household in the court of King Alfred the Great.

And there was a student of German literature anxious to examine the philosophy of Goethe. The professor in charge of his department had warned him against neglecting the genesis of that philosophy, and so had set him to work on the Gothic alphabet.

The other graduates were engaged on frankly utilitarian problems, such as the History of the Baking-Powder Controversy in the United States; the Incidence of the Mealy Bug in Oklahoma; and the 1858 Experiment with Dromedaries in Texas. Friends of theirs, who occasionally visited them, were constructing theses on The Occurrence of Bound and Free Water in Raw Prime Beef; and Differences between Seventeenth Century Classic and Current Usage of the Prepositions Employed to Introduce an Infinitive depending upon Certain French Verbs.

Such affairs as these, Juan was told, occupied the minds of intellectual young men all over America.

XII

Football, Juan discovered, was not only a game but a pageant. A football match was a tribal gathering where priests whipped the multitudes into recurrent ecstasies, and the spectacle of valour on the field became the occasion for a communal release of emotion that had slowly accumulated during the week of anticipation.

The stadium at Motley was a shallow bowl, oval in shape, able to hold sixty thousand spectators. The town of Carthage was, it is true, a very little town, but to see a good game people would drive for many miles and the bowl was generally well filled. The first game of the season, which Motley won by a spectacular number of points, was against a Baptist team, the representatives of a small denominational college nearby. Baptists, it appeared, were not very good footballers. A little soft, perhaps, as a result of so much immersion. At any rate, Methodists were much better, though even they were completely outclassed by Irish Catholics.

It was against a Catholic team that Motley would play its next game.

As at the first match Juan put on his armour, his jersey and leather-plated breeches, and ran on to the field with the team. All the reserves accompanied the team. There were about sixty of them, and during the game they sat on the side-lines wrapt up in large blanket-cloaks. The stadium was nearly full and the University band, a hundred and forty strong, marched round and round playing stirring *bummsmusik*. As soon as the band finished, on an extra loud *bumm*, the cheer-leaders became busy. These were five agile young men, four dressed in white and the centre one in red, who incited the crowd to applause. They shouted through megaphones. The crowd replied. They gesticulated. The crowd responded. Thousands of voices barked like one. The gestures of the cheer-leaders gathered speed. They pointed this way and that, spread wide their arms, stamped with impatient feet, and shook tight fists at heaven. They leapt into the air, belaboured space, turned somersaults. Faster and faster. And to every movement the crowd had an answering voice, a rumbling voice, a roar, a hiss, a noise like the cracking of whips, an exultant chorus. Quicker and quicker. Gibberish loud as thunder. Congolese cantrips. Mumbo-jumbo with a megaphone. Bean-fed Yankees – the flower of the Twentieth Century, the advance guard of civilisation – bellowing hocus-pocus to exorcise the imp of victory from an alien clan. 'M-O-T-L-E-Y!' Mass emotion escaping in a clamorous alphabet. '*Motley!*'

Savage and impressive, thought Juan.

The game began.

American football, which grew out of Rugby, has been modified by Irish and German influences. The Germans have systematised it, reduced the possible varieties of action to a definite number of types, and invented some eighty or a hundred rules with a few score amendments. The Irish have expanded the opportunities for personal contact between members of the rival teams. Whereas in Rugby it is only the man with the ball who is of immediate interest, in American football any member of the opposing side is legitimate excuse for a tumble. As soon as the whistle blows the centre, who has been crouching bird-like over the ball, hurls it through his legs to one of the backs, while on either side of him guards, tackles, and ends leap from a kneeling position into awful life. As the guards, tackles, and ends of the opposing team – many of whom weigh more than two hundred pounds – spring to action at the same moment, an appalling sodden crash is heard. The two lines have met. Meanwhile the backs, one of whom has the ball, have either tried to leap over this Briarean obstacle and fallen on to it; or to run round it and tripped over the edges; or to execute a forward pass and run clear away from it. The ball is eventually discovered under a heap of writhing players. Those who appear to be seriously injured are carried off and substitutes drawn from the army of reserves. The referee and two assistants examine the ball and decide the precise spot at which it has come to earth. A couple of men with a surveyor's tape run on to the field and measure how far Motley has advanced. And the operation is repeated.

So it appears to the novice, to the untaught spectator, but the knowing eye sees intricacy and speed, tactics and strategy, in the movement of every player.

Meanwhile at crises of the game the cheer-leaders mesmerise the crowd, turning spectators into a choir that shouts a mumbo-jumbo hallelujah or a witch doctors' *vae victis*.

'Ah!' they cry through their megaphones.

'AH!' roars the crowd.

'Bah!' they encourage.

'BAH!' thunders the crowd.

'Wah-hah-hah!' shrill the cheer-leaders in demoniac glee.

'WAH-HAH-HAH!' bellows the now intoxicated crowd, while the four cheer-leaders in white leap high into the air, their feet twinkling, and he in red turns somersaults like a fiery wheel.

The effect of this is beneficial and cathartic to the spectators. A psychic purge has been administered and their emotional waste satisfactorily discharged.

The players, exasperated by so much noise, tackle harder than ever. The eloquent Mr. Ramper has prayed over them, preached to them, wept before them. He has filled them with anger and the lust of victory. ('Fight!' said Mr. Ramper in the dressing-room. 'For the sake of dear old Motley!' he added, while tears made an island of his nose. 'Bam!' he concluded, truculently smiting a table.) Now the staccato ear-splitting *rafale* of cheering rowels them afresh. Look at Schwarzwalder bucking the line!

'A long yell for Schwarzwalder!'

See Toccata taking out interference!

'Yea, Toccata!'

And Merejkowski tossing a pass to Buck Wilkins! –

But Buck unfortunately has dropped it. Buck's girl will give him the gate to-night. Buck's friends will treat him coldly in the dressing-room. Buck must slink in corners for a week. Thumbs down for Buck Wilkins. . . .

During all this excitement Juan sat on the side-lines wrapt up in his thick blanket-cloak. When a player was hurt or began to lose speed a substitute would take his place. But there were so many experienced substitutes that Mr. Ramper never even thought of Juan.

Three Saturdays in succession he ran on to the field, sat on a bench, ran off at half-time, ran on again, sat on another bench, and then when it was growing dark and cold ran off once more. And for this he and all the other potential substitutes trained strenuously several hours a day.

The country round Carthage grew daily more beautiful as autumn came with its wine-colours, its early morning frost, and a brownish haze at sundown. The lake was a steely blue. Juan drove with Leonie on white roads that ran parallel to it along the hills. The earth was brown and the trees were all colours, yellow and brown, and green, and flaming red. Evergreens kept their look of hard and careless strength. Apple-trees still carried fruit and hundreds of rotting apples lay beneath them, making a sweet smell in the frosty air. The brightest foliage of all was on maples and sumach. The maples flared scarlet and gold, the sumach was crimson. All over these rolling uplands shone the blood-red trees, flaunting their leaves against the sky's misty blue, like a thick nest of dancing flames, and sequins of bright gold among them. Closer to earth was the deep crimson of the sumach. And the lake filled its broad trench between the hills, mile after mile, deep and silent and steel-blue.

This was clearly a nomad's country. Hunting country and wild orchard lands, with a smell of apples for comfort and a breath of frost to make the blood tingle. This was the Red

Indians' hunting ground. Here Cayugas and Onondagas, Tuscaroras, Oneidas and Mohawks had fought and trapped and slain their deer, and here the red man had vanished before the white man who, for all his innocent pallor, was so much more deadly. It was the blood of Mohawks and Tuscaroras and Cayugas, lying heavy at the roots of the maples, that made their leaves so splendid. The sap of these trees was the blood of the red hunters who had been killed by white men. The waving leaves had been dipped in their veins. And presently the white snow would come, as white men had come, and cold winds would chill the maples and freeze the crimson sumach, and tear away their bright leaves, and throw them down for the pale storm to cover. All this rolling country, now chequered in scarlet and green and gold and brown, would lie blanched and dead, level and smooth and without features of its own, under the killing democracy of the snow. . . .

When his Fraternity gave a dance Juan was thankful that he had spent so much of his time in hard physical exercise, for the Mu Chi ball would have been fatal to a weakling. It was not so much the crowded floor as the heartiness of the Brothers and their partners; it was not so much their heartiness as the clamant vigour of the band; it was not so much the band as amorous exchanges in a dozen useful corners; it was not love so much as gin, that flowed in hidden rooms and in every one of the fifty motor cars parked round the house; and it was not really gin, but the dancing crowd, the stentorian *bonhomie*, the *vox diabolica* of jazz, the succession of amiable lips, and the lethal impact of alcohol all in one flamboyant mixture that made the night an affair for heroes only – for heroes and indestructible demi-ingenues.

Leonie was very happy to be his partner, for Juan continued to please her and several female friends had betrayed jealous displeasure at her annexation of so handsome a stranger.

The saxophones gulped and shivered, a single violin wailed

in agony, and then the room was filled with a demoniac clamour of trombones obedient to the trip-hammer rhythm of drums and cymbals.

'Oh boy,' shouted Leonie in ecstasy, 'get hot!'

Her legs and the lower part of her body became alarmingly active, her spine waggled – like a pliant cane when one shakes it – and her dapper little bottom leapt from side to side. Her legs and thighs flew in all directions, as if the American hip and knee gave free articulation all round the circle. Her knees jumped out, her knees bent in. Her feet slapped the floor. Juan, assisted by natural agility, endeavoured to accommodate his movements to hers, though he would have preferred to dance in the mild, aloof, walk-in-the-park way that the English use. Leonie sang the words of the dreadful tune that the band was playing:

'I want to be *loved* by you,
Loved by you alone!'

Then a man tapped Juan on the shoulder and Leonie danced away on her new partner's arm. Her left hand, with the fingers wide apart, clung as tightly to his shoulder as it had to Juan's. Her head lay as closely on his breast as it had on Juan's. Her eyes looked up as trustfully to him, and her neat little crupper bobbed about as obedient as ever.

For some minutes Juan watched the dancers. They were all young and the girls' bright dresses jumped in and out of astonishing patterns. Now a cherry coloured frock thrust in among three different shades of green, and a peacock-blue strode side by side with a bright lemon. Here maroon and silver jostled, there cinnamon and pink. A mercy it is, thought Juan, that men wear black. The saxophones retched and heaved after an elusive melody. All the girls' legs wore thin silk stockings of various hues. Some were flesh colour and some were gold. A member of the band was singing:

'We'd make a lovely pair,
If you could only care,
But you're a frigidaire –
Don't be like that!'

Juan was struck by the assured manner of these girls as they came into the room or walked out. Their heads high, lifting a casual hand to friends, accepting the greetings of men. A half-smile on their lips, eyes alert, anticipating homage – a green and vapid homage perhaps, but still homage. Now the foghorns were quiet and the band was humming a tune between its teeth, marking the rhythm by lightly tapping a drum and a triangle. . . . With a sudden dismay Juan saw a family likeness in all the girls. Not quite all, perhaps. Some he recognised as individuals. But the majority approximated to a type. Little round faces, little plump cheeks, little noses inclining to snubness; hair groomed in stiff symmetrical waves; lips geranium-painted after one pattern, and lively little tongues that all said the same thing. They showed a family likeness because they all had the same standard of attractiveness in mind. Smooth, hot, and snappy. 'Jesus, lover of my soul,' whispered Juan wildly, and saw for one dreadful moment the womb of America, like a Ford motor car factory, emitting an endless stream of smooth, hot, and snappy blondes (or sugars) for the standardised amusement of a standard loving people. . . .

'Come and have a snort,' said a friendly voice.

The gin was strong. They drank it in the kitchen because the chaperons officially deprecated drinking, and the kitchen was safe from chaperons. Half a dozen Mu Chis and their partners sat on a long table, drinking, and eating sandwiches that a stout negress cut for them. Juan was introduced to several people. Everyone was very friendly and he drank out of many different flasks. He felt ashamed of himself for criticising such kindly hosts, and went upstairs again, arm-in-arm with the man who had detected his probable thirst. On their way they passed several lovers armoured by each other to indifference of the world. As in the Dark Ages every cave had a silent hermit, so in the Mu Chis' house each nook and cranny had its lovers, speechless and entranced.

Now Juan danced with Leonie again, and found that she also had drunk a little gin and was very animated. And then he danced with a gold-haired girl as tall as himself, who sang in his ear while she danced,

> 'Fish got to swim, birds got to fly,
> I got to love one man till I die,
> Can't help lovin' that man o' mine.'

And then with a girl in a peacock-blue dress who was, perhaps, a little drunk, for she had a look of Mongolian sorrow on her sun-tanned face – all summer and fall she had been in Southern California – and she listened greedily to the cheese-faced leader of the band, who in a strangulated tenor sang –

> 'I got a woman that's crazy for me,
> She's funny *that way* –'

and the girl in peacock-blue hung heavily on Juan, and would only dance very near to the band, and looked from him to its cheese-faced leader with her little black eyes that were set in a face tanned dark as an old boot. And the strangulated tenor – perhaps he was *castrato* – sang in his aching emasculated voice about the O-hi-o where the shy little violets grow, and when he looks into someone's eyes they tell him what he wants to know.

'Gee, that's a hot-looking man!' said a girl in red who had newly arrived and saw Juan for the first time. So boldly he tapped her partner's shoulder and danced with her while the band, brazenly arch, played a tune called *Everything is made for love*, and the girl in red sang loudly:

> 'What are rosy lips for,
> Belts for reducing hips for?
> Everything is made for love!'

Lo-o-ove, with a vibrant heavy insistence. Youth is made to sing, and love gets the poets it deserves.

'What do we learn French for,
Sit on a park bench for?
Everything is made for love!'

And the girl in red had clamped her abdomen on to Juan with the water-tight efficiency of a limpet on a rock. Everything is made for love and love gets the poets it deserves.

Then to Leonie again, Leonie pouting a little because he had not danced with her for thirty minutes, but soon forgiving enough to push him through the crowd – coloured silks and bare arms and black cloth – to a motor car parked outside in the frosty star-sparkling night, where two young women sat on the knees of two young men and drank synthetic gin from a quart bottle, and embraced each other lavishly, but welcomed Juan and Leonie with bright cries of 'Whoopee!' and making room for them gave them gin to drink, and cigarettes, and presently, all sitting in a bunch, very warm and with limbs confusedly here and there so that anyone's leg might be caressed by anyone else, fell to singing yet another song of love and the heart-searching which goes with it:

'All dolled up in glad rags,
To-morrow may turn to sad rags,
They call you Glad Rag Doll!
Admired, desired,
By lovers who soon grow tired,
Poor little Glad Rag Doll!'

Leonie, lying heavily on Juan's chest, kissed his left eye with warm and amorous lips, and cunningly found the gin for him, and stroked his hair, and held the bottle while he drank. So that when they returned to the ball-room Juan was amazed to see that the spectrum had burst, and all its dissociated fragments were wildly dancing the Charleston with black and white partners, while a band blew throbbing rhythms out of long brass trumpets that visibly expanded and, as he watched, foreshortened into the middle of the round white cheeses from which they protruded. Now mercifully the lights were dimmed to a violet blue, and the slurring noise of feet on the floor mingled with quieter music. Now from banjo and ukulele Hawaian notes twanged plaintively in the heavy dusk, and the emasculated tenor sang to a melody plucked intolerably from strings reluctant to let it go: love, love, ever more and more about love and the gratification of yielding to its jazz-crazy voice.

'You seem to think well of love in this part of the world,' said Juan.

'Of love?' said Leonie enthusiastically. 'Oh boy, I hope to tell you!'

XIII

On the following morning Juan woke with a feeling of impending disaster that was not wholly due to the distressing state of his stomach.

He lay in bed awhile, smoking a cigarette that burned his tongue. A deplorable evening, he reflected. A display of uncontrolled vulgarity, open to criticism from every angle. Very bad gin. And girls? Well, they had improved as the evening advanced.

And to be quite honest, said Juan, sitting up so quickly that a thud of pain struck the vault of his skull and a sea-sick qualm disturbed his stomach. To be quite honest I enjoyed myself after the first half-hour. I drank their chemical gin and felt better for it. I embraced their girls and liked it. I strutted to their beastly music and called for more. I too am a vulgarian. My sin is normality. Let then my virtue be honesty. . . .

The orphan children, Honesty-of-Thought and Honesty-of-Pocket. The latter, since her adoption by Public Opinion, was fairly well cared for, but little Honesty-of-Thought was still a waif in the streets, looking through a window at the rich children playing in their doll-and-rocking-horse-filled nursery, but never allowed to join them. She could see Pride on a toy throne; golden-haired Hypocrisy, her mother's darling; Manners with her picture-book; Envy stealing sweets from her brother Greed – who was regretting his last mince-pie – and All-Uncharitableness sitting on his padlocked playbox. But she herself, flattening her little nose whitely on the window, stood shivering in the rain, or the snow, or the north-east wind – for Inclement Weather is the grumbling god-parent who rarely leaves her. Of the little rich boys and girls only Greed has ever spoken to her, and Honesty does not really care for him. . . .

I might adopt her myself, thought Juan. She would be a responsibility, of course, and embarrassing at times, but she could go to bed soon after tea. . . .

It was nearly tea-time before Juan went out to face the world, and even then he felt little sympathy for its grosser activities, and looked a little pale in the wintry sun. But he joined the footballers who were receiving instruction from Mr. Ramper, and by the exercise of heroic self-control concealed his physical weakness. Indeed, by his masterly execution of a difficult movement he caught the coach's eye, and later drew Mr. Ramper's praise by the accuracy of his fielding.

The important game with Princeton was approaching, and in preparation for it the team was practising new and subtle stratagems with which Mr. Ramper hoped to out-manoeuvre his formidable opponents. He and his assistants tirelessly drilled every man in the minutiae of his duty, so that whenever the quarter-back called a signal the team might spring into concerted action, each man working smoothly as an intelligent part in the machine, and the whole becoming a formation that might elude, baffle, harass, oppress, and utterly sweep aside the Princeton eleven.

Meanwhile, of course, the Princeton team was similarly engaged in the elaboration of tactics which would confute, confuse, afflict, molest, and ruinously defeat the Motley side.

For an event of this magnitude even Mr. Ramper's eloquence was insufficient, and a few days before the game a Professor of Rhetoric – there were several at Motley – and a number of local clergymen, together with some famous footballers of the past (paunchy men with broken noses), were called upon to tell the team and the general body of undergraduates what they thought about it all.

A mass meeting was convoked, and with the aid of amplifiers the clergymen prayed to the God of Battles for Motley's success, and reminded their hearers of Joshua and David and Samson and others who fought the Good Fight. Then in simple phrases heavily charged with emotion and untrammelled by syntactical rules, the broken-nosed veterans of football spoke of the heroes of yester-year, mighty men who had larded the lean earth with sweat and trampled on the bowels of their enemies, all for the love of Motley. Chief Ramper followed them with a word or two, scarcely heard in the hoarse acclaim which greeted him. And then the Professor of Oratory, a thin and haggard man with a far-ranging voice, took fine words from Demosthenes and Ecclesiasticus and Abraham Lincoln, and drew them into his speech, and read somewhat from the Song of Roland, and finally recited the address of Henry V to his troops before Harfleur.

Visibly moved, the vast congregation then sang a hymn, rehearsed with their cheer-leaders the tribal war-cries, and listened with throbbing hearts to the pastor of the First Presbyterian Church in Carthage while, in valediction, he charged Jehovah with the duty of supporting those who wore the green and purple jerseys of Motley in their day of trial. After this a bonfire was lighted and the congregation reverted to jungle formulae, stamping and snake-dancing round the bright core of flames.

Juan had, at first, laughed at such solemn and elaborate preparations for a mere game of football, but when he realised how serious everybody else was he grew a little frightened.

Even the lecturers on Retail Distribution and Group Buying and Statistical Analysis seemed to detect a major significance in the approaching struggle. Even the students of Free Water in Prime Beef, the analysts of the Baking-powder Controversy, looked up from their note-books and threw out their chests when walking, and misused the learned technicalities of football in their familiar table-talk. Clearly this was no ordinary game. Leonie, poor girl, was almost incoherent with excitement, and though her affection for Juan as a possible member of the team increased hourly, her patriotism was greater still, and she would not let him stay out with her past ten at night. All the foregone kisses of later hours she threw like roses on the altar of football, and counted her sacrifice as nothing in the expectation of Motley's victory.

The day dawned under a white smoke of clouds, and all morning the roads about Carthage were full of motor cars bearing old graduates of Motley, their wives and their wives' relations, the mothers and fathers of present undergraduates, and their female cousins, and business friends of their uncles, with a few visiting kinsmen from Memphis and Oshkosh and Wichita, and a great concourse of people who had no connexion whatsoever with either Motley or Princeton, but loved football matches with the devotion of small boys for the circus.

Before the Motley team ran out to face the crowded stadium Mr. Ramper addressed them briefly:

'Boys,' he said earnestly, 'I've got a last word to say to you. Just a word. So listen: Those Princeton guys have been boasting that this game's a pushover for them. *I* say that you're fit to whip your weight in wildcats. Well, which is true? Then how are you going to prove that it's true? You're going to jump on them from the first whistle. Don't let them get set. Sock 'em and rock 'em from the start! Charge and hit them! Smear them! Smash, bang, and blind them! Bam! like that. That's all I've got to say, boys. Now go in and give them hell!'

A superb ovation greeted the team as they ran on to the field. The band played enthusiastically, sixty thousand spectators clapped their hands, and the cheer-leaders led their special sections through a stentorian voodoo ritual.

The game was robust enough even to satisfy the anticipations so assiduously fomented during the weeks of preparation, and casualties were not infrequent.

Princeton scored first, a touchdown, but failed with the kick that should have added another point. Then Motley, after a brilliant run, also scored, and with a good kick gained the extra point. This success raised the enthusiasm of the home spectators to ecstasy. The Motley band played louder than ever, the cheer-leaders gyrated madly, and all the old graduates drew bottles of rye whisky or gin from their pockets and drank deeply to show how happy they were.

Now Princeton attacked with increasing ferocity and skill, and in rapid succession a Motley guard and two Motley half-backs were carried off the field. But still Princeton could not score. Beaten back almost to their goal-line the Motley men fought doggedly and held the plunging attackers out. '*Ils ne passeront pas*' was their watchword, and like Verdun their goal remained inviolate. But oh, the narrow escapes it had! Oh, the successive agonies and gratitudes that shook the watching thousands! And ah, the relief when whistles blew for half-time!

In the dressing-room masseurs and underlings of various degree worked over the heroic team, rubbing their bruised arms and slapping their legs and anointing their backs with alcohol. Mr. Ramper's face was white and his eyes were embarrassingly bright and big. When everybody had been washed and rubbed and dressed anew he stood on a chair and spoke in a voice loaded, and indeed over-loaded, with emotion. He was now nine parts Evangelist to only one of Gladiator, judging that sentimentality at this stage would be the spur most likely to harass his team into harder kicking.

'Oh, boys,' he said in a hoarse quiet voice, 'if you have sweethearts go out and fight for them now! If you have mothers go out and fight for your mothers' sake! And if you have neither mothers nor sweethearts, remember this: That old Al Ramper loves you one and all, and so perhaps you'll fight for him. I'm not a demonstrative man, boys, but I just want to say that I love you all, for what you are and for what you've done for me to-day, as truly as ever a father loved his sons. And this is a secret: I'm not so strong as you think I am. The doctor tells me that I've got a very weak heart indeed, and perhaps this is the last year I'll be your coach. Perhaps before another year has come round the Grim Reaper will have called for me and I'll be standing in the purple and green of Motley before the Great Referee who sees all our fumbles and whose whistle we must all obey. Perhaps this is the last chance I'll ever have to see you beat Princeton, and if you hang on to your lead you've got them beaten. So go out and fight, boys, as you've never fought before. For your mothers' sake, for your sweethearts' sake, for my sake! For old Al Ramper's sake, boys, hang on to that goddam lead!'

Tears flowed rapidly down Mr. Ramper's cheeks. Priam was not more moved when Hector and his youngest brothers were trumpeted forth to meet the Greekish host. Not Dido wept so fast, nor Faustus, pleading respite from hell, pled more desperately than he. And the soft-hearted footballers (many of whom weighed more than fifteen stones apiece) went out with souls afire, their fingers twitching, all ready to be copy now to men of grosser blood and teach them how to war.

Stiffened by the salt of Mr. Ramper's tears they drove the Princeton men to the far end of the field, and held them there, and menaced their goal with lance-like thrusting and subtle ruse. But the Princeton team held firm and Motley could not increase its lead of one small point.

Now the Motley offensive grew slower, and play ranged back

to the middle of the field, and by-and-by into the Motley half as Princeton, rising like giants from defence, roared like giants to attack. Now was the Motley goal once more a city set upon by enemies, its towers harassed by slingers, its walls threatened by mine and sap. Now the Motley men dug their toes into the scarred earth, and set their granite jaws, and fought valorously for every inch of ground. And now Time came to their aid, striking down, like enemies, minute after minute, so that the end came near and nearer with Princeton still one point behind.

But Fate (in the person of Aloysius Werther, the roving Princeton centre) caught by the heels Tim Appleman, a Motley half-back, and threw him heavily so that his shoulder was dislocated. And Tim was the third half-back that Motley had lost in this game.

Mr. Ramper considered the forty reserves who still waited on the side-lines. Good backs were scarcer than linemen. Mr. Ramper hesitated. In practice games Juan had been playing extremely well. He never missed a signal, his fielding was accurate, his kicking strong, and he ran with a very useful swerve. But he was, of course, inexperienced. Perhaps, thought Mr. Ramper, it would be safer to send in Guggenheim. But Guggenheim, though experienced enough, had been playing poorly in practice games. . . . Mr. Ramper risked his luck and sent Juan to replace Tim Appleman.

By this time Juan had almost given up hope of ever taking part in an actual game, and while he put on his helmet his gratification was tempered by surprise. He was, too, somewhat stiff and cold from sitting so long on a bench. He felt self-conscious as he glanced quickly round at the oval embankment of spectators and listened, willy-nilly, to the spasmodic thunder of their voices. It was an embarrassing experience but rather a joke – or would be if he had someone to share it with.

For a little while he had nothing very important to do. As a short relief from the crashing fatigue of off-tackle work the backs were kicking. Juan stood behind the Motley goal-line.

In a long swift arc the ball came towards him, and expertly he caught it. Now the orthodox and proper thing to do was to touch the ball on the ground, which would automatically give Motley possession of it on the twenty-yards line. But it seemed to Juan that he had an open field to the right, and that he could run the ball a great deal farther out of Motley territory than twenty yards.

In that, however, he erred. Perhaps because of cold and stiffness his speed had deserted him. Perhaps he had misjudged the speed of his opponents. At any rate he had scarcely gone ten yards when a charge of amazing velocity stopped him dead and another almost burst his midriff. A buffalo and a python could not have attacked more robustly, but actually it was Aloysius Werther, the roving Princeton centre, and Hy Brannigan, a Princeton end, who had tackled him. Winded, stunned, suffering extreme vertigo, half suffocated, and anxious particularly for the fate of one knee, Juan had practically no idea of what was happening to him. As a matter of fact he was being hurled back to where he started from. Such was the velocity of Mr. Werther, so great the impetus of Mr. Brannigan, that the momentum of their combined charge was sufficient to carry them and Juan and the ball for several very valuable yards, and when they all came to rest it was behind Motley's goal-line – and Princeton had scored.

On three-quarters of the crowd a silence fell. As if clamour had been a coloured veil, blankness succeeded it, like a white and empty wall that is disclosed by the removal of a gaudy curtain. Blank of heart and face, stupefied by calamity, sat thousands but lately clad in the garish colours of excitement. In vain the cheer-leaders tried to rouse them. A ragged mutter was all their answer. But the minority who cheered for Princeton were roaring their delight.

Five minutes later the game was over. Neither side scored again and Motley had lost by Juan's error.

XI

On the following Tuesday Juan left hospital. He was bruised here and there and limped somewhat as he walked. But these physical discomforts were trifling in comparison with his mental unease. For he knew that he was widely regarded as something between a fool and a traitor, something worse than a criminal and little better than a pariah, the target of small boys' scorn and the object of his fellow-footballers' hate.

The doctors in the hospital had treated him with arctic disdain, and the nurses had barely conquered their repugnance at touching him. Had he not thrown away the only victory over Princeton that Motley had approached for years? Probably he had been bribed by Princeton. The nurses felt that they would sooner tend a leper than bandage such a man's flesh.

The Sunday newspapers had abused and deftly mocked him. They quoted Mr. Ramper as saying, 'Never again will that man put on the old green and purple shirt of Motley. I would tear it off his back with my own hands!' And on Sunday evening (after worshipping in the Church of Christ Scientist) Mr. Ramper visited the hospital to utter his commination in person.

Now, as Juan walked across the campus, men stared coldly at him or avoided his eye. Three or four, talking together, would fall silent till he passed and study him with baleful looks. Girls glanced at him indignantly and, had there been anything to take hold of, would have drawn their skirts aside. Three Chinamen – students of sociology – laughed at him outright.

He went to interview the Professor of Commercial Statistics; his supervisor in Business Ethics; and the lecturer on Industrial Management. They too had suffered change. Since Juan was no longer a footballer – had they not read Coach Ramper's statement in the newspapers? – his status as a privileged student would naturally be revised. He would become – nay, had already become – an ordinary undergraduate, subject to a crushing tax of work and faced with immediate demands for an essay on The Liquidity of Public Utilities, another on The Integrity of Underwriters, and a third on A Cycle Analysis of Variations in the Demand for Garage-door Hinges. Furthermore there would be trial examinations in a very short time, and failure to make a sufficiency of marks in these would be a serious matter. So said the Professor of Commercial Statistics, his supervisor in Business Ethics, and the lecturer on Industrial Management. . . . Bottle-grey eyes in glazy-grey faces, suddenly unfriendly. Puny tyrants in a paper empire. Bam! said Mr. Ramper. A Cycle Analysis of Variations in the Demand for Garage-door Hinges, said the Professor of Commercial Statistics. This is very distressing indeed, said Juan, and decided that American currency meant a great deal more than dollars and cents. It meant, among other things, that a game was no longer a game, but a cross between a commercial proposition and a romantic ideal; and he who smutched romance, he who lightlied commerce, must suffer appropriate pains.

And Leonie had deserted him. She had not visited him in hospital, nor telephoned, nor written to him. And when Juan went to a rendezvous which they had established in the Library she was not there.

By one of those harmless affectations of sentiment they had assumed the habit of meeting in the Library at the usually deserted location among the stacks where Juan had seen Leonie's eyes, tear-dimmed, above a row of books, and spoken to her for the first time. Now he stood there alone, leaning against the shelves, and with a half-absent mind reading the titles opposite. There was Hakluyt in tall green slender volumes, and there – several rows of it – the *Journal of the Geographical Society*, the colour of dirty gloves, with maroon and sage strips on the mildly rounded backs. There were the publications of the Hakluyt Society, in blue with gold lettering:

The Journal of John Jourdain, The Portuguese Expedition to Abyssinia, Andrew Battell in Guinea, Early Voyages and Travels in the Levant, Gonzalez' Voyage to Easter Island, 1770. . . .

Easter Island was in that part of the Pacific which overflows the left-hand side of the world on Mercator's Projection, and was inhabited by large stone faces; Abyssinia was an African stronghold of black Christianity, feudalism, and the descendants of Solomon's intercourse with Balkis, who had hairy legs; the Levant was where the Mediterranean looked with sapphire enquiry at the desert, and the pirate Genoese hell-raked old orange ships that rolled blood, water, fruit, and corpses in their holds; as to Guinea, that was fever country, though if one lived there was ivory and palm-oil, and Andrew Battell had taken home some fine stories of his life among the Gagas, which doubtless refreshed his old age and commended him to his neighbours of Leigh in Essex. . . .

To be brief, there were more towns on the earth than Carthage, and a university had obvious disadvantages as a place of residence. It was isolated from the rest of the world, and false standards flourished there. . . .

A hostile voice interrupted his musing. Leonie came out of the farther gloom and stood in the brightness between the walls of books.

'I have come,' she said, 'to give you back your ring. You understand, I suppose, why I no longer want to wear it?'

She pulled a jewel from her finger and offered it to Juan, who was properly amazed.

'But I didn't give you that ring,' he said. 'I didn't give you a ring of any kind.'

'I know you didn't,' said Leonie, 'and meanness is nothing to boast about either. It was Red Roper, who used to be my boy-friend, that gave it to me, but since I've been going round with you I've been wearing it *for* you, if you understand, and if you don't understand everybody else does, so I've got to get rid of it somehow, or they'll think I'm still your girl-friend, and I'd sooner *die* than have them think that. So there you are.'

With a contemptuous gesture she tossed the ring to Juan, turned on her heel, and walked mincingly away. . . .

Voyages of Foxe and James to the North-West; Cathay and the Way Thither; Purchas his Pilgrims – these were the titles that Leonie had hidden while she talked about engagement-rings. A stupid girl with a tongue like the clapper of a bell, but comforting to touch and lovely to look at. It was a pity to lose so pretty a thing. .. Far away was *Geographie Universelle* by Malte Brun, daintily mottled; and below, on dusty black volumes, German letters: *Erdkunde*, and *Erd-vôlker* and *Staatenkunde*. And on the floor-shelf huge clumsy parchment volumes, dirty white, called *Der Neue* something or other. Juan put Leonie's ring between the pages of *Cathay and the Way Thither*. . . .

In a shabby restaurant that night he fell into conversation with a strange-looking little man. He had chosen to dine – if eating so unceremonious a meal could be called dining – in a kind of cabmen's shelter on the far side of Carthage, where he could be free from undergraduate company. Most of the customers sat on little stools before a long counter, but at one end there was a table to which Juan went, and presently the little man came and sat opposite.

He carried no hat, and his hair, which was long and in colour a streaky brown and white, had been blown about in all directions. He was a thin little man with a bony red face and bony red hands, and his eyes were almost invisible because of the way in which the lids puckered over them. His clothes were ill-fitting in a curious style, for he wore a very thick green knitted jersey that was much too big for him, and over it a tweed jacket which had been made for a boy and would barely button across his chest. Lumps of green wool thrust up towards his neck and ribbed green sleeves covered his wrists that his coat-sleeves scarcely pretended to approach.

He was very nervous and shy, and sadly embarrassed by the

little problems of eating; and yet anxious for company, eager to talk. He was not very fond of Carthage.

'I'd never been in prison till I came here,' he said with a bashful laugh. He did not look at Juan as he spoke but carried his head first to one side, then to the other; not furtively, but modestly; and his eyes peeped shyly from between their puckered lids.

'What did they put you in prison for?'

'I was watching some goldfinches and a deputy-sheriff came along and said I was a vagrant. That was in the spring. The tree was covered with new leaves, all pale green and like little spear-blades bent in the middle. You know? And a whole swarm of goldfinches came and played among them, chirping and chirruping and flitting about. They came back to the same tree for several days, and I used to sit and watch them. I hadn't anything else to do, and they were pretty, I thought.'

'You're a naturalist?'

'I used to be, but I'm not much good at anything now, so I just watch things. Birds mostly.'

The little man's name was Foley. He paid his bill in pennies and nickels and dimes, which he took some time to count out, so that Juan could not help discovering that small money was a matter of large importance to him.

When they had left the restaurant Foley said with some pride, 'I made a lot of money this Fall, picking berries. There's ever so many blackberries on these hills, and blueberries too. Sometimes I made as much as eighty cents for an hour's picking. I like picking berries. I wish they grew all the year round.'

His voice was gentle and his manner of speech a great deal more cultured than that of the undergraduates whom Juan had been meeting. Partly out of curiosity in his antecedents and partly out of a natural desire to feed someone for whom feeding was perhaps only an intermittent function, Juan invited the little man to noon-tide dinner with him on the following day. And Foley in his bashful way seemed glad to accept.

XVI

Because of this casual encounter Juan slept in a barn some nights later, and Foley, snuffling lightly, lay beside him.

So long as you have enough to eat and your metabolism is normal there are many ways to happiness. If you can find a place where wasting time brings you no shame, no pangs of conscience, that is one of the oases. If you can hate and are able to contrive misery for your enemies, you are again enarboured in bliss. And if you possess the habit of mind that will depreciate what you have lost or may never attain, you have not only a bower of content but a bower that is guarded against all the invasions of envy and regret.

It was Juan's good fortune to have such a mind, and so he wasted no time in biting his fingers over the loss of Leonie, but remembered with some clarity such things as these: that her voice was somewhat thin and toneless; that she had a large brown birthmark shaped like a dog's head; that her vocabulary was unduly limited; and when he walked with her she had a vexatious habit of bumping against him. He knew, of course, that she had these contrary excellences: lips that were admirably soft and delicately moulded; the prettiest leg in Carthage; a variety of caresses; and enviable skill in dancing. But though he had previously enjoyed the latter circumstances to the almost total exclusion of any consideration of the former, the former were now magnified till Juan discovered that his unhappiness was overcome by the simultaneous disappearance of several factors of annoyance.

In a similar way he guarded himself against regretting the amenities of Motley by a perspicacious realisation of its defects. No sooner had he decided to leave it than he saw quite clearly the disabilities of university life in general and of life at Motley in particular; and the advantages of a nomadic existence became correspondingly vivid. . . . *Cathay and The Way Thither; Andrew Battell in Guinea; Easter Island.* There were such splendid places in the world that it was surely foolish to live three years in Carthage when three years were three-seventieths of all one's life, and the demi-earth of America stretched bravely before his feet.

But where to go he did not choose – though he had a vague notion to see Quebec – until he met Foley for the second time and Foley, diffidently mentioning his own plans, gave Juan an idea.

The little man sat in a flutter of excitement before his dinner, all spread out on the table before him. The restaurant made no pretence to elegance either in service or food, and to save trouble everything ordered was brought and set on the table at once, so that Foley had in front of him a dish of hash with a poached egg on top of it, a saucer of mashed potatoes and another of spinach, a cup of coffee, and a plate dangerously overlapped by a thick damp-looking slice of chocolate-pie.

Eagerly, though with the diffidence that all his movements betrayed, he picked here and there with a fork, now at hash, now at spinach, and now at chocolate-pie. The sweet stuff was so tempting that he could not wait till all his meat was eaten before trying it. And then sometimes he would change his mind while a morsel was in mid-air, and set it back upon the nearest plate, so that by-and-by fragments of chocolate-pie were nestling in the hash and spinach lay nonchalantly in alien dishes. He was evidently accustomed to a more frugal table, for when the meal was nearly over – and it took a long time with such tactics – he said, 'It's a very good dinner, but it's pretty difficult eating so much at one time.'

A little later he remarked, 'I've been thinking about walking to Buffalo. I've got a cousin there, and perhaps he'll let me stay with him for a while. It's good weather for walking now, before the snow comes.'

Juan remembered that Buffalo was on the nearest route into Canada, and if he meant to visit Quebec he might as well start that way and see Toronto as well.

'I think I'll go with you,' he said.

'That's fine,' said Foley, 'when shall we start?'

Without unnecessary delay Juan packed his trunks and stored them; forwarded by rail a suitcase to Buffalo; drew his money from the bank – six hundred dollars or so; bought a rücksack and put in it a raincoat, a rug, a flask of rye whisky, some bread, chocolate, socks and a shirt; and on the second morning after his decision joined Foley at breakfast.

There was a winter haze on the hills when they set out, bidding no farewells, but standing for a minute when through a gap in the trees they saw the small town in a smoky hollow beneath them, and beyond it the university on a hill-top, and behind it another hill, and behind that a hill, and beyond that the sky in its seven veils.

Dead grass and weeds were yellow underfoot, and bare trees stood stilly in the windless air. Here and there hedges, made of great tree-roots pulled from the earth, made a stockade of black limbs, tangled and twisted like antlers, or witches' arms, dark and sinewy, frozen in a sudden trance. The smell of leaf-mould and sleepy earth rose till the sun came out.

Foley walked with a rapid shuffling pace, stopping now and then with startling suddenness to listen, with head cocked up or bent earthwards, to some bird's chatter or mysterious rustling in the leaves. He told in snatches the story which filled the gap between his gentle voice and vagrant existence.

He had been brought up in a wealthy home, expensively educated, luxuriously amused, encouraged to marry at twenty-one. His wife had been a year younger, beautiful and frolicsome. He neglected his former amusements for her. He forgot his friends. He took her to Italy to see her against a Florentine background; to Spain that she might pose for him in a gateway of the Alhambra; to Canada so that he could worship her in the snow; and to Hawaii where she outbeautied Aphrodite in the surf.

Then he became interested in something else, and rode his

new hobby with all the enthusiasm that he had given to bride-grooming. It was perhaps significant that his second love was cold and elusive, a dainty thing ever ready to escape, chill to the touch and secret-eyed, living on rocks rather than in softness. In a word, lizards. The first to arouse his interest was a green one in Florida. Its tail came off in his hand and twitched and wriggled faintly after the parent body had vanished. Foley bought books on zoology to see how this phenomenon could be explained. He became excited by the technical description of lizards. A transverse anus was indeed a whimsical idea. And he was fascinated by the abrupt agility of the creatures. Flick! and they were gone, like the shadow of a leaf when the wind blows.

From the green ones in Florida he went to examine the sandy-brown ones of Texas and Arizona, and the viviparous horned-toads of California that had vicious thorns on their backs and were said to squirt blood from their eyes. Then he travelled to Jamaica, where the lizards had dewlaps that were all the colours of the rainbow, and puffed them out for anyone to see; prideful reptiles, as a man could tell from the cold and gem-like glitter of their eyes. But even these, he was told, were nothing to compare with certain lizards of Australia which grew three feet long and had multi-hued Elizabethan ruffs about their necks. Foley went to Australia.

'I wrote a book about lizards while I was there,' he said. 'But it wasn't a very good book. Nobody bought it.'

And when he returned to America he discovered that his wife had divorced him on the grounds of desertion, while his family had disowned him because he preferred the company of creeping things in the Antipodes to a Thanksgiving Day reunion of the Foleys in Boston.

Now such is the inconsistency of man that Foley had no sooner written his book than he lost interest in lizards, and his journey home had been occupied by dreams of his wife all night and visions of her by day. The discovery that she had left him was a profound and almost mortal shock.

'I was pretty sick for a long time,' he said. 'They put me in a home, but I got out. I felt worse than ever when I had to sit still. I like walking about and looking at things.'

And as if to show the truth of this assertion Foley shuffled with amazing rapidity across a large field; stopped under a tree to stare intently at a bird which was doing nothing more interesting than ruffling its feathers in a bored and peevish way; and walked on again as quickly as before.

Dusk fell early and they began to look for a night's shelter. Foley wanted to sleep out of doors, though there would be frost before morning. He said that he had often slept in the snow, wrapt in a coat and a blanket. Juan suggested a barn. Foley was frightened of farmers and tried to dissuade Juan of his idea by stories of solitary men who had been murdered in the straw, and rotting bodies hidden in a dunghill, and savage dogs who fed on flesh. But when a high-roofed barn loomed blackly ahead of them Juan said he would go no farther, and Foley yielded unwillingly.

The darkness did not seem to trouble him. Perhaps he had cat's eyes. Juan, following his lead, tripped over one thing after another in the untidy farmyard, and made Foley nervous with the noise of his stumbling. But no one came, and no dog barked, and they found their way into the barn. There the darkness was heavy and almost palpable to lips and cheek, but Foley felt his way to a pile of straw where they slept comfortably enough.

It was still dark when they woke – Foley because of an alarm-clock of fear that he had set in his mind, fear lest the farmer or the farmer's sons should rouse and find him helpless in a dream, and Juan because Foley tugged at his arm. There was a new element in the stuffy smell of the barn. The morning cold had filtered in, piercing the odour of sacking and vegetable decay with slivers of frost. Juan shivered as he rose and stretched himself, and they stumbled on to the road with stiff legs, neither speaking.

The ruts were frozen, not solidly, but enough to make the road alternately rough and heavy. The stars shone with a cold pallor and the silence as they walked had the chill and sunken weariness of old men asleep. But presently the sky began to lighten, and a cock crew, and a tree-root hedge took the shape of a witches' dance in the fading darkness. And when the sky had yawned day broke as suddenly as, twelve hours before, the night had fallen. Fields of dull earth sprinkled with yellow stubble became visible. Foley and Juan broke their fast on bread and milk and walked on.

Foley began to stutter a little when he talked, as if the excitement of their adventure was getting too much for him. He recurred to his few days' imprisonment in Carthage, which had apparently distressed him unduly. It was in spring that he had been thrown into gaol, and spring was the time of year when there was so much to see in the woods. He took from his pocket-book the photograph of a tree-sparrow feeding her young.

'I w-watched the nest for a w-week,' he said, 'till the old bird got used to me, and then when she took the y-young ones out on a branch I stood in a bush not more than a y-yard away and got this photograph.'

Four nestlings sat in a row, all pin-feathers and open beaks, greedily watching the mother-bird as she stuffed food into the mouth of a fifth gaping youngster.

'But owls are d-dangerous birds to ph-photograph. I nearly got my ear torn off taking this one.'

About two in the afternoon they came to a knoll and saw farm-buildings some two hundred yards below them. Foley's instinct was to make a detour so as to avoid any possible contact with the occupants, but Juan saw something that puzzled him and he stopped to stare at it with incredulous horror.

A shed stood to the right of the buildings, open towards them, and a strange thing hung in the dark embrasure. It was white, and looked alarmingly like a body. Foley saw it too. His mouth opened, and though his fell of brown and silver hair was too heavy to stand on end it seemed to grow fluffy with excitement.

'He's hanged himself,' he gasped.

'A man wouldn't undress before he committed suicide,' Juan objected.

'Then he's been m-murdered. Taken out of his b-bed and murdered!'

'Come and see.'

But Foley was terrified. His fingers undid and re-did the single button on his coat, and his eyes blinked rapidly in a face gone sallow so far as its sunburnt red allowed.

Suddenly in a high-pitched voice he exclaimed, 'I can't stand it, I can't s-stand it!' and ran down the knoll with a loose galloping pace.

Juan shouted to him, and after a minute or two followed him. But Foley took refuge in a wood, and to look for him there was almost useless. Juan climbed the knoll again and went down towards the farm.

It was a newly-killed pig that hung in the shed.

Juan spent an hour looking for Foley, but the little man had either run far or lay hidden in some thick-growing part of the wood, for he could not find him and got no answer to shouting. Juan was very distressed at this ridiculous mishap, but he realised the impracticability of further search. Foley might have taken any one of many directions and travelled several miles in an hour; or if he wanted to hide, his practice in bird-photography would make his discovery unlikely even if he were still close at hand.

Feeling very lonely Juan made his way to the nearest highway and tried to attract the attention of passing motorists. But half a dozen went by without paying any attention to his signals. Then a large motor-truck approached, travelling with reasonable speed and disproportionate noise. Juan waved and the truck-driver pulled-up.

'Going to Buffalo?' Juan asked.

'Sure. Yump in.'

The truck-driver had a round and cheerful face, very dirty, but the dirt was redeemed by blue eyes and a strand of yellow hair that escaped from his cap. He was talkative and Juan would have liked to reply and hear something of the man's ideas, and perhaps respond with a few of his own, but conversation was hampered, and indeed prohibited, by two factors: the driver, who was apparently a Swede, spoke in very broken English, and the terrible rattle and banging of the truck killed any sound frailer than a shout. Now Juan's English voice seemed as foreign to the driver as the driver's yumping and ban-ing was to Juan, so after a great deal of bawling which neither understood, but which both accompanied with hearty laughter and gestures of goodwill, a silence fell between them. And yet silence is not the word, for the loose iron clamour of the truck continued, and grew louder to tired ear-drums until wearied by its very insistence, and as it were battered unconscious, Juan fell asleep.

It was dark when he awoke, and they had arrived in Buffalo and were driving through strange streets. Juan, of course, had no definite plans. His suit-case would be at the Railway Express depôt, but perhaps it was too late to retrieve it that evening. If so he would have to look for a very small and unpretentious hotel, as two days of muddy walking and a night in a barn had not flattered his appearance. He tried to ask the truck-driver for information, and the Swede grinned cheerfully and shouted in reply and pointed straight ahead. Perhaps he understood what Juan wanted; perhaps he did not. At any rate he continued to drive on, guiding his unwieldly wagon with a kind of robust, devil-may-care improvisation of tactics.

At last he stopped on a broad poorly-lighted street where a cold wind blew.

'The depôt's yoost three, maybe four, blocks along there,' he said.

Juan shook hands and thanked the driver for his kindness.

'You bet,' said the Swede, and drove his thundering wagon down a causeway that took the clamour to its stony breast and beat it there.

It was a curious street that Juan had been left in. Not altogether a street, for in parts it was a railway siding. And beyond the siding appeared to be ships, so that it was a quay as well as a railway and a road. The cold wind that blew came off Lake Erie or the Niagara River – Juan could not tell in which direction he was facing. This was doubtless an important part of Buffalo, though not the most attractive. Juan walked quickly to find more cheerful surroundings.

But before he had gone a hundred yards he was halted by an unpleasant voice which said, 'Reach for it, sonny, reach for it!'

At the same time he felt the pressure of something small and hard on his back, and looking over his shoulder he saw an ugly rat-faced fellow, who snarled at him and bade him 'Stick 'em up, Big Boy, stick 'em up!'

Very unwillingly Juan put up his hands, and the rat-faced fellow, keeping his pistol pressed to Juan's backbone with one hand, used the other to search his victim's pockets. Hip and coat pockets first, and then he snapped 'Turn round,' and with his pistol thrust into Juan's stomach explored further. He found Juan's note-case and peeped inside it. What he saw excited him so that he was in a hurry to be off.

'That's all the money I've got in the world,' said Juan.

'Rest your jaw,' replied the yegg. 'And now turn round and keep that ritzy pan of yours on the wall, or I'll bump you off. See?'

Juan's eyes followed sadly the transference of his money to the bandit's pocket. With infinite regret he faced the wall. His knees were inclined to be tremulous, and when he persuaded himself to look round the rat-faced man had disappeared.

Juan found no prospect of consolation for his loss in contemning money. He might arm himself against regret for Leonie by thinking of her mole, and feel no sorrow at leaving Motley when he considered how narrow was the horizon of a university, but such depreciation would not reconcile him to losing six hundred and twenty dollars. Money might be the root of all evil, as some maintained, but poverty was the very taste and apparition of evil. He still possessed, in small change that the bandit had overlooked, one dollar and seventy-eight cents. A dollar seventy-eight, and he knew no one in Buffalo. The face of destitution was a more alarming spectacle than he had ever imagined. It had come so suddenly. Six hundred and twenty dollars was affluence, and a dollar seventy-eight was indigence aggravated by six hundred and twenty holes for the wind. And no warning, no gradual preparation, had accompanied the transition.

Aimlessly now, and slowly, Juan walked along. Antipathy to the cold and dismal neighbourhood had disappeared. He was more at home there than in rich and bustling streets. He should, he supposed, report his loss to the police; but it would do no good. His nose caught a smell of cooking food as he passed a shabby eating-house, and he realised that he was hungry. He turned back and went in, and because of his poverty ordered toast and coffee.

The eating-house was called Joe's Place. It consisted, like so many others, of a long counter with stools before it and a couple of tables at one end. Cooking was done behind the counter and in a small room at the back. Apple-pie and pumpkin-pie were displayed, and red hamburger sausage-meat. A glass dome covered a plate loaded with doughnuts. Coffee was on tap in an urn. One could eat a substantial meal for forty cents.

There were two or three roughly dressed men there when Juan went in. They presently finished eating and left. A serious, pale-faced, bald-headed man who stood behind the counter seemed worried, and every now and then looked into the room behind the shop. When he opened the door Juan heard a babbling incoherent voice inside, and the proprietor – so he seemed – shouted roughly into the darkness, 'Shut up, you crazy Bohunk!' But Juan was too sorry for himself to be concerned with the troubles of other men, and he ate his toast gloomily.

The mysterious voice grew louder and its incoherence gradually acquired a rhythm, and then broke indefinitely into song. The proprietor stood at the far end of the shop looking out of a window. There was nothing to see, but he pretended to be so interested that he did not hear what was going on inside. His pretence failed, however, when the song grew louder and the singer began dancing as well. He seemed to wear heavy boots. And not only were his feet active but his hands were probably gesticulating, for the crash of broken crockery and the clatter of a tin pail were added to the din. Then the proprietor clutched at his bald head, turned fiercely, threw open the door, and leapt into the hidden room.

The noise of a lively quarrel followed his entrance. Two voices contended, there was a trampling to and fro, some more dishes fell, and after a short delay a wild and dishevelled figure with black hair appeared, propelled from behind by the proprietor.

'Open the door, will you?' said the latter.

Juan obligingly held it open while the black-haired fellow was pushed out and his progress hurried by a great kick under his tail.

'The drunken bum,' said the proprietor, gasping with so much exertion, and with his apron wiped sweat from his pale forehead. 'I told him what would happen if he tried to play me for a sucker. That stew. That's the third time he's come in all shot. They're a pain in the neck, those Bohunks. I warned him, though. I told him I'd give him the bum's rush if he tried to pull that stuff on me. Walking in here with a hard jag on! I told him what was coming to him, and it did. He's done me dirt, though. He's left me without an assistant and I've stood here since eight o'clock this morning.'

Juan answered with perfunctory sympathy, but he could not pretend to much feeling for the other's ill-luck. His own misfortune was so much greater.

'What's your trouble?' asked the proprietor. 'You don't seem too cheerful neither.'

'I've just been held up and robbed.'

'Well, that's too bad. How much d'you lose?'

'Six hundred dollars. All that I had except chicken-feed.'

'Say, that's tough. That's real tough. Have another cup of cawffee. It's all right, you don't have to pay for it.'

The proprietor refilled Juan's cup and looked at him with solemn sympathy, shaking his head a little and muttering, 'Six hundred bucks. Well, that's too bad. And cleaned you out, huh?'

'Yes,' said Juan.

'D'you live here?'

'No, I only arrived half an hour ago. I thought of going into Canada.'

'Got any friends here?'

'Not a soul.'

'Then what are you going to do?'

'I don't know.'

The proprietor stared hard at Juan and seemed to be considering something of importance.

'Are you a Canadian?' he asked.

'English,' said Juan shortly.

'Yeah? My ancestor came from England. He was a lord. Lord Brown of London. Ever hear of him?'

'I'm afraid I haven't.'

'Well, maybe he was young when he left there. I don't know much about him either, except that he was a lord or a knight or something. Now listen: you're broke and I want an assistant. I don't know anything about you, but I kinda like the look of you and I'm willing to take a chance. It's worth ten dollars a week and your meals. What d'you say?'

The offer came as a surprise to Juan, for except riding after sheep in Australia he had never done any work, and certainly never even contemplated work of this menial kind. But destitution opened one of his eyes and the democratic air of America removed an Old World cataract from the other, so that after blinking once or twice he saw that it would be as well for him to accept the offer.

'That's fine,' said the proprietor. 'Just fine. What's your name? Mine's Jordan Brown and folk call me Joe. Well, I'll be getting along. I'll be back about eight o'clock. I work day-time, you work nights. See?'

He took off his apron and tied it round Juan's waist, explaining, 'There's the eggs, and the cheese, and the beans is here, and here's where I keep my milk, and there's more doughnuts through the back there. Say, d'you know how to fix a hamburger? Well, watch me and I'll show you.'

Joe cut a slice from a lump of mottled red sausage-meat, and rolled it between his hands, and thumped it, and greased a girdle on a gas-stove behind the counter, and put the hamburger meat on the girdle, and thwacked it flat with a broad-bladed knife.

'Now all you got to do is to turn on the gas and cook it first on one side and then on the other till it looks good and smells good,' he said. 'That's easy, isn't it? I'd like to stop and help you a bit, but I got a date with the girl-friend.'

He winked heavily.

'Some hot momma,' he added, and clapt a hat on to his bald head. After another wink he left the shop to Juan. The door slammed behind him.

XVI

Joe's Place had its customers at all hours of the night. Men who looked like labourers – and presumably were labourers – would come in and brusquely demand a plate of beans. Mysterious, nondescript individuals drank coffee and ate doughnuts – the American male has a sweet tooth. Inebriates, solitary or in parties, had appetites that called impartially for fried eggs and cherry pie. Generally these were merry and loud-voiced, but sometimes they were white and staggering, drunk as Davy's sow. The morning smell of the eating-house was stale and greasy.

Juan's first night there was punctuated by altercations with the customers, who disputed his methods of cooking. He was very sleepy, and the necessity of washing egg-encrusted or bean-stained dishes was a source of recurrent disgust. Promptly at eight o'clock Joe returned, ready to treat Juan as an old friend and relate for him the night's adventures in love. But Juan was interested only in sleep, so Joe told him the way to the house where he himself lodged, in which there was a vacant room that he recommended. He offered, indeed, to let Juan sleep in his own bed – since he occupied it only by night – and it was by the exercise of considerable tact that Juan at last persuaded him of the occasional inconvenience of such an arrangement.

The house where Joe lived was a dirty dilapidated building that smelt worse than an old horse-blanket, and the landlady was a tow-headed scarecrow who simpered at Juan and, after he had agreed to take the room, came back with a second pillow for his couch and simpered again. By this time she had smeared her lips with red and sprayed herself with some rank perfume.

'I'll tell you if there's anything else I want,' he said, yawning. The woman contrived a last expression of archest invitation, and when Juan turned his back left the room with a snort of contempt.

Juan went to bed and slept long and heavily. It was dark again when he woke. His room looked even more unpleasant than it had in the morning, but this reconciled him to another night of frying hamburgers and washing dishes in Joe's Place. For Joe's was more attractive than this dismal cabin. Indeed the prospect of meeting the night-birds began to seem entertaining, and though when he thought of his lost six hundred dollars Juan was desolated with sorrow, he admitted that even the inordinate grief of being robbed might have some minute compensation in forcing one to acquire a new and unlikely experience of life.

Before Joe left – to meet his woman again – he gave Juan some further instruction in dealing with beans, hot dogs, and so forth. The trade had a patter of its own. Juan, the night before, had been seriously upset by a customer who demanded 'Two western eggs and make 'em walk.' Who could have guessed that such an order meant egg-sandwiches, with a certain seasoning, wrapt up so that the purchaser might carry them away? But now Juan was armed by Joe with a whole coffee-stall vocabulary, so that he would be undismayed even were some facetious person to ask for 'Adam and Eve on a raft, face down.'

His second night passed quietly. The only interesting customers were two men who arrived about three o'clock in the morning. Both were dressed in a smart vulgar fashion. Their suits looked aggressively new, their shirts were highly coloured, and their ties extravagantly patterned. One of the men was a large and simple-looking fellow, a prize-fighter probably, retired and run to seed a little. The other was small, dark, and weaselly.

The big one asked for apple-pie *à la mode*; that is, apple-pie with a lump of ice-cream on top of it. When Juan confessed that he had no ice-cream the prize-fighter was indignant.

'No ice-cream?' he said. 'Well, I'll never come here again. No, sir. Not if you haven't got ice-cream. I eat ice-cream with every meal I have, from breakfast to supper. It's good for you. Doctors recommend ice-cream, don't they, Spider?'

'Forget it,' was all the comfort his companion would give.

When Juan had served them they talked to each other in whispers, and several times he turned round to find them watching him. Presently the one called Spider spoke:

'Been here long, kid?'

'No,' Juan answered.

'Like the job?'

'It's all right.'

'Where d'you come from?'

'How does that concern you?'

'All right, kid, all right. Take it easy. I was only being interested in you, see?'

Spider said no more to Juan, but whispered to the pugilist, who whispered back, and once more they looked at Juan in a stock-taking, appraising way.

They finished their meal and rose to go. At the door Spider turned and said, 'Good-night, kid. We'll see you again maybe.' Juan replied politely and wondered if he were already so good a waiter that he was attracting permanent customers.

He drew a week's wages the following morning in order to get his suit-case from the Railway Express Company. Joe was in high spirits and readily gave Juan his ten dollars. Another night of amorous activity had convinced him of his prowess in love. He felt like Romeo, Lothario, and the Grand Turk all rolled into one, and scratched his bald head and chuckled greasily to think of it. He tied an apron round his swollen middle.

'Just between you and me, what d'you think of her?' he asked Juan.

'I?' said Juan. I've never seen her. How do I know?'

Joe winked. 'Go on,' he said. 'You saw her yesterday and you'll see her again to-day. She told me what she thought of you, so you needn't be shy. She says you were kinda snooty with her. Tried to high-hat her. But I told her that all limeys were like that and they didn't mean nothing by it. But she wags a mean tongue. She's a real smart dame, huh?'

Joe's *chère amie*, then, was the tow-headed slattern at the lodging-house. Juan began to laugh. That scarecrow trollop; and Joe with his serious white face contorted by smirking and winks. Such rose-crowned lovers – the one false, the other fatuous, and both as ugly as sin.

'What you laughing at?' asked Joe suspiciously.

'At your fiancée's description of me. It's witty, don't you think?'

'Fiancée!' said Joe. 'You pulled a fast one there. I must tell her that. She'll appreciate it. She's an educated woman herself.'

When Juan returned to his room the trollop was waiting for him, half disguised by a heavy dust of powder and an almost tangible veil of violet perfume.

'Mr. Brown told me to do everything I could to make you feel comfortable and at home,' she said, and grinned with appalling familiarity. Her teeth were yellow and irregular between bright red lips, and powder clung thickly to the wrinkles under her eyes.

'I've got everything I want, thank you.'

'Well, isn't that fine, to be so contented. I thought maybe you'd be feeling a bit lonely.'

'Not at all. I'm very sleepy though.'

'Now I wonder if I remembered to make your bed yesterday. I'll just come and see.'

Having satisfied herself that the bed was as it should be, the trollop sighed alarmingly, languished, and remarked, 'Ooh, I'm tired! I wouldn't mind having a lay-down myself, especially after seeing that nice bed of yours. It just makes you think of laying down, doesn't it?'

'Then don't let me keep you,' said Juan, and held the door open.

The woman lost her temper.

'Say, you've got a crust, haven't you? Well, God knows I don't want anything to do with a man that doesn't act like a man. You wait, though, till I tell Joe how you insulted me. He won't take it as easy as I do, you'll see!'

In spite of aggravated household noises Juan slept soundly till late afternoon. Darkness fell so early that he had no chance to walk abroad and see what kind of a city was this strange inland port of Buffalo. He was confined to one small and dingy segment of it, and of what lay round about he was wholly ignorant. It was a curious cell-like existence that he did not think would continue very long, though his dire poverty was like a tether to keep him from going far. He did not care to write home for money because he had not yet concocted an excuse for leaving Motley so abruptly.

Shortly before eight o'clock he returned to Joe's Place. Joe wore an unusually serious expression, and as soon as Juan arrived led him into the back room, and asked 'What's this you've been saying to my girl-friend, huh?'

'As little as I could,' Juan answered.

'She says that you been making improper proposals to her.'

'Oh, nonsense,' said Juan, and assured Joe that in no possible circumstances would he dream of trespassing on a friend's preserves.

'She looked mighty upset about something, and her eyes were all red,' said Joe; but let himself be persuaded that the trollop was wrong, and had likely been suffering from the vapours, which is still a female weakness.

About three o'clock in the morning the prize-fighter and the dark weaselly man came in, and another man with them, short and thickly built, one half of whose face was covered with a bright naevus. They were the only customers in the shop at that time.

After some minutes the man with the naevus said to Juan, 'You're kinda wasting your time here, aren't you, kid?'

'How?' asked Juan.

'Well, this isn't much of a job for a big, well-educated, athaletic fellow like you, is it?'

'You seem to have a good opinion of me.'

'Sure I have, and so's your boss. Spider was talking to him this afternoon and got the low-down on you. And I can tell you're a good egg just by looking at you.'

'And what the devil has it got to do with you what I am?'

'Aw, we're interested in you, that's all,' said the man with the naevus.

'He's got spirit, see?' said Spider. 'I knew he had.'

'Just like a game-cock,' added the prize-fighter.

The man with the naevus never looked at people to whom he was talking, but stood at right angles, showing them only his unblemished profile. For this reason he was called the King of Diamonds. The prize-fighter's name was Slummock.

'How'd you like a job where you'd earn as much in an hour as you do in a week here?' The King of Diamonds faced Spider but his question was addressed to Juan.

'It depends what the job is,' said Juan, and carried a pile of plates into the back-room and started to wash them. They were disgusting plates, fouled with stale egg and cigarette ash and the nauseating brown remnants of beans. He went back to the counter.

'What sort of a job were you talking about?' he asked.

The King of Diamonds lit a cigar before he replied. Then – still facing Spider – he said casually, 'Just a little matter of importing some liquor from Canada.'

'But that's illegal,' said Juan.

'Haw, haw, haw!' roared Slummock, and Spider accompanied him with a shriller 'Heh-heh-heh-heh!' The King was so surprised that he looked straight at Juan, and the red side of his face shone like a bowl of rubies.

'Ho, ho!' he said. 'Oh, boy, that's a fast one. That's a hell of a crack. Ho, ho, ho, ho! It's illegal, Spider. D'you hear that, Slummock? What d'you know about that, huh? And we say that a limey hasn't got a sense of humour. Oh, boy, that sure was a crack!'

They continued to laugh for some time and looked admiringly at Juan who, to cover a slight embarrassment – for he was unused to so enthusiastic an audience – drew a cup of coffee from the urn; and by the time he had drunk it his customers were in a sober enough mood to talk.

'Well,' said the King of Diamonds, 'I guess you're going to join us, huh? It's a gentleman's life – not like slinging hash – and there's skads of dough in it. Is it a deal?'

'What would my work be?' Juan asked.

'Don't call it work,' said Spider. 'It's a pleasure.'

The bootleggers explained to Juan the nature of his duties. They seemed to consist mainly of motoring and motor-boating, which was better employment than washing dirty dishes. He would go to Detroit; a handsomer city than Buffalo, said the bootleggers. A smart modern city with a charming residential district full of prosperous people even now waiting impatiently for their Christmas supplies of gin and whisky, and wines too, champagnes and benedictine: these new friends of his were no cheap varnish-peddlers, no fusel-oil-mongers or hucksters of embalming fluid, but men who supplied good drink to those who could afford it. And the pay? Skads of dough. Oodles and oodles of money. He could make six hundred dollars in no time – Joe had told them of his loss. There was, they confessed, a certain – well, not danger exactly, but a risk, an uncertainty in their work that might deter a weakling and a nincompoop, but for a lad of spirit it was merely an excuse for stepping on the gas and snapping his fingers at dullards on the startled sidewalk. . . . They admitted it. There had been casualties in their ranks. Hijackers had pillaged their caravans and despitefully used their camel-hinds and muleteers; and that was why they were recruiting in Buffalo. But the hijackers had one after the other been put on the spot, and were no more, and comparative quiet now lay on the King of Diamonds' gang.

Comparative quiet, for Slummock, an amorous ox-eyed man, had got into a jam with a broad; no ordinary broad, but a Coastguard's broad, and that had led to a little shooting. But now Christmas was coming, season of peace and goodwill to men, and Slummock hoped that he would be allowed to run his cargoes across the Detroit River without bullets whistling through the air to frighten him and threaten widowhood for the ravished frail. . . .

More customers entered the coffee-shop. Juan determined that theirs were the last hamburgers he would ever fry. Outside the night was cold and vast, full of the noise of the wind that prowled across Lake Erie and darted up the Niagara River; but in Joe's Place there was only a greasy steam of cooking.

'I'll speak to Joe in the morning,' said Juan. 'I can be ready to start about nine o'clock, if you like.'

The King of Diamonds shook hands with him. 'Atta boy,' he remarked.

Spider and Slummock both showed their approval, but Slummock was impatient to leave. 'I want a chocolate sundae before I go to bed,' he said, 'and they don't sell ice-cream here. Let's go find a soda-fountain.'

XVII

Joe was very disappointed at Juan's decision, but he realised what opportunities there would be with the bootleggers for a young man of his spirit and ability, and he was careful not to let his own feelings stand in the way of Juan's advancement. Moreover his relations with the tow-headed slattern were in danger of being spoiled by Juan; for there was something amiss between them – though Joe could not tell what – and last night his love had been niggardly with her lean and sluttish embraces, full of whimsies, demanding (if he loved her) that Juan should be humiliated, and then repenting and explaining that she had only been jesting; for she had a great sense of humour. . Perhaps it would really be better if Juan were to go.

So Juan gave back five of the ten dollars which Joe had advanced – the bootleggers had paid him fifty to show goodwill – and said good-bye, and went to the lodging-house to pack his suit-case. The slattern was nowhere to be seen. She had stolen two of Juan's shirts and was keeping out of the way.

In a little while the King of Diamonds, Spider, and Slummock called for him in a handsome and powerful motor car, and Juan very gladly joined them. They drove rapidly to Niagara Falls and crossed the International Bridge into Canada, where the sight of red pillar-boxes and policemen uniformed after the London style gave Juan the hearty feeling of being at home again.

Spider was driving.

The King of Diamonds leaned forward and shouted, 'Careful, Spider. You're in Canada now.' And explained to Juan, 'It's different from the States. You got to look out for pedestrians here.'

Juan felt slightly ashamed of the Empire's backwardness.

'It's kinda hard to remember at first, but it's all right when you get used to it,' said the King in a tolerant voice.

The country was bare and wintry looking, but the weather was mild for December. They drove all day, stopping to eat their noon meal at a small town called London, and arrived in Windsor after dark. Detroit lay across the river, a mile away, like a huge pincushion stuck full of lights.

The bootleggers had a house near the water, and there Juan was introduced to three likely lads and two women of a bright and bold exterior. The King of Diamonds had business elsewhere, and two of the likely-looking lads went with him, but Slummock and Spider settled down to a quiet evening of cards and music; that is, the radio was turned on to draw an air-borne music of copper drums and conches into the room, and Spider called for those who would play poker.

One of the women was a serpentine creature called the Snake's Hips, and the other was the wench whom Slummock had stolen from the coastguard. Her name was Rosy and she had remarkable red hair that grew in a huge cluster of tight curls. The other man, Juan learnt, was a policeman in the bootleggers' pay. His name was Schenk, and his particular duty on the Detroit police force was to patrol the streets on a powerful motor-cycle and restrain automobiles that exceeded the speed limit. Now prohibition agents chasing a suspected smugglers' car would naturally, and legally, disregard all traffic regulations, and no one but a stupid policeman would try to halt them. This particular policeman, however, was paid to be stupid, and to watch the prohibition agents as they watched the bootleggers. If a car belonging to the latter – loaded deeply with beer – was in danger of being over-hauled, it was Schenk who relieved it by roaring after the pursuers, forcing them to the kerb, and threatening them with a charge of dangerous driving. And by the time they had proved their identity the bootleggers, of course, had disappeared. Schenk was very good at this game.

Slummock put glasses and a bottle of whisky on the table and they began to play poker. The whisky was excellent, but the game for some reason was slow. The cards would not fall into sequence, kings avoided kings, original hands were empty and there was nothing in the draw. It was natural, then, that more whisky should be drunk than might have been had full houses followed a straight flush, and all the courts in the pack fought manfully for a towering jack-pot. Rosy and the Snake's Hips became very impatient and threw down their useless cards with exclamations of disgust. Their language became free and imaginative as the evening progressed, and Slummock seemed upset by some of the words that Rosy was familiar with. She, however, was paying more attention to Schenk than to Slummock.

Spider won a succession of small pots without being required to show his hand, and Slummock suspected him of bluffing. Then the prize-fighter got a pair of queens and improved them with one more in the draw. Spider was again ready to bet. Slummock pushed out his chips. Spider replied with more. So did Slummock, made moody by his love's fickleness and almost sure that Spider trumpeted so loudly to conceal his lack of soldiers. Spider, with a taunting look at Slummock, increased his stake by twenty dollars. Slummock hesitated, fingered his cards, muttered to himself.

Rosy whispered something to Schenk and Slummock thought she was mocking his caution. He paid up to see Spider's hand and saw three kings.

'Aw, this is a hell of a game,' growled Slummock. 'I ain't had a break all night. I'm going out to buy me some ice-cream.'

The others laughed as he went out, but Rosy said, 'He's right. It's a bum game and I want action.'

'Let's make it strip poker,' said the Snake's Hips.

Drink had a curious effect on Rosy. It gave her eyes a marked obliquity and animated her hair. Now, applauding the other girl's suggestion, she squinted wildly at everyone in turn and her hair stood up in a kind of luxuriant abandon. The tight red curls had loosened. They stood up in the rout and swayed like serpents' heads. Juan looked at her across the table, waving her bare arms and clamouring for strip poker, and recognised Medusa.

Juan, with not much money to lose, had been sitting quietly and betting mildly. He had felt at first rather like a new boy at school, but now the fine whisky was ennobling his blood and laving his brain in a more generous ichor. He no longer felt inferior or superior to his companions. He did not feel friendless because he had not learnt their surnames, nor did he think superciliously of them because (it may be) they had no surnames. He felt, as a living thing, the brotherhood of man. Not from the same womb, it is true – there was a Chinese womb that grew almond eyes, and wombs in the Solomon Islands budded blackly, and English wombs were kindly things, and Prussian wombs bore pickelhaubes still – not from the same womb but from the same vast loins came man. Priapus, the World in Spring, it was who had impregnated China and Bolivia and Dorsetshire alike. The brotherhood of man. Some of your brothers were the sailors who stormed Zeebrugge on St. George's Day, and the Lancashire lads who fought at Gallipoli, and men who kept the peace in India; and on the other count were knaves, and many fools, and ten thousand ugly ones, and forty who were lovely to look upon; and here was a bloody villain, and there a stinkard, a pimp, a ponce, a lard-eating Eskimo, the akridophagous Piute, and a great concourse of hypocrites, with such a multitude of liars as would cover the Sahara. All these were begotten by the same desire – a circumstance in which, at ordinary times, we discover neither comfort nor pride nor even amusement. For the brain is a cold fastidious thing. But now, like an iceberg driven far to the south and caught in the warm water of the Gulf Stream, so that its cliffs have become smooth downs and all its angularity a flowing ease, now Juan's brain swam in malt, and its convolutions relaxed, its pores opened, and the criss-cross fibres of association were strings for a suite for strings, and the theme was enjoyment of the polychromatic but monogene world.

In this mood he agreed to play strip poker, which is a game where the player who loses must pay with a garment.

In a very short time Juan had lost his coat, collar, and tie; Spider was barefoot; the Snake's Hips sat in her shift; and Rosy, with shoes and garters already gone, was pulling off a stocking. The spoils lay under Schenk's chair.

A stocking may be pulled off modestly enough, but Rosy, screaming with laughter, made a great display of removing hers and showed all beneath it and much beyond, and while she lay back in her chair and waved her hands in glee, and had one foot cocked on the table, Slummock came in with a pint of ice-cream in a little cardboard bucket. He stood with a look of extreme surprise on his face, and then spoke sternly to Rosy.

'Is that the proper place for your foot?' he asked.

As though she were a child reproved for putting her elbows on the table Rosy sat in a more decorous position, and stopped her laughter, and looked sulky, and said, 'Aw, we were just having a game. What d'you want to come in and spoil things for?'

'She ain't doing nothing wrong,' said Schenk.

'That's for me to say,' corrected Slummock.

'Oh, is it?' said Rosy. 'So I'm a slave, am I? Like hell I am!'

'Stop beefing,' said Spider, and dealt the cards.

It was Rosy's misfortune to have four hearts and a diamond in her hand. To her alcoholic vision the diamond was not very distinct. It was a seven, and it lay between the six and the nine of hearts. To Rosy they all looked like hearts together. She whooped with joy.

Spider and the Snake's Hips did not bet, and Juan with a pair of tens fell out early. But Schenk had a straight and still wore all his clothes. He was in a strong position.

Rosy bet her remaining stocking and Schenk raised her by his collar and tie. Rosy pledged her ear-rings, and Schenk answered with his shoes. Rosy offered a silk scarf and the policeman bombastically replied with his coat.

The Snake's Hips encouraged Rosy to be audacious, and Spider filled her glass. But Slummock, sucking away cold gobbets of ice-cream, hung over the gamblers like a storm-cloud riding the mountains.

Rosy looked at her cards again, and though the company of red cards still looked like hearts, she hesitated. The Snake's Hips taunted her.

'All right,' she said. 'I'll put my dress on it.'

'I'll see you,' said Schenk, and everybody except Slummock laughed loudly.

'We'll all see her,' shouted the Snake's Hips.

'Will you hell!' said Rosy, and spread her hand on the table.

'A bob-tailed flush!' Spider recognised it at once.

'J— H. C—!' exclaimed Rosy, and stared open-mouthed at her cards.

The Snake's Hips jumped up and danced in malicious ecstasy.

'Take it off,' said Schenk, grinning broadly.

'No, you don't,' said Slummock, and hurriedly swallowed a lump of ice-cream. 'You've taken too much off as it is, a grown woman like you.'

'If she's taken off her dress why can't I?' Rosy pointed to the Snake's Hips.

'That stick of green rhubarb! She's got nothing to show, anyway.'

'Yes, I have!' screamed the Snake's Hips. 'I got as much as anybody has, you big sap!'

'Shut up,' said Spider, and pushed her into a chair.

Rosy began to pull off her dress. 'I lost, and I'm gonna pay,' she said, and blew a kiss to Schenk.

'Atta girl,' said the policeman.

Slummock put down his ice-cream and hit Schenk hard on the mouth. Schenk toppled over, taking his chair with him, and then fell sideways off it. He got up with bloody lips, and Slummock promptly knocked him down again. This time the policeman's head hit the floor and he lay still.

Rosy had taken her dress off and stood with it over one arm. She gaped, first at Slummock, then at the policeman, not knowing what to do. Slummock boxed her ears, loudly and painfully, and then went back to his ice-cream, taking no notice of her though she screamed and stamped her feet, and all her hair stood up like copper snakes in a hot sunlight, weaving, writhing, and nodding their glittering heads.

In a cold efficient manner Spider re-established an appearance of order. He made Rosy stop crying, and frightened the Snake's Hips out of her hysterical laughter. Then he and Juan carried Schenk to another room and put him to bed, taking off his shoes and removing his pistol from an under-arm holster.

When they had done this Spider looked at Juan and said, 'You seem to carry your liquor all right.'

'Yes,' said Juan gravely, 'I think I do. My uncle Oswald was a very heavy drinker indeed, and I have acquired his ability by a sort of knight's move in the hereditary sequence. You play chess?'

Juan was in that aloof and happy state of intoxication that permits a man to watch, without alarm or resentment, scenes of outrageous violence. He was a little enthroned, a little like Gautama on a lotos of untouchable calm.

Spider answered him respectfully. 'You sure know how to make those words behave,' he said. 'I like to listen to you. A guy that can talk like you after drinking hard liquor is a good guy. These other guys start fighting when they've had eight or ten drinks, and as for the broads – aw, hell! Well, you've seen 'em. But me and you and the King of Diamonds can drink like gentlemen, and we got brains too. We'll make this beer-running racket a knock-out, if we stick together. A regular knock-out. What d'you say?'

'I have every confidence in you,' said Juan, and solemnly shook hands with Spider.

When, sometime later, he went to bed, he fell quickly asleep on a pillow that floated, airily undulating, to a paradoxical ease – for though the pillow sailed higher and higher in swinging arcs, and sometimes stooped to soar again on gyroscopic wings, the ultimate slumber was profound as though he had burrowed far into the earth.

The following day was busy with preparations to run a cargo across the river when night fell. The King of Diamonds was going to take advantage of the mild weather to smuggle a few hundred dozen bottles of beer into Detroit. In really cold weather beer would freeze, and the unseasonable warmth was a welcome opportunity to replenish his stock.

The beer was ordered from a brewery, and Spider took Juan down to see it delivered at the wharf where the King of Diamonds' fleet lay. Several tough and surly-looking men loaded the boats. The beer was easy to handle, for the brewery packed it cunningly in sacks. Each sack held two rows of bottles with stiff cardboard outside and between the rows, and the open end of the stack was stitched up so as to leave two lugs to carry it by. When the boats were loaded they were cleared by a Customs officer. The clearing papers named the place of export, the transporter (who was the King of Diamonds), the consignee (a mythical Hiram Holloway), the port of destination (blandly said to be Nassau in the Bahamas), the exact cargo, and the time of departure.

So as to obey the last item the boats moved off at once and swung out into the river. But they did not head for Detroit. They went up-stream to another wharf where they tied up and were left under guard till night-time.

The river was a snuff-coloured, sluggish flood. Sometimes a muddy ice-floe, all but submerged, floated down. The December light seemed imprisoned between the water and the cloud-packed sky. On the Canadian bank tall chimneys grew from distilleries and breweries, and their smoke rose till it met the clouds, where it spread like a brown blanket beneath them. Here and there along the water-front were small bonfires. Bootleggers were burning the wooden crates in which their whisky had been delivered. In the chill and misty air, between their smoky background and the snuff-coloured river, the fires burnt cheerily. They looked like tropical flowers, startlingly scarlet on a gloomy tree. They shone like poinsettias in a fog. And over the river, vastly brumous, was the city of Detroit, out of which came a great buzzing and humming of factories like hives, and the agitant stridor of crowded streets.

Spider pointed out to Juan the various objects of interest and explained in detail the whole routine of bootlegging. It was really a very simple matter. The commercial problems of supply and distribution had to be worked out in darkness and executed with speed. That was all.

'You can swim, I suppose?' asked Spider. 'That's fine. Sometimes you have to. And I'll show you how to work a machine-gun. It's easy.'

A commercial problem under special circumstances. Bootlegging was no more than that.

At midnight the boats left their wharf on the Canadian shore. Juan and Slummock went together in a craft so heavily loaded that it had no more than three inches of freeboard. They ran out nearly to mid-stream and then turned till certain shore-lights were in line. The other boats had scattered. Slummock shut off the engine and for some minutes they drifted with the stream, listening. In the distance was a reiterated *thud-thud* which Slummock said was a Government patrol boat. They heard its siren braying a signal, answered from still farther away. Everything on the river was dark as a cellar. There may have been many boats abroad – faintly came the chatter of an engine – but none carried lights, and the sky was too dense for stars to pierce it and sprinkle the water with silver drops. But there were shore-lights in plenty. Detroit looked like a long softly-glowing ridge, stuck full of incandescent prickles, and from the ridge rose towers more brilliantly lighted, gaily coloured, changing from one bright hue to another. Over all, slowly and with cloudy intervals, went swinging beams.

'Let's go,' said Slummock, and started his engine.

The little boat throbbed as it raced at full speed through the darkness. A bitter wind tore past, bringing tears to Juan's eyes and making his cheekbones ache with cold. The water seemed to rise like the sides of a trough on either hand, not really visible, but felt as something moving and dangerous from which the boat was escaping, and a smoky-white wake spread broadly in their rear. Recklessly they darted into blackness, while ice-cold spray whipped their faces.

Slummock steered for a bright light lower than, and in line

with, a certain illuminated tower. They roared across the river.

Under the lamp-sprinkled ridge before them was a belt of grosser darkness. As they drew near to the bank the tail guiding-lights disappeared behind the roofs of the waterside houses, but in their place a dim-glowing green, a red, and another green appeared. Slummock stopped his engine. They heard its noise echo off the houses and then they drifted forward in a strange silence.

'Well, here we are,' said Slummock.

The quality of the darkness had altered. It was now confined and more intense, for the boat had entered a small dock with high sides. As it touched the quay Juan turned his head, startled by a harsh grating noise behind them, as though a sliding-door had been shut. The entrance to the dock was so small that a kind of portcullis could be lowered to close it off from the river.

Now, secure from pursuit, lights appeared, waiting figures showed on the wharf, and the boat was quickly unloaded. The wharf was the back-garden, as it were, of a private house, and a motor entrance in a high wall gave access to a street. Three closed Ford cars waited to receive cargoes. One boat had already arrived and discharged its freight. The cars were loaded with beer. The dock-gate was opened for another boat. More sacks of beer were transferred. The men worked quickly and silently. Within half an hour of the time when the boats left the Canadian shore all their cargoes had been safely reloaded in motor cars, and the cars had set out to deliver them.

It was Spider who superintended the transhipment. He looked at his watch as the last motor drove out.

'If I could only keep these guys off hard liquor,' he said to Juan, 'they'd be real smart guys. But they will drink.'

XVIII

That night Juan slept in the house on the Detroit shore. It was similar to the one across the river. Both were dirty, shabby, and furnished apparently from a scrap-heap. The tables were covered with innumerable overlapping circles to show where wet glasses had stood, and the walls were scarred by bottles that had missed their human targets. The beds were untidy piles of blankets. But the bootleggers all wore smart new clothes, diamond rings, and gold watch-chains.

In the morning the King of Diamonds came and talked seriously to Slummock about his quarrel with Schenk. Slummock insisted that he had been in the right, but said that he was quite ready to be friends with Schenk if the latter would keep away from Rosy.

'I don't want no fighting,' he said earnestly. 'I kept out of his way yesterday morning, just in case he'd be feeling sore. And I'll go right on keeping out of his way if you like. But if he comes hangin' round Rosy, and tries to make her undress in public – and you know what women'll do with a bit of encouragement – well, I'll sock him one. And if he doesn't stop then, I'll sock him another one. And that's all there is to it.'

Schenk appeared about midday and was sulky when he saw Slummock. But the King of Diamonds spoke sternly to him – looking out of a window so as to keep the crimson side of his face hidden – and presently the policeman consented to reconciliation, and promised that he would never again tempt Rosy to misbehave.

Juan and Slummock returned to Windsor and at night ran another cargo of beer across. This time Juan steered, and found little difficulty in picking up the guiding lights and reaching the proper harbour – theirs was not the only secret dock on the river. Many houses on the waterside had a wharf guarded by high wooden fences and a door against observation, and since public opinion in Detroit favoured the bootleggers, these smugglers' coves were rarely molested. On the river and on the road coastguards and Customs officers and Border patrolmen and Prohibition agents kept watch, and very often fired ruthlessly at anyone they suspected of carrying liquor. But the private docks were comparatively safe.

On his second day in Detroit Juan went out to admire the handsome buildings of the city – skyscrapers perforated with a rectangular pattern of innumerable windows – and later walked down Dubois Street to look for a spectacle that Spider had told him was worth seeing.

At the end of the street was a wharf and a Customs shed. On the wharf was a huge pile of empty beer barrels. Beyond the barrels was an embankment of sacks, all full of bottled beer. In the water, tied to the wharf, were forty motor-boats, crowded together, some with broken bows and others bullet-scarred. And near the door of the Customs shed an old man sat, breaking bottles of whisky with a hammer. All this was the fruit of Government victories in guerilla warfare with the bootleggers.

The old man sat on a barrel. With a brittle *tap!* another bottle was broken. Whisky ran down his bare arms, down his oilskin trousers, down a broad gutter to the stream. The smell of whisky rose like incense. At his side was a mound of sacks, ripped open, their contents displayed: bottles lying snug, with handsome labels, and wrapt – some of them – in pink tissue paper. *Tap-tap!* Half a gallon more trickled down to the river. Enough to make a whole family happy and keep it happy for hours. Enough to drive away the spectres of hate, and poverty, and pain, and futility, and failure. Enough to give a man the sensations of adventure and passion and power. Enough to compensate him – briefly perhaps, but with sufficient truth, if all is indeed illusion – for never having seen the Himalayas, or lived like Haroun al-Raschid, or heard the Jupiter Symphony, or known freedom. Enough to comfort timidity, humanise arrogance, amend the selfish, and vindicate faith that the world abused.

For a moment the old man looked up from his toil. He had a bitter, shamefaced, and tortured look. So Ixion might for a moment raise his eyes to meet the horrified gaze of men.

So regicides, conscious of their sin, might look. With such a face would the Wandering Jew peer in at lighted windows and find no home on earth. *Tap, tap, tap!* The old man broke more bottles, crouching over his work like an old man in hell. Beside him was the dirty warehouse, and behind him the icy sullen stream, and over his head a hostile sky.

Angered by the spectacle of waste Juan turned back to the city and walked for a long time in the cold and noisy streets. The Puritans and the millionaires between them had concocted this monstrous insult of Prohibition. The spirit of Calvin and the spirit of Croesus had communed and wrought by bribery and corruption an addition to the Decalogue. Because the Puritans feared happiness in themselves and hated it in others, and because the millionaires decided they would become billionaires if their workmen drank water instead of beer, they contrived a new veto to bear the old embargoes company, and beside Thou Shalt Not Kill, Thou Shalt not Steal, Thou Shalt Not Commit Adultery, they wrote Thou Shalt Not Drink. . . . Moses had talked with God before he bade the Israelites commit no murder, theft, or fornication; but the millionaires had rubbed their bellies against a desk and talked with other millionaires, and the Puritans had talked with their own mean and dismal souls. . . . Iron beat upon iron and clamour answered out of stone. Motor cars rushed by. Hundreds of motor cars. Darting and stopping. Desperate to go somewhere. From one office to another. From one shop to another. Backwards and forwards. This way and that way and all round the town. Horns brayed and brakes screamed. Not far away was the staccato insanity of a riveting-machine, and from the opposite direction came the fierce and endless wailing of syrens as a fire-engine raced to its work. Pandemonium split into traffic lines. This was efficiency. This was what the millionaires had given to America in place of Yquem and Tokay and Chartreuse that gladden the heart, and sherris-sack that makes the brain 'apprehensive, quick, forgetive, full of nimble fiery and delectable shapes; which, delivered o'er to the voice, the tongue, which is the birth, becomes excellent wit.' But wit was the last thing a millionaire would care to encourage. Millionaires were a natural target for wit, and a forgetive brain could shoot a millionaire's idea of efficiency fuller of arrows than St. Sebastian. No wonder, then, that the Croesuses frowned on wine and wit and favoured the kitchen tap, that would drown criticism and make men build and buy motor cars and radios out of sheer desperation, to deafen the everlasting rumble and splash in their water-logged bowels. . . .

'Where have you been?' said Spider when Juan returned. 'I meant to show you how to handle a machine-gun.'

Juan shuddered slightly. Though he could find no moral objection to bootlegging he detested the notion of murder.

'I'd rather not do any shooting,' he said. 'As a matter of fact I'm a pacifist.'

Spider gaped for a moment and then burst into laughter. Slummock looked up from his strawberry ice-cream – he had a little cardboard bucket full of it – and hoarsely remarked 'Haw, haw, haw!' Two or three other men sitting about also laughed. Spider reiterated Juan's earlier objection to the illegality of bootlegging, which the bootleggers had thought such a fine joke, and everybody laughed again. Then they repeated his assertion of pacifism. 'Can you tie that?' they asked, and chuckled deeply.

'That word's an earful,' said Spider, and smacked Juan on the shoulder.

Juan was puzzled by the reception of his innocent remark, and his look of bewilderment added to his reputation as a humorist.

He and Slummock presently crossed the river, the latter to see Rosy, and Juan because he had decided to bring his possessions to the Detroit side and thereafter sleep in Windsor as seldom as possible. He disliked Rosy and the Snake's Hips and he had no wish to be drawn into a quarrel about them; that they were frequently the cause of quarrels he had little doubt, since both were loose and loving. The King of Diamonds allowed no women in the Detroit house lest their presence should interfere with the transhipment of cargoes, but there were generally one or two living in the other establishment. Slummock kept Rosy on the Canadian bank to be as far as possible from her old sweetheart the coastguard.

The first person Juan and Slummock saw after landing in Windsor was Schenk. He said he had been looking for a cigarette-lighter he had left in the bootleggers' house. But Slummock was suspicious. It was only a few hours since Schenk had been told to keep away from Rosy, and a cigarette-lighter was a poor excuse for disregarding such advice.

'Did you get Rosy to help you look for it?' he asked.

'What if I did?' asked Schenk.

'I told you once before, if you start looking for things with her what you'll find is trouble. See?'

'You make me tired,' said the policeman. 'You're worse than a gutsache. You ain't got nothing on me. All that stuff about me and Rosy's just the bunk. We're friends, that's all.'

Slummock ruminated for a minute. 'Is that so?' he said, and walked on. Juan followed him.

The next time the King of Diamonds ran a cargo two of his boats were captured and a Ford sedan loaded with thirty cases of whisky was stopped no more than a hundred yards from the wharf. A few nights later, working to repair this disaster, even worse befell; a boat was sunk, its crew either shot or drowned, and another motor car was taken.

Dispirited by these reverses the bootleggers drank heavily and were always on the verge of quarrelling. The King himself found it difficult to maintain order, and his naevus grew a bright purple as he stared out of a window and shouted to unruly yeggs ninety degrees off his line of vision. The gang was losing its morale. They had only recently overcome a long hostility with hijackers, and now the authorities had seemingly declared war on them. There was no general action against bootleggers. Indeed, as though coastguards and Prohibition agents recognised the special case of Christmas, there was almost peace on the river. Only the King of Diamonds' men had been singled out for attack.

The King thought that the insulted coastguard, brooding over Rosy's abduction, was at the bottom of it. Spider pointed out, however, that she was not abducted but merely escorted away; and any sensible coastguard, he said, would be grateful to the man who had relieved him of so awful a burden. Spider's theory was that Schenk had turned traitor. The policeman had been severely beaten by Slummock and publicly reprimanded by the King. Moreover he knew intimately how the bootleggers worked and could have supplied the Prohibition agents with the precise information necessary for their recent coups. But the King was unwilling to think so badly of Schenk.

The weather grew colder and snow fell heavily. Sometimes the river was hidden by a great curtain of snow that reached from the sky to the moving water, and endlessly falling endlessly disappeared in its slow flood. Sometimes the city was silent in a white cloak, and at night, if the sky cleared, ten million lights so twinkled, and high towers shone so splendidly, that one could not see the stars. In the wealthy residential districts every house had a fir-tree in the garden, splendidly decorated with cherry and green and orange lights. Everywhere a new and special radiance had been contrived for Christmas; such a radiance as would frighten away poor shepherds, if any were foolish enough to keep their flocks in the wintry plains of Michigan; and though it might attract the kings they would find no stable in Detroit – and would a garage do for mild Mary's hour?

Now it was bitter work to cross the river, and the stream was a menace between frozen banks.

Two days before Christmas the King of Diamonds, Schenk, and Juan were sitting together when the telephone rang. One of the King's private customers wanted immediately three cases of champagne and some Benedictine. He was so good a customer that the King never thought of refusing his request, though he had nothing suitable in stock. Juan, who had learnt the necessary procedure, was sent over to Windsor to get the wine and tell Slummock, who had spent the night there, when to run it across.

But Slummock was drunk. He had had a quarrel with Rosy and found comfort only in alarming potations. When night came he was still unconscious, breathing hoarsely, with an odd petulant expression on his face. He lay on a bed with his coat off and all his buttons undone. Juan decided to run the champagne across by himself.

The river patrol worked in overlapping watches. The night watch went off at two o'clock in the morning, and the morning watch came on at one. Slummock's orders had been to cross at midnight before the watch was doubled.

It was snowing lightly when Juan went down to the wharf and started up his engine. There was a fresh breeze that drove the snow slanting before it. Sometimes a fierce flurry came, and the snow beat on him in thick and angry confusion. Juan cruised slowly down-stream to pick up the mark-lights on the Canadian bank before heading across. They came in line and he swung towards midstream, opening the throttle as he turned.

He was still in Canadian waters when a searchlight leapt out of the darkness. The snowflakes were magnified and floated brilliantly in its wavering beam. It fumbled for its quarry, moving jerkily here and there, as though blind in spite of its brightness. Juan turned sharply upstream and away from it, crouching low in his boat. The searchlight swung over him and then came back and rested on him. Almost immediately a machine-gun stuttered *tat-tat-tat* in a metallic voice that the roaring engine slightly muffled, and Juan heard the whine of bullets passing him. He swung left, and then right, and left again, zig-zagging like a snipe, and sometimes he was in darkness and sometimes in the searchlight's naked path. The boat shook with speed and the water seemed a solid unyielding thing over which it bumped and skidded. Two bullets struck the stern, but did no damage, and another burst went shrilly over Juan's head. Then came a thick flurry of snow, leaping wildly down the river in a sudden squall, and the searchlight lost its mark. Racing at full speed Juan tore through the squall, blind as a bat. There was a calm behind it where the snow fell leisurely, though the speed of the boat still made a fierce wind and the slow wet flakes slapped into Juan's face and plastered his eyes. But he had cheated the pursuit, and he could see the searchlight far in his rear, flitting aimlessly up and down. The chase, though beaten, continued and Juan fled before it.

When he dared stop his engine he was close to a reedy shore. There was a dry stirring as the wind searched through frozen rushes, and the snow came down in shapeless clots that stuck coldly where they fell. Juan shivered. In spite of the freezing air a light sweat had bedewed his body when the bullets whistled past his ears, and now little coldnesses trickled under his arms and across his chest and down his back.

For what seemed a long time – perhaps fifteen minutes – he sat still, listening, and watching for the searchlight, while the boat drifted slowly downstream again, past the rushes that whispered harshly to each other as the breeze went through them with frozen fingers. Then he started the engine and, still cautiously, ran back to where the Christmas lights shone brightest. Because he thought his pursuers, if they were still busy, would most likely be patrolling mid-stream he kept close to the American shore. Once he stopped and listened, with his heart beating violently, to a Government patrol-boat signalling to a companion with its syren. And once he was almost run down by another bootlegging boat that came roaring over the river at thirty miles an hour. He rocked in its wake and heard the frightened curses of its crew.

Because he was unusually close to the Detroit shore he had some difficulty in picking up the mark-lights, and nearly went past the King of Diamonds' dock. Then he saw its green, red, and green signal and turned into the friendly cellar-like gloom, and heard with great thankfulness the water-gate close behind him.

Spider and the King himself were waiting.

'Where in hell have you been?' asked Spider. 'And where's Slummock?'

Juan related his adventure. The others listened with close attention and congratulated him on outwitting the enemy. He was, they said, a smart fellow, and they were glad of his company. But who, they wondered, had been lying in wait for him to fire without a challenge?

'Did anyone know when he was going to run the stuff across?' asked Spider.

'Schenk,' said Juan, 'He was here when the telephone message came and he heard all the arrangements.'

'Schenk thought that Slummock would be in the boat,' added the King, showing only his unblemished profile.

'And Slummock's the bozo that he's after,' said Spider. 'He's sore at Slummock for socking him and for keeping him off that god-awful woman. It was Schenk that squealed this time all right. Well, this is the end of him.'

'We got to make sure,' said the King.

'Are you going to wait till he throws a gun on you himself?' sneered Spider.

'I want proper proof,' said the King stubbornly.

Proof, or at least circumstantial evidence, of the policeman's treachery came on the following morning when a bootlegger named Scully brought the news that Schenk was even then drinking coffee and eating fried egg-sandwiches with Bauer the coastguard. It was Bauer who had been Rosy's sweetheart before Slummock took her, and Schenk had never before been friendly with him. Half an hour later Slummock himself arrived, white and shaken after his debauch, to say that Rosy had disappeared.

'That's no loss,' said the King.

'No guy's going to take my woman away from me,' said Slummock.

Spider thumped the table. 'I got it,' he said. 'Her and Schenk's in cahoots, see? He tells her that Slummock's going to get bumped off, so she packs her grip and goes while the going's good. But she don't know the line-up. It's Bauer that knows that, because Bauer's going to do the job. Schenk's told him that Slummock was going to run some booze across at midnight, and tells him the mark-lights, so as he'll know where to wait. See? Bauer does the dirty work and Schenk gets the broad. Gee, that cop's a wise guy, huh?'

This hypothesis satisfied the King and Schenk's guilt was considered to be proved. The King retired with Spider to determine what steps should be taken to prevent further betrayals.

Juan took a nap in the afternoon, for he liked twice as much sleep as the four or five hours that he had got the previous night. But scarcely had he drifted into one of those confused and fragile dreams that come with daylight dozing when he was wakened by Spider and the King. The latter gave him a roll of twenty-dollar bills.

'There's your split,' he said. 'It ought to have been more, but we've been unlucky lately.'

Juan was gratified, however, to find that his share came to three hundred dollars. Spider and the King sat down, and the King was so impressed with what he had to say that he faced Juan squarely, and in that side of his countenance which was red as rubies his left eye shone more brightly than its fellow in the pale and unscarred side.

'We've been talking about Schenk,' he said. 'We're going to take him for a ride. Or rather you and Slummock are going to take him for a ride. D'you understand?'

'Not very well.'

'A one-way ride. He'll come here to-morrow night for his split. You and Slummock will be waiting for him – if you haven't got a rod Spider'll give you one. Then you put him in the Ford sedan. One of you drives and the other sits in back with Schenk. When you get eight or ten miles out you stop, and Schenk gets out. Then you bump him off. That's all. We thought that you and Slummock had better do it, as you're more interested than anyone else. To-morrow night. He'll be round about eight o'clock, I guess.'

'But I've never done such a thing before,' said Juan in a horrified voice.

'Aw, that's all right,' said the King. 'We all had to make a start, and most of us didn't get such a break as you're getting, with Slummock to see you through. Don't you worry, son. Slummock'll look after you and finish him off if you don't feel like it.'

'Sure he will,' added Spider. 'You got an easy break. And as the King says we all had to learn once. You'll soon get used to it. In six months you'll think nothing of putting a guy on the spot. Nothing at all. Just you see.'

The King patted him on the back in a fatherly manner, and then they left him. Juan was horror-struck at this dreadful plan and the part that he was supposed to play in it. It was easy to see why the bootleggers had chosen him to assist in the murder of Schenk. Once he was guilty of such a crime their power over him would be enormous and he would be definitely sealed as one of the gang. The prospect appalled him.

He had been badly frightened in the Chicago street-battle; he had been frightened again, after a vague fashion, when news was brought that a boat had been sunk and the bootleggers in it shot or drowned; and he had been still more frightened – though not so as to lose his wits – when the searchlight settled on him and he heard the *tat-tat-tat* of a machine-gun and the shrill whine of bullets through the snowflakes. But he had never been so frightened as he was now.

A cheap fly-blown mirror hung on a wall. Juan took it down, and carried it to the window, and stared into it. A feeling of unreality prompted him to see if his reflexion were still familiar – indeed, to see if he had a reflexion, since to a dream the mirror would show only an empty surface. But an answering image looked back at him. The eyes were too large and their pupils contracted and dilated in a manner sinister to see, for the movement was beyond his control even as external circumstance threatened to be – an owl, an owl, somewhere he had seen an owl with eyes like that, a toy in a dark corner whose eyes shone yellow and large, and shut again; or a shopkeeper's sign in a black night that winked at passers-by. He turned away sharply, and a fault in the glass distorted his mouth so that it seemed to slip into a cadaverous and twisted grin. . . .

He must escape. He could not be driven into murder, into butchering a frightened man, firing at a white face and a body that writhed in fear – and on Christmas Day. . . .

It was, of course, ridiculous to think of it. He had no intention of becoming a murderer – especially a professional one – and his only problem was how to leave Detroit and all the bootleggers in it as speedily and inconspicuously as possible. For a minute he had been on the fringe of panic. Now he felt sane again, as though he had suddenly become a spectator of all this banditry, instead of a participator in it. For he remembered that he had three hundred dollars now. He was no longer poor and helpless, but so rich that he could ride in any train he liked from coast to coast, or from icy Michigan to the hot beaches of Florida. He was so rich and powerful that he could command transportation over three thousand miles and more of bright steel rails – once he had given the slip to the King of Diamonds and his gang.

At six o'clock he was alone in the house. The idea of his leaving them had not occurred to the bootleggers. That anyone should voluntarily renounce so lucrative a calling would be to them even more incredible than moral scruples about taking a squealer for a ride. They went to supper and left Juan – who had developed a convenient tooth-ache – in peace to pack his bag.

Good fortune let him find a roving taxi-cab no more than two hundred yards from the house, and in a very short time he was safely in the thick of an enormous crowd that thronged the railway station. But he had not yet decided where to go. Here and there were indicators that gave the names of forty different towns, none of which he had ever heard of. Which were in the south, and which in the north? He had a notion to go south, not in one journey but by short stages, so as to come gradually to a hot sun and fine easy weather, savouring it well as he went, tasting the growing warmth, and watching the country turn slowly from northern bleakness to a semi-tropical luxuriance of hot-house and rainbow hues. But which of these stations lay towards the south, and which were the northern ones that he might turn his back upon?

With a sudden acceleration in its movement the crowd carried Juan in a direction to which he took unreasoning aversion. He turned, and tried to struggle through and against the mass. People frowned at this solitary opposition to their common purpose and pushed him from side to side. His suit-case was often in the way, bumping the knees of those who thrust by him. It was pulled arm's length away from him and into the bay so formed a girl was jammed, whom Juan, when the tension slackened on his suit-case, willy-nilly embraced.

She glanced up at him, indignant – and then her expression changed.

'Juan!' she exclaimed. 'Oh, Juan, is it really you?'

Juan looked at her in amazement.

BOOK THREE

OLD LOVE AND NEW

I

It was characteristic of Juan that his surprise should quickly give place to simple pleasure. From childhood he had recognised a coincidence as one of the least bewildering of world phenomena. When he lost an arrow he always shot another in the same direction and found both; at more than one dinner-party he had discovered a pearl in his oysters; and when he dined alone in a restaurant he habitually found a handsome young woman, solitary also, at the next table. Such contingencies, he felt, were no more than compensations for the unjust irrationality of life. And so at this present encounter he recovered his composure long before Dora, to whom the meeting seemed a very miracle.

While she stood there, and the surging crowd held her very close to Juan, a little stream of images passed through her brain. She saw the Chapel of Merlin College, and the Annual Ball of the Cambridge Licensed Victuallers' Association; Juan (three years younger) in various attitudes and circumstances, and her father (stern and awful in a night-shirt) roused to let her in one late night when she had forgotten her latch-key; Sir Hildebrand, statuesque and liberal with his money; and her mother, whose anger was always yielding to curiosity about the where and the when and the how often; that nightmare in the hospital, and then her sister providentially bereaved and beating her full breasts whose store had been too strong for a weakling brat; then Bob coming back from Coventry, and all his talk of America, and her innocent deception of him. . . . and the voyage out, and England so far and far away, and

Christmas services, with holly at the door, and midnight carols, and here was Juan who knew all about these things too, and was indeed part of so many of them!

She jumped up and down on her toes like a little girl and said excitedly, 'When did you come, and what are you doing here, and where are you going now? Oh, there's so many things I want to ask you! Isn't this a dreadful crowd? And you don't look a bit older. Do I? I feel like a hag. But tell me, what *are* you doing here?'

'I'm doing practically nothing at the moment,' said Juan, 'except wondering where I should go.'

'Really? You're not joking? Then you've got to come home with me. We've got a spare room – a guest room, I mean – that no one's ever slept in yet, except Bob when I had a dreadful cold once and I didn't want him to catch it. It will be lovely to have you for Christmas, and I know Bob will like having another man in the house. Men do, don't they?'

'And who is Bob?'

Dora took off her glove and showed her chubby hand with a wedding-ring on the proper finger. 'You didn't know, did you? I'm Mrs. Squire now. But we must hurry or we'll lose the train. We live in a little town called Monroe that's not more than an hour's journey away. I've been doing some last-minute Christmas shopping in Detroit. There are lovely shops here, aren't there?'

They got the last seat in a crowded day-coach and through the noise of the train Dora explained that she had been married for rather more than a year and had lived in America nearly as long. Her husband was a skilled machinist making handsome wages and they were very comfortable indeed, but oh! how homesick she got sometimes, and especially on birthdays, and Bank holidays, and at Christmas. . . . And Juan said that he had been for some months at Motley University and was now travelling to see the country.

When she spoke of home and husband Dora's manner

changed. Her childish excitement gave place to a mature and settled air. Her voice grew rounder and even her flesh seemed to acquire a new firmness. But as she became more confident Juan grew embarrassed, for he wondered more and more what had become of the child that had so unfortunately grown out of their sentimental trafficking of three years ago. Would he find the urchin waiting for them in Monroe? Probably there were toys in those parcels that Dora carried. And the unknown Bob might not be so pleased to see him as she appeared to think; many husbands being unnecessarily conservative in their attitude to conjugal rights.

How, he wondered, should he ask about the brat? – for he had a bachelorly disinclination to speak of 'our child', and (slight though his share in the business had been) it was manifestly unfair to say 'your child'.

But Dora guessed what he was thinking and for a minute her manner reverted to its old simplicity, and she put her hand on his sleeve and said soberly, 'My sister took our baby, Juan. She's married to a farmer near Ditton, you know. Her baby was born three days after mine, but it died almost at once, and she and her husband were both heart-broken, and I – oh, I'd have given anything to keep him, but mother and father were so ashamed, and she offered a way out – that was God's mercy, father said – and what could I do alone? So I gave her our Jacky. He's a lovely boy now, and they just worship him. I've got photographs I'll show you.'

'And your husband?'

Dora hesitated. 'He knows nothing about it. I didn't mean to deceive him at first. I thought that he probably knew, though we had kept it awfully quiet. But he didn't. He was working in Coventry when you were in Cambridge. Then he came back. We'd been sweethearts before I ever met you, and he asked me to marry him. He was going to America as soon as he got a place on the quota. I meant to tell him, Juan, but it's so difficult to explain things, and somehow I never did.

And then a friend of Bob's, another girl, told me that he had been carrying on dreadfully with a girl in Coventry, so I felt justified in a way. She behaved very badly, I believe. In fact——'

Dora hesitated. Then she whispered, '*There was a child.* And Bob never told me anything about that, though it's different for a man, of course, and he was really in love with me all the time. I wouldn't let him know that I knew anything about it for anything. And he never seemed to suspect about me.'

So noisy that it filled one's head with the shouting of many iron voices, the train rolled on to Monroe, and there Bob Squire was waiting to meet his wife in a motor car that suggested prosperity, and took them rapidly over snowy roads to a little house that proved it.

Squire was a large cheerful-looking man who seemed amused at his wife's acquisition of a guest, and to her annoyance refused to be impressed by the strangeness of destiny that brought an old friend to sit with them on Christmas Eve. It was Dora who kept the conversation going from supper till midnight. With her husband and an old lover for audience, and reminiscences of all Cambridge, and all her short life, and all her relations, for subject-matter, she talked briskly and happily and laughed again and again, and enjoyed herself remarkably well. Bob was naturally inclined to silence and Juan felt it wise to be reticent about his own affairs. But Dora prattled and tattled so that Bob, if he had heard nothing of it before, now learnt that Juan and his wife had once been very friendly indeed, in spite of the difference in their social positions.

And yet, Juan felt, there was nothing in her tone to suggest they had been lovers. Rather she spoke to him as if he were a brother, and a younger brother at that; a young brother come home from sea or the colonies, and entitled by reason of his absence to a certain display of interest and sisterly affection. It was very clever of her to adopt this attitude. Or was it an unconscious attitude? Three years ago she had been a shy and appealing creature, with chubby hands and widely opening eyes. But now she had a home of her own and a manner proper to such possession.

After all, thought Juan, a woman could rise from an embrace to which she had incited you and in which she had enthusiastically participated, and tolerantly pat you on the cheek, and look at you with the air of one saying, 'There now, run along and wash your face or you'll be late for tea. That's mother's boy!' A woman could obliterate the past as easily as she could remember it in false colours or evoke it in startling veracity. But it was strange to see the once ingenuous Dora display such a power.

Christmas morning found her bustling and important, a little short of patience and anxious to be left alone in her kitchen. She had no sympathy with the American habit of eating in restaurants. 'Christmas dinner should be eaten at home,' she said, with authority in her voice that reached back, at the least, to some housewife of pagan Mercia. 'Take Juan out for a drive,' she said, and Bob obeyed. As soon as the door closed behind them Dora lit the gas in the oven, and did certain things to a turkey, and considered a plum-pudding tied up in a linen cloth.

But when dinner was over and robust appetites had sufficiently praised her cooking, the efficient Dora faded and a sentimental Dora said unhappily, 'Oh, I wish I was at home again.'

'You wouldn't have got a better dinner than the one you've just eaten,' said Bob.

'But just to be in England! If only we were near the sea I wouldn't mind so much, but we're so far away. There's nothing but America on all sides of us here, and sometimes I feel drowned in it.'

'Well, I wouldn't be making seventy dollars a week in England,' said Bob. 'That's one advantage of being drowned in America. And we wouldn't have a motor car, and a frigidaire, and an electric washing-machine.'

'We wouldn't want them.'

'And you could get a glass of beer when you felt like it, and see a football match, and have all your old friends to talk to,' said Juan.

'And some of my old friends have got nothing else to do but talk. They've been out of work so long they've forgotten what it's like. And I'm making seventy dollars a week. That's £14, or £700 a year. The head-master in the school I used to go to doesn't get as much, and the curate of St. Agatha's doesn't get half as much. Do you think his wife's got an electric washing-machine?'

'But perhaps she doesn't want one,' Dora persisted.

'She would if she'd ever seen one.'

'But she hasn't.'

'Then that's her loss.'

'If you make twice as much money here you've got to spend twice as much,' said Juan.

'And I like spending money so long as I can afford to,' said Bob.

'Do you like spending twice as much to get your watch repaired, or your shoes soled, and then find that the work isn't half as good as you'd get in England?'

'There's certainly a lot of bad workmen here,' Bob admitted. 'They're in such a hurry to get things done that they can't be bothered doing them properly. When I get a job of work I like to do it well, but an American wants to do it quickly.'

'They're developing some Jewish traits,' said Juan. 'They prefer selling things to making them. Salesmanship is getting ahead of production.'

'And the children are very badly behaved,' said Dora sadly.

'But their faces are clean and you don't see holes in their stockings.'

'Oh, you're just becoming a regular American!'

'I get seventy good arguments for it at the end of every week.'

Dora sniffed. 'Well, even though they've all got motor cars and clean faces and no holes in their stockings, I don't like Americans as well as English people and never shall, so there! They're callous and boastful and noisy, and you know they are. And they're always saying that England's effete, and nearly bankrupt, and didn't win the War, and hasn't got good roads, or a sense of humour, and is just going to the dogs generally. And it isn't true!'

'But England isn't troubled by other people's opinions,' said Juan.

'Personally I like a bit of criticism,' said Bob in a comfortable voice. 'I've found out a lot of my faults since coming here, and some of them were very interesting.'

'And I've found out a lot of America's faults,' said Dora crossly, 'and they're not interesting a bit. Only nasty.'

Juan protested that he had scarcely had an uninteresting day since he landed, but Dora would not listen, and presently Bob found an opportunity to talk about the War, which was the only subject on which he ever grew really expansive. Juan found his reminiscences very boring and Dora yawned openly. She complained that Bob had made friends with a German who used to be a corporal in the Prussian Guards –

'He was a sergeant-major with the Bavarians,' said Bob contemptuously, 'and what he doesn't know about the War isn't worth knowing.'

'Well, I wish he'd forget it for a change. Whenever he comes in you talk about nothing but killing and raids and rations till I'm sick of the whole thing, and how you've remembered such nonsense for ten years I can't think.'

Juan waited with impatience for a chance to air his thoughts about America, whose institutions he was eager to defend against the biassed criticism of Dora, and some of whose defects he wanted to explain to the over-complacant Bob. He was prepared to talk for a long time without stopping. But Dora was also in a talking mood, and the usually silent Bob, stirred by his memories of war, had many things to say. The result was that no one listened to anyone else except to snatch an opening for his or her own topic; and conversation, after becoming a matter of yawns, impatience, and interrupted monologues, finally died in a silence of common frustration. The excellence of Dora's cooking may have had something to do with this, for they had all eaten too much, and excess of food without the ameliorating quality of wine is a mortal enemy to kindness.

Sadly Juan discovered that absent friends develop unlooked-for faults.

On the following day Bob went back to work and Dora showed Juan many photographs of their child, taken at her sister's house. He was a good-looking sturdy boy, and Juan felt rather pleased with the result of his folly. He did not encourage, however, Dora's inclination to dwell on the details of their liaison.

'And Bob knows nothing about it?' he said wonderingly.

'Absolutely nothing,' said Dora earnestly. 'He's the most unsuspicious man I've ever met, and of course it would only be cruelty to tell him now. Though I do wish I could have my Jacky here.'

'Aren't you going to have any more?'

'In May,' whispered Dora, wide of eye and very solemn as became the keeper of a secret.

'He'll be an American.'

'He won't!' said Dora indignantly. 'How can you say such a thing?'

'But he will be,' said Juan. 'Everybody born in the United States is a citizen of the United States, and in the next war he'll have to fight against England and will probably kill his brother Jacky.'

Dora burst into tears.

Juan realised that he was treating his hostess very rudely, and made such amends as would comfort her. He was sorry for what he had said. He had been fond of Dora once, and pleased to see her again, but now her stupidity annoyed him. She had become another person. And she was going to bear children who would be strangers to his child. He had never felt like a father before. . . .

'I shall be leaving here soon,' he said.

'Leaving? But you've only just come!'

'I'm on my way to the south, and I've got so little money that I can't afford to delay for very long.'

'Then stay here till you get some more. It won't cost you anything to live with us, and I do like having you so long as you don't say cruel things to me.'

Juan explained that he was no longer living on an allowance from his father, but that he was keeping himself by his own endeavours. He did not go into details, for Dora was surprised at the idea of him working at all, and to learn that he had been washing dishes and bootlegging would shock her profoundly.

'What are you going to do?' she asked.

'I'll take the first job I see. I never did any work till a few weeks ago, so I'm easily satisfied. I've got no professional pride, and all jobs look alike to me.'

'Then why don't you get something to do here? Bob might be able to help you, he knows quite a lot of people already.'

To stay where he was, for some days at any rate, would have this advantage: he could write to his bank in Carthage and see whether his mother had sent him a Christmas cheque. For though he spoke in a fine hearty way about work, Juan was not too bigoted to live at leisure if he had the means. A little money would give him a lot more freedom. And, he readily admitted, he was more comfortable here than he had been since leaving Motley.

So, agreeing to Dora's proposal, and making her very happy by doing so – for she had a kind possessive nature – he slept again in the guest room that was so obviously intended to be more of a toy than a useful thing (bright as new enamel, clean as a hound's tooth) and on the next day – for he insisted on finding work for himself – he walked here and there about Monroe till he saw a card in a drug-store window, and went in, and talked plausibly to the owner, and before long was engaged as a clerk; which meant that he had to stand behind a counter and serve fruit drinks, and ice-cream, and sandwiches.

II

Neither Dora nor Bob thought highly of Juan's new occupation. To Dora it seemed a menial office, and Bob thought it paltry for any man to be serving flappers with ice-cream. But Juan found it amusing.

Brightly chattering about the young men with whom they flirted, girls came in to sit on stools at the counter and order hot drinks, or cold drinks, and strange sweet confections which Juan speedily learnt to prepare with great skill. At midday many people ate their lunch in the drug-store, drinking a glass of chocolate malted milk and eating a sandwich of ham and rye bread, or some similar combination. And in the evening young men brought the girls who had already been there in the morning, and entertained them with pineapple sundaes, hot fudge pecans, and raspberry parfaits.

The soda-fountain and sandwich-bar was the important part of the shop. Behind the other counter a few prescriptions were made up, and another assistant was prepared to sell tooth-pastes and tooth-brushes, shaving-cream, face-powder, lip-stick and other cosmetics, soap and shampoo powders, eau de cologne, mouth-washes, combs, scissors, and all such toilet accessories; while in the centre of the shop brightly-coloured magazines were displayed for sale, with an odd assortment of hot-water bottles, picture post-cards, gramophone records, and dog-collars. But without the soda-fountain the drug-store would have been a meagre thing.

Juan rapidly increased the custom which the shop enjoyed.

The young women of Monroe discovered his presence and immediately recognised the advantage of eating a chocolate float prepared by so handsome a stranger. He was a mystery, grave and aloof, fascinating them by the deftness with which he drew lemon and raspberry syrups from their several taps, and brought a milk-shake to its proper pitch of bursting foam.

Dora never went to the drug-store while Juan was there, though he promised to make the most delectable dish for her if she would come and see him and admit how excellent a dispenser of ice-cream he had become in his brief apprenticeship. But Dora knew her own mind. She passed the shop one day and looked in, and saw Juan, in a white coat, wiping suds off the counter. That he, who had been so splendid a figure at Cambridge, should have fallen to this! It saddened her, for she was a fine sentimental conservative, and like St. Paul believed that every man should abide in the same calling wherein he was called. Juan, she thought, was a victim of democracy, and she mourned his fall.

Nor could Juan win Bob's approval, though the latter professed his contempt for class distinctions, and one would have expected him to be well pleased by Juan's reduction to the discipline of such a humble occupation. But in reality Bob was no more a believer in democracy than Dora. He despised unskilled labour as heartily as he disliked an idle aristocracy, and he knew that his own highly skilled work was something entitled to respect. He had the solid pride of the craftsman, and he was justly annoyed by Juan's belief that all work was alike and no work an occasion for too much seriousness.

None of the three, then, was really content with their association, and when Juan received from the bank in Carthage a cheque for five hundred dollars (his mother's Christmas present), he decided to follow his original plan of going south. But Dora, clinging to all that reminded her of England, however much he disappointed her, begged him to stay a little longer and Bob, for his wife's sake, repeated the invitation. Juan, being good-natured, agreed to stop for another week or two that meant yawning after supper, Dora tirelessly asking 'Do you remember this?' and 'Do you remember that?' and Bob talking solemnly with Otto, the Bavarian sergeant-major, about minnenwerfers and gas-attacks, working-parties, and who really captured Monchy, and the see-saw business at Cambrai.

The drug-store with its gossiping patrons was a livelier place than the Squires's house.

One morning a stranger, an arrestingly handsome woman, came in and ordered one of the simpler drinks, a mere matter of turning a tap and putting a straw in the glass. Even these commonplace movements, however, Juan performed so expertly that she was obviously impressed by his dexterity as well as by his distinguished appearance. She herself had attracted Juan's attention as soon as she entered. She was very tall. She wore a little tight-fitting cloth-of-gold turban and a shining gold coat that wrapt closely round a figure admirably proportioned and strikingly mobile. Her freedom of movement and superb muscular control were evident even in the four or five steps which she took between the door and a stool at the counter. Nor was her face less worthy of praise than her body. The jaw, perhaps, was a little heavy, but elegantly rounded. Her teeth, it may be, looked unnecessarily powerful, but they were even and white as a snowbank. And her eyes were large and velvety – but topaz-glints leapt lively in them, like tiny goldfish in the dark.

She finished her drink. Her eyes had followed Juan's every movement and were still upon him.

'I guess I'll have a Banana Special,' she said.

This was one of the most elaborate confections and took some time to prepare. A foundation of bananas, split longitudinally, was laid in an oval dish and a quantity of raspberry syrup poured over them. A hillock of chocolate ice-cream was deposited on the left-hand side of the dish and an equal hillock of strawberry ice-cream on the right. A small hand-pump was then used to force thick cream (that lay in clots and heavy whorls) over these tumuli, and a handful of crushed walnuts was sprinkled on the cream. Two glacé cherries and some sprigs of angelica completed the extravagant mess.

Juan pretended to be very serious over its preparation. He wore the intent expression of an artist busy with the problems of colour, design, spatial harmonies, significant form, and what-not, and his good-looking customer obviously admired him; for most Americans admire serious art – indeed it is the seriousness of art that appeals to them, and the superstition that all art is somehow (inexplicably and mysteriously) serious is the reason why even poets in the United States sometimes grow rich.

'You sure know how to make a Banana Special,' said the woman in a deep emotional voice.

'Thank you,' replied Juan gravely.

The confection was by now an inchoate mass of pink and brown ice-cream, irregularly bloodshot with the raspberry syrup, and still garnished in a dilapidated way with one bright cherry.

'D'you ever go to the movies?' asked the woman.

'Occasionally.'

'There's a swell show at the Orpheum this week. The picture's not so hot, but Buddy Hambone's band is a wow. You oughta hear it.'

'You've heard it already, have you?'

'Say, I'm in the show. You'd like my act, I think.'– She put her elbows on the counter and leaned forward confidentially.–'A smart intelligent fellow like you would see what's in it. My act's *different*. Outa the ordinary, see? And an artist like you – oh, I watched you making the Special, and I know an artist when I see one – you would appreciate it. You come in to-night and see me, and then I'll come back here to-morrow morning and hear what you think about it. I'd like to have your opinion on it. Honest I would.'

Her smile was dazzling.

'There's my card,' she said.

Even in the brief distance from the counter to the door she was able to reveal, beneath her cloth-of-gold coat, a divine opulence and the lithe movement of an athlete.

On her card, in small capitals, was printed OLYMPIA; and under, in running script, The Unique Operacrobat.

Juan had no difficulty in persuading the Squires to go to the cinema with him that night.

The programme consisted of a picture, a news reel, and variety turns. The picture was a foolish thing, a domestic drama of a policeman's family in which all went wrong until the very end, when the death of the villain unnecessarily put everything right again. Then came Buddy Hambone's Collegiate Jazz Band. As the curtain rose it opened with a full blare of brass that shook the house. For some minutes there was no abatement of the noise, which came in a spasmodic rhythm without melody. Buddy Hambone conducted after an epileptic fashion. His feet shuffled, his knees bent and straightened, his body writhed, his arms flapped widely, and his head jerked backwards and forwards like a vulture tearing gobbets from a carrion carcass. But there was nothing vulturine in the face that he turned to show – one beaming smile – when the opening number was done. It was a round and harmless face, with so little chin and forehead that it had to be filled up with enormous smooth cheeks, between which and pinched into insignificance by them was a little nose. And under the nose was a small red mouth. Obviously Buddy Hambone was hugely pleased with both himself and his band.

'The next number will be a little number of my own composition,' he announced. And turning to his band said with great heartiness, 'Let's go!'

At once the trombones and the saxophones brayed enormously, a drum banged, and cymbals clashed with brassy irrelevance. The noise was similar to the noise which the band had already made, and Buddy Hambone capered before them with the very movements that he had previously employed. But in a little while the din subsided, the lights were darkened, the trumpets were muzzled, and two violinists stepped forward to play a sickly air on muted strings. Buddy Hambone closed his eyes and conducted in a shuddering ecstasy. The tune was reminiscent of several popular songs that Juan had heard, and it seemed to him that violin strings had never betrayed their origin in the bowels of a sheep so clearly as these did to-night. The number, however, was greeted with enthusiasm.

Then Buddy Hambone introduced 'Poppy Delaney, one of the cleverest little girls to ever dance on a Michigan stage.'

Poppy was a blonde with a fixed smile and very little clothing. She ran across the stage with mincing steps and struck a pose in which her right hand was held aloft and her left leg bent backwards and upwards till the sole of her foot touched the back of her head. She repeated this on the other side of the stage. Then she leapt into the air several times and executed creditable twinkles. After that she turned Catherine wheels, somersaults, and handsprings, first in quick time and then slowly. The slower she turned the better pleased was the audience, because they had more leisure to observe her legs, which were bare to the groin in front and remarkably uncovered behind. Buddy Hambone waved a nonchalant baton to his band and watched Poppy with simple pleasure. In her last movement she stood on her head and made slow semaphore motions with her legs, while the band stimulated applause with a cunning crescendo.

Following Poppy came 'Old Ollie Isaacs, the World-Famous Eccentric Comedian,' a little man with a startlingly simian expression and a suit of grotesquely ill-fitting clothes. His trousers were an important part of the performance, for they were continually falling down and whatever he did was likely to be interrupted by their sudden decline. He began with tap dancing – and was embarrassed by the evasive small-clothes;

he showed hunger, and ate some buttons, his collar and tie, part of somebody's hat (this was his eccentricity) – and once again was upset by the irresponsible garments; even a string of old jokes gave them an opportunity to slip away, and finally in a gust of temper Old Ollie pulled them off completely, and after them his coat and waistcoat, and disgustedly throwing them at Buddy Hambone (who cleverly dodged them) walked off in a suit of red underwear.

Juan grew impatient for the appearance of Olympia. The band was playing again. He realised that she must be the star turn. The music stopped, the stage was cleared, and Buddy Hambone in a high voice announced: 'Ladies and gentlemen, the one and only Olympia, the star of stars, in her unique act of operacrobatics!'

Olympia bowed. In green trunks and a leopard skin she looked superb, and with the gait of a goddess walked to a rope that dangled from an unseen beam. Without warning she began to sing the Habañera from *Carmen*, and when she had observed that 'Love was like a wilful bird' started to climb the rope. She went up hand over hand with perfect ease, singing as she climbed. When she reached the top she turned down and slowly descended head-first, singing

> 'And if I love you now, beware!
> And if you love me not, beware!'

When the Habañera was finished and she had rested for a minute, she climbed up the rope again and swung towards a ring some little distance away. This she carefully fitted between her teeth and so hung suspended from it, facing half-left. With a sudden explosive release of muscular force she doubled her body up like a jack-knife – her hands were lightly clasped behind her back – so that her toes touched her chin. The downward swing turned her body through an angle of ninety degrees till she faced half-right. Again she doubled up and kicked her chin; faced half-left again, kicked up; half-right again; jack-knifed again; half-left . . . and so on. It was not a pretty movement but it showed Olympia's amazing strength, and as she went on and on, tirelessly jack-knifing first to one side and then to the other, the audience began to feel a sympathetic strain in their own teeth and necks and abdominal walls, and watched her with a curious fascination that was half a wish for her to stop and half a desperate curiosity as to how long she could continue.

At last she was done. The applause was vigorous and Dora, who had been unwillingly captivated by the powerful rhythm of Olympia's contortions, gasped with relief.

'Thank goodness I don't have to earn my living like that,' she said. 'Isn't she a dreadful creature, Juan? I should be frightened even to meet her. Wouldn't you?'

'I have met her,' Juan answered coldly. 'She's a very beautiful woman.'

Even Bob was not altogether unmoved by this revelation – after his wife had repeated it to him – and Dora excitedly demanded, 'When did you meet her? And where? Is she really beautiful? And why didn't you tell me, when you knew how interested I would be?'

'Hush,' said Juan. 'She's going to sing again.'

Olympia's voice rose – and Olympia on the rope again rose with it – in the aria 'One Fine Day' from *Madame Butterfly*. Half-way up the rope was a loop into which Olympia stuck one of her feet, and so hung head-down from it without interrupting her song. An attendant now pulled on a cord so that Olympia began to swing out over the audience, and sailing in graceful arcs her voice came in alternate crescendos and diminuendos. As she swung forward, louder and louder was heard –

'And then a little puzzled he –

'Will call, "Dear baby – (these four words growing quieter and fainter as the singer receded)

'Wife of mi-ine – (an ascending scale of loudness)

'Dear little orange blossom" – (the first three words diminuendo, but 'blossom' bursting like a whole garden of hollyhocks from the startled air as Olympia swooped forward)

'The names he used to call me when he came here'– backwards and forwards she went, and rushing through the air added to her song a whooping effect that was not without the charm of novelty. Her voice was powerful and by no means unpleasant. Not till the very last did she betray any distress, and then, as though too much blood were distending her throat, her tone became thick and foggy, and the last topmost note of the aria was no more than a whisper in the air. But Buddy Hambone's men, come cautiously on to the stage again, covered this deficiency with a great pealing and blowing and banging of their various instruments, while the audience had started hand-clapping some bars before the end and clapped on until Olympia, rather red-faced, slid down the rope to bow left and right to the grateful din and her admirers in the dark. Thrice she was recalled to bow, and thrice the habit of her gait, so lithe and powerful, filled Juan with admiration. But Dora sat motionless, without applauding in any way.

'You don't really like her, do you?' she asked, as they sat crowded together in Bob's small car, driving homewards.

'She's very beautiful,' Juan repeated.

'And do you like everything that's beautiful, or what you think is beautiful?'

'I fancy I do,' said Juan.

'Well, I don't.' Dora's voice was warm. 'Beauty isn't always a good thing, and any sensible person ought to know that. Look at the harm that diamonds have done, just because they're beautiful. I read an article only last week that said every famous diamond had caused the death of at least fifty people. And beautiful women, it said, were even more disastrous than diamonds. Anyway I don't think that she – Olympia, or whatever her name is – is particularly beautiful. She's too big.'

'Then she can't be dangerous,' said Bob solemnly.

'Unless people are foolish enough to think she's beautiful,' countered Dora.

When they got home she returned to the attack, criticizing Olympia for the stupidity of her performance, and asking very pertinently how a song could be improved by singing it upside down. Juan found it difficult to answer this. He too had thought the act rather silly, but even silliness could not obscure the physical attractions of Olympia. If Dora refused to recognise these there was nothing more to say, except that she was quite as foolish as Olympia, though in a different way.

With admirable self-discipline, however, Juan refrained from telling her so. Hospitality, he remembered, should have its proper rewards. But when he lay alone in the enamel-bright, smart little guest room he became surer and surer that Dora's narrow domestic silliness was a less agreeable thing than Olympia's flamboyant theatrical kind. How Dora had changed! Her sweet foolish innocence had become a petty and jealous intolerance, and her loving heart was full of clotted sentimentalities. Warm arms and warmer kisses, soft breasts and eyes of wonder and shy delicious laughter – that was the Dora of Cambridge. And now she was a stupid little snob. Was it a chemical change? Had the constitution of her soul and body altered in so short a time? Or had the fangs of Time stripped off the sunny flesh of youth to show the sinew and fat that had always lain beneath?

Whatever the reason, thought Juan, it's very sad indeed – and sadder still because we treat it as a commonplace – that youth is the prettiest thing on earth, and the frailest. . . . And thinking of such sadness he became sad for himself, and with delicious melancholy saw himself as a wanderer to and fro across the world, never stopping long enough to see the growth of things, but only the leaves and the flowers – and growth is better than a flower, since the one is Becoming, and so endless, and the other has Become, and so is about to die. . . . He was a gipsy, ever driven from comfort and security by something in himself that was akin to the wildness of earth, and took him into danger, and made him bedfellow with disaster.

Sheep-herders and bootleggers and old loves that had lost their savour were his companions, and there was no comfort, no hearthstone for him. . . . Through the window, that was no more than a yard from his head, he could see scattered lights of the town. With snow on the ground and a three-quarter moon in the sky there was scarcely darkness. Houses rose dimly out of whiteness, bare-faced and roofed with snow. Indigo dusk drooped over them. The yellow lights glittered frostily and seemed to be throwing their brightness first to one side, then to the other. Stars also sparkled. Only the moon was quiet, the inconstant moon, shining so calm and peaceful, and yet too beautiful for peace to last, like a great courtesan dreaming of her childhood. Now moonlight shone through a row of icicles that hung from the edge of the roof and looked like translucent silver roots, each with a core of light. They were a crystal pallisade reversed, coldly glimmering. They were moonlit fangs of ice. . . .

To Juan, waiting for Olympia to come, the next morning seemed lethargic, as though numbed with cold. He served lemon phosphates with indifference and hot malted milks without enthusiasm. And then she arrived, a tall and glowing figure in her cloth-of-gold, coming out of the bleak and wintry street. She sat down, loosening her coat, and smiled in the friendliest way.

'Well,' she said, 'what d'you think of it?'

'It's an astonishing act,' said Juan. 'I've never seen anything like it before.'

'No kidding?' asked Olympia.

'No kidding,' Juan assured her. 'You've got a charming voice, and I envy you your strength.'

'Oh, I'm not so strong as I used to be. I used to do a three hundred and sixty pound dead lift with my teeth just easy, but it kinda gives me a headache if I practise it too much nowadays. Still, I can't complain. How about another of those Banana Specials?'

There was no sign of fading strength in Olympia's appearance. Her skin was smooth as a baby's, and there was a pearly gleam in the white of her eyes. She smiled, showing teeth that looked peculiarly solid; flawless and unshakable; and her neck was like an ivory tower. Such were the grip and the muscle for lifting three hundred and sixty pounds. It was fascinating to think such loveliness was so strong.

They talked across the counter, she in the free unembarrassed way of America, and Juan with a certain reserve. When she rose to go, then, he knew more about Olympia than Olympia did about him. He knew that her mother, who was dead, had been half Italian, half German-Swiss, and an opera-singer by profession; her father was a Swedish gymnastic instructor; one of her brothers was the strong man in a circus and another a travelling salesman; she took a seven in shoes, hated pink, and was just getting over an unhappy love-affair; she didn't smoke and seldom drank, but she happened to have a couple of quarts of gin in her room at the present moment, and if Juan cared to look round after the last performance they might continue their talk, and he could meet Buddy Hambone (whom Olympia admired) and Old Ollie Isaacs and Poppy Delaney (whose real name was Sarah Slipitch, and she lived with the two violinists and was very stupid, but her heart was in the right place, said Olympia) and, if he cared, all the other people who lodged in the house; for if anybody had a bottle of gin the news spread quickly. In return for this information Juan told Olympia his name, his birthplace, his brief experience in the soda-fountain, and the fact that he would be very pleased to attend her party.

III

Buddy Hambone faced the people gathered in Olympia's room and struck a chord or two on his banjo. Juan and

Olympia sat side by side on bedroom chairs, and because there were only these two chairs in the room they seemed to be enthroned. The other guests sat on the floor or the bed. They had been invited to hear Buddy's new ballad, called 'Square-shootin' Kate', and having drunk some gin were ready to be polite about it. The gin was both bait and bribery, for though Olympia truly believed in Buddy's genius she was not quite sure that the others would recognise it, or even listen to his poem without some inducement more obvious than aesthetic pleasure. But she was lonely and a little melancholy since her lover had left her, and so in a proper mood to patronise the arts. Two bottles of gin was not an extravagant price, she thought, to pay for a successful *première*, especially as she really admired the ballad and was strongly attracted by Buddy's poetical character.

Pang! said the banjo. *Pank-a-pang. Pang!*

In a voice full of emotion Buddy began to recite:

'In the Golden West,
Where the very best
And the worst live side by side,
They tell you still
(And your heart will thrill!)
Of Chet and the Woman who Died.'

Buddy's face seemed to grow larger as he thrust it farther and farther forward over the stock of his banjo. To intensify emotion he shook his head from side to side, so that his cheeks wobbled and his voice became uncertainly tremolo. His eyes protruded, and his lips were like the rim of a red wooden trumpet. The ballad continued:

'Now Chet was a weakling son of the East
And worthless for man or beast,
But his folk were wealthy, and he could afford
To live like a duke and to dress like a lord.

And the woman who died – well, after all,
She was only a woman, and women will fall
For a lord or a duke though she passes by
A dozen red-blooded he-men like you and I!
And Kate – for that was her name – to give her 'er due,
Was honest as daylight, square-shootin', true blue!
She stuck to Chet and she saved his life
Again and again – though he never made her his wife!

So how could they win,
Living in sin
In God's Great Open Space?
No, that's why she
Never lived to see
The smile on her baby's face!'

The ballad then described the successive calamities which befell Square-Shootin' Kate and her unworthy paramour. Repeatedly she sacrificed comfort, health, money, and reputation to save Chet from his creditors, from the other gamblers whom he had out-cheated, from fathers whose daughters he had betrayed, and from sons whose parents he had tried to blackmail. For she loved him. And Buddy Hambone never tired of repeating that love could conquer all. Even when everything seemed lost and hopeless love was waiting to spring forward at the last minute, *redemptor ex machina*. Perhaps not always in this life; but was there not a bigger and better life to come? And it was in that superior existence that poor Kate – on earth deserted by the thankless Chet – found her reward at last:

'And the guy got a break,
And he went away.
But did she get a break?
No, never, they say,
Till she went Up Above,
Where, because of her love,

The angels were waiting outside of the gate.
And when they had claimed her,
Why, God himself named her
"Square-shootin' Kate!"'

Juan was surprised to find that the response to this ridiculous ballad was a genuine enthusiasm. Poppy and one of her fiddlers wept openly. Old Ollie Isaacs shook Buddy by the hand and said earnestly, 'Boy, that'll land you straight in the big time! You see if it don't.' And all the others expressed their admiration so fervently that Olympia confided to Juan her belief that the recital would have been a success even without the gin. Buddy himself grew tired of repeating, 'Aw, I don't pretend it's a masterpiece. I ain't a genius, but I got talent –'

'And personality!' interposed a young woman with a tendency to goitre.

'I guess I have,' said Buddy. 'Anyway a lot of folk tell me so.'

'That's the great thing to have,' said someone else. 'I always say that if you got personality then you can get anything else you want.'

'I believe in work,' said the trap-drummer. 'Nobody ever got anywhere without working for it. If I hadn't of worked nights on a correspondence course I'd of been firing a furnace still.'

'Personality is what I'm really interested in at present,' said the young woman with goitre. 'I've just registered for a course in it, and for another in Accounting Principles. I think that's a good combination, don't you?'

This conversation presently drew everyone into its mesh but Juan and Olympia. And Olympia was busily elaborating a suggestion that first astonished, then amused, and latterly appealed to Juan for subsidiary reasons.

She began by skirmishing. 'I expect you got a good singing-voice, haven't you?' she asked in an off-handed way.

'There were few better in Cambridge,' said Juan, who had

found the gin both strong and palatable. 'Sweetness and power are its characteristics. Listen to this:

> "Roses and lilies her cheeks disclose,
> But her ripe lips are more sweet than those,
> Press her, caress her,
> With blisses her kisses
> Dissolve us in pleasure and soft repose!" '

He soared superbly to the top note of 'kisses' and descended with power to the grave depths of 'repose.' Everybody turned to stare and listen, and then to applaud. Olympia was very much impressed and Juan took a little more gin.

The majority continued their discussion of personality, work, and other important factors in life.

'Ever since I was a little girl people have noticed that I had an unusual type of mind,' said the girl with incipient goitre.

'When I work I like to work for something really worth-while,' said Buddy Hambone.

'What?' asked Old Ollie Isaacs.

'Well, my art,' replied Buddy, blowing out his cheeks a little.

'Boloney,' said Old Ollie Isaacs. 'Give me the jack and art can go chase itself round the block.'

'Well, the way I look at it,' said Buddy, 'is that working for art and working for money is just about the same thing. Because if the public likes your art, and the way you put it across, they'll give you a bigger hand, and come to see your show oftener, and your name'll go up sky-high, and you'll have all the money you want – just because you're a good artist.'

'You've said it, Buddy,' exclaimed the saxophone players, and the girl with goitre added, 'There's nobody can contradict that. . . .'

'So there you are,' said Olympia. 'You can sing, and you're strong enough, and you got the looks. You got everything. We'd make a swell act, you and me. I know we would. And it won't cost you nothing buying costumes, because I've got another leopard rug. Eddy Quinn, that's the guy that left me flat three weeks ago, for a dis-and-dat jane with the skin you love to touch – with your boot – well, he wanted to take it with him, but I socked him with a chair I happened to pick up, and he dropped the hide pretty quick. Yes, sir! And I haven't seen Eddy since. But you're better-looking than him, and you sing better, and I guess you're stronger too. Say, you don't begin till where he left off! That's my opinion, honest it is, so what d'you say to us teaming-up for the old act with improvements? Huh?'

Juan had no ambition to become a vaudeville star, and at first the idea seemed nonsense. But the prospect of touring with Olympia attracted him strongly. She was a magnificent creature and her *naïveté* seemed, for the moment, an endearing trait. Now in this shabby bedroom, full of shabby comical people, she looked like a goddess snatched sleeping from an ancient glen in Thessaly (still her brain was not quite awake) and wrapt by jealousy in the impertinence of clothes. What right had the triviality of fashion-mongers on those large and perfect limbs, that noble bosom, her waist so white and round and stronger than mere woman's flesh? From purely aesthetic reasons (fortified but not adulterated by gin) Juan felt moved to command her, 'Off with your clothes!' so keenly did he feel the impropriety of shopkeepers' wares on that splendid body. 'Off with your clothes!' He almost said it. But there were too many people in the room. Even now the voice of the trap-drummer rose from the babbling din to relate a paltry incident:

'She socked him in the eye and then threw a cup of cawffee in his face. Bill wiped it off and said, "No lady would do a thing like that!" So she picked up another cup of cawffee and threw that in his face, only this time she threw the cup and saucer too, and Bill didn't offer any more criticism. No, sir! . . .'

This was no place for the apocalypse of beauty. Aphrodite rose from the waves of open sea, not from a puddle in the street.

Juan rebuked his irrelevant aestheticism with a little more gin and told Olympia that he would be delighted to accept her offer.

'Because,' he said, 'you are the most beautiful woman I have seen in America. Because you are probably the only beautiful woman in the world who can sing "One Fine Day" upside-down, or hang by her teeth from a ring.'

'It makes you giddy to think of it like that,' Olympia interrupted. 'All these millions of people in the world, and only me who can do what I do! Gee, it makes me feel kinda religious to hear you say that.'

'It need not,' said Juan impatiently. 'I am singularly clear-sighted at the present moment. I am in a mood to discern the essentials of life behind all its shams and the poppycock of convention, and I see no reason why you should experience any sensation of Hebrew pietism. You are pagan and Greek. Hellenic, rather. Hellenic by all means. And what I feel about you is this: your beauty – please don't interrupt me. I'm not flattering you, I'm talking coldly and dispassionately, and if you're not careful I'll forget what I was going to say. Your beauty, I feel, is a function of your vitality. That is, it's ingrain and real, not a mere adventitious prettiness. What would adventitious prettiness look like if you saw it upside down? Just damned silly. But you don't look silly at all. You look as beautiful upside down as you do downside up. I mean the other way up. And why? Because your beauty is real and complete, and Keats says Beauty is Truth. "Beauty is truth. O Beauty, if that name thou love, who art a light to guide the erring, and improve the genial sense of youth!" I think that's misquoted, but it doesn't matter, because you see what I mean, don't you?'

Olympia did not. But the frequent mention of beauty pleased her, and she was awed by Juan's easy handling of abstractions. That impalpabilities should step off anyone's tongue so smartly, so neatly clad in fitted garments! It was wonderful.

'Gee, I wish I'd your education,' she said. 'I left school

when I was thirteen. I try to make up for it, of course, by reading what I can, but it isn't easy. I'm reading a book now all about history and morals. It's a good book – it set me back three dollars fifty – but I don't seem to get the idea of it very well. Maybe you'd help me with it sometimes when we're not rehearsing for the act?'

'Never,' said Juan. 'I distrust all education, and popular education I utterly condemn. Not only is it a stupid thing – fancy putting a fox in a bag and telling him to improve himself by studying it! – but to admit a desire for education is to reveal an inferiority complex. And you can't have an inferiority complex, because there isn't a professor in the world (I'm pretending that professors are educated men, which isn't always the case) with one tenth of your strength or a hundredth part of your beauty. So why should you worry what any of them say? Because beauty is truth, which is what professors are looking for, and you're beautiful already. And if beauty isn't truth, might is right, so you've got it both ways. But education dulls your eyes, rots your digestion, spoils your temper, ruins your muscles, blotches your complexion, thins your hair, saps your courage, spikes your endurance, and devours your immortal soul. Leave it alone! You stay just as you are, Olympia – and we'll have another spot of gin to wish you luck.'

Olympia hastened to pour it out. Her heart was beating as it had never done before. Juan's masterful manner filled her with wonder and admiration, and a desire to prostrate herself before him and submit to all kinds of indignities and caresses. Men had always treated her with deference. Even Eddy Quinn had jilted her in a hang-dog apologetic fashion. But Juan reproved her, snubbed her, contradicted her; told her where to get off, in fact. And she liked it. Moreover to her American mind, with its superstitious reverence for letters, anyone who cocked a snook at education was a hero defying the gods. Her eyes shone brightly and through her parted lips came little breaths of ecstasy.

At this moment Buddy Hambone approached with a grievance. Olympia had given the party for him, and here she was paying attention to no one but this fresh guy she had picked up in a drug-store! It was too bad.

'Say, is this a duet?' he asked. 'Or can anyone horn in?'

'Buddy,' said Olympia proudly, 'meet my new partner!'

'You're kidding,' said Buddy.

'On the level!' replied Olympia.

'Say, you haven't taken long to make up your mind. How d'you know what he can do?'

'Didn't you hear him sing? And he can do anything he wants to just as well as he sings.'

'I was looking for a new violinist,' said Buddy with a sneer, 'but I suppose I needn't look any further now.'

Olympia glanced enquiringly, hopefully, at Juan.

'I used to play a little,' he said.

Buddy picked up a fiddle-case belonging to one of the band, offered it to Juan, and said 'Do your stuff, Big Boy.'

'I dislike your manner,' Juan replied, 'but don't think you'd please me by improving it. Not a bit of it. I am no missionary, but just a friendly critic who doesn't want either to destroy or to elevate the objects of his criticism. Because then there would be nothing left to criticise.'

Before Buddy could think of an appropriate reply Juan had tuned the fiddle and, with greater spirit than accuracy, was playing the Londonderry Air.

'You want a lot more practice,' said Buddy when he had finished.

'I want a little more gin,' replied Juan.

Unhappily there was no gin left. Olympia was very distressed and offered to pay for more if anyone would fetch it. But the nearest reliable bootlegger lived four blocks away, and someone discovered that it was getting late, and Poppy and her violinists felt sleepy, so they decided that the party had come to a natural end and everybody said good-night to

Olympia, who smiled at them in a queenly way and let them go without reluctance. But Juan's hand she pressed in hers till it became numb and bloodless.

And Juan, walking home through snowy streets, sang his song from the Beggar's Opera till he heard it echo off a brick wall, when it occurred to him that he might be a little drunk. So for the rest of the way he walked in silence, wondering which of the two proverbs were nearer truth: Ale is another man, or *In vino veritas*.

IV

'I believe you're going away with that woman,' said Dora.

'What woman?' asked Juan.

'Olympia. Oh, you needn't pretend to be surprised. You knew very well who I meant. There was never room in your head for more than one at a time, but the trouble is that none ever stays there. So even if you do go off with her – the great vulgar creature – I know it won't be six weeks before you're tired of her, and goodness knows who you'll fall in love with next, for there's all kinds and colours in this country. And if you're starting off with acrobats you'll probably finish with niggers or Chinese, or somebody unnatural like that.'

'You've absolutely no right to say that,' said Juan indignantly. 'Whatever I am I'm not unnatural. I have, as a matter of fact, an unusually high degree of normality, especially to-day when aberrations are fashionable.'

'Is it normal to fall in love with a whole procession of women?'

'Yes, if they're all different, and all pleasant to look at, and amusing to talk to.'

'Then Bob isn't normal, and neither am I, and I'm glad we're not! Because Bob has never loved anyone but me – he just thought he was in love with that Coventry girl – and I've never loved anyone but him – except you, Juan. And I loved you more than I've ever loved Bob – *inff!* – and that's why God's punishing me now and – *inff!* – making me so unhappy!'

Dora's bosom was shaken with sobs and her face was all wet with tears. She looked for somewhere to hide it. Juan's shoulder was the obvious place. She took a step forward and looked at him with moist entreaty. He, touched by her grief and a memory of their love, and feeling in an impersonal way that a woman in tears had a right to bury her face in any man's breast, took her into his arms and let her cry against his coat as long as she wanted to.

He had come down late to breakfast – long after Bob had gone to work – and telephoned to the drug-store to say that he was giving up his job there and would not be back. Dora was startled by this cavalier treatment of an occupation which, though lowly enough, paid respectable wages. And she knew perfectly well that Juan's lateness was a result of Olympia's party – a party which she had bitterly resented.

Why, she had asked, was Juan not going to work at the drug-store any longer?

Because he was leaving Monroe, he had replied.

'Leaving Monroe!' said Dora, already threatening tears.

'I told you that I was going south in a very short time.'

'But not yet, Juan, not yet!'

'I must, I'm afraid. My plans are made.'

'I believe you're going away with that woman! . . .'

She had become a sentimental shrew. She would have become one no matter how her earlier years had passed. But Juan remembered this and that, and was flattered by her confession that she had never loved Bob so much as him. He felt sorry for Dora, in spite of the fact that he no longer liked her.

'I'm going to Charleston,' he said. 'I've got relations there whom I want to see.'

Dora looked up, unbelieving but ready to believe.

'Honour bright?' she asked.

'Yes. My mother's great-aunt Rachel lives there. She's very old.'

'And you're not going with Olympia?'

'Why, no. Whatever made you think that?'

'Oh, Juan, I'm so glad! I don't know why I thought you were, unless it was just jealousy because I . . . But I *am* glad, because I'm sure she's an awful woman, and though I wish you would stay for ever I'm so happy that you're not going with her that it doesn't seem quite so bad now.'

When was it, Juan wondered, that he had thought of adopting the orphan Truth – or was it little orphan Honesty? One of that brood. He realised now that it would never have done, and he was glad that he had taken no serious steps about it. Little orphan Truth was left out in the snow because that was the proper place for her, the smug, self-righteous, hymn-sniffling brat that she was. She ruined the happiness of every house she entered. Much better company, and kindlier too, was the huge family of Ananias and Sapphira: Lies, Fibs, Crammers, Prevarications, Whoppers, the tumbling twins called Terminological Inexactitudes, fat Uncle Falsehood and Grandpa Guile, and old Aunt Perjury, and handsome black-moustached Cousin Mendacity, together with the by-blows Suppressio Veri and Dissimulation, and the jolly old crone Nurse Bunkum, and all the rest of them. A fine happy healthy family, and a credit to their godfather the Devil.

'Yes,' he said, 'I'm looking forward to meeting great-aunt Rachel. Her husband was killed in the Civil War.'

And presently Dora came into a state of pleasant melancholy in which she rehearsed her prospective good-byes and nursed the gentle sadness which should accompany them, and when Bob came home at night the first thing she said to him – resigned to it now, and even looking forward a little to the excitement – was 'Oh, Bob, do you know that Juan's going to-morrow?'

'Well, I knew he wouldn't be staying for ever,' said Bob.

'But aren't you sorry?'

I don't suppose he'd change his plans however I felt,' said Bob mildly.

After supper they sat and waited for bed-time. Bob sat by the radio listening earnestly to cacophonous nugacity. Juan read. And after sitting for some time with her hands folded and her head lying back so that she looked up sadly to the vacant ceiling, Dora sighed and stood up, and smiled at Juan, and ran trippingly upstairs; from where she re-appeared three minutes later, wearing a little lace-edged apron and a pair of horn-rimmed spectacles that made her face look solemn and childish. She carried a soft bundle of clothes: some shirts and vests and several pairs of socks.

'Oh, Juan, I almost forgot to do your mending,' she said. And happily sat down to darn socks, and sew on buttons, and even embroider an odd handkerchief with a portentous J.M.

Two hours or so passed slowly. Then Dora went to bed, saying good-night to Juan in a voice that seemed to forgive him for all sins past and to bless all years to come. But Bob, ranging from one station to another, made the radio howl like a troll in agony, and Dora fled with her fingers in her ears.

Presently Bob said, 'So you're going to-morrow, are you?'

'Yes,' said Juan.

'Well, I can't say I'm sorry. I'm glad you came, but I think it's time you went.'

'If I had ever thought you objected to my being here I should have gone long ago!'

'That's all right. If I'd wanted you to leave I'd have said so.'

Juan was uncomfortably surprised by this sudden disclosure of Bob's feelings. He had never felt that Bob particularly liked him, and on his part he had no special affection for Bob. But to learn that his host actually rejoiced to see him go was something of a shock.

'I'm very sorry indeed if I've imposed on your hospitality,' he said stiffly.

'You haven't.' Bob filled his pipe slowly, and lit it, and when it was drawing well he went on more comfortably: 'You see, it was this way. When I found out who you were I was in half a mind to throw you out then and there. Neck and crop. Yes, neck and crop. Oh, you needn't look bewildered, or indignant, or whatever it is you are looking. I know all about you and Dora, and that it's your kid her sister Lily's got. But I never told Dora I knew. Women like to have their little secrets, and it does no harm for a man to let them act at being mysterious. Dora's a good girl and a good wife, and I had no call to make her uncomfortable by asking questions about her past. But when you showed up I wondered if you were going to try and play the old game again, and that's when I thought about pitching you out. But I knew Dora pretty well and I felt I could trust her, so I decided to let you stay and see if you wouldn't do me a good turn. And I think you have. How? Like this: Dora used to have spells of moping, and sighing, and looking out of windows. She'd never tell me what was wrong, but it didn't take a genius to guess that she was comparing humdrum married life and her romantic episode with young Mr. Juan Motley. And married life wasn't often getting the ball out of the scrum. Well, a romance is like cheese. The older it gets the stronger it smells. So those moping fits, it seemed to me, were going to get worse and worse – and so they would have done if you hadn't come along.'

Juan wore the expression of a slightly disapproving playgoer. Displeasure concealed his embarrassment at learning that Bob knew all about his affair with Dora. At first he had flushed hotly with discomfort; then he had set his teeth in vexation; and now the latter emotion completely masked his embarrassment, the more so as he suspected what was still to come.

Bob continued: 'I've often found that things we remember as being absolute knock-outs aren't anything like so good when we actually see them again. There was a pub in Cambridge, for instance, that I used to dream about when I was in France. But it looked a dirty little place when I got back and went along for a pint, and found it closed, being out of hours. But that's the way we are. We dress things up and just ask for disappointment. And Dora's been dreaming about you like I dreamt about the pub, never thinking I'd live to see it again. But I did, and so did she, and the result was the same in both cases: we were disappointed.'

'That's very flattering,' said Juan.

'It means that she's seen you as you really are, and what you are isn't just what she pretended you were. It couldn't be, and still be human. And so I think you've done her good. You've brought her back to earth, and she won't be so likely to dream again now that she knows her dreams were all wrong. And so I'm glad you came, but now that you've done your job I think you'd better go. Because three in a house isn't a good number.'

Bob knocked the ashes out of his pipe and stood up.

'It's bed-time,' he said.

Juan laughed, though not very happily, and said, 'Give Dora my congratulations on having a husband who isn't afraid to say what he thinks. And I suppose you're broad-minded too, or you'd have been high-falutin' about the child.'

'I don't think any the better of you for taking advantage of Dora when she was just a youngster,' said Bob. 'But I don't like to judge people too harshly in case I forgot some day and used the same standards for myself. I'm a married man, and it's up to me to look after my home as best I can. But I'm not perfect any more than you are. There was a girl in Coventry when I was working there and – oh, well, I'm paying her ten bob a week for it now. It's just as well that Dora never heard of that little fly-by-night.'

V

The matter of leaving Monroe was complicated to a mild extent by the antagonistic circumstances that Olympia looked forward to Juan travelling in the train that she and Old Ollie Isaacs, Buddy Hambone, and Poppy Delaney were taking; and that Dora, who insisted on seeing him off, would expect him to travel strictly alone on his way to visit great-aunt Rachel. Paying a clandestine visit to Olympia, however, Juan persuaded her that pressure of business – the demand for raspberry sundaes, that is – would compel him to leave by a later train than hers. And by good fortune the vaudeville party's next engagement was at Toledo, a city which, lying south of Monroe, was on the road to Charleston and, as Juan explained to Dora, the proper sort of place in which to plan the major part of his journey.

'In a large city like that,' he said wisely, 'one is offered a bigger choice of routes than is possible in a little town like Monroe.'

So he bought a ticket to Toledo, and kissed Dora good-bye – her chubby hands caught at his sleeves – but even while she waved her handkerchief to the great snorting train she was making plans for a supper so unusually delicious that Bob would scarcely notice the loneliness after their guest's departure. . . . And when Juan reached Toledo he went straight to the dingy hotel where Olympia had waited impatiently and greeted him with enthusiasm.

It was decided that he should do nothing more for his début than steady the rope up which Olympia climbed, and pull the cord which swung her out in long arcs while she sang the aria from *Madame Butterfly*. And so on the very next day, in the large city of Toledo, Juan made his first appearance on any stage, and performed his simple duties ably and without a sign of stage-fright.

Moving pictures were shown in the theatre from eleven in

the morning till half-past eleven at night, continuously except for three intervals, one in the afternoon and two in the evening, when the vaudeville players gave their performance. This, Juan found, was a not unusual arrangement. Perhaps an audience grew tired of the unsubstantial perfection of people in pictures and were refreshed by the imperfect but heartier antics of people in the flesh. For the cinema was at best a tenuous entertainment: not acting, but a photograph of acting; not action, but its shadow; not a fat and coloured three-dimensional thing, but a hollow shifty affair that aimlessly drifted over a flat white screen. It did not give you a book to read; it gave you a one-sided review of a bowdlerised copy of a book. It was never more than secondary entertainment.

So Juan thought to himself as he pulled the cord which kept Olympia swinging backwards and forwards, now swooping out at the audience and now sailing in retreat, while she sang – and her voice was getting a little thick and foggy, and the band was ready to cover her failure to reach the last high note –

> 'This will all come to pass as I tell you,
> Banish your idle fears,
> For he will return,
> I *know*!'

There was nothing fictitious or unsubstantial about Olympia except her top notes. In her green trunks and her leopard-skin she put a hundred moving pictures to shame. What was photography worth beside her warm and heavy and vivid actuality? – The ultimate skylark note of the aria was a whisper in her throat; trumpets shrilled roofward; in their fuliginous cave the audience applauded; and Olympia slid down her rope, panting, her breast heaving, smiled at Juan, bowed, took his hand, bowed again, walked with him to the wings, went out to bow again, and came back to say, 'Gee, I feel great when you're at the bottom of the rope! I could go on singing for ever.'

Her leopard-skin rose and fell with happy emotion and she smacked Juan heartily on his bare shoulder – for he also wore a leopard-skin which, though it suited him very well, did not offer much protection.

'You look swell in that skin,' said Olympia.

'I was just going to say as much to you,' Juan answered politely.

'Oh, go on! I got a mole on my leg. Look!'

'So have I.'

'Well, that's cute. It's just like a lady-bug. What's mine like?'

'A lady-bug's beau.'

'And what does that mean?'

'They ought to get together.'

'Say, you're getting kinda fresh, aren't you?'

'I just say what I think.'

'So long as you aren't proud of thinking what you say.'

'Would you like to know what else I'm thinking?'

'Well, I've got my own secrets.'

'What about an exchange?'

'I got too little on to be confidential right now. I'll see you later.'

Olympia's room in the shabby small hotel where they all lodged was almost identical with the one in which she had given her party. A room that, without charm even in youth, in age had grown so tired of its ever-changing occupants, so careless of appearance, so absolutely negative, that it scarcely seemed to exist at all. Such a room would be depressing to people able to be depressed by so trifling a circumstance as a room. People who must ever be hanging up pictures and buying knick-knacks for a corner – the home-makers, that is – would certainly be made unhappy by such a room. But Juan and Olympia scarcely noticed it.

Her response to Juan's first kiss was immediate. She threw her arms round him and hugged him till his ribs crackled. For a moment Juan wondered if she were angry, and with an effort drew one hand loose from her imprisoning arms and thrust her back a little so that he could see. Her expression reassured him. Her eyes were closed and her lips parted enough to show between them the glimmer of wet pearls. It was not the expression of an angry woman.

On the following morning Juan woke first and once again was moved to admiration of Olympia's triumphal beauty. It was beauty, he knew, that might have daunted a lesser man, for it condescended to no petty allurement, it had rejected the appeal of littleness, it scorned the dimple, the bee-stung lip, and the plucked eyebrow, as if to say: The world is full of the prettiness that the silly world desires, of saucy, provocative, tip-tilted prettiness; shop-girl prettiness, twopence-coloured, cheap and curly prettiness that tickles the skin and leaves imagination sleeping; but beauty such as mine – now that it wakes no more from Parian marble or stoops from heaven to vie with mortal maids for Adon's love – beauty like mine is rare, so rare! And, it might have added, even when they find it men are too often shy of it and turn instead to the little shop-girls with their mincing, pouting ways.

So Juan was doubly happy: intensely gratified by possession of Olympia, and very pleased at his own ability to appreciate her. To find that the human body could so transcend itself was a wonderful thing. To see that such utilitarian matters as a breast and a belly and a knee might be so lovely and yet not have their utility impaired, made one think better of mankind. And to know that one recognised beauty when one saw it, to be aware of one's palate, that was surely an occasion for happiness almost as genuine as beauty itself.

Olympia stirred, opened her eyes, yawned, and stretched herself. As if it were a lagoon shaken by some vast submarine catastrophe the bed moved with her. The counterpane heaved like billows, the mattress rocked, and as a quire of harps the bed-springs jangled. During these turbulent seconds Juan remembered that morning does not always approve what night has done, and it occurred to him that Olympia might be less willing to find him in her bed than she had been to invite him to it. One acted on impulse and sometimes one was sorry for it. There was such a thing as regret. And though Olympia seemed too noble a creature ever to entertain that snivelling emotion, one could never be quite sure. Juan waited anxiously.

But he had less cause to fear her displeasure than her affection.

'Oh, boy!' she said on the heels of her yawn, and before he could answer a word her arms went round him and her lips had visited his neck, foraged on his cheeks, invaded his eyes, fared sumptuously on his mouth, and coolly on his brow. He almost drowned under the torrent of kisses.

'How I love you is just nobody's business,' she said.

Clearly she had no regrets. No conventional regrets, that is. For presently her forehead wrinkled and she said with some displeasure, 'You'll have to pay for your room.'

'I suppose so,' Juan agreed. 'One generally does in a hotel.'

'But you haven't used it much.'

'I've no complaints to make.'

'But it's a waste of money to pay for what you don't use. Of course you can't get out of it this time, having made your reservation, but as soon as you're dressed you go and tell the manager you won't be needing Number 17 to-night. Tell him you're sleeping with me now. Of course we'll have to pay a bit extra for this one when it's occupied by two, but we'll each save something, splitting it. Perhaps you won't think it much, but it mounts up in time.'

Olympia's financial acumen was a hitherto unsuspected trait. Her businesslike regard for the future was also remarkable. Juan was very impressed by the efficiency with which she made an affair of one night seem a prelude to respectable permanency. Perhaps, he thought, and looked with awe at her white broad forehead, her heavy but elegant chin, perhaps their association would be permanent. Could one break with young Niobe? Would ever a caryatid jilt him? He really did not know. For the present it was a great relief that Olympia should be so completely unembarrassed by their association.

Nor were the other members of the troupe unduly excited by it. Buddy Hambone was not pleased, for in a doubting, frightened way he had sometimes paid court to Olympia himself. But though the music he conducted and the songs he often wrote all testified to the ubiquity and invincible nature of love, yet his heart was too weak to know itself and too timorous to experiment with so majestic a woman. With a sigh he had watched her monopolise Juan at her party. With a sigh he had seen them – leopard-skin clad on the untidy stage – exchange smiles far fonder than any histrionic grimace could be. And with a sigh, not with anger or even surprise, he heard of their liaison.

Poppy Delaney was mildly disappointed, for she was losing one of her violinists – he was leaving to take a more profitable position with his brother, who was a barber in Atlantic City – and she had thought that as Juan was going to take his place in the band so he might also play his part in her *ménage à trois*. But she was a sensible creature and not really perturbed by the contrary news.

Old Ollie Isaacs cackled and winked, but that meant very little, for he always cackled when he heard of bedrooms, pyjamas, nightgowns, keyholes, and so forth; and winked lewdly at any mention of love, birth, or young mothers. And the members of the band made little jokes that had done previous service on many similar occasions. Juan's appearance and the tone of his voice had at first somewhat overawed them, but the readiness of his surrender to Olympia (so they construed it) persuaded them of his humanity, and they were no longer abashed in his presence.

The troupe stayed three days in Toledo and then moved to the next town, where Juan's duties grew appreciably heavier.

He became a member of the band and with the other violinist assiduously practised a melody called 'What'll I say to my sugar when I see my sugar again?' They played this *lento con molto espressione* on muted strings in a dim blue light between a full band number and Poppy's tumbling act. Juan rapidly became expert in extracting from his fiddle the tone of agonised yearning which Mr. Kipfer (his companion violinist) instinctively produced. The result was a glutinous compost of inanity and Hebraic sentiment which proved extremely popular with audiences in Ohio and Indiana, and very often Juan and Mr. Kipfer were made to repeat the air.

Then Olympia had plans to enlarge her operacrobatic performance, and Juan, for one reason or another, co-operated with her in the most amiable way. The very first time she heard it, Olympia decided that Juan's voice was too good to be wasted in idleness, and now she was all agog to add a duet to her act. For a while she thought it would be pretty if he were to strike an attitude and sing to her while she swung far overhead and replied like Juliet suspended from the balcony by her heels. Then it occurred to Olympia that perhaps Juan could also be taught to sing upside down, for she, who had devised the inverted pose for opera, was naturally enthusiastic about it and thought the habit might profitably spread and bring credit to its innovator. Juan, then, was persuaded to practise simple tunes while hanging head-down from a trapeze.

Olympia had a wide knowledge of the more popular operas. A week before she was born her mother had been one of a chorus of villagers in *Cavalleria Rusticana*, and two weeks after her birth returned to the stage as an Egyptian priestess in *Aïda*. Olympia grew up in communal dressing-rooms, and her childhood was naturally influenced by the constant metamorphoses of her mother, whom she saw one night as an Italian peasant, the next as a vestal of Isis, and again as a Spanish gipsy. She learnt songs and snatches of recitative instead of her multiplication tables. She accepted the tenets and mores of opera as the tenets and mores of life, and naturally looked forward to life with the utmost confidence. She saw that everything was constantly changing and yet mysteriously remained the same. People were always rushing about, brightly clad, in seemingly turbulent but really disciplined groups, to sing agreeable comments on this and that, to chant a warning, to point a moral, to congratulate a bride, to mourn disaster, and to greet the young baron, the strolling players, or soldiers from the nearest garrison. People so interested in their neighbours must be kindly souls, and life itself a simple and hearty existence where every act came to its appointed end and the sorrow of death disappeared in a fine funeral song.

By Olympia's tenth birthday her mother was too fat even for opera. She could no longer rush to and fro on congratulatory excursions from the wings to the footlights. She impeded the chorus of rustics, and when all the other village girls perched lightly on their soldiers' knees – sitting in the tavern and heartily banging tankards on the table-tops – there was never a soldier strong enough to bear Olympia's mother. So regretfully she said good-bye to the stage and philosophically decided to live with her husband, whom she had irregularly but amicably visited during the fifteen years since their marriage, and who was then doing well as a gymnastic instructor in Milwaukee.

He very soon recognised the latent possibilities of his daughter and at the earliest opportunity took her to the gymnasium. There he performed miracles of strength and grace on the parallel bars, the horizontal bar, the horse, the rings, the high trapeze, and other apparatus. Olympia immediately fell in love with her father and burned to emulate his prowess on the horizontal bar. She demanded a lesson. He lifted her up. At her first attempt Olympia circled the bar. Father and daughter hugged each other delightedly and exchanged the most rapturous kisses. Their breath was equally flavoured with chewing-gum. Olympia pulled her father's moustache. He turned her over and with pretended severity smacked her bottom. They laughed at each other's pranks and walked home hand in hand.

It was natural that the gymnasium should appeal to Olympia more strongly than singing, and for a year there were frequent altercations as to whether the child was to be educated as a prima donna or an acrobat. Both father and mother thought well of their own professions, but they were more sensible and good-humoured than people often are, and so after only a year of wrangling they reached a compromise by which Olympia was to have singing lessons and gymnastic lessons on alternate days. Mondays, Wednesdays, and Fridays were reserved for *Rigoletto*, *Pagliacci*, *La Bohème*, *Traviata*, and other works of that nature, while Tuesdays, Thursdays, and Saturdays were more strenuously occupied with up-starts, long arm balancing, vaulting, and similar exercises. On Sundays Olympia and her father went to a Lutheran church, her mother and brothers to a Roman Catholic one; and in the afternoon Olympia helped her mother with the weekly household budget.

These details and many others Juan learnt from Olympia's pillow-chatting. He also discovered that she regretted her lack of a literary education and frequently attempted to repair the deficiency by reading the autobiographies of self-made men and some of the knowledge-without-tears publications in which the country abounded. From these works she drew a feeling of pious depression that she rather enjoyed.

After a week's practice Juan was still unable to sing more than ten words head-down without a feeling of suffocation. But Olympia was undaunted.

'Of course it takes time,' she said, 'and some people would never learn. Plenty of people can't neither sing nor hang upside down, but you can do both separately and some day you'll manage them together, if you don't lose heart.'

'Do you think it's worth while?' asked Juan a little wearily.

Olympia was indignant. Her face reddened. 'Say, d'you mean my act isn't worth doing?' she demanded. 'Then let me tell you you're making the hell of a mistake. It'll be on Broadway inside of a year – *we'll* be on Broadway if you don't talk hooey like that "worth while" crack.'

Juan assured her that it was his own physical ability that he doubted; that he wondered if it was worth training a cab-horse for a race, as it were.

'Aw, you're underrating yourself, honey,' said Olympia earnestly. 'You mustn't say things like that or you'll get an inferiority complex. Sure you will! It said so in a book I was reading only last week.'

With such slight exceptions as this Juan and Olympia lived together very happily for some time. It was inevitable that minor differences should appear, especially as the inconveniences of a trouper's life were new to Juan, for he found the constant moving from place to place rather wearisome. They never stayed in a town for more than three days. Then everything had to be packed up and off they went to the next halt, a dull little town exactly like the last, with perhaps the same pictures being shown, and their act to be repeated three times a day.

The weather was harsh and wintry. Ten degrees below zero was not an uncommon temperature. They travelled from one town to another through an unchanging landscape of level snow-swept farmlands. On both sides lay white fields out of which peered at intervals almost shapeless houses. And snow drove blindly against the windows of the train. But Olympia moved tranquilly through all discomforts, for she was quite unaware of them. She enjoyed everything she ate and never felt cold. Under the snow-laden roof of a cheap and chilly lodging-house she would say cheerfully, 'It's warmer to-night, isn't it? I do believe that spring is coming.' And then she would throw half the clothes off the bed.

This, not unreasonably, made Juan angry, so that Olympia, at once contrite and ashamed of her thoughtless behaviour, would get out and retrieve the blankets and wrap Juan up so carefully that he wished he had shivered instead; and she would wake him three times during the night to ask if he were warm enough.

Often her love became frolicsome, and in such moods Olympia was definitely dangerous. A weaker man than Juan would have been seriously injured by some of her embracings, her jocular buffets, her friendly clips and clasps. She loved a rough and tumble like a six-months' old lion cub, and Juan was grateful more than once for his training with the football squad at Motley. Thanks to that he gave as good as he got except when Olympia used her teeth, and then he was no match for her. She delighted in showing the strength of her bite. She could crack Brazil nuts or hang by her teeth from a padded ring for nearly an hour. Often, in her liveliest moods, she would snap Juan up by the band of his trousers and carry him as easily as a dog would carry a bone, and in the same way.

But on the whole they lived together very happily.

VI

Olympia had chosen for their duet the song of Rodolphe and Mimi in the first act of *La Bohème:* Rodolphe, in the moonlit garret, has said that he is a poet. 'Who are you?' he asks, and simply the girl replies, 'They call me Mimi.' And presently they sing together and in a little while go off, still singing, through snowy streets to the Café Momus where Marcel and Colline and Schaunard are waiting for them.– And never had so robust a Mimi appeared on any stage before.

For three or four weeks Juan sang his part in a more or less orthodox manner – that is, from a stationary and upright position – while Olympia, reversed, swooped overhead. But during this time he was also practising the more arduous, and so honourable, position. Every morning, on a deserted stage, he swung head-down from a trapeze and sang scales or such simple airs as John Brown's Body, Sally in our Alley, or *Sur le pont d'Avignon.* Gradually he improved, and the suffocating sensation that at first attacked him after a dozen words became slowly less terrible, until he could withstand it for several minutes. Olympia waited impatiently for him to achieve something like her own degree of proficiency. As soon as he could sing a whole verse of Sally in our Alley she made him practise Rodolphe's part in the duet, and when he tumbled down with his face the colour of port-wine, his ears ringing and his eyes all wet, she would kiss him twice or three times and bid him try again.

With so much to do he saw comparatively little of the towns in which they stopped, but as these were all alike and not very interesting that did not matter much. He saw enough to discover that their necessary and invariable features were a certain rectangularity, two or three cinema theatres decorated with a gaudy extravagance, a vast multitude of motor cars, some smart shops for women, the drug-stores, the Presbyterian, Methodist, and Baptist churches, a large new hotel, and a complacent newspaper.

They were self-revealing towns, and what they did not actually tell about themselves was easily inferred. There was never a tortuous wynd, a moated grange, or hermit's cave to hide secrets and breed a mystery. They said what they were (or what they would like to be) in a florid ungrammatical way, and all one had to do to arrive at the truth was to knock a substantial discount off their recital. And his fellow-troupers, Juan found, were as artless as the towns. Their characters were not complex. Fundamentally materialistic, they often streaked their selfishness with sentimentality; under a cynical surface they were really very gullible; their boasting was the beating of a hollow drum, and the objects of their ambition were mostly procurable for cash.

The troupe moved slowly southwards, and one day Olympia said to Juan, 'I do wish you'd be ready to do your stuff when we get to Cincinnati. It's a real city, see? and they'd appreciate it there if we was both to sing upside down.'

'When do we reach Cincinnati?' asked Juan.

'A week to-morrow.'

'All right. I feel that I shall be able to sing in any position you like next week.'

'Say, that's swell! I knew you'd do it once you'd made up your mind. Aw, honey, you've no idea how glad I am that I went into that drug-store in Monroe and found you there, fixing chocolate sundaes as though you'd been born to do nothing else. You that can do anything you like! You're just the cream in my cawffee, Juan. Honest you are!'

Olympia's face was radiant with generous emotion. She glowed as if with that ineffable light that bathed the figures of the gods. Then wisdom came to cool her enthusiasm.

'Perhaps it would be better if you did it for a few days before going on to Cincinnati,' she suggested. 'Then you'll be confident and it won't be no strain to you, thinking you're trying out something new in a big city like that.'

'Just as you please,' said Juan, who was in his most affable mood. 'This day, next day, some day, never. You say the word and I'll hang like a bat and sing like a lark.'

That morning he had remained upside down for an unusually long time without distress, and his consequent optimism was ready to father any kind of an undertaking. But the following day he was a little costive, and a little queasy too, and in the evening, an hour before attempting to fulfil his promise, he felt a premonition of failure.

The early part of the performance was the same as Juan had first seen at Monroe, except that Buddy Hambone had introduced his ballad of 'Square-shootin' Kate'; and, of course, since Juan was now a member of the band, he had to face Buddy instead of watching his back. This was unpleasant, for grotesque as his antics had seemed from the audience, the spectacle of his face at close quarters was still less agreeable.

His small eyes half-closed, his large fat cheeks wabbling, he faithfully looked his part of midwife to a saxophone, the *accoucheur* of jazz. The other musicians were also ugly and stupid men. They swayed from side to side as they bumbled and blared; they put their instruments down, and smiled archly, and showed their teeth. Sometimes, in a cold impersonal way, Juan hated them all – all except Buddy, for Buddy, though he looked the most blatant of all, was troubled by a secret diffidence, by little draughts of doubt, by a scarcely articulate musical ambition. There was still a peep-hole for grace in his heart.

This evening he recited his ballad with extraordinary unction, maltreating nearly every vowel for undeserved emphasis and so mouthing his deplorable sentiments that the audience clamoured for an encore.

While this was going on Juan, in a small and shabby dressing-room, changed his dinner-jacket for his leopard-skin. He shivered as he took off his shirt. His qualms had become a definite reluctance to sing in so foolish an attitude. But, he realised unhappily, it was too late now to tell Olympia that he had altered his mind.

Old Ollie Isaacs shared the dressing-room. He grunted and cleared his throat as he painted red wrinkles on his face. His clothes, full of the dust of innumerable stages, had an ancient smell. He drank half a glass of gin before going out to face the audience.

Juan stood in the wings and watched him dance. Tap-a-tap, tap-a-tap, tap, tap, tap; tappitty, tappitty, tap-a-tap-a-tap-a-tap; tappitty tappitty *tap*. He looked like an old grey chimpanzee dressed in a gorilla's cast-off Sunday suit, but his feet were smart enough. Then his trousers fell down. Old Ollie Isaacs was a picture of simian embarrassment. He pulled them up and almost furtively began to dance again. Again his trousers slid down. Infinitely abashed, Ollie ate his collar and tie, some buttons, and a bunch of flowers. Casually he began to tell his usual stories:

'. . . and he said, "What lady was that you was riding with yesterday?" and I said, "That wasn't a lady, that was my wife." Well, anyway, the next thing he asked was what had happened to my face. So I told him. I told him I'd had an argument with a fellow about driving in traffic. And he said, "Why didn't you call a cop?" "What," said I, "*another* one?" . . . But his sister was queer too. She was the most unselfish girl you ever seen. Even her prayers was all for other people. She used to kneel down and say, "Dear Lord, I don't ask anything for myself. Just you give mother a son-in-law." *And He did.* It pays to think of others. . . . She was a lot luckier than my sister Alice. Of course Alice could have married anyone she pleased; but she never pleased anyone. I been married three times myself. The last time was a swell affair. Yes, sir. They even used puffed rice. . . . Well, I ought to be dancing again, but I got a corn on the bottom of my foot. I ain't grumbling though, because if you got to have a corn that's the best place for it. Nobody can step on it but yourself.'

Old Ollie Isaacs' trousers fell down yet again. . . .

Hand-in-hand Olympia and Juan walked on to the stage. Olympia sang the Habañera and did her jack-knifing act. Its rhythmical violence always compelled applause. Her neck was a column of pliant marble, her abdomen rippled with muscles like a pond in the wind, her legs rose and fell. . . . And watching her Juan wished that the theatre would take fire before he had to hang like a flittermouse and sing like Rodolphe.

But no flames appeared. Olympia mounted her rope, put one foot into the loop, and hung from it in perfect comfort. Slowly Juan climbed to a trapeze, gripped the bar under his knees, and hung down. An attendant pulled on a cord and he began to swing backwards and forwards.

Now by a serious oversight Juan had done all his practising on a stationary trapeze, and the unexpected motion upset him badly. The band was playing, and Olympia swooped to and fro with the swift assurance of a bird. She sang even more strongly, more sweetly than usual, for she was elated by Juan's proximity and the fructification of her desire.

She listened for Juan's answering voice.

But Juan, after his initial effort, was silent. At the extremity of every arc he was frightened of falling and in the middle he felt sick. The blackish audience rose and fell. The bright stage flashed past him dizzily. His knees were weakening and his stomach heaved. Dimly he heard the band and dimly Olympia's voice. He knew that he should be singing, but he feared to open his mouth.

The band grew perturbed. Olympia was alarmed in her flight. And the audience realised that something was amiss.

Then they heard Juan's voice – but not in song.

'Let me down!' he shouted, and immediately clapt one hand to his mouth and with the other caught at the trapeze, to which he clung desperately till it came to rest and he could slide floorwards.

The audience bellowed and hallooed with joy. They roared their delight. The house was full of their mirth, for was not this the oldest and best joke of all – a man pretending to do what other men could not do, and being discomfited in the midst of his pretence?

Olympia wept openly; a terrifying spectacle, for she raised her arms as if in supplication, and lifted her face as though indeed she wept to heaven. Buddy Hambone drove his band into their concluding number, but even above the clamour of brass rose the noise of Homeric laughter as the audience held to their merriment in the dark.

It was useless for Juan to contend that nausea was an accident which might afflict anyone at any moment. Olympia could no more control her disappointment than a child who had lost her doll. She felt that Juan was to blame for the catastrophe. He had not taken his vocation seriously enough. He had doubted his own ability, and once asked 'Is it worth while?'

'That's when the trouble started,' she sobbed. 'As soon as

you said you didn't think you could do it you got an inferiority complex. Yes, you did. I read a book that told just how it happens. All you got to do is to say "I can't," and there's your inferiority complex. It's like laying an egg. And by-and-by the egg hatches, and you get sick on a trapeze and ruin *my* act.'

For three days Olympia sulked while Juan maintained an appearance of bland indifference, and tried to persuade himself that laughter had no critical significance, but was merely a physical reaction to any chance disclosure of the basic frailty, impropriety, or incongruity of human life.

And before he had made up his mind on this matter Olympia was ready to resume a more amicable relationship. But it was a dangerous truce, for her confidence had been destroyed, her professional pride injured, and Juan's contentment in her was also fading. He had begun to think that so much beauty would be the better for a little intelligence; that without the salt of wit it might go bad.

VII

On their first night in Cincinnati Olympia and Juan lay reading in bed. There was a striking difference between their pillow books. Juan read a frivolous farcial novel of no social, intellectual, artistic, or moral import whatsoever. But Olympia lay with a work entitled *How to Think*, and wrinkled her smooth forehead over it, and stared respectfully at its momentous pages.

How to Think was an interesting book not so much for what was in it as for what had happened to it. A hundred and fifty thousand copies of it had been sold in six months. Its author was a Spaniard, unusually perspicacious, and a master of adroit penmanship. He had lectured for some months in America and discovered that the characteristics of its people included an insatiable desire for novelty. He saw too that a clever minority of men – inventors, manufacturers, contrivers of petty knick-knacks – took advantage of this unwearied hunger and reaped a handsome profit by feeding it with seasonal mouthfuls of bonnets, scarves, motor cars, cigarette-lighters, perfumes, and a thousand gewgaws valuable only for newness and their power to satisfy a want that nothing but their appearance had created. It seemed to the Spaniard that where others reaped so might he, and he searched his brain for something that he could offer for sale among the bonnets and cigarette-lighters. He wanted a genuine novelty. . . . But looking around at the riches of the great democracy it appeared they had everything that the brain of man could devise and the hand of man create. . . . And then, waking very early in the morning, it occurred to him that there was one thing a great democracy never did, never had done, and in all probability never would do. It never thought. The ideas of flying, motoring, travelling in submarines, wearing all manner of garments, playing forty different games, eating a hundred kinds of food – these were familiar to it. But the notion of *thinking?* 'By the late spatulate pontifical hallux of Pio Nono,' said the Spaniard, 'here is Manoa, Eldorado, and the wealth of Croesus! For here is the first hair on the milk-white chin of Novelty's bridegroom; the teething-cry of Novelty's youngest child; the virgin rustle of love in the breast of Novelty's grand-daughter. *Terra Incognita*, *Terra Nova*, *Terra Novissima*. Whoever thought of thinking as a popular entertainment? I am the very precursor, the herald, the voorlooper of Innovation!'

And forthwith he wrote his description of the practice of thinking.

Constitutionally unable to ignore *le dernier cri*, America leapt joyously to its feet – dropping pell-mell its newest cos metics, diseases, flying machines, murders, and plans for world-peace – and reached with a myriad hands for this guide-book to Thought. No one had ever thought of thinking before and here was a Spaniard saying that anybody could do it. What a world we live in, with new discoveries pouring in upon us every day! Leave your radios, you sons and daughters of democracy, and learn to Think in six chapters with an explanatory diagram of the cerebrum on page 13 and a record of what thinking did for Julius Caesar, Christopher Columbus, General Grant – and what it might have done for George III!

For several weeks America *thought*. With the earnestness that glorified its golf and the publicity of the motion picture trade it *thought*. The newspapers had a daily list of What To Think About This Evening. The popular magazines offered prizes for The Twenty Best Subjects for National Thought. And the Spaniard bought a yacht with his royalties, and might have bought an island on the Dalmatian coast as well, had not a new mouth-wash been invented, the advertisement of which distracted America's attention and interfered with its thinking; and then a new talking-picture was put into circulation, and after that no one thought about Thought any more, and *How to Think* gradually disappeared from the bookshops.

Olympia was behind the times, for she had only heard of the idea after almost everybody else had forgotten it. But she read the book with as much care as though it had been really new – while Juan amused himself with a frivolous and useless novel.

But Olympia was the first to fall asleep. She lay with one muscular arm outside the bedclothes. She looked larger than ever when sleeping, and a shadow magnified the power of her jaw. An hour earlier she had demanded caresses. She had pinched Juan with fingers that could bend a coin out of shape, she had hugged him with arms of steel, and nuzzled his cheek and ear with the furious simplicity of an affectionate tigress. To all her movements there had been an accompaniment of tinny gibbering as the rusty bed-springs made their mouse-music; squeaking of twisted wire; tin slats that rattled again. O voice that breathed o'er Eden! And then, simple as ever, a tigress with an earnest soul, she had reached for *How to Think* and settled in her pillow to read awhile.

This it was to love a female acrobat who sang arias upside down. Juan put away his novel to contemplate the droll chapter he had reached in his life. Could anything be more blissfully ludicrous? . . . He thought of his friends in England; an urbane periphery circling about a hostess who asked, in a voice clear as the tinkle of her spoons on porcelain, 'One lump or two?' Young men gossiping over the smoky China tea, and young women, charmingly dressed, listening with a sprightly air for a chance to interpose their arch and bird-like contradictions, or to laugh with pretty shallowest assurance. Theirs was the bright patina of social grace, while he lay abed with a thoughtful tigress who made her living upside down and tried to improve her mind in the intervals of connubial excitement. . . . What if his father could see him now? – Sir Hildebrand with his orders of the Bath and SS. Michael and George and the British Empire; Sir Hildebrand regardant in a portal of the Ministry of Rebuttals; Sir Hildebrand coming into this frowsy bedroom to find it a tigress's cave and be entertained with extracts from *How to Think* – or if he knocked at a neighbouring door he would meet a comedian with perpetually falling trousers who would say to him, 'That wasn't a lady, that was my wife' – and on the other side the leader of a jazz band who would recite:

> 'Then she went Up Above,
> Where because of her love
> The angels were waiting outside of the gate,
> And when they had claimed her,
> Why, God himself named her
> "Square-shootin' Kate!" '

Juan started to laugh. . . . Olympia telling a hypnotised audience to 'Banish your idle fears' while she hung by one foot from a perilous rope and half the blood in her body sank chokingly to her head; nightly laughter at trousers that would not stay up; his father's horror; slobbering saxophones that the people loved, and a conductor who thought of God as a kind of perpetual Grand Master of an Elks' Convention; his own ridiculous misadventure on the trapeze – it was too much. Juan's laughter spread from his brain to his throat, and from his throat to his belly, so that the bed-springs responded – mouse-music again, and the clatter of tin slats – and the bed began to shake. At this Olympia woke. She thought it was a fresh summons to the connubial office. And she was ready.

When she realised that Juan was laughing she was scandalized. No one with proper feelings, she thought, would laugh in bed. It was like laughing in church, or while Buddy Hambone was reciting 'Square-shootin' Kate.'

'What's the big idea?' she asked suspiciously.

'Ho, ho!' said Juan, by this time caught helplessly in the quicksands. 'Ho, ho, ho! Hoo-hoo. Hoo-hoo-hoo-hoo-hoo. Ho-hoh! Hoo, hoo, hoo!'

There were tears in his eyes and his face was flushed and creased with laughter. He patted Olympia's large and muscular arm. She was beautiful as well as ridiculous. He continued to laugh.

Olympia grew angry.

'What d'you mean,' she demanded, 'waking me up and then laughing, huh? Have you gone nuts, or what? All you English are goofy, anyway. Say something, can't you?'

It made no difference. Juan continued to laugh as heartily as ever. He could not speak, but he tried to comfort Olympia by patting her shoulder. Indignantly she repulsed this foolish courtesy, and gripping Juan under the arms exerted a moiety of her enormous strength and threw him out of bed.

She followed and stood over him menacingly, and loudly gave tongue:

'Think you're going to get fresh with me, huh? You and your classy line of talk! Going to treat a girl like dirt, are you, just because she's all alone in the world and hasn't got the strength she was used to? But I'm nobody's fool. I'll show you,

you big sap! You can't high-hat me. Lay off that ritzy laugh or I'll sock you, see? What's the game? Come clean, will you? To think I called you the cream in my cawffee!'

So storming, and tramping to and fro, her muscles rippling and her glorious topaz eyes flashing furiously, Olympia filled the room with clamour and threatened Juan's life with flimsy furniture that she brandished in the air.

But Juan only lay in the corner where she had thrown him, and laughed and laughed.

VIII

This second insult – as she saw it – had a serious effect on Olympia. She had fallen suddenly in love with Juan, and suddenly her love turned to hatred. Having no sense of humour herself, she was mortally afraid of laughter. To her it always seemed a destructive force, and twice within a week she had been compelled to listen to laughter of the most violent kind. The first time was bad enough, for the dreadful laughter of an audience could easily kill an acrobat, or a dancer, or a singer. But Juan's laughter was worse, because she could not understand it.

When at last he had grown quiet – and everybody in the house was beating at their door before that happened – he had got into bed again, not daring to apologise for fear he should start to laugh once more, and Olympia, choking with rage but impotent because of her perplexity, had followed him, and put out the light, and lain in a silence that only her heavy breathing broke. It occurred to Juan that she might try to strangle him, and indeed she contemplated murder of some kind, but the effort of thinking made her drowsy and she fell asleep instead.

She woke with her anger set as in a mould. Juan tried to explain his unmannerliness, but Olympia would not listen. At the afternoon performance she sang flat, and in the evening she would not let Juan on to the stage. He, with nothing else to do, walked back to their lodgings and went early to bed.

When Olympia came back her anger had grown to such dimensions that she could barely restrain it. She hoped that Juan would be waiting for her return, to laugh at her again, and then her wrath would leap to battle like cavalry charging. But Juan slept; and sleep, when Olympia trumpeted for a fight, was insolence indeed.

She snatched the bedclothes off him. He lay on his right side, with his back towards her. Olympia stooped over him. His pyjamas were made of strong stuff. She gripped them at the waist, the double thickness of jacket and trousers between her teeth and a fold of Juan's skin as well, and lifted him as a dog would pick up an enormous bone. Juan woke with a cry of pain to find himself in an almost hopeless position, for Olympia had her hands free to guard herself when he tried to clutch her.

'What are you trying to do?' he demanded, and with an effort kept his voice calm.

Olympia growled and walked to the door. Juan caught at the door-posts but she beat his hands off.

In the house where they lodged there was a central well round which the staircase climbed, and their room was on the top floor. Olympia stepped deliberately toward the banister that guarded the well and Juan, seeing her intention, raised a loud shout for help. She tried to thrust him over the edge, but he caught at the rail and Olympia did not want to release her grip till he would fall clear. She hit his hands to make him let go.

'Help!' shouted Juan.

Doors opened on all sides. Poppy and her violinist, saxophone players, Buddy Hambone, Old Ollie Isaacs – everybody rushed out in shirt-tails or knickers, and seized Olympia and took hold of Juan, and pulled them back from the well, and exclaimed shrilly or harshly at so terrible a scene, and by their outcries attracted all manner of other people from the lower floors. Many of these had also been interrupted in their undressing, and the spectacle they presented was very indecorous.

Olympia let Juan go. She took two deep breaths and licked her lips, and then she shook off those who held her. They expostulated. Buddy Hambone told her to calm herself. Others offered similar advice, and the crowd was growing. Olympia looked about her. She stood a head taller than the chattering, excited, inquisitive throng.

'Bah!' she said in a tigress's voice, and clouted a saxophone player on the head, and hit Poppy's violinist in the face. Arms shot up to restrain her. She gripped two wrists in her left hand and two in her right, and pulled their owners towards her. Then she encircled their necks with her strong arms and banged their four heads together. The crowd sagged and swayed as those in front tried to escape and those behind pushed forward. There was a lot of noise – though Olympia herself fought in silence – and both men and women took their share of hard knocks. But no one even thought of calling the police.

They urged each other on to the attack, and Olympia buffeted them, knocked them down and trod on them, ripped their shirts off, tore their hair, and kicked their naked shins. The press was thickest in front of her own room. She forced her way through the crowd, hitting, using her elbows, knees, and feet. Two men and a woman fled before her into the room, whom she caught one by one and threw out. She stood in the doorway and confronted her assailants. Someone had scratched her face and the blood ran down it. But her adversaries too were bloody and torn and panting for breath.

Olympia's eyes shone as she looked at them. Her self-satisfaction was returning.

'And now you can all go to hell, you pack of yellow dawgs!' she shouted, and slammed the door.

Juan had taken no part in the brawl, but had found a quiet place in which to examine his side. Olympia's teeth had torn it and it was bleeding freely. He made a pad with a handkerchief and stopped the blood. Then he discovered that the crowd was preparing to force Olympia's door, and because he was tired of violence he pushed his way through them, and turned, and asked rudely, 'What's the sense in starting another row? Can't you leave her in peace now that she's left you?'

The crowd muttered, and fingered their bruised cheekbones, and pulled at their torn shirts.

Juan observed that he was in a heroic position; he was defending a woman against an angry mob; and the temptation to act up to the situation was irresistible.

'You won't get into this room while I'm here to stop you,' he said in a determined voice.

The crowd, quick to see the unreason of this remark, expostulated loudly and pointed out that they had originally come in response to Juan's cries for help. This was indisputable, and before he could think of an answer the door was unlocked and Olympia, who had been listening inquisitively, stood in the opening as fierce as ever.

'Say,' she demanded of Juan, 'where d'you get that stuff? D'you think I can't look after myself without a sap like you hanging around? Go chase yourself outa here, you big boob!'

The crowd was amused. They advised Juan to assert himself, and with shameless fickleness cheered Olympia's tirade. She, not satisfied with words, now began to throw all Juan's clothes out of the room. Suits, shirts, ties and socks flew out; hairbrushes, handkerchiefs and shoes followed them; and last of all came a big brown suitcase.

'There!' said Olympia, brushing her hands. 'Now beat it! I never want to see that pan of yours again!'

She closed the door with a bang.

Slowly the spectators returned to their rooms, while Buddy Hambone and some of the saxophone players helped Juan to gather up his clothes and pack them into the suitcase. He went into Buddy's room to dress and contrive a new bandage for his lacerated side. He decided to find other lodgings at once.

Buddy was morbidly fascinated by the marks of Olympia's teeth.

'She's a swell dame,' he sighed, 'if only she wasn't so darned strong.'

He was sorry to lose Juan's services in the band, but he was too frightened of Olympia to oppose her edict of expulsion. He shook hands and said good-bye facetiously: 'Well, don't do nothing I wouldn't do!'

Juan paid his bill, got a taxi, and drove to the best hotel in Cincinnati. He slept till noon of the following day and woke with a luxurious feeling of being alone and in a more comfortable room than he had occupied for some time. Solitude and comfort were the proper salves for such humiliation as he had suffered the previous night. Bodily comfort would always shrug its shoulders at wounded pride, and solitude could whisper, There's nobody here who saw your disgrace; why worry about a secret fall? And indeed, thought Juan, there's little chance of ever seeing those people again. I shall always remember that I have been carried between a female acrobat's teeth like a dog's bone, but I am unlikely to meet other people who remember and one's own knowledge should not embarrass one. What happened yesterday will not affect me to-morrow. I am different from a man whose habitation is settled, to whom yesterday is important since its deeds remain with him. But I can leave yesterday a hundred miles away, for I am a free man – or very nearly free.

Pertinent to this thought Juan got up to count his money and found that he had seven hundred dollars in traveller's cheques. Because Olympia disliked wasting money he had lived economically, almost within his salary as her partner and a member of the band, and so his mother's Christmas present and the bootleggers' dividend were practically intact. Seven hundred dollars was a comfortable sum. He recalled his intention, now two months old, to go south. The vaudeville route had taken him in the right direction, but very slowly. Now he decided to move quickly, to find a train that would take him straight to Charleston, or Savannah, or Miami, and waste no more time in cold grey weather but go and live happily in warm sunlight.

Over his lunch he read a newspaper which was full of a great event imminent in the capital city of Washington. The inauguration of a new President was to take place in three days' time, with all the pomp and circumstance proper to such an occasion. Washington was already full of soldiers and sailors practising for the parade, and of distinguished visitors come to acquire more distinction by their participation in such notable proceedings. Washington, said the newspapers, was at present the Mecca of America and the cynosure of the world.

This was enough to modify Juan's plans. Washington was not much more than four hundred miles away, and four hundred miles was a trifling distance in America. It would be foolish, he thought, to miss a Presidential inauguration when it was so near at hand. He would find out when there was a suitable train.

BOOK FOUR

IDYLL WITH VARIATIONS

I

THERE had been a Presidential campaign the previous autumn. The candidates were good men either of whom would have made an admirable President. Politically there was only one difference between them, and that was according to custom and perhaps even statutory: one was a Republican and the other a Democrat. And between the Republican and Democratic parties there was also but a single difference: one was in office, and the other out. In these circumstances the election had to be conducted on personal lines, and the personal differences between the candidates were many and varied. It was indeed a little strange, and perhaps a little depressing, to a student of Government to think that either of these men, who as men were the poles apart, would make a satisfactory President and that a hundred and twenty million people might live as comfortably and contentedly under one as under the other. But, of course, no one interested in politics ever considered such a thing.

Mr. Brown, for instance, the Democratic candidate, was a Wet, and Mr. Boomer, the Republican, was a Dry. But both were aware that whoever became President would preside over a country officially Dry but actually drinking as much as it could afford or its gastric mucosa dispose of without becoming perforated. So that made no difference. Then Mr. Brown was generally referred to by his Christian name, which was Mike, while Mr. Boomer was more respectfully called by his surname. This again was relatively unimportant to Government. Mr. Brown was a man of exceptional personal charm, and Mr. Boomer an engineer of singular ability and the architect, in the past, of great humanitarian enterprises. But either would find his personal opinions slighted and his suggestions disregarded by a stiff-necked and haughty Senate. So that made little difference. Then Mr. Brown was the son of extremely poor parents and he had risen entirely by his own ability; while Mr. Boomer had made his name in foreign countries and succeeded solely as the result of his own endeavours. So that each was an equally useful inspiration to the youth of America. And lastly Mr. Brown was a Catholic and Mr. Boomer a Quaker. Now as Mr. Boomer, being such, would not commit sins, and Mr. Brown, being a Catholic, would promptly confess his and receive absolution for them, that might not appear to be very important either. But it was.

For America is a very religious country in many ways, as well as being excessively irreligious in others, and even above its God – or any of its gods, for they are many – it cherishes its independence from the rest of the world. Knowing that only too well, certain unscrupulous Republicans whispered here and there through the land that it would be a bad day for America's churches – Methodist, Baptist, Presbyterian, Christian Science, Episcopal, Adventist, Mormon, and all the rest of them but one – should Mr. Brown become President. For Mr. Brown, they whispered snakishly, was a creature of the Vatican and, should he be elected, his master the Pope would promptly say good-bye to Rome and take a house in Washington, an apartment on Park Avenue, a camp in the Adirondacks, a lodge in the Rockies, and rule iron-handed over the United States with the despicable Mr. Brown as his satrap.

This whisper, cunningly disseminated, spread on the wind and became a shouting in the presbyteries and synods and church-halls and back alleys of the Protestant people of America. A rumour got about that the Papal Guard had mobilised and were doing gas-mask drill daily in preparation for the invasion of the United States. Patriots of every kind sprang to arms and denounced the Scarlet Woman and all her ways. The Daughters of the American Revolution and the Ku Klux Klan (two well-known secret orders) issued daily manifestoes, and a Baptist minister declared that the Pope was anti-Christ and Mr. Brown – saving his American blood – just as bad. This seemed to dispose of Mr. Brown's hopes of becoming President.

Undismayed, however, even by this deadly attack, the more desperate and conscienceless members of the Democratic Party invented some counter-slanders about Mr. Boomer and put them into rapid circulation. These alleged his affection for negroes. Now there are many million negroes in the United States, and many million white people who dislike them heartily, and not a few who are afraid of them. Cunning Democrats, then, ran about and whispered to such that Mr. Boomer was a nigrophile. His favourite dancing-partner, they said, was a very large negress. Every night he used to foxtrot with her. And his stenographer was also a negress, they averred, a very black one, and she read all his private letters. And should he become President he intended to make her brother Secretary of State for the Navy, and would probably create a few nigger admirals as well.

Furiously the Republicans denied these assertions, and categorically stated that Mr. Boomer had never, never, never foxtrotted with a negress. Nor even in quadrilles had there ever been so much as an octoroon in his set. But the very suspicion of such things lost the Republican party several million votes.

Between the Scarlet Woman and the Black, then, the contest became fairly warm, and not till the very last phase was the issue settled, and then the relative culture of the candidates became the deciding factor. It happened in this way:

Mr. Brown made a speech that was broadcast to an audience estimated at fifty million people, not counting Mexicans and Oklahoma Indians. In this speech he several times employed the word 'radio,' referring to the device by which his words were transmitted to so many listeners. But unfortunately he chose to pronounce the word 'raddio', with a very short *a*, whereas every one of the fifty million knew that the proper way to say it was 'radio,' with a long flat *a*. And as he repeated his initial blunder the audience in their many homes began to laugh at him, for all Americans are either well-educated men and women or bright children sitting close to the top of their class. And nothing, of course, moves well-educated people so swiftly to mirth as the spectacle of ignorance in others. So when Mr. Brown said 'raddio' for the fourth or fifth time there were peals of happy laughter all over America, and that night's work lost him many million votes.

The Democrats, however, knew that he still had a chance, for on the following evening Mr. Boomer was going to make a speech that would again have a fifty million audience, and they thought it just possible that he also would mispronounce an odd word or two, and so level the score. Eagerly they waited for his voice to come thrilling and throbbing out of the ether, mangling some simple word as it sped to Pacific Coast and Atlantic, to the Dakota prairies and the lush swamplands of Florida. But they were disappointed, for Mr. Boomer's speech contained very few words indeed. It was nearly all figures. The only remaining hope was that he might be guilty of miscalculation, and the Democrats prayed that this would be so. His speech ran something like this:

'In 1924 under a Republican administration the United States exported $7,363,011 worth of automobiles; $4,107,865 worth of locomotives; $20,103,719 reputed worth of cinema films; $2,304,108 worth of household appliances . . . amounting to a total of $5,000,983,010. In 1927, still under a Republican administration, we exported $9,461,023 worth of automobiles; $5,078,101 worth of locomotives; $35,765,113 reputed worth of cinema films; $3,105,678 worth of household appliances . . . amounting to a total of $9,163,045,500. That is an increase of $4,162,152,490, a gratifying result largely due to the integrity, industry, and commercial astuteness of Republican advisers. If you elect me as your President there will be a further increase of five thousand million dollars in our export trade in the next four years.'

All over the country, from Maine to Catalina Island, from the Dakotas to Palm Beach, men and women sat with paper and pencil jotting down these remarkable figures, adding up the one side, totting up the other, skilfully subtracting, checking the answer – and then from millions of throats rose the triumphant affirmative, 'He's right, he's right' – and from millions of others the surly admission, 'He's right.'

Mr. Boomer had done his sum correctly. He, like all good Americans, was an educated man. In this way he acquired many millions of votes and was duly elected President. . . .

Just before he left for Washington – while indeed he waited for a bell-boy to bring down his luggage – Juan was able to give some small assistance to a lady whose skirt had caught, and held her fast, in the revolving door of the hotel. She was a lady with a commanding appearance and a dignified bosom. Even when imprisoned in one quadrant of a revolving door she retained her dignity; she frowned, but her frown showed impatience, not perturbation; 'Tch!' she said, and her annoyance was at the door, not at herself. When Juan had released her she thanked him without effusion.

Her husband, standing outside, said 'Why don't you wear short skirts like all the rest of the women?'

'I'm past sixty and I dress to please myself,' she replied with composure.

Her husband was a genial, pot-bellied old gentleman with a red face, twinkling eyes, and white hair. He winked to Juan and said, 'That door couldn't catch a flapper's skirt without jumping its grooves.' Then he followed his wife into a cab.

They also were going to Washington, and in the club car at the end of the train Juan met the old gentleman again. He was reading a novel, but when Juan sat down beside him he closed it decisively as though glad of the excuse, and said, 'Another of these belly-aching German war books. Who started the War, anyway?'

'I forget the latest theory,' said Juan.

'Theory?' bellowed the old gentleman. 'You don't need theories about a thing like that. It's as plain as a pikestaff. It's as – you're not a German, are you?'

'I'm English.'

'Then you ought to know better than to talk about theories.'

The old gentleman was chewing tobacco – his quid did not impede conversation – and now he wanted to spit. He looked for a cuspidor. There was none in sight, and his mouth was full. He showed some annoyance and glared up and down the car until the man opposite observed the situation and uncrossed his legs to reveal the spittoon which they had hidden. The old gentleman spat hard and true, a long brown jet that hit the very centre of the cuspidor. The man between whose feet it lay comfortably recrossed his legs.

The old gentleman asked Juan how long he had been in America and what he was doing.

'I was at Motley, for some time,' said Juan.

'And why did you go there?'

'For various reasons. A family connexion was the real one, I suppose.'

The old gentleman's eyebrows shot up. 'A family connexion?'

'My mother was a Motley – and still is, curiously enough.'

'Which one?'

'Charlotte.'

'Lowell's daughter who went to England and married her cousin? For the Lord's sake! My wife was at your mother's wedding, boy. Who are you – Noel or Juan?'

'Juan.'

'That's a bad name to give a boy. What did your mother want to rake up that old scandal for?'

'Fun, I expect.'

The old gentleman told Juan that his name was Carey Dekker. He was a former Governor of West Carolina. And, he said, Juan must now come and meet his wife, who would be delighted beyond measure to find that their acquaintance of the morning was the son of her friend Charlotte Motley whose wedding she had attended; for Charlotte's Aunt Abbie was her school-time friend and had insisted on her going, and then the Bloods – Harley and Lettice – had travelled with her –

'But what's that to you? I'm chattering, just chattering, and you'll have to hear it all from my wife anyhow, so you'd better come right along.'

And so, in the Dekker's compartment, Juan listened for more than an hour to Mrs. Dekker's description of his mother's wedding and the guests thereat, and answered a hundred questions very tactfully, and caused great astonishment by admitting that so far he had been to see none of his American relations.

'You haven't been to visit your grandfather and grandmother, or your great-aunt Abbie Rothmer, or your Uncle Edward, or your Uncle Bryant and Aunt Ruth Maitland Motley, and your cousins Clifford and Francis, and Marcia and Sylvia and Russell?' Mrs. Dekker looked over her bosom with eyes of wide amazement.

Juan explained that when he landed in New York they were all holiday-making in distant parts of the continent, and since leaving Motley he had really had no opportunity for visiting.

'Of course,' he added, 'I do know most of them. My grandfather Lowell was in England just after the war, and Uncle Bryant and Aunt Ruth stayed at Mallieu a year or two later. The two girls were with them – Marcia and Sylvia – but they were very young and I didn't see much of them.'

'They're very lovely girls,' said Mrs. Dekker impressively.

'It would be worth your while to see a bit more of them now,' added the Governor with a ponderous wink.

'You know a lot about my relations,' said Juan.

'I have known your great-aunt Abbie Rothmer for fifty

years,' Mrs. Dekker explained, 'and I should consider myself remiss indeed if I didn't know *everything* about all my friends. And I should think the worse of them if they forgot the names of my aunts and cousins and children and grand-nieces, yes, and my servants too.'

'We're interested in people,' said the Governor, 'and in the South we've still got time to write letters and read them.'

'And in West Carolina we do know who our grandfathers were, and we like to know about other people's as well. Not that your family had anything to do with the South, except your mother's great-aunt Rachel Legaré in Charleston, poor thing. Are you going to see her?'

'I had thought of it,' said Juan.

'Be sure you do, for she's the sweetest old lady I've ever known. She won't have anything to do with the Yankee Motleys, but you're English, so you'll be all right.'

'Where are you going to stay in Washington?' asked the Governor.

'I don't know yet,' said Juan.

'Then it's a good thing that we met you, for if you haven't reserved a room you'd never be able to get one now. Washington's just as full as an egg. You come along with us to the Mayfair and we'll fix you up.'

'That's extraordinarily kind of you!'

'Your great-aunt Abbie and I were at school together,' said Mrs. Dekker, 'and if she wouldn't do as much for a grand-nephew of mine I'd want to know what was wrong with her. Friendship has its obligations, and personally I love to meet them. Now tell me, does your mother think of coming to America while you're here?'

II

The Mayfair Hotel was a huge pompous building, its opulent main floor crowded with guests, its elevators full of more guests, its restaurants and coffee-rooms constantly busy, and bell-boys always running here and there or calling people's names in a loud piercing voice. Juan got a small bedroom in the Dekkers' suite and was very comfortable there.

Washington, he found, was instantly recognisable as a national capital. Its architecture was dignified and official. There were open spaces well-gardened and overlooked by numerous statues. Clearly its growth had never been straitened by commercial pressure, but was moulded by art and taught in lordly ways. . . Anyone would recognise Washington as a capital city, but no one would guess that it was the American capital, for it looked European. There was little of the towering rectangularity of New York or Chicago or Detroit, but plenty of handsome curves, balconies, dignity happily rounded and often sustained by portly columns.

Even the rain – for it was raining – seemed more amiable in consequence of such stately flexures, and fell in kindlier fashion on the dome of the Capitol than it ever showed to the angles and stiff sides of a skyscraper street. . . .

The Governor and Mrs. Dekker were attending a semi-official dinner party and Juan supposed that he would be left alone on the evening before Inauguration Day. But the Governor had no intention of leaving his newly-found guest without suitable entertainment, and in the late afternoon he introduced Juan to three acquaintances whom he had found in the hotel: Senator Auber of Minnetonka, Mr. Boles of Baltimore, and Colonel Handyman of the National Guard.

'These boys will look after you,' he said, 'They're all dining here, and they've got a friend coming – Alfred Adelaide.'

'I've heard of him.'

'That's not difficult,' said the Governor. 'Well, I hope they give you a good time. You can depend on the Senator's whisky, but don't play poker with him.'

The Senator was flattered, but protested that he played poker very indifferently and acually disliked the idea of winning money at cards – and indeed he was a solemn pious-looking man, very unlike a gambler in appearance. The Governor winked and called him an old hypocrite. ('So he is,' he whispered to Juan.) Mr. Boles, a solid man, remarked that hypocrisy was only another aspect of statesmanship, and Colonel Handyman, who was very untidy and badly dressed for a soldier, said that during the war he had often played poker for extravagantly high stakes. Twenty minutes was spent in such conversation as this, and then the Governor had to go and get dressed; and taking Juan with him said confidentially, 'They're not just the brightest conversationalists in America, but they're the best I could find for you at short notice. Everybody's dining out to-night. You may find Adelaide amusing, though. I never read his stuff myself but he's got a big public.'

Though comparatively few people had seen him, Mr. Adelaide was one of the best-known men in the United States. He was a journalist. Every day he wrote a newspaper column of topical criticism – ten little paragraphs that might be advice to doctors, sermonettes, or impressions of an aeroplane journey – and as this column was syndicated it appeared simultaneously in a hundred different papers all over the country. Mr. Adelaide was an ardent patriot. He believed that America was not only the largest and richest state in the world, but the most artistic, humane, and intellectually enlightened as well, and this made him very scornful of other nations. He did not, of course, ignore them. He frequently mentioned the European countries, to remark in happy conclusion how much better it was to live in America. In spite of the fact that this blessedness was his he was not altogether a happy man, for his patriotism was continually exasperated by thinking about the British Navy and the continuance of the British raj in India. Because of this he was hawk-eyed for signs of decadence in Britain, and being ingenious as well as patriotic, and credulous of marvels even as he was omniscient, his column was frequently filled with such matters as:

'There is a cow on Mr. So-and-So's ranch in California which holds the world's record for production of milk. Every day last year this cow produced three and a half gallons of Grade A certified bacteria-proof milk. And not only last year but *every day for the last three years* it has done this, without missing a day. No other cow in any country in the world can equal this record.

'Long ago "Merrie England" used to be famous for its cows, but English cows, like the British Navy, are not what they used to be. They do not give as much milk as American cows, and what milk they do give is not so good. England can still do many things, but she is losing her prowess in the dairy as well as her hold on her colonies.

'The population of China is more than 400,000,000. This is a very large number of people, but their individual purchasing power is low. Millions of coolies in China live and die without ever seeing a motor car, and many millions more *would* die without ever seeing one were it not for the genius of American engineers and the industry of American business men. Because of these two factors at least sixty per cent. of the people of China now know what an automobile looks like. So our civilisation benefits the whole world.'

Mr. Adelaide's appearance was disappointing. Juan had expected that the highest-paid journalist in the world – his salary was $150,000 a year – would be a notable man to look at: something of a prophet, steely as young Napoleon, eager as

Shelley and like him showing in every gesture his soaring impatience. But Mr. Adelaide looked like none of these. He was curiously indescribable. He seemed to have collected his features, his clothes, and everything about him in a haphazard way and let them grow together without ever having been able to make a satisfactory whole of them. He might have borrowed unremarkable items – a nose, a pair of eyes, a dinner-jacket, and so on – from various unremarkable people and forgotten to return them. He was like a composite photograph of some hundred nonentities, and Juan found it impossible to remember his appearance for even a minute. While talking to Senator Auber he would hear the columnist's voice and think perplexedly, What does he look like? A few minutes later, listening perhaps to Mr. Boles, his attention would again be distracted by some statement of Adelaide's, and again he would try to recall his appearance. But it was useless. The image would not stick. Only the voice was unforgettable, and that was like a huge cracked bell.

When dinner was over there fell a brief expectant silence during which everybody glanced at the Senator and glanced away again. He at last cleared his throat and said, 'Well, gentlemen, I'm not a drinking man, as I think you know, but the weather's inclement and I happen to have a bottle or two of rye in my room. Would you care to come up and sample it?'

Everybody rose with alacrity and on their way to the elevator the Senator told a bell-boy that he wanted a couple of siphons of soda-water. When these arrived they slightly diluted the whisky that, not to waste time, had already been poured out, and drank the health of the incoming President of the United States.

'And here's a continuance of our national prosperity,' exclaimed Mr. Boles.

'You can't stop it,' said Mr. Adelaide.

'Not under Boomer you can't,' declared the Senator. 'Now if Brown had got in there might have been a different story.

He might have declared himself in favour of repealing the Eighteenth Amendment, but Boomer won't stand for any monkey tricks with Prohibition. No, sir. He told me so himself. Prohibition's safe for the next four years, and so long as we have Prohibition the country will remain prosperous.'

'Well spoken, Senator,' said Mr. Adelaide, and emptied his glass. 'Do you know,' he went on, 'that Prohibition has diverted fifteen billion dollars from the liquor trade in less than ten years' time? Instead of being wasted on drink that vast sum has been used for productive and constructive buying. Just to give you an example: In 1919 there were two thousand electric refrigerators in the United States. To-day, under Prohibition, there are a million and a quarter. In 1919 there were just a million electric washing-machines, and to-day there are no less than six million. That's what Prohibition does. Think of it, gentlemen! There are few homes to-day too humble for an electric washing-machine, an electric refrigerator, and a radio, and all these civilising, almost cultural, influences are bought with that fifteen billion dollars that might have been thrown away on rum!'

'That certainly does make you think,' said the Colonel.

'Fifteen billion dollars!' sighed Mr. Boles. . . .

Conversation depended on finance, politics, and personalities. Juan heard sententious assertions like 'Stocks haven't begun to discount prosperity' and 'This is a new era in investments.' He half-listened to dull scandals about an oil magnate, a Presbyterian bishop, and a lady who had been friendly with the last President but one. The Senator declared that the Senate did more legislating than the House, and was altogether more important. He spoke of the nation's pulse. . . . Juan wondered if words meant anything at all. Certainly they rarely meant as much as their users thought, and often they were meaningless as a bullfrogs' chorus. Nine-tenths of all words were parrot-noises, not weighed, savoured, and tested, but merely repeated; a token coinage, defaced by long usage; there were whole sentences that lay on the surface of public memory and were paid out ten thousand times a day – flipped off the tongue, rebounding from the tympanum – without a thought to give them life; and to nine-tenths of this vain nine-tenths no one listened. So that it was doubly vain. A minute disturbance in the air. *Brek-ek-ek-ex*, *koax*, *koax*. 'The Senate is, if anything, a deliberative body, and by virtue of its deliberative powers a safeguard of liberty. . . I want to go on record as saying. . . . They accorded me a like honour. . . . The mind of the people. . . .'

An hour was spent in this way. Everything the Senator and his guests said they had said at previous times and would repeat on future occasions. . . . Men talked because men had the capacity for speech as monkeys had for swinging by their tails. Talk passed the time away that would otherwise hang like a millstone about a man's neck. Men swung from day to day by their long prehensile tongues. . . . And not content with speech alone men had discovered the processes of fermentation and distillation, and found in alcohol time's perfect solvent. Minutes dissolved in it like sugar in hot water. It melted hours away. A whole evening might be drawn into a bottle as though it were the model of a sailing-ship. . . : Pleased with his fancy Juan sat up and began to pay more attention to the conversation in which, despite his disillusioned attitude to conversation, he now wished to have a share.

'We're a great country,' the Senator was saying. 'Fill up your glasses and drink hearty.'

'This is very good whisky,' remarked the Colonel.

'We've got good bootleggers in Washington,' said the Senator.

Mr. Adelaide asked Juan what he thought of America.

'It's rather difficult to put into a few words,' Juan began, 'but I've come to the somewhat unusual opinion –'

'Of course,' said Mr. Adelaide, 'it must seem unusual to you as to anyone coming from the Old World. You see that the American people have created a new heaven and a new earth, and you're rightly astonished. We have thrown away the old things, and in their place has come a glory never previously enjoyed by any people of our world.'

'That isn't precisely what I meant to say,' objected Juan, but Mr. Adelaide motioned for silence and continued:

'Last year the women of America spent sixty billion dollars. A great deal of that money bought what you would term luxuries, but what the Old World considers luxuries we regard as necessities. Now a million dollars is a lot of money, and a billion dollars is a thousand times as much, a very great deal of money indeed. But sixty billions is colossal. It would be an incredible sum to anyone who did not know the inexhaustible wealth of America. Would the women of France or Germany or England spend so much in a year? I don't think so. I don't think so for a minute. In fact I know they wouldn't, because they haven't got it to spend. Why then should our statesmen pay any attention to what France and Germany and England think and do?'

Mr. Adelaide poured himself a little more whisky and looked triumphantly at Juan.

Senator Auber was telling Mr. Boles and Colonel Handyman the secrets of political success:

'It has been my life-long habit,' he said, 'to be out of bed by six-thirty. I take a short walk before breakfast, which consists of a little fruit, not more than half a cup of coffee, and a home-made cereal made by boiling together two parts of bran with one part of oatmeal. Plenty of roughage, you see. After this frugal meal I exercise on a vibrating-machine which I keep in my room. That starts the day well. And as to rules of conduct for the day's work, I have for long observed the wisdom of frequently differing with my subordinates but always loyally supporting my superiors.'

'Very sound advice and a very good regimen,' said Mr. Adelaide, who had pricked up his ears at the Senator's mention of breakfast foods, for dietetics was yet another of his favourite topics. 'I hope, Senator, that you don't neglect spinach. Spinach is a very valuable food indeed. I was recommending it to Bishop Vent of the Methodist Church only the other day. He has been having gastric trouble, and his doctor put him on a milk diet. But I told him that was all wrong. Man cannot live on milk alone. Only the new-born child can do that, because of the peculiar constitution of the infantile liver. But adults need iron, and spinach is just full of iron. "Eat spinach," was what I told the Bishop. "Don't disregard your doctor's advice, because every American professional man has had an excellent education, knows what he is talking about, and is worthy of our deepest respect. But you add spinach to your diet and see if you don't feel the better for it." The Bishop was much struck with what I said.'

'That reminds me of what I was going to tell you,' said Juan, 'when you asked me, some time ago, what I thought of America.'

'Just a minute,' interrupted Mr. Adelaide. 'This matter of spinach has another aspect. Everybody who eats it has a double satisfaction. He is doing good not only to himself but to the spinach-growers, and as American spinach is the best in the world – no other kind contains so much iron – its growers deserve our hearty encouragement. Now Mr. Motley, what were you going to say?'

'It doesn't really matter,' said Juan.

'Everything matters,' said Mr. Adelaide severely. 'If it didn't matter our Creator wouldn't have taken the trouble to create it.'

Colonel Handyman sipped his whisky in a meditative fashion. 'Is that story about Judge Moper's party true?' he asked. 'Of course it's been hushed up, but I hear that several of the guests are still blind, and the doctors have given up hope.'

'Quite true,' said the Senator. 'It's nothing short of a

tragedy. There are three of them stone-blind. Young Moper, a most promising boy; his uncle from Kansas, a worthy man indeed; and young Moper's fiancée, a charming girl, I'm told. That's what comes of employing an unknown bootlegger. There was wood-alcohol in the stuff they were drinking.'

'It paralyses the optic nerve,' declared Mr. Boles.

'But can you really rely on any bootlegger?' asked Juan. 'Isn't there always the risk of an accident? There might be wood-alcohol in this whisky for all we know.'

'For heaven's sake don't even suggest such a thing,' exclaimed Mr. Adelaide, and emptied his glass with a shudder. 'Blindness! I can't bear to think of it.'

'You're safe enough with this,' said the Senator.

'It doesn't taste quite as good as it did a minute ago,' said the Colonel.

'Do you mean that?' asked Mr. Adelaide nervously.

'Nonsense,' said Mr. Boles. 'He's taking you for a ride.'

Mr. Adelaide slowly recaptured confidence while Mr. Boles described a crisis on the Stock Exchange. It was an exciting story about traders who rode a stock for the last penny, and people who hung on for a long pull, and stocks that fell two or three, or even five, points between sales, and selling orders that piled up over-night; about stocks that sold 'at the market' and others that went to the traditional thousand. What it was all about Juan had no idea, but he listened attentively, nodded his head with apparent intelligence, and applauded the dénouement. . . . The whisky was working in his veins, carrying its familiar cargo of confidence to every parish and hundred of his body. His blood, lighter and more valiant than strictly sober blood, came adventurously from his heart, passed carelessly through his arteries, thrust with unfailing pertinacity into the backwater of meagre capillaries, and returned with bland assurance through canal-like veins. He felt that he could meet a financier on his own ground. He would have debated the Higher Criticism with a bishop, military strategy with a general. Very soon, he determined, as soon as he got a chance, he was going to tell these eminent Americans what he thought about America. . . .

'Wealth in the service of humanity,' said the Senator dreamily. 'That is what I live to see. Perhaps you'll open another bottle, Colonel?'

Mr. Adelaide assured him that that ideal was fast approaching. 'Last year there were 11,000 cases of murder in America. Out of that number there were only 249 convictions and thirteen judicial executions. So our courts daily become humanitarian and men deal more charitably with their brothers' frailties. Now as Emerson once prophesied, "The quality of mercy is not strained".'

'Does this bottle come from the same place as the others?' asked Mr. Boles. 'It seems to have a different flavour.'

Mr. Adelaide tasted it anxiously. 'I hope it's all right,' he said, and tasted it again. 'It's very strong, isn't it?'

'Of course it's all right,' said the Senator testily. 'You've made them all nervous with your suggestion about wood-alcohol, Motley.'

'If there's anyone who can be relied on to have good liquor it's a United States Senator,' said the Colonel gallantly, and filled all the glasses.

'Hear, hear!' said Juan, and bowed to his host.

'Humanity,' mused the Senator again. 'The very sound of the word is inspiring. When you consider the mighty force that holds the universe together, and remember that the same force also shapes the tear-drop on a mother's face – h'm. Well, it's a very illuminating comparison and should teach us all a lesson. Don't you wish, Mr. Motley, that your country would adopt a more humane attitude to India, for example? What a lesson to the world if the British could be induced to deal with the poor Hindus as we have dealt with our Indians.'

Juan was somewhat startled by this suggestion, for he knew that nearly all the North American Indians had been killed off, and Senator Auber seemed too mild a man to be advocating a Hindu pogrom. Nor had he, of course, any such idea in his head.

'Don't you think that those mild-mannered people ought to be left in peace,' he asked, 'as we have left our surviving Indians in peace, on suitable reservations, to live their lives without interference and in accordance with their own spiritual values? I think so. In fact I mean to introduce a measure in the Senate at the earliest opportunity to consider – in the friendliest terms, need I say? – the restoration of India's independence on lines such as I have indicated.'

'What is your opinion about that, Mr. Motley?' asked Mr. Adelaide, licking his lips. 'The British are facing a very serious crisis in India, aren't they?'

'I don't think so,' said Juan coldly, 'and in any case I should prefer to tell you what I feel about the United States.'

The Senator and Mr. Auber smiled in a superior way but Juan's manner prevented them from interrupting. – It was curious that a little whisky often made him philosophical; a little more, combative; and still a little more, pontifical. – He continued:

'I am usually a silent man. I seldom talk at any length. I see all kinds of things and I reach very interesting conclusions about them, which I generally keep to myself. But now I want to explain why I cannot subscribe to the opinion that you and most Americans hold, namely, that America leads the world in all the arts of civilisation. The foundation of your belief is an abundance throughout the country of mechanical contrivances such as aeroplanes, bath-rooms, and gramophones. Such things, I admit, are modern enough. But in spite of them America is really a quaint old-fashioned land. Personally I like it. But that does not blind me to the fact that it is the last abode of romance and other mediaeval phenomena. There is, for instance, more crime in America than England has known since the Wars of the Roses; your people are as apathetic about the central government as serfs and villeins were; you still resort to patronage and jobbery to get anything done; you believe in soothsayers and alchemists so long as they speak from Wall Street; the Volstead Act is a class measure like the Plantagenet game-laws; universities encourage a tiresome mediaeval industry; your newspapers are as full of personalities as the Prologue to the Canterbury Tales, and your casual friendliness – a charming trait, I admit – is very like that of Chaucer's pilgrims.'

At this point, while Juan was taking a deep breath and everybody else was clamorously interrupting, contradicting, and protesting, a sudden violent blackness descended on the room, and with it silence.

The silence endured for a moment only, and then Mr. Adelaide's voice rose in a terrified scream, 'I'm blind, I'm blind, O God, I'm blind!'

Juan blinked in the darkness. Shadowy blue and green suns floated before his eyes. Could it be true? He didn't think so, and yet he felt a prickle of fear.

'Oh, oh, oh, I'm blind!' wailed Mr. Adelaide. 'I *knew* I was drinking wood-alcohol!'

'Nonsense!' shouted Mr. Boles, the Colonel, and the Senator all together. 'The lights have gone out. That's all.'

Juan laughed. 'Of course they have,' he said in a confident voice.

'Can't you see either? Then you're all blind too. Our eyes have been taken from us' – sobs interrupted Mr. Adelaide – 'as young Moper's were, because we've broken the law. Blind, blind! And I've been a sinner all my life. I've encouraged pride and haughtiness, I've told lies, I've used my neighbours despitefully, and now I'm blind. Oh, oh, oh!'

'For heaven's sake be quiet,' said the Senator angrily. 'Hasn't anybody got matches?'

But nobody could find any matches except Juan, who promptly put them in his pocket, while Mr. Adelaide, who had drunk more than anyone else, shouted:

'I won't be quiet! I'm going to repent. I'm repenting now, because I've told lies and fomented discord among nations. I've spread slander and murdered God's truth. I've been a fool and a sinner and God has punished me with blindness. I'll never write another word, never, never, never, if God will give me back my sight. Oh dear, oh dear, oh dear!'

There was a sound of paper being torn. Mr. Adelaide was destroying the notes that he had in his pocket; notes written to fill front-page columns in newspapers all over the country. Then, thrilling the darkness, the telephone rang, and the Colonel, who was nearest, stumbled towards it and found the receiver.

'Hullo,' he said. 'What's that? A fuse? Yes, just what I thought. All right, thank you.'

He spoke to the unseen room. 'A fuse has blown. The light will be on again in a minute.'

The light raced his words, and everybody blinked in the unexpected brilliance. Mr. Adelaide, gaping of mouth and eye, stared round him. His hair stood on end and his cheeks were beslabbered with tears. He stammered and stuttered, and first a look of childish joy, then of shame and humiliation, crossed his face. It was noticeable indeed that everybody was now painfully sober, though a minute before they had been very animated.

'Well, Adelaide, and what does it feel like to be blind?' asked Mr. Boles cruelly.

The columnist sniffed and gulped, opened his mouth like a small kitten trying to say *miaow* – but for a second or two no sound comes – you see a pink emptiness, a vainly curving tongue – and then there is a feeble innominate squeak.

'E-e-eh,' said Mr. Adelaide.

He got noisily out of his chair, his limbs still shaking, and dashed from the room.

The Colonel and Mr. Boles laughed unkindly, and the Senator said, 'He never could carry his liquor.'

Juan thoughtfully picked up some of the scraps of paper which Mr. Adelaide had torn and scattered on the floor.

On one fragment he read: '. . . forty-eight states without a trade-barrier between them. What would Europe not give to enjoy such a position?' On another: 'When we can afford to build as many cruisers, battleships, and submarines as we like, why should we listen to any pleas for the reduction of armaments?' And on a third: 'All honour to Mrs. Una Hackett, of Bowling, Ky., who has just given birth to her second set of triplets in twelve months. Six children in a year is a good record, not likely to be equalled outside America.'

III

At breakfast the Governor and Mrs. Dekker were too busy with anticipations of the day's ceremony to examine Juan very closely on his evening's entertainment. They asked him how he liked Senator Auber and whether Mr. Adelaide had been good company; but before he could reply they bade each other hurry, for they were late, and the streets would be so crowded that no one could say how long it would take to get to the Capitol, where Mr. Boomer was to become President Boomer; and then they made clucking deprecatory noises about the weather, for the rain had fallen all night and was still falling steadily, sometimes blown aslant by the wind, sometimes descending in straight lines, but never growing thinner or promising to stop. The parade would be ruined, said the Governor. All the poor soldiers! exclaimed Mrs. Dekker. And the sailors too, she added, though they would be used to water, of course, and might not mind it so much.

The streets were full of motor cars, shining-wet, and people who carried dripping umbrellas. It was not far to the Capitol, but it took the Dekkers and Juan a long time to reach it and find their seats where so many were bent on the same errand.

Over the broad flight of steps leading down from the Capitol a platform had been built and an open pavilion erected in which Mr. Boomer would take the oath. On either side of the pavilion were seats for privileged people – ambassadors and embassy staffs, senators, members of the new and old cabinets, governors of states, and so forth – while before it, making a half-moon in the plaza, stretched a huge amphicircle of benches almost covered by a black roof of umbrellas.

In due time the old President and the new arrived, with the Chief Justice and many other important people, and Mr. Boomer kissed the Bible and loudly answered 'I do!' to a question which the Chief Justice asked him, and so by the grace of the People became successor to Washington and Lincoln and tenant of their White House.

When the ceremony was over the Dekkers returned to their motor car and drove to another erection of benches beside the White House where they settled to watch the parade. Ever since the day when as a small boy he had seen English soldiers swinging endlessly down a road in Gloucestershire, the sight of troops on the march had been to Juan one of the most exciting of all spectacles, and now he bent forward eagerly to watch the American army salute its new President.

Because of the rain the soldiers wore greatcoats which made their movements ponderous, and they marched in column of platoons – or its American equivalent – so that the parade, with its broad frontage and rain-darkened khaki, seemed like an avalanche, a huge heavy thing not easily stopped, that rumbled on and on and on. Horse, foot, and guns they came, an army with banners under the grey sky. At regular intervals a band appeared, bravely puffing and blowing as they marched, rolling a little in their stride or trumpeting at ease on horseback. . . . Here was a regiment that wore broad-brimmed hats and marched with an easier, prouder swing than the others.

'Marines,' said the Governor.

Their N.C.O.'s were hard-bitten men, like a cross between

cowboys and centurions. After them came a still livelier band and sailors in white caps and blue uniforms that were not spoiled by the rain. . . . And then more khaki, more and more of it, till, beautiful among so much drabness, scarlet shone, white-belted scarlet tunics, and blue tunics, white breeches, busbies and shakos. These were the volunteer militia regiments in old-fashioned uniforms.

'The Richmond Blues,' said the Governor proudly. 'The Connecticut Foot Guards.'

But khaki was the dominant colour of the parade, khaki that absorbed the rain and marched on with sombre strength. Mrs. Dekker grew a little tired of watching its recurrent monotony.

'I shan't be sorry to leave Washington to-morrow,' she said. 'This dreadful weather does make one appreciate Florida. I was very unwilling to leave it, but the Governor had business to do in Cincinnati, and then it was our duty, I suppose, to come here and see Mr. Boomer's apotheosis. Not that our presence does him any particular good. . . .'

Negro troops were passing, some of whom grinned broadly with unsoldierly happiness. And overhead, out of the farther mist, without warning came a great grey airship with a wreath of cloud about its nose, followed by two smaller chubbier airships. Because of the wind they had difficulty in keeping their course. They were blown sideways. . . .

'Why don't you come back to Florida with us?' asked Mrs. Dekker. 'We're motoring down from here. We drove up ten days ago and took the train from here to Cincinnati because it was turning cold. You really must see the South.'

'I should like that very much,' said Juan. 'Who are these people with umbrellas?'

A company of men dressed formally in morning clothes was passing. They marched in a spirited manner, swinging their unoccupied arms and carrying over their tall hats pink and white umbrellas.

'I'm sure I don't know,' Mrs. Dekker admitted, 'but the Governor will tell you.'

'The Republican Club of Pittsburgh, or Indianapolis, or – I don't know where,' said the Governor.

'Carey, my dear,' said Mrs. Dekker, 'Mr. Motley is coming to Florida with us.'

'Well, that's fine. I was going to suggest it myself. I was, I assure you. But what's coming now?'

'It's charming of you,' said Juan, still somewhat surprised but very pleased by the suggestion, which promised to look after his immediate future in the happiest way possible.

Cowboys rode past, splendidly mounted, and after the cowboys Red Indians, some on horseback with bright feather head-dresses, and others, showing less spirit and no thought of incongruity, packed tightly in motor cars. Then, on a grey rain-soaked pony, came a solitary figure. He was naked and arrogant, and as he rode aloof from those behind and those in front something cold and lonely broke the solidity of the procession. Among the spectators astonishment bore him ghostly company. The rain glistened on his brown skin, his naked thighs gripped the flanks of his rough-clipt pony, and three feathers drooped from his wet black hair. He, in so great a procession, yet seemed alone. He looked neither to left nor to right, unaware of the crowd, not come to do honour but to show himself and say, 'I am America. I am he who first saw the caravels of Columbus, who first talked with the English in Virginia, who fought Spaniards and Dutchmen, French and English. It is my blood that paints the maples red and glorifies the crimson sumach. All else that comes here changes, but I have not changed. Yet am I America.'

The procession passed. . . .

'Charleston is a little off the main road to Florida, but we might go that way to see your Aunt Rachel Legaré.' Mrs. Dekker had not been thinking about the Indian – she had seen Indians before and rated them much lower than negroes –

for her mind was occupied with plans for her guest's entertainment. She was one of those busy kindly women who, liking such part of humanity as decent manners recommend, find hospitality a natural virtue, and by their deft practice make it one of the most agreeable of all virtues. Already she was considering which of the personable young women in Miami she would invite to her first party; which of the young men Juan might enjoy riding and swimming and playing tennis with. . . .

And the rain fell as though it would never stop. The gutters were full of water, roofs glimmered wetly in the grey afternoon, and every road was washed clean. When darkness came and the city grew quieter it seemed to fall more heavily still, making a liquid noise as it sifted through the air and splashed in countless tiny fountains on the pavement, or beat insistently at window-panes. Nor was the deluge confined to Washington, for nearly all the Eastern states were being simultaneously pelted with storms, some of which came from the north and some from the mountains.

'We're going to see floods if this doesn't stop,' said the Governor.

'It will be fine to-morrow,' said his wife in the comfortable voice of one whose wishes were generally respected. And in the morning she was able to say, 'I told you so,' for the rain stopped for a little while and they drove off in high spirits, crossing the Potomac under a watery sun that made everything shine like old silver; and they felt assured of a pleasant journey.

But they were wrong. By midday it was raining again. The red soil of Virginia was sodden. Its woods, that grew carelessly in great irregular patches, hung heavily under their weight of water, and all the rolling haphazard countryside that might have looked so gay was listless and dull.

'Usually it has an untidy light-hearted appearance,' said Mrs. Dekker, 'like a cavalier in his shirt-sleeves, with his hair unpowdered and a glass – or even a bottle – in his hand. Such an attractive country; a little harum-scarum, a little dreamy, and able to make you feel very happy. I'm sorry you're not seeing its nicest complexion.'

'But it's better to see it like this than not at all,' added the Governor. 'This is the best of America, in spite of all they may say in the West. When I think of America I think of the thirteen original states. They gave the world a new and splendid gift: not only the ideal, but the visible fact of freedom. They enriched the whole spirit of the world. But the rest of America has pandered to its body.'

The Governor's motor car was a large enclosed Rolls-Royce. It travelled smoothly and almost noiselessly except for the susurrus of its tyres on the wet paved road. The Governor sat in front beside his chauffeur. One side of his face bulged with a quid of tobacco. At intervals he spat, neither inelegantly on the floor nor vulgarly out of the window, but into a plated spittoon, let into the floor, that was perhaps the most unusual fitting on his car. Now and then he turned and spoke to his wife and Juan, jocosely, wittily, wisely, or to reiterate, 'We're going to see floods, I tell you.' For confirmation he pointed to streams that were already bank-high, and to rivers swollen and discoloured.

They lunched at Richmond and drove on. The red earth of Virginia gave place to the sandy soil of North Carolina. The country grew flatter. The rain still fell. And Mrs. Dekker questioned Juan pertinaciously on the ramifications of the English Motleys: Sir Hildebrand's brothers and sisters, Oswald, Caroline, Cuthbert, and Anne. Poor pimply Cuthbert who had died on a South African kopje, Oswald who lived curiously in Capri, Caroline who had married into the Church, and Anne whose husband was killed at Cape Hellas. And then, still unwearied, she asked about the families of that Thomas who had been Collector of Cooch-Parwanee, and Major-General William Motley, and the Australian Motleys, and other houses into which the daughters of old Horatio had married. Of Noel and

Rhea she seemed to know more than Juan. Afterwards she told him further things about the American Motleys, and her own family, scattered north and west so that she, who had been accustomed always to a house full of people, was now a lonely woman – or would be did she not bestir herself – and the ties that bound the Dekkers to the Motleys were such and such and so and so. . . .

'But what do you care about all these people?' she exclaimed at last. 'I must have been boring you for hours. Now let me tell you about your Aunt Rachel Legaré in Charleston – I think we should go by Charleston, don't you, Carey? – for her story is really interesting.'

While Mrs. Dekker was composing her thoughts for this narration, however, they drove into the small and lovely town of Raleigh – lovely even in the rain – where they had decided to spend the night, and where they heard disquieting tales of rivers already in flood and still rising. But the Governor was sure that no advantage lay in deferring their journey, and so they set off again in the morning with some expectation of adventure and their eyes alert for strange sights.

But nothing untoward befell or confronted them for some time, and Mrs. Dekker could tell the story of Aunt Rachel without interruption; how as a girl of sixteen she was staying with friends in Richmond, and on that very day in April when the guns opened fire on Fort Sumter she plighted her troth to young Francis Legaré. Her relatives in the North were furious. In any circumstances they would never have approved her marriage to Legaré; poor, proud, alien to them in temper and manners. But now war was coming, and how could a family be divided against itself? Brother Reuben hurried to Richmond, damning his sister for dragging him from the business and money-making that he loved; and found her gone. For Rachel had spirit as well as beauty, and wedding Francis – he suddenly aflame to fight and she caught by this new unselfish ardour – she was willing to wed the whole cause of the South. They fled to his home in Charleston, where Reuben could not follow even if he had cared to, for South Carolina was already at war. . . . And the rest of the tale was what one might expect of such romance, whose end is traditionally the wilderness. Francis – Captain Legaré since sundown of the previous day – was killed at Gettysburg, and Rachel's baby died of hunger and diarrhoea and the bitterness of her mother's grief; and Rachel lived for many years in poverty among a beaten people, hating her friends in the victorious North, and Francis's sister Sally with her, five years younger than Rachel and feeding her anger, for one grew fierce whenever weeping mollified the other . . . and then her mother died – Annabel the ship-captain's daughter – and left her poor child her love – all her love, she said, for Father Sam Motley had died a month before, and Reuben was so hard and greedy that Annabel shrank from him – so at the last all her love, and her money too, went to little Rachel whom she had not seen for thirty years and more, and then as a school-girl going off on holiday; and that holiday, because the gallantry of the South in arms had captured her heart, became a lifetime of no holidays at all.

'I always grow garrulous when I speak of her there in Richmond,' said Mrs. Dekker. 'A child, faced suddenly with the double problem of marriage and national loyalty, and choosing in the grand manner the bright and difficult way. Carey says there was no problem, but I believe she made her choice in full consciousness of what she was doing, for she refused to be taken home after the war was over, and she never regretted having said yes when Francis asked her to marry him. She's a strong woman, though a little one. She only took the money her mother left her because if she hadn't it would have reverted to Reuben. . . .'

They crossed the State line into South Carolina and the threatened flood came nearer to reality. Here and there the wild sandy waste was already inundated and bushes were robbed of half their height. Now the flood-waters were blackly pock-marked with rain, and now flogged with wild cloud-shadows. Sometimes the road, higher than the adjacent country, was like an endless bridge trying to span a bankless river, and once or twice they drove through water-splashes hub-high. They encountered cars hurrying north whose drivers shouted as they passed that the road was gone, the bridge was washed away, and they should turn back while there was time.

'We might as well see what we can see,' said the Governor, and bidding his chauffeur drive on, spat with a musical *plop!* into the plated cuspidor.

'We were in San Francisco when they had their earthquake,' said Mrs. Dekker with a sigh. 'The Governor did enjoy himself, and insisted on staying till the fire was over.'

'Now, now, my dear,' her husband protested, 'there's no danger in a drop or two of water. You'll give Mr. Motley a very foolish impression of me if you talk like that.'

'I'm fond of sight-seeing,' said Juan. 'I should hate to turn back now.'

'Well then, it won't be my fault if we're drowned.' Mrs. Dekker settled herself more comfortably and looked at the changing view.

They came to another flood area. A deserted negro store stood on a tiny island, the water lapping to its door-step. It was made of wood that had never been painted, gone an old ash-grey in colour, and propped against one side was a notice-board that said 'No Loafers.' The rain had stopped and the afternoon sun shone through a cloud to make the waters livid with great streaks of light. . . . The cloud blew seawards, and the sun showed itself clear and strong. The waves then shone like a great pool of yellow wine, and black branches that thrust above them were tipped with unsuspected green. More and more clouds joined the retreat to the sea, and as the flight became a rout the sky flaunted banners of exultant blue.

'I thought it would clear up,' said Mrs. Dekker.

The clouds were showing long brown tails, and the blue banners filled the sky with their cerulean triumph. The roads shone with a dazzling gleam and the flood-waters were yellow and bright.

Where the road curved sharply a policeman stopped their car and told them they could go no farther; the bridge, though not down, was unsafe. They could drive another quarter of a mile or so to look at it, but it would be a fool's game to try and cross.

'All right,' said the Governor, 'we'll just go and see what it looks like.'

Two other cars and a Red Cross Ambulance stood at the bridge-end, and their occupants watched the huge expanse of orange-tawny water, frilled here and there with white foam, that swirled and eddied before them. The bridge was not a simple arch or suspension or cantilever bridge, but a viaduct of alternating embankment and span that crossed a wide swamp through which, in normal times, the river ran sluggishly in many separate channels. But now the channels were one river, fierce and magnificent, shining like a tiger in the westerly sun. It was road-high and lipped the bank. It rushed past, covered with small noisy waves and vanishing strips of foam. A pig went by, swimming desperately, too lean to cut its throat as pigs often do. After it followed a dead cow, and far off the gable of a house showed, caught by the bridge.

The Dekkers and Juan stood with the other watchers and heard the news. The Red Cross men had just fished a dead nigger boy out of the water. There would likely be a lot of casualties and a lot of damage to property, but if the water got no higher than this it would not be serious. Not really serious, that is.

A mule came down the river, shot under the bridge, and with a valiant effort turned and got into the backwater by the abutment. It tried to climb out but the side was too steep. It fought determinedly, showing its yellow teeth and the brown-flecked yellow of its eyes.

Juan got down to the edge and tried to help it, while several people told him to take care and Mrs. Dekker called to him to come back. The mule wore an old straw-stuffed collar, torn in several places, and Juan took hold of this. The collar had swollen with long soaking and Juan's hand, sliding under it, was caught firmly between it and the mule's neck. The mule was contrary as all mules, and on the point of being rescued decided that danger was better. It shook its head, plunged violently, and sheered off down-stream.

Because his hand was tightly held Juan went with it. He fell with an ungainly splash and filled his mouth with water that tasted of the swamp. The river was cold, but the nervous shock which he experienced was so great that he scarcely realised any physical discomfort. His head rose from the water and he saw the figures on the bank – the Dekkers, the Red Cross men – standing in attitudes of horror. Then, for the mule was travelling at a lively rate, a bow-wave broke over his head, he swallowed more water, and lost sight of the shore.

IV

Juan pulled himself up to the mule, caught its collar with his left hand, and wrenched his right free. After a struggle he got on to the animal's back. He brushed the water from his eyes and for a minute looked about him. Wrinkled with speed, the orange-tawny river flowed into what seemed an ocean of water whose untidy surface was sprinkled with débris and occasional tree-tops, and was everywhere ribbed with swift dissolving lines. They were heading for the very heart of the ocean and already the bank and the bridge were far behind.

Then the mule tried to bite Juan's legs. With incredible viciousness and a neck that appeared supple as a snake's, it twisted its head first to one side and then to the other, and snapped at his shins. But Juan deftly and repeatedly kicked it on the nose until it tired of biting and attempted to roll him off. Then it tried to buck, and because there was nothing solid under its feet a very curious motion resulted. Juan was frequently in grave danger of being thrown off, but by exercising all his strength and skill he managed to retain his seat. When all its devices failed the mule began to sulk. It closed its eyes, and hung its head, and let the water come over its nostrils. Juan was alarmed by the thought that it meant to commit suicide, and reaching back he grasped its tail, which he twisted very vigorously. The mule responded immediately. It pulled its nose out of the water, looked round at Juan with something like admiration in its brown and yellow eye, and swam rapidly down-stream.

Relieved from the fear of immediate drowning Juan was able to compose his thoughts. At first he had experienced nothing but a sense of bewilderment at an experience so unexpected and indeed unlikely, but now his astonishment yielded to reasonable unhappiness. He glanced over his shoulder: the Dekkers and the very bank on which they had stood were vanished from sight. He was alone with a mule of uncertain temper in a vast flood; he who, a few minutes ago, had been driving comfortably in a Rolls-Royce motor car, befriended by jovial, wise, and kindly people. Fate had never treated him so violently as in this violent – and, he felt, unjustifiable – translation from luxury to cold and loneliness and danger. He shivered. Though bright orange behind him the river was growing shadowy ahead, for the sun was already low. A damp warmth, generated by the mule, comforted his thighs, but his body was chilled in its dripping clothes. The swirling water made him a little dizzy. Far off were tree-tops, but Juan could not tell whether they grew on dry land or thrust their branches through the water. He saw a table, floating with its legs up; a bundle of hay; a wooden box with a hen sitting on it; a privy; a cane chair; a dead sheep; a little swimming island of reeds on which three swamp rabbits crouched wetly. There was no sign of anything to comfort him or help him except a clear sky and the seeming vitality of his mule.

Driven by the absence of all practical expedients to a more academic consideration of his plight, Juan discovered that he was an unusually adaptable person. He had often suspected as much, and now he considered it indisputable. An experience as fantastic and improbable as this would, he felt, evoke in most people an emotion so strange, so unlike any previous emotion, as to be overwhelming in its effect. But he, having once overcome an excusable bewilderment, found that he could ride a mule in a flooded Carolina river with a philosophical acceptance of such a state of affairs and its contingent phenomena. True, he was cold. True, he was unhappy. True, he was dizzy when he looked too closely at the water. And true, he was somewhat afraid. But coldness, unhappiness, nausea, and fear were not the tramontane strangers one might have expected in such circumstances. They were familiar visitors with whom Juan knew how to deal. And, except for such commonplace annoyances, he ceased to be perturbed by his unusual situation.

The mule swam unweariedly. As if satisfied with its initial perversity and the battle when Juan first mounted it, it made no further attempts to unseat him. It even showed signs of friendliness, for when Juan patted its neck and spoke commendingly to it – for an Englishman will talk readily to animals, however reserved he may be with human strangers – the mule nodded comprehendingly and flapped its long ears to indicate, perhaps, a mulish enjoyment of the adventure. Darkness came, and still the beast was undismayed. It avoided entanglements with occasional tall tree-tops and yet snatched a mouthful of leaves as they passed. Once or twice it made an effort to swim across the current, as though realising there were limits to the flood somewhere, but the stream was too swift, and very soon, with a sensible acquiescence in fate, it turned its head down river again.

Juan felt very lonely after it grew dark. The river made a mournful noise, and there was no horizon, no moon. The stars came out, but the stars were dead and distant prickles of light. The orange river had turned to a velvety blackness, and the ears of the mule had a lost, bedevilled look.

'Good boy,' said Juan, smacking the brute's neck; and wished for the first time since he had left her that he was sleeping in Olympia's bed again, with all that stalwart beauty to warm and comfort him. He let his mind go back, sleepily, luxuriously, to midnight enjoyment of her shoulders and sides; and almost fell off his mule. . . . Mules, he thought, were untroubled by such visions, being sterile and so not chained by love whether old or new; which was why mules were devils and jesters and given to humorous adventure. There was much to be said for a mule, that took neither after its Tory father the horse nor its Christian mother the ass, but lived its own life, wild, and illegitimate, and unhampered by progeny. . . .

'Much to be said for a mule,' said Juan loudly, to oppose the river-noise that surrounded him; and clapped his beast heartily on the withers, and shivered violently, and yawned, and counted the stars to keep himself awake.

V

A long way down the river two nigger families were roosting in the tree-tops. The few acres which they farmed were under water, and their cabins, built on slightly higher ground, had the flood at their door-steps. The river had reached that height at noon and showed no signs of rising since. But old Zed Kinney and Rose his wife, and Silas Hooker, and his aged mother and her still more aged aunt, and even big Jake Hooker, had been terrified by the remorseless advance of the waters and were convinced that their only hope of safety was to remain in the branches till the flood receded.

There was plenty of room in the big live oaks, and even some comfort, for a few blankets and a pillow or two had been arranged in a fork of the branches, and there the two old women lay, bewailing the deluge and watching the sun paint it orange and clay-colour. Close beside the old women were Zed Kinney and Silas Hooker, and higher up in the tree were several Kinney children and four or five little Hookers. In a neighbouring tree – their farthest growing leaves were contiguous – Zed's wife and her marriageable daughter Missy Lou had taken refuge, and with them was big Jake Hooker, a slaughterer from the Chicago stockyards home on holiday. Several pigs had been rescued and carried up the second tree, where, tied to suitable branches, they lived uncomfortably, alternately grunting and squealing. In contrast to the pigs a large number of hens sat with apparent satisfaction on the lower branches.

Silas Hooker had some reputation as a preacher and his prayers helped to pass the time very pleasantly. During the first hour or two of their sojourn aloft, while excitement stood high as they, he had addressed the Lord with unfailing power. He had reminded God of His excellent judgment in saving Noah, his sons and his sons' wives and all their household animals, from a peril very similar to the present one. He had recalled the strategic use of water to preserve the Israelites from the pursuing armies of Egypt, and Christ's mastery of Galilee in storm; clearly God could do whatever He liked with sea-water, rain-water, and river-water too. 'Praise de Lawd!' shouted his congregation. 'Hallelujah!' they exclaimed. Then Silas remembered Paul and his voyage to Malta, another peril comparable to their own; and was not Paul delivered from the hunger of the waves? 'Amen, amen!' cried his audience. . . . Silas scratched his head. He could think of no other escapes from drowning except Jonah's, and he did not want to suggest a whale to the Lord if the Lord could be persuaded to organise any other form of rescue. So he diverted His attention to Shadrach, Meshach, and Abednego (whose plight was altogether different), and to Daniel, and lastly, with exceptional felicity, to Jacob and his Ladder. 'Hallelujah!' bawled the roosting flock.

After the prayers Zed Kinney, who had a very powerful voice, started a hymn – suggested by Silas's discourse – in which everybody joined:

'Pharaoh's army drowned in de sea,
O Lawd, I'se thankful dat it wasn't me.

Pharaoh's army got far from de shore,
O Mary, don't you weep no more!

De sea ob evil am wide and fair,
All de sinners gonna perish there.

When I get to Heaben I sho' will ride
On two white horses side by side. . . .'

And so on. It lasted a long time and mingling with the sound of the river made a very pretty and lugubrious noise. When it was done Mammy Kinney, on the opposite tree, was taken with fear that her individual danger might have been overlooked and began to sing:

''Tain't my father, tain't my brother, but it's *me*, O Lawd,
Standin' in de need of prayer;
'Tain't my mother, tain't my sister, but *me*, O Lawd,
Standin' in de need of prayer!'

The two old women, Lizabeth and her extremely aged aunt Malindie, were very moved by this hymn and rocked about in their nest of blankets as they sang. Their ancient voices were cracked and tremulous. Aunt Malindie, ill with pellagra, was a very pitiful sight. Her skin was so parched and dry that she looked like a mummy except for the excited gleam in her eyes. Her thin white hair was pulled tightly back from her wrinkled forehead, and when with the artificial vigour induced by the hymn she waved her skinny arms in the air, they looked like burnt twigs.

The small Hookers and Kinneys, perched in the higher branches, had recovered their equanimity soon after taking to the tree, and they were now thoroughly enjoying themselves. The poor old women struggling with emotion and song appeared very comical to them as they peered through the leaves and hung perilously from their swaying limb. And presently little Vincent Hooker – an unspoiled product of equatorial Africa – kicked, in his delight, little Eva Kinney – a pot-bellied, chocolate-coloured, very kinky-haired child – who loosed her hold and fell with a heart-rending shriek. The hymn-singing stopped short, and so fortunately did Eva; for her dress caught in a lower branch and there she hung in a horizontal position, making vain natatory movements with her arms and legs and howling dismally. The other children shrieked in sympathy and the old women wailed. Mammy Kinney shouted instructions from the other tree and Missy Lou threatened hysterics. The dogs, of which there were several tied to branches, barked excitedly, and, sitting lordly among its hens, a cock began to crow.

Old Zed Kinney shouted for silence. His first shout was unregarded, his second cut the clamour in half, and his third reduced it to a mere fretful whimpering. Zed knew how to get obedience. He had been for many years a Pullman attendant with the Union Pacific Railway, and he had acquired the habit of command in the natural course of his duties. He had regularly bullied his white passengers to bed by nine o'clock, and shamed them into getting up by half-past seven. He had lolled luxuriously in untaken compartments, and read the white folks' magazines. For twenty-three years he had ruled like a czar between Chicago and San Francisco – on a narrow territory, it is true, but undisputed in his sovranty – and now his personality once more became evident. Even little Eva herself was quiet while Zed directed her rescue.

'Yo' Jake,' he called. 'Yo' come 'cross and climb up and get dat chile!'

'Do yo' think Ah wants to drown mahself?' roared Jake.

The water between the trees was no more than ankle-deep, but Jake's huge muscular body trembled all over when he looked down at it. Its muddy wind-flawed surface hid all kinds of terror for him.

'Never yo' mind 'bout drowning, yo' wuthless nigger. Jes' yo' come and save dat po' chile when Ah tells yo' to!'

Hearing herself called a poor child Eva once more began to howl, and Missy Lou added her entreaties to Zed's commands. Big Jake slowly and reluctantly climbed down, hung for a long time while he measured the depth of the water with one foot, and at last stepped into it. A gasp of apprehension rose from both trees. Jake trod warily, his eyes rolling from side to side and his shoulders hunched up like a man in a snowstorm. With a gusty 'Thank Gawd!' he reached the other tree, and climbing up retrieved the child without difficulty. Then he splashed and returned to his original perch beside Missy Lou, where he puffed bravely and smacked himself on the chest, and made her beam with admiration for his courage.

The discussion engendered by this incident lasted another hour, and afterwards everybody watched some interesting débris float by. Then the sun set and darkness quickly fell.

Every limb of the live oaks took on a new and hideous aspect. They became twisted and sinister, like serpents writhing, or clutching hands, or the limbs of agony. And beneath them was water that made a rushing sound; not the solid stable earth, but a surface that ever vanished and a depth without stability. It rushed along, stopping only for an instant to chuckle malignly round the trees. Then the stars came out to glimmer furtively through the leaves, and the leaves rustled ghostly in a wandering wind. From somewhere not far away came a banshee cry that might have been a wild-cat screaming.

All the little Hookers and Kinneys, already alarmed by the strangeness of night, wept loudly, and fled to the blanket-nest of the two old women, who with their aged eyes were also seeing ha'nts and hags. In the other tree Missy Lou and her mother clung closely to Big Jake, and Big Jake told them in a tremulous voice of the adventurous life he lived in Chicago; but all the time realised that a South Carolina swamp was a more fearsome place than any tough city joint. He looked up at the dark sky and groaned to think how long it would be before morning broke.

Silas began to pray again, but in the darkness his voice seemed different, like a stranger's voice, and the way it went out of his mouth and disappeared among the unseen leaves frightened him into silence. An owl hooted, and Aunt Malindie moaned in terror. But the children kept her and old Elizabeth warm, and presently they went to sleep. The others, in their several perches, fell into a restless doze, and the rushing of the river was sometimes only a dream in their heads, and sometimes a fearful reality that swept dreams aside and woke them with its loudness. Were the waters that they could not see still rising? – Their clucking malignant laughter sounded nearer and clearer. – Was not the tree already rocking for its fall? – 'O Lawd, sabe yo' chillen!' muttered the negroes between sleep and waking.

Time passed. . . .

At last, waking among his hens, the cock crew and everybody roused stiffly, and rubbed eyes open, and shivered in the cold before dawn. The children whimpered and the old women groaned, for darkness still clung to the tree and the river seemed so noisy that they feared it was invading the branches. But when the first gloom of waking had gone they felt more cheerful, for the darkness, grim and permanent though it looked, would be gone in an hour. They bestirred themselves, called to each other, and stretched their cramped legs. Zed counted the children and found them all safe. In the opposite tree Zed's wife began to sing:

> 'When Sis' Mary took a hop out o' de willow-tree,
> She hop right ober into Galilee!'

And with that and other songs the last hour of darkness was scattered, and suddenly they looked down and saw through the branches the flood, pale and vast, stretching endlessly beneath them. Day had come, and so far brought no comfort with it.

'O Lawd,' prayed Silas, 'gib' us a sign! Show yo' chillen a sign, like yo' done show to Noah yo' bow in de clouds.'

'Amen!' said his hearers, in hoarse and quavering tones. 'Gib' yo' chillen a sign, O Lawd!'

'Gib' us a sign dat yo' ain't gwine to send no fifteen cubits ob water dis time. We ain't got no ark, Lawd, and dey ain't none of us can't swim. Don't be angry with us, Lawd, but draw back dis yere flood into yo' sky and gib' us a sign like de rod you gabe Aaron or de mighty signs of yo' 'postle Paul!'

'Yes, Lawd, gib' us a sign!'

The light strengthened rapidly and the flood shone whitely. The waters had not yet begun to recede.

'Sen' yo' chillen a sign,' prayed Silas.

Those on the other tree could see far up the river, and suddenly Missy Lou pointed wildly and shrieked, 'Hallelujah! Praise de Lawd!'

'What de matter?' shouted Silas.

'De sign am come!' yelled Missy Lou, her black face all bright with excitement. 'De sign am here! De Lawd hab' sent a sign to tell us he ain't gwine to drown no po' niggers dis time. Hallelujah, praise de Lawd!'

Feverishly Zed and Silas shuffled out to a branch from which they could see what Missy Lou saw. The children scrambled perilously to the top of the tree, and even the old women crept out of their nest and blinked through the leaves. On the other tree Mammy Kinney clasped and unclasped her hands in bewilderment, and Big Jake stared suspiciously.

Soon no one could doubt that what they saw was sufficiently unusual to pass for a sign. It was a man sitting upright in the midst of the flood. What he sat on could not be discerned at first, for it seemed all one with a dark reflexion in the water. But he came nearer and nearer, and the rising sun shone straight on his pale face. Then they saw that he was riding a horse, or a mule, or – could it be a donkey?

'Oh, sweet Jedus!' cried Mammy Kinney, and everyone was filled with a wild surmise. One of the little Hookers wept loudly and hid his face.

> 'O John, Jedus comin',
> O John, Jedus comin',
> O John, Jedus comin','

shrilled Missy Lou.

'Dat ain't no Jedus, dat's a buckra,' said Big Jake contemptuously.

'Shet yo' face, yo' good-fer-nuthin' nigger!' shouted Missy Lou. 'Do yo' think Jedus am a black man like yo'? Well, yo' don't know nuthin'!'

Then she sang loudly, and the others joined in:

> 'Ah'm gonna walk and talk wid' Jedus,
> One of dese days;
> Yes, Ah'm gonna walk wid' Jedus,
> One of dese days;
> Sister, Ah'm gonna talk wid' Jedus,
> One of dese days!'

This joyous noise startled Juan as he sat, stone-cold and weary to the bone, on his half-drowned mule. There was no feeling in his legs, and his arms were so tired and heavy that he did not know what to do with them. The mule had again taken to sinking its nose in the water, as though willing to drown, and every few minutes Juan had to pull it out by the ears. The night had seemed endless. Sometimes he had shivered so violently as almost to lose control of himself, and at others he had sunk into a state of dull acquiescence in misery.

Daylight had cheered him greatly, and when the sun rose he saw the big live oaks, so high out of the water that they promised dry land beneath, and urged the mule towards them by tail-twisting and tugging its right ear. Then he heard singing. At first it frightened him, for he thought it a product of delirium. But as the mule, drifting and languidly swimming, took him nearer to the live oaks the song grew louder in his ears, and he saw figures in the trees, and the red kerchief that Mammy Kinney had tied round her head. He felt relieved and grateful, but he was too tired to be curious about the reception that awaited him, or what manner of people these were. Even the singing, once he was sure that it was singing, did not interest him. It had no significance beyond that of a human noise.

The mule stumbled aground, tottered and fell, and threw Juan into the shallow water between the oaks. Immediately Zed and Silas ran forward and picked him up. They, and all the others except old Aunt Malindie, had come down from their trees when the stranger drew near, and waited mid-shin deep, trembling with excitement, to receive him. In Juan's half-conscious ears sounded a score of lusty 'Hallelujahs!' He saw dimly many black faces with eager bright eyes and white teeth. He recognised, without understanding, an exaltation in their manner. And then he fainted.

VI

When Juan recovered he found himself lying in a crotch in one of the trees, half-undressed, with Mammy Kinney rubbing his legs and Missy Lou his arms. Hot pains ran up his limbs. Mammy Kinney smiled expansively at him and he asked her where he was.

'You're safe in dis yere tree, honey,' she said, 'and you're gwine to be safer still when de water goes. We sho' is grateful to yo' for comin' to tell us dere wasn't gwine to be no flood dis time. Yes, suh! It made our sperrits dance wid' joy to see yo' ridin' in de ribber and to know dat we wasn't born to be drowned. We knew yo' was a sign from Heaben jes' as soon as eber we seen you.'

'We thought you was Jedus,' said Missy Lou, and looked lovingly at Juan, who was very embarrassed.

'And sho' enough yo' was a sign,' Mammy Kinney went on, 'fo' de water's been gwine back to de ribber eber since you came. Jes' yo' look and see!'

The children were splashing and paddling between the trees. When they stood still the flood-water rippled against their ankles. It was flowing back to the river.

'Even if you ain't Jedus,' said Missy Lou, 'you sho' is de han'somest son of a bitch Ah ever done see.'

'Dat ain't no way to talk!' said her mother indignantly.

'Ah don' care. Ah jes' says what Ah thinks.' Missy Lou rubbed Juan's arm caressively and smiled in the most generous way.

By evening the cabins stood on ground which, though not dry, was all visible. An island of soft untidy mud had emerged from the waters which were still receding. The old women and their blankets were carried down from the tree and taken to Silas's shack. Juan managed to walk as far as Zed's, where Mammy Kinney had found enough dry wood to start a fire. She and Zed sat before it, warming their bare mud-caked feet and smoking short pipes, while Missy Lou cooked a supper of peas and bacon and cornbread. The smell of this mingled with wood-smoke, a heavy odour of dampness, and a suggestion of goat. The cabin grew warm and Juan, lying in Mammy Kinney's bed, began to scratch. His legs still throbbed and he lay in a state that was half lightheaded and half a curious dreamland. At one moment he was tossed helpless in a whirlpool, and the next he opened his eyes to see black faces in the yellow glow of a kerosene lamp. Now he heard the rush of the river and now the treble laughter, quickly hushed, of some small Kinney. He was not quite sure which of these things were real and which imaginary.

But in the morning he woke with a feeling of perfect well-being. The sun was shining, the children playing, the ground was drying fast – steam rose from it – and all the country was full of delicate bright hues like a painting in water-colour. The men had gone to see what damage their fields had suffered in the flood. Mammy Kinney stooped over her fire. And Missy Lou, her face newly polished with lard, sat and smiled happily at Juan while he dried his money in the sun.

No one except old Aunt Malindie, whose brain was affected, now entertained any extravagant notion that he was anything but an ordinary human being. The older people believed that he had been sent as a token of God's mercy to them – was not everything in the world signed by that large Hand? – and so they treated him with great respect and gratitude. But their idea that he might be the Redeemer in person had not lasted long, and now it seemed a matter for unashamed and hearty laughter. The circumstances had been so plausible. He had come riding on the foal of an ass and walking the waters at the same time! And then he turned out to be an ordinary buckra after all! Mammy Kinney held her sides and shook with mirth to think of it.

'We sho' is a lot o' fool niggers,' she said. 'But de Lawd made us, and if He likes us dat way we ain't got no cause to grumble.'

But Jake, who came slouching across from the Hookers' cabin, was not so good-natured. He puffed out his enormous chest and sneered at Juan.

'Right from de start I knew you wasn't no Jedus,' he said. 'I ain't one of dese country niggers. I lib' in Chicago, and we don't believe nobody's Jedus dere. No, suh!'

The women interposed and told him that nobody would care where he lived if he spoke as unmannerly as that. Jake was particularly hurt by Missy Lou's reproof and by her obvious sympathy with Juan. She was a strong and comely girl, and as Zed Kinney was known to be very wealthy after his long service with the Pullman Company, Missy Lou would not go undowered to the altar. Jake had come home with the idea of marrying her, and at first she had been greatly attracted by his muscular person, his sophisticated air, and his exciting stories about Chicago. Jake had plumed himself on an easy conquest. Then the river had flooded, and he was conscious that he had not been seen to great advantage in the ensuing danger. But that would be forgotten very soon. The serious obstacle to his wooing was this mysterious stranger who, without doing anything to deserve it, now engrossed all Missy Lou's attention. She polished her face for him. She had daubed her hair with some stuff that half-straightened the negro kink. And she had concealed the delicate odour of goat that was natural to her under a shower of perfume.

Jake scowled heavily and sat on the doorstep beside Juan.

'Do you know who Ah is?' he asked. 'Well, Ah's de best hawg-killer in Chicago. Dat's who Ah is.'

'How interesting,' said Juan

'Ah kill millions ob hawgs ebery week. Mah arms is covered wid' red blood to de shoulders when Ah's workin'. Dey's lak' ribers ob blood, and de noise ob de hawgs yellin' is louder'n fo'ty fire-trucks wid' all deir syrens hootin' togedder. It's de biggest noise in de city of Chicago, and Ah's 'sponsible for it. Dose hawgs look at me and dey know Ah's goin' to stick 'em fo' sure, and so dey yells good and hard. Ah makes 'em make dat noise!'

'And you like to kill them and to hear them yell?'

'Sure Ah likes it. Ah's de best hawg-killer in Chicago. Ah couldn't be dat if Ah didn't like it.'

Jake had been talking equally to Juan and to Missy Lou, and to his annoyance the girl had taken no notice of his boasting. She sat and looked at Juan with eyes that were soft and round as a full-moon.

'Ain't he got de prettiest hair yo' eber seen?' she asked.

'Hair! What's hair?' snorted Jake. 'Hab' yo' eber killed a hawg, mistuh?'

'I never have,' said Juan.

'Ah thought as much.' Jake stood up, spat, looked triumphantly at Missy Lou, and stalked away.

'Dat nigger thinks dey ain't nuthin' in life 'cept stickin' hawgs,' remarked Mammy Kinney.

He was indeed the one unfriendly note in the rural harmony which had succeeded the flood. The damage done had been slight, and as Juan had presented Zed with his mule the Kinneys had nothing at all to bemoan. The mule had speedily recovered from its ordeal and proved, as Juan had inferred, an animal of exceptional strength, vitality, and independence of spirit. Juan's title to it was unquestioned even by himself. If he was a token sent by Providence, then the mule had obviously been bred, reared, consecrated and ordained for his riding; and if their joint adventure had been nothing but an accident, then let those who helped them both, by their timely presence and their hearty welcome, be rewarded with what means were present and proper.

So Juan thought, and looked at the blue Carolina sky, so huge and empty except for a line of flocculent clouds to seaward; for the sea was not very far distant, and as if in emulation of its enormous neighbour the country was also spacious and careless, and lay loosely under the sun and the wind. The river still ran in a channel twice as wide as its normal one, and its colour was still orange or bright clay. Except for evergreens the trees were not yet in full leaf, and the fields, in their sandy way, looked empty but not desolate. There were birds in plenty: tanagers, mocking-birds, cat-birds, and brown and yellow meadow-larks; mourning-doves and red-headed woodpeckers; woodcock and coots and water-rails of different kinds.

Juan felt that he could live here very pleasantly for some time, in spite of a few lice in the bed and the fondness of Missy Lou. Here were the ease and freedom he had wished for in the winter-bound towns of the north. Here was comfort: not the bought and confected comfort of a drawing-room, but the comfort of Nature, who didn't mind who spat in her parlour, or wore his braces visibly, or ate from his fingers. Here a man could sleep in the sun and walk with the whole hemisphere of sky for his companion. And though some people might object to consorting with niggers, Juan found them much pleasanter than the bootleggers with whom he had lived, and more interesting than Dora and her husband.

His only care was to let the Dekkers know that he was safe, and as soon as the roads were passable one of the Kinney boys went off on the mule to the nearest post-office (which was by no means near) with a telegram that told so much, but offered no information about Juan's future plans.

The Arcadian existence which he anticipated lasted only a very short time, however. For two or three days more he enjoyed fishing in the river, making jokes with Mammy Kinney, and listening to Zed's reminiscences of life in the Pullman cars. There was humour in Zed's views and a homely imagination in his thought.

He spoke of the Union Pacific line from Chicago to San Francisco. 'Hab' yo eber seen a watch-chain stretched tight across de wescoat ob a big fat Senator? Dat's what dat railroad track am like – a silber chain across de big corn-filled belly ob Uncle Sam.'

Then the little Kinneys and the little Hookers danced with great agility whenever they felt like dancing, and sang:

'If you want to bake a hoecake,
To bake it good and done,
Jes' slap it on a nigger's heel
And hol' it to de sun.'

Or Mammy Kinney would sing in a deep fruity contralto:

'When yo' see dat gal o' mine,
Jes' tell her for me, if yo' please,
Next time she goes to make up bread,
To roll up her dirty sleeves.'

And Missy Lou occasionally chanted with happy insinuating glances at Juan:

'Oh, a white lady sleeps in a fedder bed,
A yaller gal does de same,
The po' black gal makes a pallet on de floor,
But she sleeps dere jes' de same.'

Indeed somebody was singing nearly all the time; not always a full-length song, but perhaps half a dozen words to which a few casual notes were given – and straightway the remark became a comical bird that sat on a bough and sang till its owner grew tired of it and sought another.

Their laughter too was a pleasant thing to hear. It had much in common with their songs, being rich and mellow in sound, uncontrollable as hunger, natural as thirst. . . . White people singing and laughing were performing social tricks with their larynx and palate. But tickle a nigger and he answered like a fiddle, all over, because it was his nature to. This, it might be, was the result of forcibly transplanting a people from one continent to another, using them in slavery for several generations, and then bestowing on them a nominal freedom and a position beyond the pale of society. They had neither past nor future, no memories of greatness and no excuse for ambition. They had no shame to live down and no false pride to live up to. Their spirits were not wearied nor their flesh corrupted with luxury. Tar-black by nature, they could touch pitch and not be defiled. They had lost the whole world and saved – well, the ability to sing like bull-angels in a wine-cellar, and laugh and be lazy in a bird-haunted swamp, while the heaven-born, English-German-and-Italian-born, white-pink-or-sallow-faced, victorious, earnest, and important peoples of the north slaved in a frantic medley of cold and noise and bewilderment to make money to keep themselves alive and buy the goods whose manufacture and profit would keep alive other pink or grey men (and their pink or sallow wives) in the same bewilderment of discomfort, and frustration, and hope that some day there would be leisure to sit down and think what it all meant; and conclude, of course, that it meant just nothing at all. . . .

Sitting on a fallen tree by the river Juan philosophised in this way – which is indeed a way of philosophy that anybody may use – and then wondered if the English were conquered by the Brazilians (for instance) and led into captivity up the Amazon, and despitefully used for two hundred years, they would at the end of that time be a lazy and light-hearted and tunefully-minded people singing battered versions of *Who is Sylvia*, and *Drink to me only with thine eyes*, and *Good King Wenceslas* – or some of Gilbert and Sullivan's songs – or the rude songs about Samuel Hall, and the Tinker, and the Ram of Derby Town? Think of the English living in Brazil, taking their ease, and laughing, and singing catches all day! It was a humorous and handsome thought which pleased Juan greatly. . . .

This black Arcadia had its villain, however, and the shadow of Big Jake frequently stretched from the Hookers' cabin to the Kinneys'. He was an unhappy villain, for Missy Lou would now take no notice of him except to snub him. She spent all her time admiring Juan and embarrassing him with hearty compliments. If Jake came slouching over she paid no attention to him until he made her, and then she would turn angrily and say, 'Go 'way, can't yo! D'you think me and my friend Mass' Juan wants to segashuate wid' common Chicago niggers like you? We're talkin' 'bout impo'tant things and we ain't got no time to listen to yo'.' But Jake never went far away, and every now and then Juan would look up to see his fixed and foreboding scowl.

One night, however, when Juan had been with them for a week, Jake apparently put away his animosity and came over to the Kinneys' in a mood of great amiability. He carried old Aunt Malindie in his arms. She still believed in her half-witted way that Juan had come straight from Heaven, and wished to comfort her fading spirit in his presence.

Jake's purpose was to invite Juan down the river to hunt alligators. He said that he had heard one bellowing, and though it was early for them to emerge from hibernation – they did not usually rouse till early April – he believed that the flood, by sending cold water into their winter caves, must have wakened some and driven them out. So he had collected bait and tackle, and if Juan would go with him they could start early in the morning. 'Gator-fishing, he said, was mighty good sport, and he knew all the best places. Would Juan come?

Jake's manner was engaging. His scowl had vanished, and he smiled in a large, frank, and genial way, so that Juan, who could always say yes more easily than no, accepted the invitation very unwillingly. All the Kinneys and all the Hookers were present, and as everybody grew animated at the suggestion of sport, for the rest of the evening Juan listened to exciting stories of the chase. White-tailed Virginia deer, 'possums, 'coons, and wild-cats were discussed and despatched; fish of all kinds brought to shore; snipe and duck and wild turkey shot; buzzards, rattle-snakes, foxes, and water-moccasins mentioned in passing; great hunters of the past summoned from the shades and lauded extravagantly; and when it grew late Silas brought the topic to its end by the story of a negro who had all his life hated alligators and killed an immense number of them, putting their skulls in a little field which, by the time he was eighty years old, he had succeeded in filling with heads. Then like Ezekiel he went in to prophesy to the dry bones, and immediately there was a noise and a shaking, and the bones came together, and the skin covered them, and breath blew into them. . . . That at least was the supposition, for the old negro was never seen again, and in the morning there was not one bone left in the field.

During all these recitals old Aunt Malindie sat close to Juan, at intervals touching his sleeve and looking up at him with an expression of childish ecstasy on her shrivelled face. Now and then she muttered something unintelligible. When it came time for the Hookers to go she cried and held on to Juan, who pacified her with an old silk handkerchief, which she clutched delightedly.

Before it was light again Juan and Big Jake were paddling down-stream in a roughly made canoe. When the sun rose it shone straight in their faces, and the river looked like a broad shallow trench between its palisades of trees. The alligator-tackle lay in the bottom of the canoe: a long tough rope, stakes of wood sharpened at both ends and attached to wire traces, and some dead rabbits for bait.

The alligator, Jake explained, would swallow the stake endways, with the rabbit impaled on it. A tug on the line turned the picket round, and then, its points sticking in the brute's throat, the battle would begin. Jake drove his paddle into the water with still greater energy. The alligators hibernated in caves in the river-bank above the level of the water, and these caves were far away. They must hurry if they were to have time for proper fishing. Jake's manner was hearty.

About ten o'clock they drew in to the shade of a tree that overhung the water, and ate some cold bacon and cornbread. The water, still yellow, was dappled with leaf-shadows and the air was warm. A hundred yards away the river seemed to encounter a dense wall of jungle and to go no farther, but actually it split into three narrow channels, each of which wandered almost invisibly through heavy growth, lapping on their way the roots of cypress trees and darkened by the Spanish moss which overhung them. Nothing, thought Juan, could be pleasanter than this idle, entertaining country. . . . He glanced round and saw that Jake was looking at him in a curious, speculative way.

'What are you thinking about?' he asked.

Jake hesitated, and then said slowly, 'Ah was thinkin' 'bout them hawgs Ah used to kill in Chicago. Hab you eber seen de stockyards? Well, dose hawgs is hung by dey hinder feet on a cable, side by side, jes' like dey was shirts hung up to dry. And de cable keeps movin' all de time, jes' carryin' up new hawgs. And dere's me standin' wid' hawgs squealin' on one side ob me, and hawgs kickin' on de odder. Yes, suh. Dey's all squealin' mighty hard till dey reaches me, 'cause Ah sho' is de bes' killer in Chicago and dey knows what am comin'. Ah sticks 'em in de throat, jes' once, and dat lets out de squeal and 'bout half a bucket ob blood, and den de cable carries him 'way kickin' jes' as hard as he knows. Dere dey is, thirty or maybe fo'ty all togedder, wid' deir throats cut and de blood spittin', kickin' jes' like they'm tryin' to dance. Sometimes they dance de Chahlston, sometimes dey ball de jack. Ah seen 'em cuttin' pigeon-wings and dancin' de cake-walk. Dey can dance jes' any dance yo' like, and dey is all dead. But dey can't squeal no mo' 'cause Ah's let de squeal out.'

'A curious recollection for a morning like this,' said Juan.

'Well, dat's de way Ah's made,' Jake replied, and pushed the canoe out into the stream again, and very soon guided it into a channel over-arched with trees. Grey moss hung from the branches and sometimes a big white flower starred the gloom. A water-moccasin swam across their bows.

'Dey's plenty ob dem cotton-mouths 'bout here,' said Jake, 'and dey's bery poisonous.'

In a mood of apparent satisfaction he sang:

> 'De blues ain't nuthin' but a bad nigger gal
> On a good nigger's mind.'

The channel wound through the jungle in such serpentine fashion that Juan lost all sense of direction five minutes after they left the main river. He could seldom see more than ten yards ahead or ten yards astern, and what lay ahead looked just like what they had passed: a tree-roofed alley lit by wavering sunlight, festooned with Spanish moss, and floored with brown, slowly-swirling water that grew more and more sluggish as they advanced. Here and there were tributary or diverging creeks. Sometimes a bird made much ado in the branches. The air was warm and heavy and smelt of the swamp.

By-and-by they came to a small clearing with a little muddy beach, and Jake said they had reached their goal. He drove the bow of the canoe on to the beach.

Juan stood up and looked about him. 'I don't see anything that looks like an alligator or an alligator's cave,' he said.

'Dis am de place,' Jake answered stubbornly, and Juan stepped ashore.

Freed of his weight the bow bobbed up, and with three powerful strokes Jake swung the canoe clear of the beach, turned it, and held it pointing upstream.

Juan looked round and was greatly surprised to see an expression of ferocious triumph on the negro's face. It was split by a snarling grin in which the teeth looked alarmingly white and big. He shook his paddle at Juan and yelled, 'Dat am de place fo' you but it ain't de place fo' me. I sho' was gettin' tired o' de sight ob you, you po' buckra, you Gawd-dam white trash. But I ain't neber gwine to see you again, and you ain't neber gwine to see me. I'se gwine to leabe you here, and if de 'gators don't get you de rattlers or de cotton-mouths will. And if dey don't get you you'll stick in de mud. Or if you don't stick in de mud you'll sho' lose yo'self and stahve to death, and den de buzza'ds 'll come.'

'What the devil are you playing at?' shouted Juan.

'Ah ain't playin' – '

'Bring that canoe in here at once!'

'Ah ain't bringin' no canoe dere. Ah's gwine to leabe you dere so's you won't steal mah gal no moh.'

'Do what I tell you and don't be a damned fool!'

Juan began to wade out to the canoe, but his feet sank in soft mud, and Jake drew a razor from his shirt, the blade of which he bent back across his knuckles in a handy position for slashing.

'Jes' you remember dat Ah's de best killer in Chicago,' he threatened. 'When Ah cuts 'em dey sho' stays cut.'

Juan retreated to firmer ground and attempted reconciliation.

'I've never done you any harm,' he said.

'You steal mah gal. Eber since you come she won't look at me, 'cause all de time she'm rubberin' after you.'

'I've never touched your girl, and I don't want to.'

'Maybe you don't. But she wan' to touch you plenty. Ah knows women and Ah knows what she'm thinkin'. And if she hadn't neber seen you she'd be thinking' dat 'bout me. Dat's why Ah's leabin' you here, so's she won't neber see you no moh.'

Jake put down the razor and took up his paddle again. With three strokes he drove the canoe twenty yards away.

'Come back!' Juan shouted.

Jake turned his head and shouted, 'Nobody won't see you no moh 'cept de 'gators and de cotton-mouths and de buzza'ds!'

'You can't leave me here, Jake!'

'Ah's lef' you dere!' Jake roared with laughter, thrust again with his paddle, and drove the canoe round a leafy corner and out of sight.

Juan tried to run along the bank, but before he had taken six steps he charged into a thick growth of vines that seemed impassable. They hung in a green network between the trees, and as he tore at the tough stems he could hear Jake's wild laughter – that full-bodied negro mirth which he had thought so splendid. And then Jake started to sing, and his voice, growing fainter and fainter, carried through the swamp:

> 'De blues' ain't nuthin' but a bad nigger gal
> On a good nigger's mind!'

VII

Silence followed Jake's song. A mosquito trumpeted. Juan stood with his hands full of vine-leaves and pliant stems, facing a green barricade, and tried to control the suggestions of panic which, like dark bubbles, rose in his brain. Once again he had been abruptly translated from security to danger, from peace of mind to a state of intense alarm and bewilderment. He was deserted, and lost, and imprisoned by intricate waterways and the tangle of jungle growth. He tore foolishly at the rampart of vines and disturbed from their shadow a whole troop of mosquitoes that sang joyously and bit him on wrists and ears and the back of his neck.

This acute irritation brought Juan to his senses and persuaded him to think seriously, for it was obvious that either anger or panic would lead him quickly, and by way of increasing discomfort, to a position even more perilous than his present one. He therefore returned to the small beach where Jake had landed him and tried to recall the various turns and deviations of their way thither. But he found it impossible. Their route had been too tortuous and too empty of landmarks to remember.

The sun was overhead. There were no clouds in the sky, nor had been all morning, to make a wind-vane and give him his direction. And indeed, though there had been clouds, there was no wind to make them move. Everywhere the leaves hung motionless and the blue sky stood still. Even the water before him was too sluggish to flow, and on its brown surface a dead branch floated motionless, half of it looking black in shadow and half grey in the sunshine.

There was nothing to help him find his way back to Zed Kinney's. And even if he knew the way there was water to cross, with soft mud under it and cotton-mouths swimming in it – and beyond the water dense growth of trees and matted vines, and rattlesnakes waiting malignly for careless travellers – and beyond the jungle more waterways – and over all the blazing sun with invisible specks in its brilliance that were vultures waiting more patiently than the rattlesnakes. It seemed that Jake had nothing more to fear from his rival, and that clear thinking would only persuade Juan his case was hopeless.

He walked up and down the small muddy beach. A jay called hoarsely and scuffled in the leaves. Idly Juan looked round, but the bird was invisible. Then he looked up, and high above him saw a white gull sailing. . . . A gull! And suddenly he remembered that the sea could not be far away, and that beside the sea in all probability there would be a beach on which he could walk somewhere or other; somewhere out of this labyrinth of trees and vines.

The Atlantic was probably nearer than Zed Kinney's house, and was certainly a larger mark to aim for, and a better one too, for the sea always offered ways of escape. It was a synonym for freedom.

But in which direction did it lie? Juan sniffed first to one side, then to the other. But there was no smell of salt in the air. Nothing but the heavy, half-rotten odour of the swamp. And yet as he turned this way and that, a feeling slowly grew that the sea was *there*. He could neither see it, nor hear it, nor smell it, but as surely as there is a difference between land and water he knew, when he faced the mark left on the mud by Jake's canoe, that the sea lay to his left and most of the American continent to his right.

With all the excitement of hope then, and no small fear of snakes, Juan turned left and began his march to the sea. For a hundred yards the undergrowth was so dense that it seemed impossible to make any headway at all. His arms were constantly entangled with creepers and vines, his feet sank deeply into semi-liquid mud, and soft thick leaves lay closely on his cheeks while their stems half-throttled him. Once he seemed helplessly caught in manacles of green and gyves of an unseen root, and while he struggled against their hold a great cloud of mosquitoes settled on his face, and to the tune of their tiny harps and trumpets pricked and bit and stung him again and again. Frenzied by the unyielding creepers and exasperated beyond endurance by the multiplication of petty pains, Juan filled the immediate air with a roar of curses against the unspeakable Jake – a huge wave of commination that carried with it, rumbling like boulders and rattling like pebble-stones, the names of Heaven and Hell, of the fluids of the body and its excrement, the circumstances of birth and conception (juristical and physiological), and of several perversions, of God and the Son of God and the Mother of the Son of God, together with the Devil and the more noteworthy furnishings of Hades – its styes and sinks and lupanars – and the conditions of torment therein, aggravated as they were by all manner of bodily ailments and itchings, and finally some incongruous flamboyant combinations of the afore-mentioned names and estates.

Reluctantly the creepers parted, and Juan stumbled forward, free. To keep off the mosquitoes he plastered his face with mud which stank vilely. His shirt was badly torn and his fore-arms were streaked with blood. But presently he came to easier country, where the vines grew less profusely and the leaves were not so thick and heavy. Then he swam one stream and waded another, very slowly, for he was frightened of losing his shoes in the mud – and within three yards of the farther bank he did lose one, for he saw a water-moccasin swimming towards him, its white mouth wide-open, and as he leapt desperately for solid earth his left foot slid out of a resisting shoe and left it on the bottom.

In spite of constant difficulties, however, he kept to a fairly straight line in the direction which he had chosen; the direction, he believed, which would lead him most shortly to the sea. And by-and-by he was doubly gratified, for the sun, though ever so slowly, began to slide down from its mid-noon altitude and to beat not on the top of his head but the back of his neck, which showed that he had guessed aright and was really heading eastward; while the growth of the swamp became gradually thinner, so that even with only one shoe he was able to maintain a steady advance. But he grew very tired, for excitement had drained some of his strength and battling through creepers and vines had spilled much more, and now he was limping, and his head ached under the hot sun. Where he was not wet with swamp water he was soaked with sweat. He had small idea of the time, and a little fear began to wake in his mind that he might not be able to get out of the jungle before night fell. This unhappy thought kept him from sitting down to rest, or made him compromise with his weary legs by saying, 'I'll have a rest when I've counted a thousand.' Then, while he struggled forward, he would count seven or eight hundred and say, 'Oh, I don't need a rest yet,' and give up counting till his legs persuaded him to start again.

When he had reached seven hundred for the seventh time he decided to continue to a thousand and really to halt for a little while, and lie down perhaps. The ground was growing harder. He stumbled over a rock. The trees ahead were less in number but grew taller. He counted as far as eight hundred and fifty. The ground was definitely firmer. With a great flapping noise a heron flew up among the tree-tops. Juan started the ninth hundred, but before he was half-way through he stopped and looked at what lay before him with dismay that banished all thought of numbers.

The ground was harder because it now formed a natural

embankment, and beyond the embankment lay a curious twilit lake. Its waters were perfectly calm, like a shaded mirror, and growing through them were innumerable cypress trees. They rose straight from the water, tall and slim, and the water faithfully mirrored them and the garlands of Spanish moss that depended from their branches. Among them, like burnt-down candles and little black cones, emerged the knees of the cypresses. These too were reflected in the dull silver of the water, so that everything was double and mysterious, as the nave of an old cathedral would be, whose floor had been polished enough to mirror the high arches of its roof, and the faded battle-flags on its walls, and, like patches of white sky, the clerestory windows. For the cypresses, tapering as they rose and growing flatly together at the top, had an inverted Gothic look, and their reflexion was truly Gothic.

What dismayed Juan, however, was not the Gothic twilight of the lake, but its size. He could see that it stretched far to the north and far to the south, and its opposite bank was hidden behind a ghostly multitude of trees. The Atlantic, it seemed, was still a long way off. His heart sank, for he had been hoping for a different spectacle to this, and straining his ears for the soft crumbling sound of waves on a beach. But here were only a cypress lake and no sound at all.

He sat down and stared gloomily at the stillness of the waters, at the silver floor and dark columns and bannerets of grey moss. A white bird flew down the broadest aisle. How long a détour would he have to make to reach the sea? The American scene was done on so lavish a scale that the lake before him – though he was certain that it could not be very broad – might be twenty miles long, and as it was certainly fed by the many wandering streams into which the river split, to walk round it might be a journey of considerable difficulty.

Juan scratched some of the mud off his face and cursed his luck; not grandly and vociferously, as he had cursed Jake, but in a mild and gloomy way. Another white bird flew across the lake; through the transept, as it were. It flew northwards and disappeared. Juan rubbed his bare foot and wondered which way to go. Reluctantly he got to his feet and, because the birds had gone that way, turned northwards. The ardour of journeying had left him, and in its place weariness fell heavily on his shoulders. He became conscious of the discomfort of wet clothes, and he limped tenderly on his bare foot that hurt him more at every step. He bent stiffly under a bough and with dull hands pushed aside a pliant branch. Green images in the water were no longer beautiful, and the silver mere was only another barrier to escape, a barrier so huge that he scarcely bothered to wonder how long it would take to get round it. He walked on, unhappily admitting the prospect of a night in the jungle.

And then – he almost passed it unnoticed – he saw something which instantly altered the complexion of his distress, and transfigured the whole situation with the liveliest colours of optimism. A canoe lay beached on the margin of the lake. Juan's first impulse was to shove it out and board it immediately, but a second thought suggested that it might have an owner and to leave him marooned would be churlish behaviour. So Juan walked on another twenty yards, briskly now and careless of his bare bruised foot, and two or three times shouted 'Hallo!' But he saw no one and there was no answer to his challenge.

Without hesitating longer he pushed the canoe into the water and got aboard. He dipped his paddle twice. Then a shrill howl of grief startled him, a wail, a piercing ululation, and turning he saw a small nigger boy standing on the bank, with his knuckles dug into his eyes, while his open mouth emitted a continuous treble agony. He was dressed simply in a pair of ragged trousers, and a fishing-pole lay at his feet. Though Juan must have passed close to him the bush in whose shelter he had been sleeping had concealed him from that perfunctory search.

Juan drove his canoe ashore again, and the nigger boy ran

at him in a sudden childish temper. Juan held him at arm's length while his small black fists whirled viciously but ineffectually. Great tears rolled down his face and his body shook with fear and anger.

'It's all right,' said Juan. 'I'm not going to steal your canoe.'

Gradually the boy's rage subsided, and through his sobs he chattered in incomprehensible Gullah.

'That's not much help,' said Juan. 'Suppose you get in, and we'll go home. Home, do you understand? – wherever your home is.'

The boy stared at him with enormous eyes on whose lower lids tears still balanced, and when Juan tried to pull him into the canoe he broke away, and howled again, and stamped his feet in the mud.

To try and bring him to his senses Juan pushed a few yards off shore. The effect was immediate, for the boy screamed with fright and rushed waist-deep into the water. He nearly upset the canoe as he climbed into it.

'Now, which way do we go?' Juan asked, and pointed enquiringly in several directions. The youngster would not help him, but sobbed and sniffed and gulped his tears, shaking all over with fear in which anger was not quite extinguished.

Juan decided to continue in his old direction, seawards as he hoped.

It soon appeared that this was not going to be easy, for by-and-by the cypresses and cypress-knees were all around them, growing out of the water like great columns and black candles. Aisles opened here and there, meandering lake-ways that closed again under an olive-green roof from which depended bannerets of Spanish moss that sometimes reached their images in the silver flood. Here was bright sunshine and there cool twilight. Now the water grew shallow and the bow of the canoe thrust into a scum of floating weed that crumpled before it and rose, so thick it grew, into green wrinkles. Now the moss hung down like a curtain to the level of the lake and they brushed through it blindly. It felt dry and crumbly. Now they frightened from its nest a great blue heron and now an egret, small and so dazzling-white that its reflexion in the dark water seemed like a flame rather than a bird. Now snake-birds turned and twisted long thin necks at them, and dived neatly, leaving not a ripple on the surface.

Completely bewildered, Juan once more tried to persuade the nigger boy to guide him, who at the first question threw himself face down and sulkily refused to answer. Juan made his voice as persuasive as he could, but the boy paid no attention. Then Juan thought of bribery.

'Look at this, you sulky little devil,' he said, and took out his watch. It had not gone since his mule-back journey down the river, but its appearance was handsome, and when curiosity at last overcame the child's sullenness, and he looked round with a suspicious eye, it captivated him at once.

Juan explained with much reiteration and pantomime that the watch would be a reward for proper piloting.

The boy wriggled into a kneeling position, his dark eyes fixed on the watch. He held out his hands for it. But he hesitated, and suddenly, as if he had remembered a dreadful warning, howled again and scrubbed his eyes in miserable perplexity.

Utterly puzzled by the child's incomprehensible reluctance to guide him through the lake, Juan set about soothing him and presently was rewarded with another stream of Gullah in which the only recognisable words were Missy Someone-or-other; Missy Lal, it sounded like; or Lal with an uncertain suffix. She, it appeared, was the cause of the boy's terror, though for what reason Juan could not divine; unless, he thought, she was a recluse who forbade the presence of strangers, and he had unconsciously trespassed on a private domain. It seemed unlikely that this wilderness lake was private water, but he could think of no other solution to the mystery.

The child continued to protest, but his eyes returned to

the watch. He sniffed and snuffled, but the lure was too bright to be resisted . . . He took it in eager paws, put it carefully down where he could see it while he steered, and, still sobbing quietly, picked up a paddle.

He found his way through the labyrinth of trees without difficulty, by twisting lanes and under screens of grey moss, until they reached the outer border of the lake, and left it to paddle up a narrow waterway that was almost entirely hidden by over-reaching trees. After some time the channel grew broader, the vegetation sparser, and the water gave out a brackish smell. They were approaching the sea. And presently, though the difference was hardly perceptible, their surroundings were materially altered. They were no longer on a piece of land intersected by many water-channels, but on a piece of sea studded by many islands. Of these the largest and most difficult to find was Egret Island.

They came to one that seemed larger than its neighbours. The landward end was swampy, and in a grove of cypresses egrets nested. They coasted it for some little distance until they came to a narrow channel up which the boy turned his canoe and presently beached it.

But now his fear returned, and when Juan would have landed he shrilly objected, and by signs indicated that Juan should stay in the canoe till he had seen the mysterious Missy Lal and, presumably, obtained permission for him to come ashore. Juan agreed impatiently, and sat down again. Tightly holding the watch, but slowly and with obvious doubts of his reception, the nigger boy went off by a narrow path that lost itself in the trees.

Juan lay down in the canoe to await whatever might happen, and before he could hazard more than three or four conjectures as to what awaited him, fell fast asleep.

When he awoke the sun had gone down and darkness, though not yet fallen, was imminent. He felt stiff and cold, but his discomfort vanished when he saw who had wakened him.

A girl in a green dress stood by the canoe, and to Juan she appeared both extremely attractive and vaguely familiar. But his wits were still half-asleep, and before they could rouse themselves they were startled by her cold and hostile voice.

'What are you doing here?' she asked.

Juan told her.

'And how did you get into the swamp?'

Juan explained that too.

I don't believe you,' said the girl. 'Who are you, and where do you come from?'

Juan told her.

'Those don't look like English clothes,' she said.

'They don't look like clothes at all,' Juan agreed.

'Well, I think your whole story's very suspicious,' said the girl, 'and you can't expect any help from me.'

'Then what do you propose to do?'

'I'm going to send the boy back with you to where he found you. He'd no business to speak to you –'

'He didn't, except in Gullah.'

'He's been forbidden to go to the lake at all, so I can punish him by sending him back there, and get rid of you at the same time.'

She turned and called to the nigger boy, who was waiting unhappily some distance away.

Juan laughed. 'No, you can't,' he said. 'I'm going to stay here.'

The girl flared superbly into temper and shouted, 'You'll do what I say, and instantly! No strangers are allowed on this island –'

'But I'm not a stranger,' said Juan. 'I can't claim to be an old friend, but I've seen you before and spoken to you. Only a few words, it's true –'

'Are you trying to make a fool of me?' the girl demanded.

Juan shook his head, smiling. He felt extraordinarily pleased with himself – though the mud on his face spoiled his expression of it – for his half-recognition of the girl had become certainty, in spite of her cold hard voice that assorted so badly with his memory of her.

'We were fellow-passengers on the *Corybantic*,' he said.

The girl stared at him.

'I crossed in her about seven months ago. You were in a private suite and one night I spoke to you through your cabin window.'

The girl came closer, looked at him intently for several seconds, and asked 'Do you mind washing your face? Whoever you are you're unrecognisable under that mud.'

Juan immediately knelt down by the water's edge and began to sluice his face, and while he scrubbed he described the plague of mosquitoes and the other hardships of his journey that were responsible for the unsightly spectacle that he made; knuckling his eyes, scouring the back of his neck, rinsing his hair, and talking busily the while, so that a certain intimacy began to invade the scene. When he had finished washing he stood up, his cheeks now very red, and faced the girl, who looked at him without speaking for half a minute.

Then she said slowly, 'I think I remember you. '

Juan was so pleased that he started to explain how vainly he had sought for her on the ship, and how disappointed he had been not to see her again before disembarking.

'I even went to Chicago to look for you,' he confessed.

'Why did you expect to find me there?' The girl showed some astonishment.

'Because your – ' Juan stopped in some perplexity. He meant 'Because Red-eye Rod Gehenna went there,' but as he did not know her relationship to Red-eye he hesitated between father and husband, and finally chose guardian.

'Because your guardian went there,' he said.

'You mean?'

'Rod Gehenna.'

'My father,' said the girl. 'You know all about him?'

'Not all,' Juan admitted, 'but I read the newspapers and they often discuss him. And while I was in Chicago I heard a lot, of course.'

'Of course,' the girl agreed, and studied Juan for another half-minute or so. Then quite suddenly she laughed in a bold and hearty way.

'What fun to find you here on Egret Island!' she exclaimed, and offered him her hand.

'Then you're going to let me stay here?'

'Why, certainly! Do you think I would let you go away and lose yourself in the swamp?'

As this had clearly been her first intention Juan answered with a non-committal smile and stepped ashore.

'You're not too tired to walk, are you?' she asked. 'It will be dark in a few minutes, and we've got four or five miles to go.'

She led him up the path that wound through the trees, and neither spoke for some minutes. Juan's gratification at seeing Red-eye's daughter again was so great as scarcely to leave room for surprise at the curious chance of finding her on a Carolina swamp-island. He recalled his brisk pursuit of her nearly six months ago, from the *Corybantic* through a New York speakeasy to Chicago and the battle over Cola Coloni's funeral; and he was ashamed – for she was very beautiful – to think that after his wound was healed he had scarcely given her another thought. But now his old emotion revived. The pain and misery of his passage through the swamp disappeared like morning vapour. There remained a residue of physical weariness and the discomfort of legs still heavy with mud, waist all wet with perspiration, and neck puffed-out with mosquito bites. But fear and anxiety had vanished as quickly as poor relations when her ladyship calls – and when was my lady ever so lovely as this, with dark eyes and pale red mouth, a green dress and a girdle of twisted gold, and overhead dark branches and a sky that rapidly grew black as the cypress trees?

The need for speech re-asserted itself simultaneously in

each of them, so that Juan's query where they were going met in headlong collision the girl's assertion that his trousers smelt vilely of the swamp.

'But don't let that upset you,' she said. 'I've a keen nose but it isn't over-delicate and little things like a smell don't worry me.'

So frank and free was her manner, so void of maidenish affectation, that their conversation thereafter was of the friendliest kind. Juan described his misadventures in Chicago and his more recent mishap with the mule, and Lalage – for that was her name – explained that after landing from the *Corybantic* she and her old nurse, under Rocco's charge, had come by sea to their Carolina home, where she had stayed ever since very happily indeed, for of all places she knew she loved best this wild and solitary country. She was, it appeared, a Child of Nature. Not the plaintive and timid Wordsworthian child, but the real pagan kind, self-sufficient, open-hearted, kept fresh and dewy by an innocence that is the very reverse of Christian innocence, for it accepts and is familiar with all the facts of physical life which the latter shrinks from, but is maintained in its innocence by ignorance of their occasional impropriety. It is true that Lalage did not immediately speak of these matters – except inferentially when she talked about the birds that were busy with their mating, and the mating of birds is a subject very nearly as harmless as the fertilization of plants; so reticent is an egg, so neutral its appearance, that its progenitors' knowledge of sexual matters must be slight indeed – and yet her manner gave Juan the feeling that here was a joyous pagan, no Greek simpleton or blue-ribboned romantic dairymaid, but a child of the modern earth and ancient, still generous sun. A Lalage of a more unsugared sweetness than Horace's, in whom it is likely there was too much of the confectioner's art, not wilderness honey but strained and urban stuff. *Dulce ridentem, dulce loquentem, Lalagen amabo*, he remembered. I wonder? he thought.

'Is your father at home?' he asked.

Lalage laughed. 'Nowhere near,' she said. 'You wouldn't be coming with me if he were. Strangers aren't allowed on Egret Island.'

It was obvious that any stranger would meet with difficulties in finding his way about on it, for the path was fantastically tortuous. Lalage explained that the island was seven or eight miles long, narrow and irregular in shape. The egrets from which it took its name were found only at the marshy westward end. The rest of the island was firm and dry, and near the eastern extremity rose to an eminence thirty feet above sea level. On the seaward slope of this rise Red-eye had built his house, a large building in Colonial style. Behind it and on either side were live oaks, and in front of it palm-trees through which glimpses of the ocean were visible – but it was night long before Juan and Lalage arrived.

His admiration for her pagan efficiency steadily increased as she led him without faltering in the darkness. She walked fast and confidently, laughed when Juan tripped over trailing roots, and shouted mocking answers to an owl whose close and eerie cry would have raised goose-flesh on an ordinary skin. She told Juan nothing about other occupants of the house they were going to, nor, after his enquiry for Red-eye, did he ask; such was her independence that he guessed there were only servants there.

The front of the house was softly lit. A yellow glow stained the colonial columns and overflowed into the darkness beyond. The door opened, and immediately a stout old woman pounced upon them, her voice shrill with disapproval. It was the ancient short-legged nurse whom Juan had seen aboard the *Corybantic*. She had been waiting for Lalage's return, ready to upbraid her for lateness, but unprepared to find a stranger with her. A dozen words were so near the tip of her tongue that they flew off before she saw Juan. Then, her carefully-dressed sentences forgotten, she stared wildly, flung up her arms (they were too short and would not rise easily or far), and screamed like an angry cockatoo.

'Hush, Vittoria!' shouted Lalage. 'Hush, you old fool! Mr. Motley is going to stay here. Be quiet, I say. Go and see that dinner is worth eating, and have a room got ready for him.'

Vittoria answered fiercely and volubly in Italian. Her voice was high-pitched and rough, and as she screeched her opposition her fat grey cheeks shook under their purple coat of powder. Lalage listened for some moments and then replied in the same language, yelling almost as loudly as Vittoria herself. The old woman's throat grew thicker and thicker as the big veins swelled, and her round black eyes protruded like a lobster's. Lalage stormed and threatened and stamped her foot. A door at the far end of the hall opened to disclose half a dozen negro servants, men and women, who stared in a dark and terrified ecstasy at the quarrel; and Juan waited with some surprise but more composure till it should end. Presently the old woman's throat grew dry with rage and her voice sank to a low saw-like note. But she continued to argue and protest. Then the last of Lalage's patience went. She seized Vittoria's hair, which was dyed a dull black and piled on top of her head, and hissed, 'Do what I tell you, you fat stupid old woman, or I'll break your neck!' Vittoria screamed hoarsely, now because of pain, not temper, and with tears making paste of the powder on her cheeks submitted. Her plump shoulders shook and her head jerked up and down with half-swallowed sobs as she went off to spend what was left of her anger on the cook.

Lalage called to the servants, who advanced with timid alacrity, and bade one of them take Juan to his room. She was quite untroubled by the altercation. She looked at Juan with a whimsical expression.

'Vittoria is a good soul,' she said, 'but her temper's dreadful. I know how to deal with her, though. Now hurry up and get a bath, because I'm hungry.'

Red-eye had furnished his house, or had it furnished, with extravagant taste. Juan's bedroom was luxurious and his bathroom elegant in green and silver. While he bathed the servant found clothes which would approximately fit him: flannel suits belonging to Red-eye, and a large selection of shirts, neck-ties, and other haberdashery.

When he went down to dinner he found Lalage dressed with a sort of careless splendour in red Chinese silk. She sat with her legs over the side of a chair and waved a long bare arm to Juan as he came in.

'Vittoria's friendly again,' she said. 'She wanted to know all about you, and now she thinks it will be nice for me to have a little company. She likes to have a man in the house, though her own time's gone.'

The dinner was admirable: a shrimp cocktail dressed with an exquisite and poignant sauce, an omelette of chickens' livers, a roast duckling, and an iced soufflé. They drank an Amontillado sherry, a bottle of Château Yquem, and some very good Cockburn's port. Juan thought of Red-eye Rod Gehenna with increasing respect, but it struck him that Lalage's attitude of a Child of Nature was ill-suited to so cultured a menu.

After dinner they sat on the piazza and looked out between fluted columns at the darkness where palm-trees rustled and the sea murmured with enchanting languor. Lalage talked of her family.

Her mother, who was dead, had been born in America of Irish and Greek parents. Her father was a Neapolitan by birth, but he had left Italy while still a boy and found more scope for his talents in New York. There he became associated with gangsters, among whom he showed a remarkable aptitude for leadership. Prospects in Chicago being still more promising, he had gone to the Middle West with a growing reputation and endless ambition. Five years of unremitting labour had placed him at the head of his own organisation, with a private brewery and a fixed tribute (by way of protection) from laundries, pawnbrokers, dyers' establishments, brothels, hat-cleaning shops, gambling houses, and other places of business or pleasure. Then had come the two years' war with Black

Reilly's gang, that left Gehenna with his staring wounded eye and a national reputation which, like that of all great men, was now almost independent of further deeds and thickened by mere existence. He was the wealthiest beer-baron in the country, a maker and destroyer of politicians, a symbol of lawless monarchy, a household word. Reflecting on these matters Juan thought of Lalage as indeed a sovereign's daughter.

She spoke of her father with apparent detachment. He was illiterate, she said, but understood people of his own kind very well, and was brave without being rash. He had a natural air of authority and a lot of low cunning. A born autocrat, in fact. His Irish-Greek wife had had a sense of humour and once laughed at him – but only once. Two years later, with the memory of his tyrannous displeasure vividly in her mind, she had reached the end of her decline and died. And during his brief infrequent visits to Egret Island Red-eye was a czar at whose anger the household grew faint, and whose pleasure was attended with obsequious speed.

Lalage laughed. Her father, she said, had lately become ambitious in a social way. It was for social reasons they had visited Europe the previous year: a question of her marriage. Her father had contemplated her alliance with an Italian princeling, envisaging for himself retirement to his native land and a position not far from the Duce's throne. For the princeling was an ardent Fascist, well thought of by Mussolini. Red-eye had interviewed the Duce, who favoured the nuptials at a price which was, perhaps, not excessive for the privileges that Red-eye desired, but nevertheless was far greater than he meant to pay. The scene grew tense and dangerous as the Autocrat of Italy and the Master of Chicago faced each other and discussed the propriety of a tax of half a million dollars on a patriot who wished to re-enter his native country and marry his daughter to a pillar of its society. Red-eye had controlled himself long enough to withdraw in safety, and then returned to America in great wrath.

It was a dull journey, said Lalage, for they had travelled in some state, as befitted their position, and she had been required to behave meekly while under her father's eye, who approved of domestic habits and expected females to be modest. Very boring indeed. She had been glad to get back to Egret Island.

'How long have you lived here?' Juan asked.

'Most of the time since I was husband-high.' Lalage yawned, and then abruptly said good-night. Juan sat for some little time listening to the rise and fall of the palm-trees as they shook their heads that the wind was combing; and thought how handsomely Jake had served him by luring him into the swamp after alligators.

VIII

In the morning Egret Island woke to a gaiety beyond compare. The palm-trees flaunted their tufts in a breeze that seemed to sparkle as it blew, and between their swaying tops shone the bright azure of the sea. Across the lawn flew jays and scarlet tanagers. Sunlight danced on white walls and tall white columns, and in the distance small waves made a joyful noise as they clattered on the beach. Birds whistled blithely, and from the servants' quarters sounded the shrill voices of negro children.

Juan sang as he bathed:

> 'Roses and lilies her cheeks disclose,
> But her ripe lips are more sweet than those –'

Even while shaving he sang, out of the side of his mouth, for it was a pleasure to use one of Red-eye's good razors after the unguarded blade he had been borrowing from old Zed Kinney –

> 'Press her, caress her,
> With blisses her kisses –'

And never a thought came to his mind of the last time he had sung that song, for such a morning was not meant for memory but present joy –

'Dissolve us in pleasure and–'

The fine tie he was knotting was a Leander tie that Red-eye had bought in England; and what, Juan thought, could be more suitable when Hero awaited him?

They met as happily as maypole dancers encountering face to face while they wind their bright ribbons round the shameless tree. It was dancing weather. Spring was abroad, tickling the world with wanton fingers and whispering thoughts of improbable bliss in all kinds of ears: prettily finished white ears, and flapping ears of red, and old men's loose long-lobed ears with sprouts of whisker in their holes, and pointed devil-ears, and ears that blushed coy-pink as they hid under their wearer's sweet-smelling hair. Spring was abroad. Primroses grew on mossy banks and Priapus stood shouting on a hill. Leda's cob was swimming on the lakes, and in lush meadows mild-eyed Europa's lover lowed. Cooks came forth hot from their kitchen-fires to quench hot policemen on their beat, and sparrows strove lustily on the house-tops. With hearts quick-beating, nymphs ran down the forest-rides and passing shepherds swooned at the lovely sight of their leaping breasts – but satyrs in the brake whistled with shrillest glee and bounded after. May-fly were on the water and gallant undulations shook dull marriage beds. To old tunes new words were furnished, and new vows for old were gaily given. With all her company of maidens and youths, ancient beaux with bent knees but sturdy hearts, dryads and goat-foot fauns, fat counsellors of state and ivory terns of the sea, with flowers and bulls and dancing girls, Spring was abroad again. . . .

For Juan and Lalage the morning passed quickly and yet not too quickly, and in the afternoon when the wind had gone down and the sun shone more hotly they found themselves sitting under a palm-tree, silent. She sighed, and Juan looked thoughtfully at the sea. Then, moved by a single impulse, each turned to the other and in a moment – so comformable to desire are human bodies, for all their gangling look – they were locked like wrestlers in a tight embrace.

Presently Lalage freed herself and said thoughtfully, 'We're very wise to trust to our instincts, aren't we? Intellect and reason are all very well in their way, of course, but it's only by intuition that you ever really behold the heart of life.'

'I expect you're right,' said Juan, somewhat surprised by this justification of a situation which to his mind required no such labour.

'So Bergson says,' continued Lalage.

'Who?'

Lalage bit her lip. 'Oh, nothing. I just happened to remember something, that's all. What I mean is that it's best to live simply and frankly, and give oneself wholeheartedly to natural pleasures. If you love me, why shouldn't you say so? And if I love you why should I conceal it?'

'Don't,' said Juan.

'I won't,' said Lalage, 'because I believe in being natural.'

It occurred to Juan that a Child of Nature does not often *believe* in being natural, since such a belief predicates a condition of sophisticated self-consciousness; but circumstances did not favour a hyper-critical attitude. He drew her into a more comfortable position and patted her leg. . . .

'Did you say something about Bergson a little while ago?' he asked.

'I had a tutor who used to talk about him, but we didn't get on well and she left.'

Juan admitted to himself that she could be a Child of Nature though she had heard of Bergson. 'Nature is made better by no mean but Nature makes that mean,' wrote Shakespeare; and Aristotle had said something to the same purpose. With heart at ease Juan continued to pat her leg.

Lalage was none of your heavy-lying, shut-eyed, shrinkaway,

or passive lovers; she gave kiss for kiss and kissed with open eyes that had a pleased and lively look in them. She hugged Juan with as good a will, though scarcely the same strength, as he hugged her; and if she gasped for breath her gasps at once became laughter and she pressed closer to be again encircled. When Juan stopped stroking her hair she began to stroke his. Her breath was sweet and her skin, even from close kissing distance, as flawless as a petal. Before they had been under the palm-tree for half an hour Juan was deep in love.

And then, between love and the knowledge that the battle was his but for the last charge, he grew perverse. He felt the cold hand of conscience on his shoulder. He remembered that nature, despite all praise of her, is remorselessly logical. For every action she has an appropriate sequel, and though civilised man out of his impious ingenuity has contrived means to deprive certain acts of their due consequence, yet here in this wilderness Juan possessed no such means and believed it impossible to procure them. . . . The white man's burden, thought Juan, is a kind of traffic signal, a recurrent injunction to Stop!

In order to think more clearly about this problem Juan stood up and suggested that they walk to the other side of the island. Lalage was plainly surprised by such a proposal, and more than a little hurt in her self-esteem. But she did not care to refuse and so they walked for a long while, rather aimlessly and without much conversation, until it was time for dinner.

When they returned to the house they were affectionately greeted by Vittoria, whose alarm at Juan's presence had completely vanished. Now she chuckled delightedly as she told Lalage the news of the day and made Neapolitan jokes about young men and maidens. Vittoria shared her mistress's views on nature and was prepared to take a vicarious delight in all its works.

Even a dinner as perfectly cooked and more richly chosen than the previous night's, even the champagne they drank with it, could not reconcile Juan's difficulty with his conscience. When they sat again in darkness on the piazza, and wild perfumes blew about them but none so enticing as that which Lalage used, his gestures of affection were lukewarm.

At last, with the candour of a child of earth, Lalage asked him what was wrong.

'If one blindly follows nature one must be prepared for natural consequences,' he pointed out.

Lalage's intuition was excellent.

'Contraception has delivered us from slavery,' she explained. 'We can follow nature freely nowadays.'

'Yes, but – '

'Oh, that's all right. There's no need for you to worry,' she said; and sat comfortingly on Juan's knee, where she had no further cause to complain of his laggarding, for she immediately found herself being carried upstairs and into the Ivory room, which was hers.

There in the morning Vittoria wakened them with tea and fruit, and such was Vittoria's prescience that there were two cups, two plates, and two oranges on her tray. Such too was her string of Neapolitan jokes about sleepiness and other bedroom matters that Juan – though he could not understand what she said – thought she must have lain awake half the night rehearsing them; and until Lalage at last told her to go she was still finding new ones.

For some days they lived in a cloudless delight. Love, with its peculiar quality of radiant insulation, narrowed their world to an enchanting present. Neither past nor future existed for them, but only a vernal actuality. Happiness has neither art, nor history, nor philosophy. It is or it is not, and when it is it is sufficient. They talked, it is true, but to repeat the words they used would not recapture their conversation; for lovers' talk is sweet as cherries, but their words, coldly remembered, are no more than the dry blanched stones of the cherries.

Partner in the idyll was the island itself, with its palms and red-birds and snowy herons, the dancing Atlantic wind and the sun-pointed sea; and on the periphery (like clowns in an old play, not of it but near it, and useful to keep things comfortable) were Vittoria and the servants: Vittoria slapping her sides, wheezily chuckling, bringing new jokes to the Ivory room of a morning – a humorous, short-tempered, immoral old godmother who waddled to and fro bullying the niggers; and the servants themselves, ducking, curtsying, broadly grinning – a lazy and laughing company well pleased to have some new subject for their gossip.

At the end of a week, however, Lalage grew thoughtful, a little impatient, and abstracted. For a whole day she appeared occupied with ideas she would not share, and on the following day, after some hesitation, excused herself, saying she had work to do. What the work was she would not explain, but she disappeared for several hours. On the next day and the day after that the same thing happened, and Juan was somewhat displeased both by the solitude in which he was left and the secrecy – which appeared to him both foolish and unnecessary – that Lalage maintained. She refused point-blank to tell him either the nature of her work or where she did it, and with her first sign of unfairness said, 'I know I can rely on you not to try and find out.'

One morning soon after she had vanished in what was now her customary manner, Juan went to the Ivory room to fetch a book that he had left there. As he picked it up he heard a faint metallic tapping which apparently came from behind one of the four doors in the room. Of these doors one opened into the corridor, another into a bathroom, the third into a large wardrobe, and the fourth was kept locked. Lalage had told him that behind it there was a small dressing-room that she had never put to its proper use, and was now filled with half-wanted possessions, nursery relics, unhung pictures, and the like. It was behind this door that Juan heard the small irregularly punctuated noise.

He knocked and tried the handle. The door was locked. And the noise stopped.

'Are you there, Lalage?' he called.

There was no reply. He repeated his question and knocked again. No answer came.

Later in the day he spoke to Lalage about this curious experience, but she only laughed at the idea of there being any mystery in the house.

'It was probably a cricket you heard,' she said, and sustained her explanation by a series of caresses.

On the following morning, however, after Lalage had left him, Juan again went up to the Ivory room and heard the faint irregular noise. It was certainly not a cricket, and what it did suggest was an article unlikely to hold Lalage's interest.

The Ivory room was at the south end of the long rectangular building. It was a large room occupying the whole depth of the house, with a window in the east wall and another in the west, but between it and the outside southern wall were the bathroom and this locked dressing-room. The dressing-room (as one could see from outside) had a window and a small verandah beneath it; but this verandah was not continuous with the larger one under the eastern window of the Ivory room, and had indeed no access but from the dressing-room itself. It would be possible to get a long ladder and climb up to it, but Juan was unwilling to parade his curiosity in so marked a manner. He preferred to wait for some friendly chance.

In so lazy and delicious a life even curiosity grew mild, and Lalage's daily disappearance, though always attended with regret, became a matter of routine. Her diurnal absence, indeed, gave zest to the idyll by dividing it into chapters; and to every instalment she brought new charm.

They explored the island from the dark cypress swamp at one end to the open beach at the other. They picked flowers and watched the birds, and Lalage would discuss the merits of naturalism with unfailing interest. Then, when she had finished, and sometimes before, if there was nothing else remarkable to see, the manner of her walking was in itself an entertainment to Juan – how keenly he remembered his excitement at Le Havre when he first saw that rhythmic progress across the *Corybantic's* deck! Upright as a palm, with an indolently seductive lateral movement of the podex! It was irresistible. Juan would linger behind to watch it, and after a minute of rapturous observation leap forward and embrace her with ever-renewed enthusiasm.

Or they would swim in the sea that was still too cold to linger in. Five or ten minutes would be enough and then, bright pink from head to heels, they would run up and down the beach to warm themselves, and lie in the soft dry sand beyond the tide-mark, rolling in it till they were powdered like fakirs, and so had to go back into the sea to wash the glittering dust away.

It was exasperating when, in the midst of this gaiety, Lalage turned serious, reminded Juan that she had work that could not wait, and without more argument busily put on her clothes and walked away. To relieve one of these lonelinesses Juan went one day to the negro quarters at the back of the house and spent an idle hour watching the children play. The same small boy whose canoe had rescued him from the cypress lake had a captive raccoon which he was endeavouring to tame, but the 'coon showed no inclination to be civilised and presently bit its owner's nose and escaped. Now a block of low buildings – a laundry, an engine-house, and so on – extended backwards from the north end of the house, and on one of their roofs the 'coon took refuge. At once the whole flock of children pursued it with shrill cries of lamentation, led by the weeping owner all bloody about the nose. They stood and cried vainly for it to return. The 'coon stayed where it was, its little beady eyes shining brightly and a tip of sunlight on its sharp black nose. In a rash moment Juan offered to retrieve it.

He had no difficulty in getting on to the first roof, but as soon as he got there the 'coon retreated to the next, which was a little higher. In this way Juan soon found himself, far from the ground, on the roof of the house itself. And yet he was no nearer to the 'coon, which was retreating southwards. Doggedly Juan followed it along the ridge. It reached the very end of the roof and appeared for a moment to be cornered; but in another second it slipped daintily down the slope. Still Juan followed it, for the roof was not steep. Half-way down the 'coon went over the edge and on to a verandah. By hanging at arm's length Juan found that he could reach the balustrade. He did so, and leapt lightly down. And then he realised that he was outside the window of Lalage's mysterious dressing-room. He forgot all about the 'coon and peered through the glass.

The room was neither a dressing-room nor a lumber-room. The wall opposite the window was lined with a bookcase full of volumes in sombre colours, indigo, calf, and maroon. In front of it was a square business-like table at which Lalage sat with her back to the window. Juan could hear an irregular metallic tapping. She was busy with a typewriter.

While he still mused on this curious discovery Lalage's attention was caught by the darkening of the window. She looked round quickly, and at first Juan scarcely recognised her.

Her hair was combed tightly back to show a high naked brow, and like a hurdle over her face were heavily-rimmed tortoise-shell glasses. She wore a plain dark blue dress nothing like the gay frocks that Juan had always seen her in. Even her nose looked different. Under those preposterous spectacles it stuck out like a pale bleak emblem of enquiry, and Juan stared at it in amazement. But his amazement did not equal Lalage's. For a moment she could not move. Her nerves were too shocked to carry a single impulse. Then they tingled under the burden of forty struggling for priority. Anger, dismay, and indignation contorted her face, and with incredibly rapid movements she snatched off her spectacles, tugged a handful of hair across her bare forehead, and thrust a mass of papers into a drawer.

She pulled open the window and demanded passionately, 'What do you mean by coming here? What right have you to pry and peer through windows? Didn't I tell you to leave me alone? How dare you spy on me like this!'

'I got here entirely by accident,' said Juan.

'That's a lie! You couldn't get here by accident. You came deliberately to spy on me! I hate you and I wish you'd been left in the swamp to be bitten by cotton-mouths and eaten by buzzards!'

'I got on to the verandah by accident,' Juan repeated. 'In any case I don't see why you should go to all this trouble to conceal a library – unless, of course, it's an improper one, in which case I'd like to look at it.'

Juan climbed through the window in spite of Lalage's active opposition and the rage in her face. She stamped her feet and swore, first in English and then in Italian. Her English maledictions were viciously pronounced but few in number, for it is only by skilful combination of the elementary words that English swearing can be given much variety. Her Italian imprecations, however, flowed in a stream of sibilant ferocity, now breaking into explosive rapids, now running swift and solid as a mill-lade, and anon falling in clouds from a great height of temper.

Juan looked at her books and read such names as Croce, Bergson, Ellis, Russell, Freud, Jung, Krafft-Ebbing, Rank, Flügel, Ferenczi, Nordau, Spengler, Poincaré, Einstein, and Pavlov.

Good God!' he exclaimed, 'then it isn't poetry you're writing. I thought that's what you were keeping dark.'

'Why do you think anything about me? What right have you to look at my books and laugh at them? Can't I read what I like without asking you? Oh, why ever did you come here!'

'What are you writing, if it isn't poetry?'

Juan took a step towards the drawer into which Lalage had bundled her manuscript, and immediately she leapt at him like a wild-cat, hitting, scratching, and kicking. Her nails tore his cheek and Juan lost his temper long enough to take both her wrists in his left hand and with his right catch her a ringing smack on her face.

Lalage howled

'Be quiet!' said Juan, and slapped her again.

Lalage slid to the floor and crouched there whimpering with pain and anger while Juan opened the drawer and took out her manuscript. The top sheet bore a legend: 'THIS PETTY PACE. A Novel.' On another, picked at random, he read:

'Masha pondered. That oval pinkness pierced and lit by eyes in the tall silver mirror (but candles flickered) was her face. What did it mean? To mean nothing was to be dead flesh like the starfish she had once picked off a beach. It must mean something. But what, what? She must know the truth, probe smooth mystery for truth, since truths unburdened, truths hidden in the subconscious dark, turn cancerous and itch and feed on life. She must know the truth about herself, or how could she truly express herself? And not truly to express oneself was not to live truly. She must have no fear. Did not Croce say – "True ethical volition, the really moral will, is a creator and promoter of life. It need therefore have no fear of contamination in using life to obtain greater and fuller life." '

Juan put down that page and read another:

'Her breathing grew faster. Her hands felt blindly for him. Her body tingled with a thousand pin-points of fear and rapture. Her throat felt dry, but a little perspiration broke on her forehead. . . .'

Lalage could stand his silence no longer, and jumping to her feet cried, 'Put it down! Please, please put it down!'

'But it's a novel, isn't it? And novels are meant to be read,' said Juan mildly.

'Not till they're published,' Lalage snapped like a turtle.

Juan's eyes returned to the book-case with its store of richly bound learning.

'Do you want all those books on philosophy and physiology and physics to write a novel?' he asked.

'A novelist is supposed to be an educated person nowadays,' said Lalage sullenly.

'And education is no longer the Three R's but the Three Ph's?'

'You need more than that. There's psychology and music and anthropology and painting and history at the very least that you've got to understand before you can write a novel to-day.'

'But I thought you were – well, a rather happy-go-lucky person who laughed at books. A Child of Nature.'

'I can't help what you thought.'

Juan felt that this was not quite true, but he did not argue the point. Instead he asked, 'What is your novel about?'

'A woman.'

'And is she a psychologist, or a painter, or a physiologist?'

'Don't be a fool. She's just a woman. But she meets people – men mostly – and one of them is a painter, and another a philosopher, and – well, people have got to talk about something, haven't they? And these are the things that modern people do talk about.'

'You mean in novels?'

'And in real life too, I suppose.'

'But still I don't understand why you should have wanted to keep all this secret.'

'Well, it wasn't any business of yours, and you wouldn't have understood, and – and you'd have been on your guard.'

'Against what?'

Lalage kept sulky silence.

'Against what?' Juan persisted. 'Tell me. I want to know.'

'You wouldn't have said things to me. You wouldn't have –'

Lalage bit her lips, her cheeks grew red, and then in a voice that was half defiance and half a wail, 'You'd have guessed that I was taking notes,' she cried.

'Taking notes?' repeated Juan with a crescent horror in his voice.

'Well, I had to learn from someone, hadn't I, before I could write a book about it?'

'You mean?'

'Taking notes on you, you idiot, and how you make love, and what I feel when you do. Now you know all there is to know, so go to hell, will you? Go to hell, I say!'

Juan stood in such a daze, so numb with the shock of finding himself anatomised and his nakedness written into a book, that without protest he let Lalage open the door and push him rudely out. She closed it with a bang and he heard the key turn in the lock.

IX

That night Juan dined alone, and slept alone in the room he had first occupied. The next day he spent alone, conscious of hostility in all about him. The servants no longer wore friendly smiles, and Vittoria, when he saw her, glared like a raddled Medusa. Lalage stayed in her room. She would not answer when he knocked. Even the raccoon, that had been the cause of all the trouble and was now safely in its cage again, showed its teeth and tried to bite when he went to visit it.

Juan was very properly irate. He had been put in the wrong through no fault of his own. True, he had slapped Lalage's face, but she had deserved it – three raw strips on his cheek showed what her nails had done. And it was also true that he had profaned the mystery of her literary retreat. But his profanation had been objectionable only because he himself was the subject of her exercises. He groaned to think of the things he had said and the things he had done, the half-articulate extravagance of love, not meant to be remembered beyond the moment of utterance, but now perpetuated by Lalage's typewriter. Love under cover of the darkness was proper in all its fancies, its whimsical invention, and sudden helplessness. But draw back the cover, turn on the light, and love will blush with a scarlet shame. And while Lalage's body had been so joyously and enthusiastically his partner, her brain had stood aside, marking this and that, storing impressions, recording the minutiae of action, to put them in a book! It was intolerable. The more he thought of it the angrier he became. The angrier he grew the more he remembered what might have gone to fill a chapter. And the more he remembered the more awful the whole business seemed. The surprise of finding that Lalage was by no means what she appeared – a simple Child of Nature – was almost lost in the shock of discovering the repellent nature of her secret activity.

He walked about nursing his injury, so that it grew and grew, until by very excess it lost significance. Add Pelion to Ossa and you reach the magnificence of the clouds; but pile Olympus on Pelion and both will tumble back to earth. Indignation was seldom more than a luncheon-guest in Juan's mind.– He lacked, it may be, the moral qualities necessary to sustain it for long periods.– At any rate, his anger began to give way before the cuckoo-like crowding of laughter.

This weakness in himself gave rise to sympathy for Lalage – after all he had slapped her severely and it was distressing to have a secret spoiled – and sent him off to make his peace. But Lalage's door was still locked. She was not yet prepared to forgive or be forgiven, and so for another night Juan slept alone.

But on the following afternoon he found her door open, and visible through it Lalage lying face-down on her bed.

'I thought you were never coming to forgive me,' she said in a tone of quiet and confirmed sorrow.

Juan contented himself with offering the belated comfort she wanted.

Presently she said: 'You don't really mind me writing about us, do you? Nobody will recognise you in the book because I'm making several different men out of you. You've no idea how helpful you've been.'

'I don't fancy being used as material for research,' said Juan. 'Did you coldly invite me here just as a biological specimen?'

'No, of course not. I liked you as soon as I saw you properly and remembered talking to you on the *Corybantic*. And I was so lonely. Then after you had come I fell really in love with you. I love you still, in spite of the way you've behaved. You slapped me dreadfully hard.'

'That will give you something else to write about.'

'It may,' said Lalage thoughtfully. 'As a matter of fact I made some notes about how I felt just after you left, in case I decide to give Masha (that's the woman in my book) a really brutal paramour. You've been so helpful. I think I've got enough material to give her six different lovers, and that ought to be enough for one book, don't you think? Since you came I've been writing two or three thousand words a day, and before that I often used to sit down and find that I had absolutely nothing to say. It's awful when you're writing a novel and have nothing to put in it.'

'Then why did you want to write one?'

'To express myself, of course. Our duty as individuals is to express ourselves. A living being is a centre of action, and if we don't act – and act as individuals – we forfeit our right to be considered living. And we're not only living but conscious beings, and as free will is a corollary of consciousness, to say that we're free means that we know what we're doing. But how can we know what we're doing if we're not doing anything? That was my trouble before you came. You gave me a chance to exercise my free will and realise my consciousness in action.'

'Did your tutor teach you all this?'

'No. I went to college for four years.'

'So you haven't lived here ever since you were husband-high? And your simplicity was only a pose?'

'It wasn't a pose! I'm often quite simple and enjoy it tremendously, and I really honestly believe in an ecstatic surrender to love. But you can't expect me to think one way all the time any more than you would expect me never to change my dress. It's just as natural to change one's ideas and want to read philosophy as it is to be *simply* natural and trust to intuition. Surely you see that?'

Juan said that he did. She protested so earnestly that it was the least he could do, and she looked so charming, pouting her philosophy, that he took her in his arms to soothe and further re-assure her.

'You see,' said Lalage from the midst of endearments, 'life is so very complicated that we have constantly to re-arrange ourselves in order to deal with it. And yet we really ought to express ourselves as independent social units. We have a duty to ourselves and yet we've got to pay tribute to life. It's very difficult, isn't it? Sometimes I don't know what to do.'

'Well, don't worry about it,' said Juan. 'Perhaps it doesn't matter very much anyway.'

'It matters dreadfully! Think of the eternal struggle between Free Will and external circumstance! If we believe in Free Will it's our duty to line up behind it – and of course you do believe in Free Will?'

'Oh, of course,' said Juan.

At this moment they were startled by a succession of screams in which terror and bewilderment were equally mixed. For some minutes they had been half-conscious of chattering voices outside. The servants were gossiping over something. They had gathered in front of the house and were somewhat excited. Their voices rose to a higher tone. But the gradual crescendo left Juan and Lalage undisturbed till the sudden climax of Vittoria's wild screaming – there was no other voice on the island which could produce that heron-harsh note of fear.

Lalage turned white as mist and hurried to the window which overlooked the main entrance.

X

Clustered round the portico, making a great to-do, were all the negro servants, their wives, and families. Up the wide path that wound across the smooth palm-studded lawn came a little procession of sailors, staggering under the weight of the bales and packing-cases that they carried. And frosty-white against the blue sea, only half-visible through the feathery palm-tops, was a steam-yacht at anchor.

While she stared at these portents and read their instant meaning, as if to remove the last doubt of their significance there sounded a man's voice, harsh and domineering, that quelled the now weakening screams of old Vittoria.

Lalage felt a hand on her shoulder.

'What's the matter?' Juan asked, and was amazed by her expression when she turned to answer him. Such a countenance had he who

> 'So dull, so dead in look, so woe begone,
> Drew Priam's curtain in the dead of night,
> And would have told him half his Troy was burned.'

'It's father,' said Lalage.

Juan, who had forgotten all about Red-eye, immediately felt depressed at the prospect of another emotional scene. He detested such things, and having just lived through two he thought it hard that he should have to face a third. And with a father on the stage the action would probably become heroic – more tears, defiance, recrimination, and manly attitudes. Juan damned his luck and asked, 'What can we do about it?'

Lalage shook her head dismally. 'Nothing. It's too late. Oh, why should he come at this time?'

She seemed stupefied, as if by the arrival of an ogre.

'Well, he can't eat us,' said Juan with doubtful cheer. Before the last word was over his lips the voice they had already heard cried loudly, 'Lalage!'

It shook Lalage out of her torpor. 'Quick,' she said wildly. 'Out of the window – on to the roof – hide yourself or he'll kill you!'

Nearer now, the voice called again, 'Lalage!'

'Pretend you're glad to see him,' Juan suggested.

The door was flung open and Red-eye came in, stooping under the lintel. He took a step forward and stopped. He was very smartly dressed in a blue jacket and white trousers. The light fell on his great hooked nose, his yellow skin, and the bright red gleam under his right eye. He said nothing. Lalage, shaking with fright, tried to greet him. He did not answer, but his eyes moved inquisitively from one object in the room to another. His mouth opened slightly, down-drawn at the corners. Still he did not speak.

Angered by his theatrical silence Juan said, 'I suppose you want to know who I am and how I came here. It's rather a complicated story, but –'

Red-eye whistled twice, and Rocco and Wonny the Weeper appeared in the doorway behind him: Rocco looking red and hard enough to be bullet-proof, and Wonny whom Juan had last seen shooting between the lilies at Cola Coloni's funeral.

'Take that guy outa here,' said Red-eye.

Rocco and Wonny produced automatic pistols which they pointed at Juan. Lalage shrieked and flung her arms round his neck. With some little trouble her father pulled her away, and Juan, forgetting the gunmen, hit over her shoulder and felt his fist thud bonily against Red-eye's cheek. Then Rocco hit Juan on the head with his pistol-butt. Juan felt a thunder-clap of pain, and swung round to face the gunman. Unfortunately in doing so he turned his back to Wonny, who hammered him more soundly than Rocco had.

When Juan recovered consciousness he was in the room where he and Lalage had eaten so many exquisite dinners and drunk such splendid wine. Great cracks of pain assailed his head and the light hurt his eyes. Rocco and Wonny sat near him, talking together. They watched him casually, but paid no other attention when he groaned and tenderly felt his wounds. Their conversation continued. It was about some recent excitement in Chicago, but their words meant little to Juan. He only wished they would stop talking.

While her lover lay in this discomfort Lalage submitted to her father's questions. That Juan was his daughter's lover he soon discovered; there was clear evidence of Juan's occupation of the room, and Lalage in spite of fear was too proud of their relationship to deny it with any conviction. Red-eye's dramatic composure gave way to anger. His neck swelled, his face flushed darkly, and the red streak under his eye glittered amazingly. He said that she had disgraced him. He said that he had a name in the world which she by such infamous conduct had tarnished. He hissed and bellowed and snarled. He shouted the sacrifices he had made, the wealth he had lavished on her – even now were there not packing-cases full of rich gifts waiting at the door? – and he roared like a dragon on the theme of chastity and the incalculable torments that awaited those who bartered its holiness for the lewd pleasures of an impious world.– For Red-eye had lately been inclining to a religious view of life.

Like all men who have a position in the world he was anxious to keep it, and it seemed reasonable to his superstitious mind that one way in which to ensure his tenancy was to placate the gods. His social aspirations, which were daily growing, might also be assisted by the estate which was intermediate between him and the Jealousy Above. With these ends in view he had had several conversations with a priest, and made some handsome contributions to a church, and discovered that piety was a natural inhabitant of his soul.– Racketeering, rum-running, bribing the police, a little murder now and then, and drawing a dividend from brothels did not invalidate this discovery, for racketeering, rum-running and so on were his business, and a man must live – else where were the glory to God? Red-eye's religion was a compact with his Maker of the same sort as the compacts he made with the police: live and let live, with a handsome gratuity for tolerance.

His sudden and unexpected appearance on Egret Island was due to a crisis in Chicago's underworld. The only important gang not subject to him was Buck Maloney's, and a week before, to teach Buck a lesson, Red-eye's men had captured seven of Buck's followers and shot them in cold blood. But so far from being cowed by this, Buck was immediately imbued with a passion for revenge, and swore to have Red-eye's life. His first attempt miscarried, but Red-eye thought it wiser to leave his lieutenants to carry on the war while he and his bodyguard retired to the south. The shock of a narrow escape from death, moreover, had strengthened his religious convictions. And so to find that his daughter had contravened one of the most earnest of churchly ordinances – and contravened it with an invader of his secret island, an invader who might be an enemy and a spy – was bitterly wounding.

His wrath reached its apex and then slid down unhappily into self-pity.

'You sleeping here with that fellow,' he cried, 'while Buck Maloney was trying to put me on the spot! Don't you know that God's watching you all the time? And how can He look after me in all the danger I live in if He's watching you sleep with a dam' limey?'

Any reference to the Deity roused Lalage fiercely to deny him. Psychology, physiology, and physics had combined to fill her with such scorn of the idea that she could never lose an opportunity to express the most dogmatic incredulity. Now, although a minute earlier she had been quivering with fear at her father's anger, she sat up straight and said determinedly,

'God is merely the expression of man's incurable narcissism.'

Red-eye stared blankly. 'Are you saying something against religion?' he asked.

'Religion is only a social anaesthetic,' Lalage declared.

'D'you mean it's a bum show? Say, I've just given a hundred thousand bucks to the church of St. Mark in Chicago, and d'you think I'd pay a hundred grand for protection if it wasn't worth it? Not on your life. If you had the responsibilities I have you wouldn't sneer at religion in that ignorant way.'

Red-eye crossed himself and looked at Lalage with a solemn eye.

'Honour your father and your mother,' he continued. 'That's a commandment, isn't it? Well, d'you think you're honouring your father by sleeping with someone he's never seen? Of course you're not. You're committing mortal sin, and you're being immoral as well.'

'I have not been immoral! You don't know anything about it. Spencer says that "the highest conduct is that which conduces to the greatest completeness of life," and that conduct is moral as it makes the individual more integrated. My life wasn't complete till Juan came, and now it is. I've been integrated, if you know what that is.'

'Yes,' shouted Red-eye. 'You've been integrated and now you will have a baby, eh? Well, that young man will never integrate anybody else!'

He turned angrily to the door, but Lalage threw herself upon him and frantically pled for the acquittal of that innocent word. Red-eye listened sullenly.

'He comes to my island, he sleeps with you, and hits me in the face,' he said. 'If I don't kill him everybody will laugh.'

'You can't kill him,' Lalage sobbed. 'I love him more than anything else in the world.'

'I'll kill him with my own hands!'

'Then you'll kill me too.'

'No, Lalage, no! Not you, just him.' Red-eye relapsed into

melancholy. He was rich, he had a position in this world, and he had recently paid for his reception into Paradise. With so much to lose he could not bear to lose anything, certainly not the daughter on whom he had spent so much money, who was so beautiful in spite of her wickedness, and for whom he still meant to acquire a distinguished husband.

Lalage pled in vain.

'I must kill him,' Red-eye explained. 'If I let him go he will tell about my island.'

'Then why not let him stay?'

This suggestion threw Red-eye into such a passion that he nearly went off to murder Juan on the instant. Lalage's exuberant grief stopped him at the door. And now, in desperation, like a climber on a bare cliff seeking everywhere a finger-hold, she thought of her father's new-found sense of religion and begged for Juan's release on Christian grounds. Red-eye listened with growing consternation to her talk of charity, the Golden Rule, the commandment against killing, the injunction to turn the other cheek, the equally unreasonable advice to love one's enemies, the God who marked a sparrow's fall, and the terrible God who made vengeance his own prerogative. . . . Was this the religion to which he had contributed a hundred thousand dollars? he asked.

It was, said Lalage. And should he commit so grievous a sin as the murder of his guest – Red-eye protested in vain at this ascription – then his hundred thousand dollars would be wasted, for the Catholic who loses the life of grace by such an act, though he may still belong to the body of the Church, is no longer in the soul of the Church, and dying with that weight upon him will as surely burn in hell as atheists, heretics, and those who spit upon their mother's grave.

Red-eye cowered. As a business man he could not bear to contemplate the loss of so large an investment, and as a man who might any day have a bomb thrown at him he feared the thought of hell. And yet what could he do? For if he let Juan go free the story of his secret island would be published far and wide.

'Juan will promise to say nothing about it,' said Lalage.

Red-eye shook his head. He put small faith in promises. The young fool, being in love, might even try to find his way back to the island.

Then Lalage had a cunning idea. 'He will keep his promise if I say that he must for my sake, because you would revenge yourself on me if he told anyone about Egret Island.'

Red-eye was finally persuaded that under these conditions Juan might keep his word.

'To save his life I will tell him that,' said Lalage. And privately she thought: Before he goes I will see him in secret and make a rendezvous in England; because father will surely take me to Europe some time soon again – or even if he doesn't I shall be independent when my novel is finished, and able to go wherever I like.

Presently they went downstairs and Juan, who had fallen into a painful doze, woke to see Lalage before him, looking cheerful in spite of eyes inflamed by weeping.

'Father has promised to spare your life and let you go free if you will promise never to say anything about the existence of Egret Island, or your acquaintance with him or me, and never to return or try to return here,' she said.

Now Juan, although he had seen something of Red-eye's power in Chicago, and knew through his association with the bootleggers of Detroit that very many people were murdered in America without much notice being taken, could not help being annoyed at an offer to spare his life when it was made by someone who had obviously no right to do anything else with it. And in spite of his aching head he attempted to say what he felt on the matter.

'I should like to know what title you have to interfere either with my life or my death,' he said to Red-eye. 'To pretend that you have any jurisdiction over me is absolute nonsense, and the sooner you realise it the better. You're a megalomaniac –'

'Give him a sock on the jaw,' said Red-eye, and Rocco promptly obeyed. Lalage cried and hid her face.

Juan came to the conclusion that it was wiser, though undoubtedly galling, to hear in silence whatever Red-eye had to say. Slowly he got to his feet. The blow had aggravated the pain in his head and he felt very unhappy.

'Now listen,' said Red-eye. 'I'm a reasonable man. If I hadn't been a reasonable man I wouldn't be where I am to-day. You ask anybody in Chicago and they'll tell you I'm a reasonable man. And that evidence ought to be enough for you and everybody else. But there's limits to everything, see? So you'd better realise that what I say goes. I don't take my orders from no one. I *give* orders. There's no guy tells me where to get off. I tell them – *and they get!*'

Juan offered no comment. Rocco sat and watched his chief with an expression of admiration on his face, and Wonny looked mournfully out of pale eyes that his bulging embryonic forehead threw into shadow. Lalage bit her lip and then pretended to be at ease by patting her hair and smoothing her dress.

Red-eye continued: 'You come to my island without me knowing anything about it, you sleep with my daughter, and you give me a sock in the eye. Now all those things are wrong. They're immoral, and I don't like them. Do you think I would go live in somebody's house who I didn't know, and then ruin his daughter and hit him in the face? No, sir! And why? Because it isn't good ethics to do those things, and we all ought to respect purity and good ethics. You've acted all wrong to me – you've acted lousy to me – and have I gave you the works? No. Have I tell Rocco to bump you off? No. I am a reasonable man. I turn the other cheek, I love my enemy, and – and I watch the sparrows fall.'

Red-eye paused. Lalage had certainly mentioned sparrows –

and with apparent significance – during her exposition of the Christian attitude; but now they seemed to have lost their meaning. He frowned. He could think of nothing else to say, though a moment ago ideas and words had come easily enough. He concluded gruffly, 'And so I let you go free.'

'I don't like the way you refer to my relations with Lalage,' said Juan. 'In the first place you've got no business to keep her mewed-up on this island –'

'Rocco!' cried Red-eye in another access of temper.

Rocco got up and hit the protestant on the very bruise that his last blow had left.

When Juan opened his eyes he saw Lalage bending over him, and into the vertigo of returning consciousness her voice sounded: 'He can do anything he likes, whether he has the right to or not. For my sake be sensible, and don't argue. Just promise to say nothing about Egret Island, or I shall suffer. I shall be safe if you promise now.'

Her eyes entreated and her lips formed soundlessly, 'Promise, promise.'

'All right,' said Juan weakly.

'Make him swear to it,' said Red-eye.

Juan swore never to mention the existence of Egret Island, never to return and look for it, never to see Lalage again, under the penalty of grevious hurt to Lalage herself. . . .

'Good-bye,' she said, and wore a look of renunciation that deceived her father but puzzled Juan; for it seemed like play-acting, and he did not know his cue. Then he was taken roughly to a cellar and locked in it, while Lalage was shut in her Ivory room with old Vittoria – frightened to death and her purple cheeks sagging lifelessly – and Rocco at the door. Lalage believed that it would be some days before Juan was taken off the island, and before he left she could find means of communicating with him. Her plan might have worked had it not been for Wonny the Weeper.

As soon as the prisoners had been removed Wonny shook an

extra large pinch of cocaine on to the back of his hand and snuffed it up. He did not approve of Juan's life being spared but neither did he wish to argue with his chief, who was obviously in a difficult mood. Under the influence of cocaine, however, he conceived a plan, simple yet interesting to the executants, which would enable Red-eye to keep his promise to do no murder and yet obviate the danger of setting loose someone who knew the secret of Egret Island. No sooner was the plan evolved than Wonny sought an interview with Red-eye and propounded it. Red-eye was immediately impressed by its advantages. When, he wondered, should they carry it out?

'To-night,' said Wonny, impatient to see his idea put into practice. And Red-eye agreed.

Wonny's plan for disposing of Lalage's lover was perfectly simple. Between ten and eleven at night Juan was tightly trussed, thrown into a canoe, and towed out to sea behind the motor-boat which served as tender to Red-eye's yacht. Several miles from land the canoe was cast adrift. Fortunately Juan's conscious agony was brief, for he fell speedily into the coma of delayed concussion, the result of the hammering his head had got from the gunmen's pistol-butts. In this state he lay all night, and under the hot morning sun, while the canoe rocked perilously and on several occasions nearly turned over altogether. Luckily the sea remained calm, and what wind there was carried the canoe shorewards.

BOOK FIVE

CATHAY AND THE WAY THITHER

I

Graham Druten was cruising over the sea in his new monoplane when he saw something that interested him and steered towards it. He was a wealthy young man whose father had made several million dollars in the Californian oil-fields and lately bought a large house in Charleston, being attracted by the aristocratic reputation of the town. Graham Druten, however, was more interested in flying than in social distinctions.

The floating object which he had discerned proved to be a canoe, and as Druten flew round at close range he saw to his surprise that there was a body in it. He immediately turned back towards Charleston, landed there safely, and borrowed a motor-launch from the Yacht Club. With this he returned at full speed to look for the canoe.

After an hour of careful searching he found it again, and bringing his boat alongside discovered that the body in it was firmly tied about the wrists and ankles with rope. He and his companions lifted it into the launch and as they were laying it down they were relieved to see a sharp twitching movement agitate its arms and shoulders. They quickly cut away the ropes and while the launch headed for Charleston did all they could for the young man whose death they had so narrowly prevented. . . .

Juan lay unconscious for another thirty-six hours and returned to life in a hospital bed. Having asked where he was and been told Charleston, he offered the comment 'Where my Great-aunt Rachel Legaré lives,' and promptly lapsed into heavy slumber. Mrs. Legaré was notified of this circumstance, and as she had received from the Dekkers an account of their pleasure in Juan's society until his unfortunate disappearance with the mule, and later a welcome assurance of his survival, she did not hesitate to identify the young man as her grand-nephew. And as soon as the doctors discovered that it was safe to move him – for Juan was suffering not only from concussion but also from sunstroke and general collapse – he was taken to the old house near the Battery where Mrs. Legaré lived with her sister-in-law Sally.

Mrs. Legaré was a very small and delicate old lady who concealed, behind a manner of apparent timidity, great firmness of character. Miss Sally, on the other hand, was tall and strongly made, and in spite of eighty-three years carried herself with an air of assurance. Her manner was as confident as her appearance. She would say, 'Tut, tut, my dear sister,' or 'Nonsense, Rachel, nonsense!' in a loud and business-like voice, but none the less her nature was much more pliant than Mrs. Legaré's, and it was the latter who usually got her own way.

Miss Sally was so much influenced by Juan's good looks that she wore her best dresses, of lavender silk, and grey silk, and white silk with a black pattern, all the time he was in their house, and would have let him get up and walk about as soon as he said he wanted to. But Aunt Rachel, with an air of great timidity, said, 'No, no. You must stay quietly in bed for a long time yet,' and when he grew restless she sat with him and read the works of the nineteenth century Charleston poets (of whom there were several) who had all written long poems after an eighteenth century fashion.

When Aunt Rachel had finished reading Miss Sally would come busily in followed by a stout negress carrying chicken soup, or curds and cream, or perhaps beaten biscuits and stewed raspberries; and while Juan sat up and ate what was brought the two old ladies would watch him in the kindliest way, while Hannah the old negress, who was not really old, being barely over seventy, would chuckle delightedly to see his growing appetite, and sometimes even clap her fat sides with pleasure.

By-and-by he was allowed to get up and sit in the garden – though not in the sun – and then, very carefully and tactfully so as not to worry him, the old ladies began to enquire how he had got into so strange and pitiful a plight as that in which Graham Druten had found him. Juan's explanation that he had sworn to say nothing of his captors or the place of his captivity did not satisfy them by any means.

'You can't tell who tied you up and treated you in that abominable manner?' exclaimed Miss Sally indignantly. 'Nonsense! Of course you must tell, and they will receive long terms of imprisonment.'

But Juan refused to unravel the mystery. Though Red-eye had broken his share of the compact – in spirit and very nearly in fact – and so partially justified Juan in breaking his, there was Lalage's safety to consider, and after so convincing a demonstration of Red-eye's savagery Juan was afraid to jeopardise her position in any way. To think of her still on Egret Island was very distressing, and Miss Sally's questions aggravated the pain till Aunt Rachel, seeing his unhappiness, said mildly, 'It's really no concern of ours, sister, and I'm sure that Juan knows how to conduct his own affairs without our interference.' To which Miss Sally replied, 'Fiddlesticks!' but asked no more questions, restraining her dissatisfaction for later discussion with Aunt Rachel, when she ascribed the lawless state of the country to the Yankee victory in 1865. 'It was Sherman who set the national fashion in lawlessness and brutality!' she declared. 'Sherman is to blame for it all!' – And then they sat silently, thinking how much pleasanter it would have been had the South, and not the North, won that terrible war between the states.

Miss Sally was still interested in war. Sitting in the garden with azaleas behind her, snowy white and pink as coral, she would talk with relish of the European conflict.

Were you in it?' she asked Juan.

'I was only thirteen when it finished,' he said.

'You could have gone as a drummer-boy. There were lots of drummer-boys no more than twelve and thirteen years old in the War between the States. And when they could they picked up a gun and took a shot at the dam' Yankees too!'

'I don't think there were any drummer-boys in the last war,' objected Aunt Rachel in her mild and quavering voice.

'No drummer-boys? Nonsense!' Miss Sally was extremely scornful. 'How could there be a war without drummer-boys?'

'All the same,' said Aunt Rachel, 'I don't think there were any. Perhaps that's why it lasted so long.'

There were roses in the garden, Maréchal Niel and Malmaison, and beside the azaleas, white and purple irises, and wisteria, and jessamine that smelt more sweetly when the sun went down. There was a pool that reflected, in water like thick green glass, the pink azaleas and dogwood starry and cool. And in the water were gross fat tadpoles, four or five inches long, bulb-headed, fleshy-tailed, mottled grey-green, that clung like leeches to the water-weed at the side of the pond. Jays and scarlet tanagers flew between the trees, mocking-birds called in the branches, doves murmured softly, and common little brown sparrows hopped about unperturbed by all this gorgeous company.

In these surroundings Juan rapidly regained his strength, and the nightmares which at first plagued him became less frequent. He was very melancholy for some time to think that he and Lalage had been parted in the middle of a reconciliation that might have introduced a new era of delight – even against a new background of literary significance – and he sadly regretted the carelessness which had permitted Red-eye to take them by surprise. But relief at his own escape and the natural happiness of convalescence allied to combat this sorrowful dealing with the past, and his spirits slowly returned with bodily strength.

Aunt Rachel had sent a long cable to his mother, who replied at even greater length, displaying much concern and then assuring Mrs. Legaré that no number of adventures would harm Juan, who was, she asserted, peculiarly adapted to endure the vicissitudes of fortune. She sent five hundred dollars to assist in restoring his morale.

Graham Druten called frequently to enquire after Juan's health, and when the latter was able to move about freely they swam together off Sullivan's Island and the Isle of Palms, played a little tennis, and took some short flights in Druten's aeroplane. This last exercise alarmed both Aunt Rachel and Miss Sally, but they concealed their anxiety lest Juan should consider them older and more old-fashioned than they really were, since they took great pleasure in his company and liked to think that he found some in theirs. They enjoyed taking short walks with him along the Battery, or showing him such sights as St. Philip's church, the old Slave Market, and the statue of Pitt that had one arm broken off, so very long ago, by an English cannon ball. And Juan delighted in their entertainment, and would have willingly walked about Charleston all day looking at such things and at the negroes who so out-numbered white people on the streets – enormous mammies gossiping at the corners; men who leaned negligently against lamp-posts and amiably chatted to girls with arms akimbo and chocolate smiling faces; a woman black as coal with a cherry-coloured hat and a leaf-green dress; the flash of pink gums and white teeth when they laughed; a little old man with a straw hat and a high collar and gold spectacles on his flat black nose; girls with short skirts and white stockings that looked dingy because of the colour beneath –

'We've never had any trouble with the negroes here,' said Aunt Rachel. 'They were always well-treated in South Carolina.'

After Juan had been there for some weeks and their tenuous blood-relationship was buttressed firmly by friendship, Mrs.

Legaré showed him a miniature of her husband, Captain Francis Legaré, who had been killed at Gettysburg. He was, in spite of his whiskers and his youth, very like Miss Sally, and it occurred to Juan that Francis's grandmother, had she been living when the miniature was done, may have looked to Francis just as Miss Sally did that evening to him. But Miss Sally still regarded Francis as her elder brother, and Aunt Rachel still remembered him as the strong and splendid lover. They did not think of him as someone like Juan, sixty years younger than they, for their hearts had not grown old with their bodies but were still proud and tender in the habit of youth. Their hearts' contemporaries were the young Confederate soldiers who fell at Gettysburg, and they thought of war in terms of drummer-boys, and of life as something lovely and exciting and irrevocably sad.

Juan listened to their tales of the Civil War, the long siege of Charleston, and the gallantry of a lost cause. It seemed a splendid thing to fight in a war that was passionately waged for principle alone, and the old ladies' stories excited him so that he felt he could no longer stay in this quiet town, but must set out to look for adventures of his own. – Yet the desire to go was oddly mingled with a desire to stay where he was, for nowhere else in America had he found such comfort and easy sweetness.

But the old ladies, for all their charm, were very old, and he could not stay with them indefinitely, so when Graham Druten invited him to fly across the continent to Southern California Juan accepted without much hesitation. Like everybody else in America he had considered the possibility of visiting Hollywood, and so Druten's suggestion conveniently fitted his own ideas. With his mother's five hundred dollars he was very well off, for he had in addition most of the seven hundred with which he had left Cincinnati – for Wonny had forgotten to pick his pockets before setting him adrift. The bills were unpleasant to look at, as they had been once sodden by his mule-back passage down the river – and subsequently dried in the sun outside Zed Kinney's shack – and then smeared with mud during his progress through the swamp; but they were still useful. He had bought some new clothes in Charleston, but not many, for the Dekkers had sent on his suit-case as soon as they had heard where he was. And so he was very well equipped for his journey, and whatever circumstances California might offer at the end of it.

II

Great-aunt Rachel and Miss Sally were very disappointed when Juan told them of his intended departure. Miss Sally indeed drooped badly, and sighed for a whole day until Aunt Rachel said, in her quavering but cheerful voice, 'Perhaps when Juan returns to England we shall pay a visit to Mallieu Hall. We haven't been away for such a long time, and I think we ought to have a little holiday while we are still able to enjoy it.' – Then Miss Sally's face became radiant, half its wrinkles disappeared on the spot, and she thought of seeing the dressmaker to order the proper additions to her wardrobe . . . .

The old ladies saw Juan off from the airport – standing a safe distance from the aeroplane as it roared and shook with excess of strength – and waved gallantly as it raced down the field, rose and turned, and came past them on a long slant that led far into the sky. Then they went home to a house that seemed suddenly and unaccountably larger and emptier than the one they had left.

Juan too felt very unhappy at saying good-bye, and in the monotony of the engine-din he found so apt an accompaniment to melancholy that he almost suggested to Druten their turning back to Charleston. He felt no cheerful anticipation of new experiences, but only a vast and vague dissatisfaction with those past. Pictures of Lalage came into his mind, and memories of an idyll curiously distorted by literary ambition. He saw her reflected in a green pool, now straight and clear, and now shaken (as if by a breeze that had no business there) with her novel-making and the duty of self-expression. Then the green pool turned into the pond in Aunt Rachel's garden, with its fat tadpoles and a bright image of dogwood and azaleas, and Miss Sally in her lavender dress. The picture of Lalage returned, and the powerful, cunning, stupid figure of Red-eye . . . His confined position in the aeroplane grew irksome, and the aftermath of sentimental day-dreaming was a restlessness that nothing would appease. Juan was very thankful when they reached Memphis, on the western border of Tennessee, where they landed and spent the night.

The next morning, after re-fuelling, they set out again with the hope of reaching Albuquerque in New Mexico. The forenoon passed without incident – flying for long periods Juan found to be as monotonous as railway travel – and they landed at a small town for lunch. They rested for a while and then re-embarked. The weather was fine and the sky clear. Nothing untoward happened till mid-afternoon, when they ran into a storm. Clouds formed mysteriously all round them and the air became very rough. The monoplane pitched and rolled alarmingly, and Juan looked at blue turbulent mountains of cloud, and long angry streamers of cloud, and clouds that opened in the most sinister way to enfold and swallow them.

Druten, trying to get above the storm, climbed higher and higher, but though he found occasional smooth areas these were no more than impalpable islands surrounded by angry gales.

'I've been through worse than this,' he told Juan. He was a careful and good pilot, but as the storm continued and they seemed unable to get through it Juan felt increasingly ill-at-ease. Lightning now began to dart from cloud to cloud, very bright and vicious and disconcertingly near, and the roar of the engine was dwarfed by shattering peals of thunder. The aeroplane drove into a hole in the air, and with a forward lurch fell through space. Then it climbed doggedly to its former height.

'Been through worse than this,' Druten shouted encouragingly. A moment later the engine began to misfire. Instead of the level monotonous roar there came interruptions, staccato bursts of noise, and almost before they realised their danger a thin fierce pennant of flame shot up and, like the crest of a wave, was blown back by the wind.

Druten kept calm and acted with remarkable celerity. He turned downwind so that the flame should be blown away from them, and at the same time shouted to Juan, 'We've got to jump for it! Let's go!'

With a horrible feeling of numbness Juan discovered that he had to throw himself into this vast and empty turbulence, eight thousand feet from the solid spinning earth. All day and the day before he had sat on his parachute as though it had been an ordinary cushion, and felt its harness round his waist and shoulders. But he had never expected to use it as anything but a cushion. And now he had to trust so frail a thing of silk and cord to carry his body gently through the clouds and the tempest. He, so solid and yet so soft and vulnerable, must dive head-foremost into eight thousand feet of angry wind!

Druten was already climbing out of his seat, and Juan, feeling very frightened, followed suit. The wind caught him. He fell, pushed off by the wind as he had once seen a great lout of a fellow push a small boy off the side of a wharf. He fell clear, and as he fell fumbled for the rip-cord that hung at his chest. He found it and pulled. The parachute opened with a bang and a huge tug that almost broke him in two.

Then he sailed down comfortably, blown by the wind, swinging like a pendulum, but scarcely conscious of downward movement except through his eyes, for he saw the clouds go up past him and lightning dance under his feet that did not stay for him to tread on it. He saw the aeroplane, like an enormous resinous torch dashed into the wind, fall nose-down in a wild spiral of flame. He craned his neck and saw Druten, who had jumped a moment later, following him closely. He too swung in great arcs and seemed to be dancing in the air, and Juan, suddenly relieved of all fear, began to shout with laughter. It was an exquisite motion, an enchanting sensation, to be thus suspended in the sky and hail-fellow with the clouds. – He plunged into a giant bed of cumulus that swallowed him alive, and as he laughed, deep belly-laughs, he sucked in cloud and blew out great gusts of smoke. Under the cloud was a greenish ocean with a purple floor and billowing canvas walls. Lightning darted across and across it, as if invisible drunken giants were duelling, and then as though the sky had been shaken like an iron carpet, thunder bellowed. For a moment Juan's laughter stopped. Then he shouted, and the sound of his voice was so small, so tiny and gnat-like a whimper after the thunder, that he laughed again, shaking in his harness, to think that he, an atom vulnerable at all points, a thing of fragile bones, a coil of guts and two quarts of blood packed in a tenuous envelope of skin, should ride the air and – if he cared to – break wind against thunder in its native place. He did. O potent humanity! O brave and splendid man that could take Leviathan on a hook, and fill the empyrean with his songs, and leap the equator like a skipping-rope, and dance above Aurora Borealis! Think of the foetus curled so miserably in the womb, its box-like gloomy head too big for its feeble paws to hold, the picture of defeat, crouched there in darkness with an ever-growing dread of the terrible world that lay beyond its mother's side – and *this* was the world! Not, as it thought, fear, misery, and decay, but a barony in cosmos. Yet that foetus-attitude, crumpled, ever bent down by a huge and melancholy head, was even the attitude of many grown men in the spinning world below. Fools, fools! Buy a parachute, you pessimists, (thought Juan) and come to puff against thunder on equal terms to taste the sweet sovranty of Man!

And he began to sing with a very pagan delight, but curiously impelled to pay tribute for his exaltation, *Te Deum Laudamus.*

Before he had sung more than five or six verses the light became brighter, the cloud above him dissolved into rain, and a thousand arrows of water struck him at once. Here was a new joy, for the rain, because he was falling with it, did not strike hard as on earth, but came with a cunning and whimsical softness. For the thousand arrows that struck him, too, there were a hundred thousand that missed and fell alongside – he could watch them as they came, and watch them pass and pierce downwards to become a myriad points of light beneath him. He was dropping to earth in a cascade of soft silver wires. He flung out his arms as if to catch a sheaf of them, and cupped his hands to see if they would fill with water or quicksilver. They filled instead with yellow liquor that turned to blue and then flushed rosy-red, for at that moment Juan slid through a rainbow, and for three seconds shone with all manner of faint unearthly colours.

Because of the wind he and Druten were not falling straight but in a long irregular slant that would take them down some miles from where the aeroplane, that fell like a plummet, had crashed to earth. Druten was only ten yards away. He also, because of his freedom and safety in the air, was exultant and shouted as they sailed down to some country unseen and unpredictable.

Presently he shouted for a more material reason. He had seen the earth, or rather a peninsula of earth thrust into a sea of cloud, and now both he and Juan wondered what they would find when they had come through this last dissolving flocculence.

It was open country, a drab yellow and brown, to which they were descending. They could see a grey streak that was a road, and a few trees. Then they saw a dark and inchoate stain on the road; something straggling and innominate . . . It proved to be people, and an array of motor cars. A procession? But what was a procession doing under pouring rain and in this empty country? They would soon see, for they were falling straight towards it . . . They dropped closer and discovered that it was not a procession, but an undisciplined crowd who had for some reason all abandoned their motor cars together. There was, it appeared, a centre of attraction towards which they pressed in a disturbed and impatient manner. Then one of the crowd chanced to look up and see the strange sight above, and immediately communicated his discovery to his fellows who all turned their faces skyward at his bidding, so that Juan and Druten suddenly beheld a pale flowering of that dark cluster – and almost at once, for they were close to earth now, the crowd broke up with loud and fearful cries, as though smitten by panic, and fled to their motor cars.

While still bewildered by this frantic dispersal Juan touched earth, and before he could unbuckle his harness the capering parachute dragged him across the road and into a wire fence. Druten's landing was also inexpert, and by the time they had picked themselves up and discovered no bones were broken the whole concourse of men and motor cars had gone. With a whirring of starters and jarring of gears they had fled precipitately, lanced with superstitious fear in their guilty souls, leaving nothing but the stink of their exhausts and one pitiable-looking figure at the roadside.

'Now what the devil was the meaning of all that?' asked Juan.

The figure at the roadside was a negro. He had been roughly treated, for his shirt and trousers were torn in several places and stained with blood. A cut on his forehead still bled slowly. And round his neck was the running loop of a rope.

'It seems that we've interrupted a lynching party,' said Druten.

The nigger was too overcome by fear to answer their questions. He muttered and moaned, and his eyes rolled upwards till only the whites were visible. His skin had turned a curious cold grey colour, and a dark red worm of blood crept down his left temple and dissolved in the rain on his cheek.

'The lynchers may come to finish their party,' said Juan. 'We frightened them badly, I suppose – after all one doesn't often see two men dropping from a cloud – but they may come back out of curiosity.'

Druten questioned the negro once more, but got no answer except moaning. They pulled him to his feet, but as soon as they let go he fell down again, and lay on the wet road trembling and twitching.

'This rather complicates things,' said Druten. 'Still, let's pack up the parachutes, then all we need is a new 'plane.'

While they were folding the parachutes a motor car appeared from the direction opposite to that taken by the lynchers. It was a closed car of ordinary appearance except for a kind of keel on the roof. The driver stopped when they waved to him, and Juan saw that on one side of the keel was painted in gold letters:

'WHY GO AROUND HALF-DEAD WHEN WE CAN BURY YOU FOR $39.50?'

And on the other:

'EPHRAIM SPOOTH AND SON. FINEST FUNERAL-PARLORS IN THE STATE.'

The driver was a young man with thick waved hair, expressive eyes, a long, fleshy, reddish nose, and a very long upper lip. He listened attentively to Druten and made little clucking noises of sorrow, both when he heard of the destruction of the aeroplane and of the lynching that had been so narrowly averted. He looked critically at the negro.

'About a hundred and thirty pounds,' he commented. 'He'd have hung quite a little while before he passed away. They don't use a drop, you see. They throw the rope over a branch and haul the nigger up. It's a good thing you folk came when you did. This lynching gives a State a bad name.'

The young man was friendly and helpful. Juan and Druten quickly learnt that he was the Son in Ephraim Spooth and

Son; that they were in the state of Oklahoma, not far from the Texas boundary; and that young Mr. Spooth was going to visit his fiancée – and pay a few business calls as well – in the town of Sayre, to which he would be glad to drive them and from where, if they so desired, they could take train to the West. After displaying some reluctance he also consented to take the negro, though this would expose them to considerable danger if they met the returning lynchers.

Druten offered to sit in the back seat with the negro, and Juan got in front with Mr. Spooth. For the sake of conversation he presently asked how business was in the undertaking line.

'It's good,' said Mr. Spooth in a tone of solemn satisfaction. 'Yes, *good*. I hear other other professional men complaining, but I assure you there is no sign of depression among us morticians. Our parlours, I'm thankful to say, are never empty. We're in the happy position of being able to depend on a steady supply all the year round. There's a little seasonal fluctuation, of course. The older ones generally depart in the winter or early spring, but to balance that there's a lot of young folk pass over in the summer, when the number of automobile accidents is always considerable. And we cater for all classes. Our rock-bottom price is $39.50, or $49 in monthly payments, and we have a standard *de luxe* interment at twelve hundred. We make a good profit out of high-class orders, but the cheaper ones are just charity. Yes, charity. When you consider not only the cost of materials, and the furnishing of a good parlour – I believe in sparing no expense to procure a really reverent and distinguished atmosphere for the last rites – when you think not only of that but of the initial outlay on my education, for instance, you've got to admit that $39.50 for the last rites is pretty near a hundred per cent. charity, though there's a fair amount of advertising value in being able to quote so cheap a rate. You saw our slogan on the roof?'

Mr. Spooth accepted Juan's congratulations on the aptness of his business motto, and continued:

'That was one of my little ideas. I must say that my education was pretty thorough. I graduated with highest honours as a Licensed Embalmer and Funeral Director from the University of Minnetonka just two years ago, and since I came back from college our turnover has doubled. Yes, sir. Just doubled!'

Juan was surprised to hear of so elaborate a preparation for undertaking, but Mr. Spooth assured him that the more up-to-date universities now recognised the extreme commercial importance of dying, and were prepared to supply dead bodies as well as living with attendants carefully trained in a scientific fashion.

'At the University of Minnetonka,' said Mr. Spooth, 'I studied Anatomy, Bacteriology, Chemistry, Business Organisation and Funeral Management, Psychology, Comparative Religion, and Fine Art, as well as the actual science of embalming. Those are the bare requisites of a man in my profession to-day. The successful embalmer must be a scientist and an artist, as well as a man naturally imbued with reverence for his task and sympathetically inclined to suffering humanity. One day, for instance, I might study decomposition, putrefaction, and fermentation; the next day my work might be colour mixing, lighting arrangements, and the art of modelling with its application to the rebuilding of the human body; and on the day after that, we'll say, the Professor of Psychology would detail the best modern methods of comforting those in distress and, at the same time, persuading them to make the proper purchases. Bereaved relatives are often found in a highly emotional state, and some of them are unwilling to buy a funeral of sufficient dignity and beauty. But if you're a trained psychologist you can persuade them to do almost anything. You can get under their skin and tell them, so as they'll realise how true it is, that no cost is too great for the last sacred rites of those we love. Only last week there was a lady called me in to get her husband fixed for his journey to that bourne from which no traveller returns. He was a big, fine-looking, well-known man, an Elk and a Rotarian, and she didn't want to spend more than three or four hundred. But I talked to her, and showed her what was due to a public man like her husband had been, and in the end I sold her as nice a little seven-hundred-and-fifty-dollar funeral as the town had ever seen. That's psychology. It helps you to understand the moral significance of the occasion, and it improves your salesmanship too.'

Mr. Spooth's expressive eyes shone with a fine serious light when he spoke of his work, and his long upper lip looked like a pious sponsor of every sentence that issued beneath it.

'I was always fond of flowers,' he continued after a little thought. 'I guess that influenced me in the choice of a profession, for a mortician's life is full of flowers. Flowers and beauty. I think a great deal of beauty, not only because it helps trade, but for itself. Sometimes when I've finished with a body, and she's lying in the casket with flowers in her hand, the relatives come in and scarcely recognise her. It's a real comfort to them to see their dear ones looking their best like that. The injection fills them up, of course, and then I give the face and neck a good massage before applying the cosmetics. You've got to be mighty careful to use the proper shade of rouge and lipstick or it won't look natural. Then I always co-operate with the relatives and advise them how to dress the body. It pays to buy a new dress for a lady – they always look their best in a new dress – and a smart new tie for a man. I like them to be properly clothed too. I mean, to have good underclothes as well as something good on top; or in special cases to wear something characteristic. That's the artist in me, of course. If you're naturally artistic you like to do a thing thoroughly, and I'm glad to say that most of my customers appreciate my artistic qualities just as much as I do myself. And they like the way I put things to them. I remember once burying a young lady who was very fond of swimming, and we tried first one dress on her and then another, but none of them seemed to please me somehow. And then I had an idea. I said "We'll bury her in a bathing costume." Now her relatives didn't think much of the idea at first, but when I pointed out how *different* it would be, and how very characteristic of the young lady – she'd won a fancy diving competition once – and quite likely what she'd have chosen herself, why, they came right round and were just tickled to death. So we put her in a swimming-suit, and lined the casket with green silk, and gave her a big water-lily to hold, and everybody who came to see her just broke down and cried like a baby, she looked so natural. . . . But there it is: you got to be interested in your work if you want to make a success of it to-day, with so much competition everywhere. That's the secret of success. Be interested in your work!'

Juan was so fascinated by Mr. Spooth's conversation that the journey to Sayre passed very quickly, and not till they reached the town did he consider the embarrassment of being saddled with a negro who, it was possible, had but lately raped or murdered someone. Druten, however, had decided that the best thing to do was to take him to the railway station, give him some money, and put him aboard the first train that stopped. The negro, who had recovered from some of his terror but could still give no sensible explanation of his recent plight, was well pleased by this decision. He expressed his gratitude in tears and incoherence. His cheeks were no longer drawn and grey, as they had been when he sprawled, paralysed with fear, on the wet road. Their contours had returned, firm and round, and their colour was once more a fine healthy black. He smiled doubtfully through the window of the day-coach, frightened still, but only waiting till the train gathered speed before he dared be happy. . . .

Mr. Spooth – interested in all his fellow creatures – had waited with Juan and Druten to see the nigger off. He was anxious to know their future plans. He would be glad to introduce them to his fiancée, who was staying with friends in

Sayre. Her father was a florist, said Mr. Spooth. Or could he help them in any way at all?

Juan and Druten, however, decided to continue their journey without delay. The aeroplane had probably fallen in the Wichita Mountains, far from human habitation, and their luggage would certainly be destroyed. It would be waste of time to return and search for it. A train to Amarillo, in Texas, was shortly due, and from there they could go by the Santa Fé road to Los Angeles.

So Mr. Spooth said good-bye, handing to each of them one of his business cards – with the slogan 'Why go around half-dead when we can bury you for $39.50?'– and assured them of his prompt compliance with orders of any nature or from any part of the country. 'You never know,' he said, looking from one to the other with big solemn eyes. 'To have one of my cards in your pocket might mean all the difference in the world in the way you were handled. I've a good memory for faces, and I'd recognise you no matter what condition you were in. . . .'

Presently they took their train to Amarillo, a warm and tedious journey, and there got places on a better one that carried them by day and night through New Mexico and Arizona, over the Rio Grande, over mountains and plains under a blazing sun, through bright, hot and dusty Indian country, over the dried-up bed of the Colorado River and the torrid desert of the Mojave, until at last, weary of travel and their beards sprouting darkly, they reached Los Angeles: the Spanish City of Our Lady the Queen of the Angels.

III

Graham Druten stayed only one night in Los Angeles and then left to visit his father's oil-fields. He was an engaging young man whose conversation consisted of aeronautical technicalities and reminiscences of his university days – a pleasant companion when plenty was happening, but one who would grow tedious in calm weather.

As soon as he had gone Juan looked for a lodging of moderate price and very soon found a pleasant enough room in a dentist's house, for which he agreed to pay twenty dollars a month. The dentist was a good domestic man who worked all day, listened to the radio or went to the moving pictures at night, and on Sunday took his wife out motoring. They were both keenly interested by what Juan told them of the aeroplane accident, and in return directed him to the shops where he could most suitably buy such clothes and toilet articles as he needed; for he had nothing but what he wore.

When Juan had bought all he wanted he began to take a livelier interest in Los Angeles, and found it a curious place. It was much larger than he had expected and it sprawled untidily over a wide area. The centre of the city was firmly built, but between that and a wild periphery of subsidiary towns there was a chaos of cheap haphazard houses, commercial structures, and streets that looked like a compromise between an Oriental bazaar and a Continental market. Hundreds of small shops stood side by side filled with such oddments and rubbish, gew-gaws and penny trash, as none but incurable rustics or newly breeched Indians would want to buy. And indeed Juan saw on the streets many Filipinos, Mexicans, and indeterminate breeds who looked very like newcomers to civilisation.

The more affluent inhabitants, the people in restaurants, business men waiting to cross a busy street, ladies out shopping – these displayed as a common characteristic invincible satisfaction with themselves and their surroundings. By this time Juan was well acquainted with the national habit of self-regard and the complexion of American optimism, but never had he seen such complacent assurance as now, like a garden of sunflowers, hemmed him in. And with it went a large and blatant amiability. Strangers accosted him – while he was eating his lunch, buying a newspaper, riding on a bus – and finding he had but lately arrived, told him smugly that everybody came to Los Angeles sooner or later. 'What d'you think of it?' they asked, and before Juan could reply (so sure they were of unstinted praise) they would tell him the annual increase in population, its wealth, the advantages of its climate, some facts about the motion-picture industry, and the number of bathing-beaches within easy distance. It was, they assured him, the city of the future, the metropolis of the Pacific coast, and favoured by such weather as no other metropolis in all the world could boast.

With all these advantages, it pleased Juan to discover that the inhabitants retained a simple village-view of life. They were so engrossed with their own affairs that they lived in complete ignorance of the rest of the world. Their newspapers were like an immoral parish magazine. They contained nothing but local news: graft in the various municipal services, misappropriation of public funds that should have built sewers or pavements, and a selection of the neighbourhood's most recent crimes of violence; remarks passed by prominent citizens, with polite attention to their marriages, divorces, and deaths; feats of the parish champions on the baseball field, the tennis court, or in the air; and a vast quantity of gossip, scandal, and anecdote about the directors of moving-picture companies, their actors, and above all their actresses.

These were to Los Angeles the objects of passionate interest. Every day many columns were written about their clothes, their amours, their parties, their motor cars and yachts, their new houses, their modern furniture, their opinions of each other, their hints on etiquette, their professional engagements, their views on life and death, their perfumes, unguents, depilatories, toilet-creams, hair lotions, bath-salts, hobbies, pet dogs, attendant mothers, favourite novels, and the extraction of their appendices. Every day the inhabitants of Los Angeles discussed these matters with deep seriousness, recalled the histories of their favourite entertainers, and speculated on their glorious future. Every morning they learnt the latest incident in the career of some major luminary of the films or newly risen twinkler, and every night they went to bed – this million of villagers – happy in their proximity to the stars and secure in the knowledge that they were not only the most favoured but the most important community in the world.

With such limitations as these the villagers were quite obviously real human beings, but when Juan went to Hollywood he immediately found something that seemed unreal. It was a very hot day, and under a heavy blue sky even the hills seemed artificial. They rose in a brown range behind the town, burnt bare and dusty, and they looked like a painted backcloth. They had no depth. They were stage properties, not real earth and rock. . . . And everywhere he saw artificial-seeming people, men quaintly clad and girls of extraordinary beauty but so painted, so uniformly dressed for exhibition, that one suspected they were puppets.– Were they at nightfall put into a box? Did Hollywood disappear after dark?

Not if all he had heard were true, thought Juan; and looked with some amazement at a moving-picture theatre which he happened to be passing. There were many of these theatres in Hollywood, some of them built with grotesque extravagance. This was the Hebraic conception of a Chinese pagoda. Signs of a Semitic renascence were frequent indeed, more especially in interior decoration, where there was such a wilful splendour of carved flowers and pomegranates, knops, palm-trees overlaid with gold, pillars of brass and golden hinges, as would have made Solomon's house of Lebanon look bare as a barn.

This Jewish exuberance jostled Spanish and Indian styles Marble was neighbourly with adobe walls, and a Moorish window looked at an imitation English thatched roof without surprise. . . . It was strange that people who lived in houses so diverse should themselves be so alike. At Motley it had once seemed to Juan that most of the girls had come from the same mould, and now as he walked about Hollywood and looked at women whose faces were devoid alike of blemish or individuality the thought recurred. So many of them were beautiful, and their beauty had become a smooth conformity to type. Only in their houses was originality proper, and there it crowed with great spirit. . . .

Eating his lunch in a crowded restaurant, Juan fell into conversation with a man who asked where he came from and how he made his living, discussed the merits of Los Angeles and Hollywood, mentioned some intestinal trouble from which he suffered, and showed with importance a cut finger. Juan in return made a remark about the waitresses, who were as monotonously lovely as the ladies outside, and his neighbour explained that all the prettiest girls in the country came to Hollywood with ambitions to act in moving pictures, and failing to find such employment became waitresses, clerks, and stenographers.

When the friendly man had gone, Juan sat for some little time not so much in thought as on the outskirts of thought. He played with material for thought: the brightly coloured noisiness of his surroundings, the architectural variety, the busy people whose business was about a puppet-show, and the curious air of unreality which they breathed with apparent satisfaction – for they looked healthy – and in which the Spanish houses, the synagogues, the Pueblo Indian houses, and the Old English cottages bared their walls without embarrassment.– He toyed with the idea of these things, but he was not so tedious as to resolve them into an indictment of Hollywood. He was, on the contrary, well pleased to find it different from an ordinary town.

Presently he walked out into the brilliant yellow sunshine that filled the streets so thoroughly, with such a look of tightness, that they resembled an illuminated aquarium tank, and shadows, sharing the strength of the sun, were like dark blue girders. Idly turning a corner here and a corner there Juan soon found himself beside a long wall over which he saw, side by side, a turreted castle and an ocean liner. Here were the precincts of the Tantamount Motion-picture Production Company, one of the largest in Hollywood.

Contemplating the mediaeval turrets and the ship's funnels, Juan decided to become an actor, and without further consideration called at the office of the Tantamount Company. There, however, he was told by a man who scratched his nose and looked at him through half-closed eyes that they engaged unknown people only through a casting agency. And at the casting agency Juan found a crowd of men and girls with vacant expressions, and the young woman who attended to him yawned while she took his name and address and a small fee, and said she would let him know when there was any chance of a job. She did not pretend that there was any real prospect of employment.

But Juan was now convinced of his ability to act, and spent the next two or three days in determined canvassing of every studio and casting agency he could find. None offered him any encouragement. Occasionally somebody looked at him and said he might be useful sometime. But not now. Certainly not now. Hollywood was full of unwanted extras. Wait till a few thousand died or went home to Sioux City and Oshkosh. . . .

While he was returning dispirited from his third day's quest, Juan saw ahead of him a figure that looked familiar, and hurrying on discovered Isadore Cohen, the little Jew whom he had met in New York.

'Well, well,' said Isadore, 'and what are you doing in Hollywood, eh?'

'Oh, everybody comes here sooner or later,' Juan replied.

'Say, you've got acclimated, haven't you? That's what they all tell you. I've been here three months now, and I like it pretty good, though it's dull sometimes.'

Isadore insisted that Juan should dine with him, and talking volubly all the way led him first to his lodgings, where they had a drink, and then to a small restaurant. By the time they were seated Juan had learnt the story of Isadore's marital unfortune, for it was conjugal infelicity, not the desire for adventure, that had driven him to California. His wife, so far as he knew, was still in New York, and he was in constant fear that she would discover his whereabouts and follow him. For he had run away. For as long as ever he could he had endured Mrs. Cohen's two ideas (one of them was hats) and her hundred-and-twenty word vocabulary. His life had been a misery, but he was a home-loving man by nature and he had suffered patiently for a year, hoping that somehow or other things would take a turn for the better. But they never did. Mrs. Cohen began to sulk and used no more than half of her hundred and twenty words. She bought more and more hats and became more and more insistent on her conjugal rights.

'I just couldn't stand it, see?' said Isadore. He took off his spectacles and wiped his eyes. 'I used to love that girl like a million dollars, and I'd of gone right on loving her if she'd been sensible. But she wasn't, and so I beat it out here. Maybe she couldn't help not being sensible, but I couldn't stand it anyway. That's why I came here. I like it pretty good, but it's often dull, of course. There's so many people here.'

Juan offered his sympathy, and over dinner gave a brief description of his wanderings to which Isadore listened with close attention.

'I told you that anything could happen in America,' he said excitedly when Juan had come to an end. 'Just anything. Bootleggers, niggers, getting lynched, singing upside down, and seeing Red-eye Rod Gehenna – you got to come to America for things like that. I told you that anything could happen, didn't I?'

'At any rate I haven't been dull.'

'It all depends on how you feel about things,' said Isadore. 'Sometimes I think I'd like to live on a farm and just do nothing but walk about and kind of consider everything quietly. But I've never been on a farm, and maybe I wouldn't like it when I got there.'

'What are you doing in Hollywood?'

'I got a job in a private orchestra, and I play in the Tantamount studio orchestra as well.'

'That must keep you busy.'

'The first's a sinecure,' Isadore explained. 'Ever hear of Julius Pumpenstempel? Well, he's the eighth richest man in America and he owns a private symphony orchestra. He's got a home here in Pasadena with a concert hall a hundred and twenty feet long in it, and that's where his orchestra plays when he wants to hear some music. But he's never at home, see? He's always in Venice or Italy or on his yacht. He just likes to have an orchestra of his own to give him something to talk about. That's how it's a sinecure. All we do is sign a receipt for our wages every month and practise once a week. Well, I mean we don't exactly practise. We go out to Pasadena and Nikitin counts us to see if we're all there, and then we go home again. Nikitin's the conductor, and he makes us get together once a week because he's conscientious. He's a Russian, see? He gets a split out of our pay-roll, about fifty per cent or maybe more, but as we don't do any work that's fair enough.'

Juan was extremely interested in this lordly conceit of Mr. Pumpenstempel, and enquired more closely about the orchestra. Isadore confessed after some hesitation that it was now only an orchestra in name. In the beginning, when Mr. Pumpenstempel's newly found enthusiasm for music was strong, its members had all been efficient and even distinguished performers. But then Mr. Pumpenstempel bought a yacht, and discovered Europe, and became very fond of the Lido, and consequently had not visited Pasadena for a long time. And Nikitin, who was an ingenious though melancholy man, began to replace his original musicians with instrumentalists of less ability, to whom he naturally gave smaller wages though continuing to show the old expenditure on the monthly pay-sheets which were sent to Mr. Pumpenstempel. Most of the present members of the orchestra were in fact lay figures. Some of them were old musicians brought by long drinking to decay.– Nikitin himself drank rather heavily, said Isadore, and so was sympathetically inclined to such. Others merely looked like musicians, and some could perform after an amateur fashion. They made a striking appearance on the platform, but Isadore hoped that he would never have to hear them play. 'It'd be god-awful,' he said solemnly.

'I should like to meet Nikitin,' Juan told him.

'Sure you'd like to meet him. He's a real good guy except when he's feeling melancholy, and then he's like a deaf mute who's just lost his mother. What d'you say we go see him right now?'

Nikitin had once been a conductor of repute, but his best days were over before he entered Mr. Pumpenstempel's service, and during his idleness while in charge of the orchestra that never played he had rapidly gone to seed. Isadore and Juan found him sitting alone at a large table on which stood a bottle of whisky and a tumbler. He rose courteously to greet them.

He was a tall massively built man with a completely bald head and a square red beard. His head looked as though it had grown nakedly out of the mass of bright hair. His eyes were mild and he had a large mouth with thick red lips that gaped half-open in a pathetic, rather childish way. He spoke pleasantly to Juan and in a little while his wife brought glasses of tea for them. She was a small drab woman with colourless hair and no eyebrows. She put down the tea and left the room without speaking more than five or six words.

'She is *enceinte* again,' said Nikitin with a sigh. 'But she will miscarry. She always miscarries. It doesn't really matter perhaps, but it's disappointing to her, and I should like to have a son. Though what I would do with him I don't know.'

They finished the tea and Nikitin poured glasses of whisky

for them. He swallowed his own neat, and sighed profoundly.

'It is difficult to know what to do,' said Juan, affected by Nikitin's melancholy and remembering for some reason his Great-aunt Rachel Legaré. 'Now if there was a war we could believe in, or some tyranny to rebel against, that would make life easier for us. But tyranny to-day is so diffuse and impalpable that it's almost impossible to fight against.'

'Revolution is no good,' said Nikitin. 'There was a revolution in Russia and my wife lost all her money. Perhaps money is a bad thing, but so is poverty. When I was a young man I was very poor and I found it impossible to be good in heart because I was always wishing I had money, and working so long at music that my heart grew muscular and fierce. Now I am rich – I have forty thousand dollars in the bank – and because I am rich I am also hard and unjust. I give no money to charity and I avoid people who will try to borrow from me. But if there was a revolution and I lost all my money I should be still worse.'

'There won't be any revolution in America,' said Isadore.

Nikitin agreed. 'The people are all too clean. They spend all their time changing their shirts and washing themselves. You can't feel fierce and revolutionary in a bathroom.'

Presently Juan mentioned his unsuccessful canvassing of the studios. Nikitin looked at him earnestly with his fingers stuck in his beard as though he were hanging on to it. His mouth was pulled open by so much weight depending from his chin.

'If you want employment I shall give you a position in Mr. Pumpenstempel's orchestra,' he said. 'One of my violinists has left me to go and work in San Francisco.'

Isadore laughed. 'Now you got the smoothest job in California.'

'I only play in a very amateurish fashion,' said Juan.

'You will not need to play at all,' Nikitin assured him. 'Mine is the best orchestra in the world, because it is the only silent one.'

He swallowed half a glass of whisky, loudly puffed his cheeks, and said with considerable vigour: 'I no longer believe in man's music. Man spends all his wits and all his strength in trying to conquer nature, though nature is the handiwork of God. The music that Beethoven made is better and more beautiful than any of the music that nature makes. Is that right or is it blasphemy?'

'But Beethoven was a part of nature and so just as much the handiwork of God as the rest of it,' Juan objected.

'No,' said Nikitin. 'There is a devil in man. I know, because there is one in me. And as Beethoven was greater than I he must have had a greater devil. His music was not nature but art, and art is the enemy of nature. That is why my orchestra never plays.'

'It never plays because he's too god-dam lazy to conduct,' whispered Isadore.

'I spent my strength in learning this devil's art,' Nikitin continued in a gloomy voice. His lips drooped red and sadly, and he slowly shook his head. 'None of the arts has a technique one hundredth part as difficult as the technique of music, and for thirty years I used my strength in learning it, till now I know it all, all music, and I no longer believe in it. Once I would thrill all over to read the words *allegro molto con brio*, but now I care nothing for *brio*, nothing for *sostenuto*, and *molto cantabile e grazioso* stinks in my ear. They make you too good for God, all these things. You hear a cadenza for solo violin, glissandos on the harp, a great chord in E minor, perhaps only a piercing trumpet F, and they are so beautiful you feel too good for God. But what are they after all? Nothing but wind, air coming through little holes or running away from a quivering string. And who is the Prince of the air? The devil. The devil laughs to think what a little of his wind can do if someone calls it *andante con variazioni!*'

Nikitin's wife re-entered with more tea, set down the glasses, and silently went out again.

Nikitin pointed to the door. 'Now that I no longer believe

in music I want to study astronomy. But she won't let me. She says that star-gazing is nothing but idling.'

A dismal silence followed. Nikitin mournfully looked at nothing, with large bewildered eyes. Now and again he drank some whisky. His mouth gaped half-open, its thick red lips drooping in sorrowful curves. Sometimes he tugged at his beard so that his mouth opened wide. Then he let it go and his teeth met loudly. Juan tried to make quiet conversation with Isadore, but the Jew muttered, 'It's dull. I told you it would be dull if he was melancholy.'

Nikitin said, 'I used to be puzzled by the later quartets that Beethoven wrote. There is confusion of thought in them. But now I understand. Now I know that he knew what I know now, but would not admit it.'

After another hour his wife brought more tea.

'She is *enceinte*,' said Nikitin. 'But she will miscarry. She always miscarries.'

IV

On the following day Juan met Isadore in Hollywood. The Jew had promised to introduce him to Mr. Sheen, one of the assistant directors at the Tantamount Studio, whom he knew well.

'Sure he'll give you a job,' said Isadore. 'He's a very good friend of mine, we go to the same synagogue. He'd do anything for me.'

Mr. Sheen was an alert, nervous, irritable man with oily black hair and small brown eyes. After some diplomatic hesitation, after he had impressed Juan with the magnitude of his favour, he was as good as Isadore's word and promised to enlist Juan as an extra for their forthcoming picture, *The Deluge*, in which a multitude of early Israelites would be required. The picture was going to be the greatest spectacular triumph of all time, said Mr. Sheen. Several hundred strong swimmers were required – Juan could swim? Then that was all right – to endure the waters of the Flood. They had already built the Ark, to Biblical specification as far as possible, though they had not been able to acquire any gopher wood. Noah was to be played by the great character actor, Huntley Roads, Japheth by Derek Dirke, and Miriam, who was bethrothed to Japheth, by Phryne Fuller – three stars of the first magnitude. *The Deluge* was to cost a million dollars, no expense being spared either on cast or settings. They had dammed a river in the hills to provide water, and when that dam burst there was going to be a flood that would have scared real Noah out of his wits. After the inundation the story leapt forward to modern times with a parallel theme developed on the battle-fields of the World War. Derek Dirke would then play a captain of American infantry . . . and so on. Production was due to start in a few days' time, and meanwhile Mr. Sheen was busy. They would excuse him for hurrying away? They would, and parted with amiable gesticulations.

Isadore was in high feather at this demonstration of his influence with so great a concern as the Tantamount Corporation, and assured Juan that he was starting his new career under the happiest auspices. He mentioned Phryne Fuller with grave respect.

'You'll see her,' he said, 'and maybe the prince as well. He often goes with her. She married him about two months ago, so she's a princess now. I guess she found it dull being just Miss Fuller when there's so many misses in America. She keeps her own name for business, see? but she's a princess in private life and folk call her that. I know her and I know him too. He's a good egg.'

'Who is he?' Juan asked.

'Prince Alto of Pretzel-Oppenheim – say, you know him too! You've seen him!'

Isadore excitedly waved his hands in the air and repeated, 'You've seen him, you've seen the Prince yourself. I forgot you was there. Don't you remember that *brauhaus* we went to in N'York where the waiters sang German songs? And the big handsome guy with a moustache? Well, that's him. He's a prince now and he's married to Phryne Fuller.'

Juan remembered very well the magnificent waiter with the golden hair, the lyrical eyes, and the heroic build of Siegfried.

But how, he asked, could a waiter become a prince?

'He says he was a prince all the time, but for reasons of state he had to keep it quiet. His life would have been in danger if he'd told who he was, because he had a rival to the throne. He hasn't really got a throne, of course, because his people put a stop to it, but there was a rival to what used to be the throne, and it wasn't till this rival died of consumption that he could say who he was, see?'

'Do you think he really is a prince?'

Isadore shrugged his shoulders. 'I don't know. I never saw one before. But he's got his court chamberlain with him – he's the fat guy who sang about the *schnitzelbank* – so it looks like he was speaking the truth all right.'

'I'd like to see the fat one again.'

'Well, maybe you will. I'll introduce you to the princess if I get a chance. She don't high-hat you though she is a princess, and she talks to the extras sometimes just like she was one herself, so long as they say "Your Highness" to her.'

Isadore showed no surprise at Alto's elevation from waiter to Prince of Pretzel-Oppenheim. Such a process seemed to him a perfectly normal affair, and this ease of acceptance – he swallowed news as a bird its food, without tasting – was one of the main reasons for his boredom with life. Juan, on the contrary, was delighted by the waiter's metamorphosis. Hollywood was living up to his expectations of it.

V

In two or three days' time a huge crowd of supers assembled

at the Tantamount Studio for preliminary instruction and the issue of Israelitish costumes. The picture was to open with a few rapid scenes depicting the wickedness of the land: revelry on a large scale, profanation of temples, stoning of unpopular leaders, and so on. Now and again Noah would appear to protest against these evil practices, but whenever he raised his voice a mob used to collect, deriding his grey beard and untimely puritanism. Men who could laugh with a villainous expression were placed in the front row of such crowds, and their sneering faces contrasted dramatically with the piety of Phryne Fuller who, as Japheth's sweetheart, came to give comfort and strength to old Noah. She faced the mob with a vestal calm that all their anger could not dismay, and considered the corruptness of their hearts with unfailing pity.

An extra's life was fairly strenuous. Juan had to be at the studio by eight o'clock, dress himself in the simple garments that the Art and Historical directors of the Tantamount Corporation thought proper for Noah's contemporaries, and have his face painted. The application of make-up did not take long. It was done by a spray, in the way that motor cars are painted, and subsequent refinements were left to the individual. Then the whole army would be paraded and drilled in a variety of movements. Every scene was repeated again and again, in the manner of a theme with variations, until some particular juxtaposition of effects happened to satisfy the producer, the directors, and the assistant directors. In the first part of the picture only a minimum of speech was required, for the turbulence of a world about to be drowned could be suggested more dramatically by a confusion of noise and incidental music.

His fellow supers Juan found to be amiable people except in the revelation of their common obsessions. Most of them were native Americans, but enough Russians, unassimilated Germans and Italians, Englishmen, Greeks, and Bulgarians were among them to give their grievances an international character. They generally considered their salaries inadequate, their personal merit peculiar but unrecognised, the worth of their neighbours over-estimated, the characters of those more eminent in their profession curiously spotted with vice, the future to be golden, and that all these circumstances deserved frequent discussion. Otherwise they were amiable people.

With two girls called Jill à Becket and Genevieve Crewe (all the extras had distinguished names) Juan became, first by conditions of their work, more friendly than with the others. It was they who, in one of the orgy scenes, lay in his arms and spilled wine on his face. With them he mocked the aged Noah and shrank away muttering from the virginal rebuke of Japheth's sweetheart. When the dam released its waters he would share a log with Jill and Genevieve – Flotsam on the Ocean of God's Wrath – and with them be carried to apparent destruction.

Neither of them looked any more like a pre-Israelite than Juan did. In many ways, however, they resembled each other, for both closely approximated to that type which the air and demands of democracy had evolved in America. Both were five feet four inches in height, with straight slim legs, slender arms, and small low breasts. They wore no corsets and did not need them. Both were blonde, though Jill's hair inclined to a silvery pallor and Genevieve's to a ruddy hue. Their *coiffures* were identical: their hair was short, cropt close at the nape, and elsewhere compressed into smooth symmetrical undulations. Their eyebrows had been so plucked that mere brush-marks were left on their little foreheads, and under these slender arcs their eyes were round, wide-open and guarded by lashes groomed with mascara to minute *chevaux-de-frise*. Jill had grey eyes, Genevieve brown, but each pair was enlivened by the same ingenuous look of calculation, a kind of shallow and lively shrewdness. Their noses were unremarkable, being small and without sufficient callus to give them a definite shape. They were not snub noses, neither were they Greek, Roman, or eccentric Gothic noses. They had little pretty nostrils, but otherwise they were no more than undistinguished ridges between plump cheeks. As for teeth, both Jill and Genevieve could claim perfection, and the lips that parted willingly to disclose their even whiteness were apparently modelled with equal success. A closer inspection, however, showed that the Cupid's bows were artistic emendations of an original form which in Jill's case was a little too loose, and in Genevieve's a shade too meagre. The modelling of cheek and chin was pretty and agreeable, but there was no permanency in it. The curves were too mild and full to last, and in a few years' time would need massage, astringents, and bandages to cure their growing flaccidity. But meanwhile they were charming. In the matter of make-up both used a coral rouge, a cardinal-red lipstick, and a cream-coloured powder. And their perfume (which the advertisements described as a 'subtle *odeur*') came from the same bottle – or, as they preferred to call it, a *flacon*.

Nor was their resemblance confined to looks. In the same sort of voice (a small and undistinguished pipe which did well for tenuous laughter, and little expressions of admiration or surprise) they made the same kind of conversation: gossip about moving pictures, some scandal, a few pert quips, a dozen tiny witticisms, the minor technicalities of motoring, a brisk to-do with the dressmaker's vocabulary, and familiar exercises in flirtation. This similarity occasionally led Juan into the error of addressing Genevieve as Jill or telling Jill some small pleasantry that he had intended for Genevieve.– Their physical resemblance was general, not detailed, and the eye was never puzzled to distinguish one from the other. But mentally they were twins (or multiplets rather, for their brains were replicas of many other young women's brains in Hollywood and other parts of America) and when Juan's eyes were occupied elsewhere his mind – cynical perhaps, or lazy – would sometimes refuse to distinguish between them. Then Juan would be reproved –'Say, where d'you get that stuff? I'm not Jill, I'm Genevieve. Take some interest in your little pal, won't you?'

Or if the case were reversed Jill would complain in similar accents, 'How d'you get that way, Big Boy? I'm not Genevieve, I'm Jill. Snap out of it, can't you?'

They had their good points. They were lively, fairly good-humoured, always ready to be amused, and grateful for amusement. They were not mercenary. They were more entertaining together than singly, for one encouraged the other to indiscretion and supplemented her naïveté with ingenuous comment. They discussed their own affairs with artless candour, and artlessness characterised all their remoter speculations. About love they were wistful and romantic, but about lovers they had no illusions. Though ignorant of most things they knew how to handle a man, and were proud of their knowledge. Much of their conversation dealt with victories over the enemy.

'You remember So-and-so,' Jill would say, 'and how he tried to play me for a sucker? He thought I was Dumb Dora, but I showed him who I was. I bawled him out all right. Gee, you oughta heard me! O boy, I was good!'

And Genevieve would counter: 'Just like that big guy Whozis. He tried to pull a fast one on me, and I listened like I was in a hop-dream. Then I put the skids under him. Gee, that guy was sore!'

'He took me out and gave me a fifty-cent Dago dinner,' Jill explained, 'and then started to shoot off his mouth. Youda thought that guy was President and he'd given me a steam-yacht to hear him talk.'

'Whozis was a tight-wad too,' Genevieve continued. 'Gee, how I hate a tight-wad! Going out on a party with him was like living in Scotland.'

'There's nothing wrong with a fifty-cent Dago dinner if you choose your company,' Jill admitted, 'but when a guy you've never seen before, and don't much like the look of anyway, tries to get fresh on the strength of a meal that only set him back four bits, a girl's justified in giving him the razz – and I don't mean maybe!'

'Whozis wanted me to go down to Tia Juana with him,' Genevieve elaborated. 'He thought I was the girl-bride from Hicksville, Ky., till I told him two or three things I knew about him. They were true too, right off the police-blotter. You oughta seen that guy wilt.'

Such conversation was conducted with great animation, gestures, *oeillades*, and laughter; and Juan found it amusing. When he had been a week or two in Los Angeles he bought a motor car for three hundred dollars – only the most indigent inhabitants of California had no motor cars – and in his spare time drove here and there, up the coast and down the coast and into the hills. Often he took Jill and Genevieve with him, but never one of them alone, for taken singly he felt there was nothing else to do but make love to them; and with memories of Lalage he had no fancy for new love-making.

Mr. Pumpenstempel's orchestra assembled for practice on Monday evenings, and as the Tantamount studio was generally busy with talking-sequences on a Monday, that was an easy day for Juan. His salary as a violinist was thirty dollars a month – how much more went into Nikitin's pocket he did not know – but Juan felt that he was well paid with what he got.

Mr. Pumpenstempel's house in Pasadena was worthy of a man who owned an orchestra. It stood in large and elaborately gardened grounds where many varieties of palms, cacti, and other exotic plants grew with an air of unbending prosperity. The house was a vast building in the Spanish style of architecture. It had white stucco walls, curly red tiles, Castilian arches, Moorish grilles, balconies with bright awnings over them, casement windows, and heavily-hinged doors. Masses of brilliant flowers clustered against the pale walls that sometimes looked blue in shadow, and the lawns were kept bright green by dozens of water-sprays in which minute rainbows quivered. But within the walls was more splendour than anything without them could show, for the house was built round a courtyard conceived by someone who had distantly recollected the Alhambra. In the centre stood an alabaster fountain supported by marble lions, and all around were marble pillars and arches magnificently embellished with brightly coloured arabesques. The transition from external stucco to internal marble was perhaps a little strange, but Isadore Cohen, who accompanied Juan on his first attendance, saw nothing to weaken his admiration, and Juan, who was no snob, agreed that the Pumpenstempel mansion was a remarkable building.

He was equally impressed by the members of the orchestra, some of whom had a pallid stucco look, while a few resembled statues of old stained marble. These were lifeless and dilapidated, like something left to the wind and the rain and the starlings that haunt a ruined house. Others again – the brasses particularly – had a hearty rococo appearance. Several of them wore curly moustaches, their hair was done in quiffs, they had red and bulbous noses, a sprinkling of warts, a squint or two, an eccentricity in their dress, and they talked loudly to their friends. One of the harpists looked like Herod the Tetrarch and the other seemed to be his ingle. Among the wood-winds were striking doubles of Philip IV of Spain, a Murillo peasant boy, and Leech's idea of James Pigge. It seemed to Juan indeed that he could recognise the models or subjects of several famous painters: one or two jaundiced lanternesque specimens who might have been used by El Greco, a desperate prison-hospital-looking fellow like a caricature of Goya's, two or three more out of the *Rake's Progress*, and a brace of second fiddles by Daumier. Half a dozen or so were decent-seeming men who supplemented their salaries from another source with this easy increment; all the rest were dregs, riff-raff, decadents, and failures who were glad to live in idleness on whatever Nikitin cared to give them.

The practice was soon over. The members of the orchestra arranged themselves in an orthodox manner while Nikitin stood at the far end of the concert hall and watched them.

Then with a firm swaggering step he walked up, mounted the rostrum, and picking them off with a baton counted his troupe.

'Some of you were late in arriving,' he said gruffly. 'That will not do. You must come punctually to your practices or they are no good. Remember that, if you please. Now you can go.'

As the orchestra stumbled and fumbled, tottered and shuffled and scuffled away, Nikitin called to Juan and Isadore.

'Let us go to a restaurant,' he said, 'where we can sit and watch young ladies dancing.'

Neither Juan nor Isadore had anything better to do, so they got into Juan's motor car and drove to one of the large hotels where such a spectacle might be enjoyed. On the way there Nikitin said solemnly, 'I was a little drunk when you came to see me, and more drunk after you left. What did I talk about?'

'God and Beethoven,' Juan answered.

Nikitin sighed. 'I am a religious man, but I never show it unless I have been drinking. Perhaps drunkenness is a good thing after all.'

'And you said you didn't believe in music,' Isadore added.

'There is foolishness as well as virtue in being drunk,' Nikitin admitted.

When they got to the restaurant he said, 'Now let us go in and see the young ladies.' He walked up the crowded floor in a fine splay-footed masterful way, his arms swinging and his stomach thrust out. When he passed a comely young woman his eyes brightened, he smacked his lips, and said 'Ah-ha!' in a loud appreciative voice. They were given a table from which they got a good view of the dancers and Nikitin settled down contentedly.

After a little while he said, 'I do not disbelieve in music any more than I disbelieve in these young ladies. But – well, I like to look at young ladies, but I no longer want to make love to them all. And also I like to think about music, to listen to it in my brain, but not necessarily to play it. It is a nuisance to teach an orchestra how to play Tchaikowsky's Concerto in B flat minor, and when by thinking about it I can hear it all in my brain why should I trouble to teach them? Besides, I may not want to hear it all. I may want to listen to one small piece and then choose to hear a little Mozart, or something by Brahms, Ravel, or Rimsky-Korsakov. But can an orchestra shift like a bird picking crumbs from one to another? No. Only I in my brain can do that. Now, for instance, in spite of all this noise, I am listening to the Andante movement of Schubert's Unfinished Symphony. I hear the pizzicati of the strings under wood-wind and horns – and then that so lovely melody by clarinet and oboe – and now bouff! come all the basses!'

Nikitin smiled happily and tugged his beard. After a few minutes he said, 'Now my brain is playing the Marcia Funebre from the Eroica Symphony. . . . Beautifully, beautifully! Ach, it is far better to hear such music in the head than to make sixty men play it when so often they play it badly.'

'That orchestra of ours couldn't play it at all,' whispered Isadore. 'But he's conscientious and tries to make excuses for himself, see?'

'I only disbelieve in music aloud,' said Nikitin, and pushed his chair back from the table. 'Now let us stop talking of such things and look at the young ladies instead.'

VI

The Princess of Pretzel-Oppenheim was not inclined to be so friendly as Isadore had predicted. Sometimes Juan saw her in the distance, but he never observed her fraternising with the humbler members of the company. She was a beautiful woman, older than she looked, and practised particularly in the expression of yearning, sorrow, innocence, and maidenly pride. Her body was lithe and supple, with seductive curves and movements carefully schooled to allure. Its slender suggestion of luxury had not been acquired without difficulty and pain, for Phryne had a large appetite and easily put on weight. At one time her career had been in danger from fat which accumulated on her breast and arms and haunches with the obstinacy of falling snow, and, like snow that lodges on cupolas and arches, exaggerated their curves with clumsy loads. Neither diet nor exercise, massage nor Turkish baths could rid Phryne of her adipose burden, and with wilful irrepressibility it escaped and overflowed the most rigid corseting. Then, when she was almost in despair, a friend had suggested a remedy drastic in its nature but guaranteed to be effective. He had procured for Phryne the head of a tape-worm enclosed in an easily digestible capsule, and this she swallowed between a shudder and a glass of champagne. She began to lose weight rapidly. The snow melted from arch and cupola and her arms regained their youthful grace. Her manager was delighted and Phryne, as she watched her slimness re-appearing from its blanket of corpulence, came to think of her parasite with something like gratitude. In a very short time she was thinner than ever before, and her body was able for serpentine cajolery that sometimes contrasted oddly with the persistent virginity of her face.

One day as Juan left the Tantamount studio he noticed Isadore talking with two men who sat in a superb blue and silver limousine. The little Jew hailed him excitedly:

'Come and meet the Prince! Prince, this is my friend Mr. Motley, who I was talking about. Juan, meet the Prince of Pretzel-Oppenheim and Baron Schnapp.'

Juan murmured politely, the Prince bowed cordially, and Baron Schnapp raised his small green Homburg hat, after which he took no notice of anyone but sat in a fat stiff silence. In ordinary clothes the Prince hardly looked so magnificent as he had in Tyrolean costume, but he was a handsome figure and did not seem oppressed by his rank. He made some commonplace remarks in an amiable voice with a strong German accent.

While they were chatting a group came to the door of the studio, and Phryne Fuller emerged with several friends in attendance. A little smile was on her face, a royal smile that could pass with scarcely a line changing from the condescension of greeting to the courtesy of dismissal. She looked from side to side as if expectant of applause.

As soon as she appeared the Prince and Baron Schnapp sprang from the car. The Prince hastened to greet her, and the Baron, hat in hand, stood by the door. Isadore, now with some diffidence, introduced Juan.

'Charmed,' said the Princess in a cultivated voice. 'Charmed indeed. You must come to see us some time.'

And then without more delay she got into the car, and the Prince and the Baron followed her. Before they had settled themselves the Princess, in a voice altogether different from that in which she had spoken to Juan, snapped to the chauffeur, 'Step on it, Big Boy, I'm hungry as hell!'

The limousine slid rapidly away.

'She's temperamental, of course,' said Isadore doubtfully. 'All the real stars are temperamental.'

'I liked seeing the Baron again,' said Juan, 'though he doesn't look as happy as he did in the *brauhaus*.'

'He's got a position to keep up now,' Isadore explained. 'You can't be a baron without showing it somehow.'

Juan's acquaintance with the Princess would probably have gone no further had it not been for a serious accident during the production of *The Deluge*.

For the flood scenes, the most spectacular part of the picture, most of the company went into camp in the mountains where a river had been dammed and a skeleton town built all ready to be knocked down by the bursting waters. Some anxious days were passed in dry rehearsals, and then, when everybody had been thoroughly drilled, when cameras had been posted at every tactical point, the dam was pierced.

At the first trickle of the waters a crowd gathered, ready for panic. The king – some early anonymous king – stood on his palace steps aghast. Soldiers – in Assyrian dress – forsook their posts. The waters rose. The frenzied crowd assailed the palace, dragged down the king, beat soldiers from the ramparts, and staggered in the growing flood. Towers impended, tottered, fell with a great sounding splash. A gateway rocked in the torrent, buckled, gave at the knees, and noisily wallowed into the stream. Water swirled at the palace gates and the crowd grew wilder. Little groups ran hither and thither, waving desperate arms, climbing on to walls only to be dragged down by their frenzied companions or washed away by the tempest. Strong swimmers sank beneath the water, and everywhere camera-men assiduously recorded the various phases of destruction.

Juan's duty in the general ruin was first to wrestle with a soldier and throw him off a parapet to make room for the two girls. Genevieve became giddy at the sight of the leaping swirling waters and had to be helped in earnest. Juan himself grew excited. Everybody was excited. The flood was not merely realistic but real, and shrill cries rose from the inundated streets that were more than histrionic exhibitions. The directors, the watching technical staff, and the camera-men were delighted.

By and by, as the water rose, Juan and the two girls were driven from their parapet to a baulk of timber that by special arrangement came floating by. Genevieve whimpered as she swam, and Juan had to use all his strength to drag her across the log. They made a fine picture of despair as they swept past the waiting cameras.

Phryne Fuller, naturally enough – for she was supposed to be safe in the Ark – had no part in this rough work, but as the spectacle was unusually interesting she had chosen a position from which to watch it, as she thought, in safety. A channel had been dug into which the waters converged to be led back to the dry bed of the river, and where they converged was a high point which offered a view of the ruined town and all the wreckage that came sweeping past. There Phryne stood to enjoy the scene.

Unhappily the force of the water was so great that it undercut one side of the channel, and when the flood was at its height the bank on which she stood crumbled suddenly and in the midst of a muddy subsidence Phryne fell into the torrent. Even in so much surrounding tumult her piercing screams attracted attention. A director and an assistant-director danced excitedly on the bank, and Juan, who at this moment was passing on his baulk of timber, jumped off and swam quickly towards her.

He could make little progress across the current, but as they were carried down stream they converged and he caught her while she was still strong enough to struggle in his grip. She was frantic with terror, and had not Jill, who was a good swimmer, and Genevieve, who had conquered her nervousness, come to his assistance Juan could not have done very much. But the three of them, swimming with the stream, brought her to land in a very short time.

A small and half-hysterical crowd waited for them. Mr. Strunk, the principal director, was there with Mr. Sheen and two score underlings attracted by calamity. Dripping figures gathered round as the extras, their duty done, emerged from the flood. Doctors who had been waiting for an accident thrust their way through and by skilful manipulation of Miss Fuller's body forced her to expel a large quantity of dirty water. She returned unwillingly to her senses and sobbed with terrifying persistence. They gave her brandy. Mr. Strunk and Mr. Sheen wrung their hands, and all the underlings, all the extras, stared silently at their half-drowned star. Till she recovered enough to speak sensibly no one paid any attention to Juan or the two girls. The safety of Phryne Fuller was more important than her rescuers.

But when the brandy had taken effect Phryne's first thoughts were of them. She sat up and demanded, 'Where are the heroes who saved me?'

Several people pushed Juan forward.

'You saved my life!' said Phryne with awe in her voice. 'And you too,' she added, looking at Jill and Genevieve. 'You helped him to save me. You are heroes. Mr. Strunk, they must be suitably rewarded!'

Then she fainted.

Fortunately the camera-men had all kept their posts, and so no part of the scene was wasted. For the rest of the day there was great commotion in camp. Many of the extras had had stirring adventures and escapes of their own, and while none was inclined to under-estimate Phryne's danger all were determined to relate their own, so that Juan was surrounded by people who first congratulated him and then described their private perils. After a while he grew weary of this heroic atmosphere and would have escaped had not a messenger from Mr. Strunk intercepted him. Mr. Strunk was magnificent in his thanks. Jill and Genevieve, who had also been summoned, listened with ever-increasing delight to all he said. He promised them advancement in their profession. He promised to make them all Tantamount stars – and in the middle of his promises the Prince arrived, summoned by telephone to his wife's bedside, and he in broken English added his gratitude to Mr. Strunk's.

For a day or two Juan suffered, Jill and Genevieve basked, in the rewards of their minor heroism. But their companions' admiration soon dissipated, the air became normal again, and in a week's time the adventure was almost forgotten.

Not by Phryne, however. Every day or two she reiterated her gratitude. She thrilled the crowd of extras by coming among them to look for Juan, for Jill and Genevieve, to tell them yet again how marvellous had been their courage, their presence of mind, and skill in defeating the angry waters. She brought the other stars to talk to them, Huntley Roads – awful in Noah's beard – and Derek Dirke, who had acquired the reputation of an intellectual by thinking long and seriously about himself. 'His real name's Elmer Doublebottom,' Jill whispered.

Then they were all invited to a reception at Phryne's house in Beverley Hills. The invitation cards were embossed with the arms of Pretzel-Oppenheim, and stated that the guest of the occasion was to be Dr. Julius Salvator, whose name Juan did not know, but found on enquiry to be that of a person of some fame.

He was, it appeared, the founder of a cult that had attracted many people in Hollywood and Los Angeles. It would undoubtedly have attracted more but for the presence of so many rivals, for religions of all kinds flourished exceedingly in southern California. Any Oriental creed from Yoga to Lao Tze's could attract believing if not practising adherents so long as its apostle had a white beard, went abroad naked, or sugared his doctrine with sufficient eloquence. Evangelical preachers sprang up like burdock in a dirty field, drawing easy sustenance from rank credulity and a greedy demand for spiritual comfort. Their extravagance culminated in the Holy Rollers, in whose congregations foam spattered from pew to pew and epilepsy was regarded as the finger-print of God. An independent pastor gathered a flock by his proposal to re-arrange the books of the Bible in alphabetical order, arguing not only the business-like nature of such an alteration, but also the artistic quality of an orderly progress from Acts through Amos, Chronicles, Colossians, Corinthians, Daniel and so forth to the logical conclusion of Zechariah. Christian Science prospered on easy optimism, murky varieties of Spiritualism drew thousands of glycophagous simpletons to their altars, and any Presbyterian church could fill itself with the aid of a few saxophones, a jazz organist, and a hot soprano.

Despite these counter-attractions Dr. Salvator was doing well. His creed was ninety-five per cent physical. He believed in the cultivation of the body to the deliberate exclusion of the mind, whose activity he distrusted, not only for its notorious ill effects on bodily health, but because he was opposed to the very existence of mind. Often he declared, 'Thought is a symptom of cerebral decay. Every serious thought is the epitaph on a brain-cell. Every time you think it means that a cell has died and decomposed, and the product of that putrefaction is your thought. My advice, my message to you all, is Keep Your Brain-cells Healthy *by not thinking*!'

This was welcome advice to the majority of people who heard it, who knew that thought was a wearisome business, and when Dr. Salvator added to his contempt for the mind a very generous consideration for the body, his success was inevitable. For in modern America the human body is more seriously regarded, more slavishly catered for, more pampered with sun-baths, anointings, lavings and massage than ever in the world since the Epicurean days of Rome. Now, as then, bodily health has become an obsession. Now, as in Rome, the art of medicine has a sacramental character, a liturgy, and a priesthood of fantastic power. Dr. Salvator was so supremely fortunate as to be the prophet of a popular creed.

The Pretzel-Oppenheim mansion was a handsome building – though not to be compared to Mr. Pumpenstempel's at Pasadena – and when Juan arrived, with Jill and Genevieve, he found a large assembly of guests, most of whom bore famous names in Hollywood. They walked about the grounds with the splendidly assured manner of people who have little more to do than attend garden-parties.

The Prince and Princess stood by an Italian fountain to receive their guests, and immediately after greeting their hosts visitors were offered cocktails and sandwiches by ubiquitous waiters. The opening movements of the reception were characterised by dignity and even hauteur. On all sides were heard voices controlled for the occasion to a thin formality, or sounding richly out of a society stop. When everybody had arrived the waiters put down their trays and with great speed arranged a large number of chairs in a thick semi-circle. As soon as the guests, with bright anticipatory chatter, had seated themselves, the Princess led Dr. Salvator to the steps of the Italian fountain and briefly introduced him.

His presence was remarkable. Tall, with thick brown hair, a broad forehead and an expression of heroic eupepsia, he wore a morning suit cut from white broadcloth and a dull orange stock. Even in Hollywood his appearance attracted attention. As soon as he was ready to speak, Phryne's guests became a trained audience. Their private conversations died, their laughter was stilled, and they attended with faces smoothly prepared to respond to every velleity of meaning. The doctor's introductory remarks were of a general nature, a broad statement of his philosophic position, and then more acceptably he passed to specific illustrations of his theory.

'I want you to consider a panther,' he said. 'Now a panther combines grace, power, and efficiency to an enviable degree, but does a panther think? Certainly not. A panther is too wise to think. It is certainly aware of everything that it sees, hears, feels, or smells – and aware to an extent of awareness that we with our dull, warped, and muffled senses can scarcely imagine – but it does not think about them because it already knows. A deer, a flower, the wind, a drinking pool – all these things are simple and perfectly comprehensible things so long as you trust to your eyes. But if you refer them to your brain, what do they become? Products of evolution, physical phenomena, chemical formulae, variants of a sub-species of a botanical genus. They lose their natural significance and become words. And words are fundamentally meaningless. Words are the fraudulent currency of speech, and speech is the cry for help of thought, and thought is the pustular eructation of a putrefying brain-cell. No wonder our behaviour is futile, full of hesitation and dismay, when the stimuli to which we should react are so padded with meaningless meanings that they can no longer prick us into decisive action. Normal behaviour is a true reflex excited by external circumstance, but human reflexes generally have to travel through such a slough of thought that they fail to make the grade. How much wiser than man is the panther, whose reflexes sock it on the seam for a home run every time! How much more beautiful and efficient than any of us here! For the panther, my friends, does not think. It lives and is aware. But no one can be fully aware whose blood-stream is poisoned with those gaseous products of cerebral decomposition that we call thought. . . .'

Juan's interest began to wane, and would have slept had not the doctor mentioned his School of Thoughtlessness, a colony which he had established in charming surroundings on the coast not far from Los Angeles. He had already enlisted thirty or forty scholars, who pursued their lack of studies naked except for loin-cloths. Dr. Salvator explained that the loin-cloth was a symbol not of prudery but of that aesthetic sensibility which was native to man. 'When Adam and Eve plucked fig-leaves in the dawn of the world, their action was a true reflex to an aesthetic stimulus,' said the doctor.

He continued: 'Nakedness needs little defence to-day, for happily we are all beginning to realise the beauty of our bodies that has for so long been shut away in musty clothes, as if in a dark cupboard. But beauty should not be hidden. It should be brought boldly into the sunlight. And when we offer our bodies to the sun we find that a wonderful development – indeed two wonderful developments – begin to take place. First, the body acquires new beauties of shape and colour by proper exercise in the open air; and second, we stop thinking. The ever beneficent sun inhibits thought, kills it at birth, as surely and as cleanly as it kills and inhibits the growth of micro-organisms in a dirty wound. The sun makes our brains aseptic and thoughtless. We sit in the sunlight, no longer poisoning our blood-stream with the septic products of cerebration, but content to be healthily aware of our surroundings. We know that what we are sitting on is sand, that in front of us is the sea, behind us the mountains, and all around us the beautiful brown bodies of our friends. That is all we know on earth and, I am bold enough to say, all we need to know!'

No sooner was the lecture over than the waiters re-appeared with trays of cocktails and the guests, made thirsty by thinking hard about thoughtlessness, willingly accepted everything that was offered. Here and there people discussed Dr. Salvator's theories, and some who had heard about Behaviourism talked about that, while others assured their friends of the benefits of abdominal exercises – but in terms guarded and circumspect, for they were determined to maintain their conversation on the high level befitting their social position. They exchanged the most amiable nugacities, and in sedulously cultured accents trifled with politest gossip or the dinner-table droppings of artistic friends. Derek Dirke wore a grey top-hat and beneath it his cheeks were moulded to an easy smile. Everywhere faces were tactfully animated or correctly attentive, and as Juan passed from group to group it seemed to him that nowhere had he seen such uniformly charming behaviour.

Meanwhile the waiters briskly carried their trays through the crowd.

Presently Juan encountered the Princess, who took him off to meet Dr. Salvator. The doctor was talking to a remarkably beautiful Chinese girl, who was introduced to Juan as Miss Kuo Kuo.

'Miss Kuo's grandfather was a mandarin, but her father became a friend of Sun Yat Sen and she herself is very interested in the Youth movement that is a feature of the world to-day,' explained Dr. Salvator.

'She ought to join your colony,' suggested the Princess, and walked away to entertain other of her guests.

Juan scarcely noticed her go, and though he pretended to

listen to Dr. Salvator, who continued to talk about Youth, his attention was really taken by the Chinese girl. She was small, and her delicate oval face had the clear pallor of moonlight. She seemed to be smiling as she listened to Salvator. Her slanting eyes under exquisite eyebrows, narrow as a jenny wren's leg and black as jet, gave her an expression of being amused, but whether it was her present surroundings or something far away that caressed with ironical fingers her Celestial sense of humour one could not divine. Her chin was pointed like a gull's egg, and her small full lips were a dark rose colour. She wore a black silk tunic, high in the neck and reaching to her knees, and black silk trousers. A gold dragon with a tortuous body and a fantastic lion's head twisted and sprawled on her tunic. Compared with the dresses of the other women, that offered to the public air legs, arms, backs, and bosoms, her costume was armour impenetrable, a black wall guarded by a golden dragon that hid her from neck to toe, from wrist to wrist....

'A subject for the most interesting speculation,' Dr. Salvator was saying, 'is what will happen to the youth of our time.'

'I suppose they'll grow up,' Juan absently replied.

'That is not precisely what I meant,' explained the doctor a little stiffly. . . .

'What are you doing in Hollywood?' Juan asked when Salvator had gone.

'Looking for a Superior Person,' said Miss Kuo. Her voice had a tinkling, fountain sound which was very pleasant to hear, but Juan found her meaning obscure.

'Perhaps you have not read Confucius,' she said.

Juan admitted that he had not. 'But you don't think Salvator is a Superior Person, do you?'

'When there are no real Superior Persons it is amusing to meet those whom others believe to be superior.'

'As some people like to collect the world's worst books?'

'Yes. And a butterfly collector takes ugly specimens, little hairy moths, as well as pretty ones.'

'And you would enjoy sticking pins in them.'

Kuo Kuo laughed. 'I haven't got any pins,' she said.

'I'm not so sure,' said Juan, looking at her slanting eyes that might be bows to shoot barbed and feathered pins of discernment at all manner of fluttering pretences and comical specimens. Behind the reticent loveliness of her face there could be hidden quivers full of arrows, pointed with Chinese wisdom that no Occidental would ever dream of, for though all the western world was plain to see and understand, delectable mysteries were still native to Cathay – or should be, when it showed a complexion so bewitchingly inscrutable. 'I'm not so sure,' he said.

'And what are *you* doing here?' asked Kuo Kuo.

'I'm a kind of an actor at present.'

'I think you could play some parts very well.'

'I like to be my own director, though.'

'Because you're ambitious – or disobedient?'

Juan had never bothered himself with ambition more than a yacht looks for cargoes, but as he was more interested in Kuo Kuo than in discussing his own character, he felt no temptation to enlarge on this peculiarity. Instead he parried the question and presently returned to the original topic of her Confucian quest.

'You must find the Hollywood idea of superiority rather commonplace,' he said.

'In China we have never despised the commonplace. Much of our poetry is commonplaces expressed with the art that Western peoples keep for loftier matters.'

'And China is supposed to be the abode of wisdom.'

'Perhaps it is. Yet more of our poetry shows the poet lamenting that he is not nearer the sea, or the mountains, or some big city. And always to be wishing you are somewhere else is not very wise.'

'But to follow your wishes and go is sensible.'

'Until you become disillusioned?'

'Did you come to Hollywood looking for disillusionment?'

'I came to look for a Superior Person.'

Miss Kuo's expression was more enigmatic than ever. She might have been amused at her own quest.

'And what would you do if you found one?' Juan persisted.

'Try to learn the secret of his superiority.'

'But how would you recognise him?'

If he combined great knowledge and great happiness I think he would be worth studying.'

'Then you're really serious?'

'Of course!'

'But you still find time for incidental amusement?'

'Amusement grows by the roadside, but it isn't the terminus.'

'And if your terminus is a long way off –'

'The more amusement you find on the way to it.'

'If you travel leisurely.'

'I'm not an American!' protested Kuo Kuo, and as she half-turned to see who at that moment had called 'Juan!' the dragon on her tunic stretched its long glittering neck and raised its golden head as if to bark with laughter.

The interrupter was Jill who, with Genevieve beside her, came to enquire where Juan had been hiding himself for so long. They were very cheerful after the several cocktails they had drunk, and talked with excited commendation of the party. Juan introduced them to Miss Kuo, but the introduction scarcely interfered with their bubbling loquacity. They interrupted each other and talked together, and so similar were their voices, so identical their vocabularies, such consanguinity had their habit of thought, that it might have been one person speaking with two tongues. They prattled and clacked with great animation, chattered and gabbled and gasped with little spurts of laughter, and some time during this shallow and noisy gust of small-talk Kuo Kuo silently and unobtrusively retired.

'Oh gee, it's a swell party!' cried Jill, and Genevieve asked

Juan if he had noticed how many of the distinguished guests were the better for their cocktails.

'The Prince has got a snootful,' she said, and Jill with an embracing gesture added, '*Everyone's* pie-eyed!'

Juan looked round and discovered with some surprise that while he had been talking the complexion of the garden-party had materially altered. Formality and punctilio had disappeared like poor swimmers in a rising tide, and loud laughter back-slapping, vociferous gaiety, and badinage of the most boisterous kind had taken their place. Faces were flushed, and beneath the decorum of Paris frocks and morning dress the guests were all hot and lively. They shouted to each other, and cracked broad jests, and laughed tumultuously. Groups of people formed, coalesced, broke apart and formed other groups, and as they moved about in brightly coloured or sombre raiment the garden looked like a huge pot to whose boiling surface spring pieces of carrot, turnip, green peas, white onions, red beef – and now a bubble bursts, the water swirls, and out of a seething flurry leaps a spurt of steam – and then the peas and the carrots and the leeks all dance again with the restless energy of unstinted heat.

Baron Schnapp had taken off his coat, and with a napkin over his arm was serving drinks with the other waiters. He had returned in spirit to the jovial nights when he worked in a New York *brauhaus*, and as he carried round a tray on which stood tall glasses of beer his bald and shining head glistened with innumerable beads of sweat, and down his fat cheeks, all creased with jolly thought, trickled tiny streams that glittered in the westering sun.

Phryne and her director, Mr. Strunk, were in high humour, and in a strident voice she demanded of her husband, 'Aren't you lucky to get a girl like me to go over the bumps with? Aren't you lucky, Big Boy? Don't I give you a swell time? You bet your sweet life I do!' – But the Prince was watching Baron Schnapp with a kindling light in his eye, and when a nearby guest shouted impatiently for a drink he turned and bellowed at the startled fellow, '*Komme gleich, mein Herr!*' and ran with giant strides into the house. In a moment he re-appeared, coatless like the Baron and with a napkin over his arm, carrying another tray on which stood enormous glasses of beer. These he rapidly distributed, stooping hugely over his tray and here and there wiping with his napkin imaginary table-tops. '*Drei dollar zwanzig*,' he roared, flourishing his napkin, and when a humorous guest threw some money on his tray, '*Danke schön*,' he shouted, and protesting to another, '*Komme gleich, mein Herr, komme gleich!*' hurried off for a new cargo.

The spectacle of their host serving in person gave new enthusiasm to the guests, who applauded this royal jest with unstinted mirth and, to encourage him in a pastime at once humorous and beneficent, redoubled their demands for refreshment, so that in a very short time they consumed a prodigious quantity of beer and still continued to enjoy the joke. The Prince and the Baron far excelled the other waiters in activity. They swerved like football-players as they carried their trays through the crowd, and swayed like ballet-dancers beneath a glittering load of empties. The glasses they brought were all brimfull and crowned with top-gallant-sails of foam, but never a drop did they spill and scarce a fluff of froth was wasted. The Princess shrieked with laughter at her husband's behaviour, and over a dozen empty tumblers kissed him enthusiastically.

Presently, after a brief consultation with the Prince – the latter stooped, listened, guffawed, and smacked his thigh with loud delight; the Baron's face glowing ripely in a mist of sweat like a ruddy September moon – the Baron disappeared for some little time, and when he returned carried not beer but an easel, a roll of canvas, and a pointer. He set up the easel and hung the canvas upon it, and as it unrolled Juan recognised its array of pictures. Here were the flowers, the domestic utensils, and the whittling-bench about which he had heard Eitel, the fat waiter, and all the people in the *brauhaus* sing so jovially. But now Eitel was Baron Schnapp, and his chorus was to be the high fashion of Hollywood. Juan waited impatiently.

The Baron cupped his hands to his mouth and shouted: 'Bay attention, blease! We will now *ein hübsche Liede* sing. It is galled *Die Schnitzelbank*, and I will der questions ask und you *die Antworte* make. *Zum Beispiel*, I boint to a rose und sing, '*Ist das nicht ein' blaue Rose?*' Den all togedder you sing, '*Ja, es ist ein' blaue Rose!*' Und der ghorus is, '*Eine schöne, eine schöne, eine schöne Schnitzelbank!*'

The Prince, with his hair towsled and his shirt-sleeves rolled back to display colossal fore-arms, assumed an expression of gravity and added this explanation:

'This song,' he said, 'is an old song which always at my castle in Pretzel-Oppenheim on Saturday nights we used to sing. For my father Prince Otto and my grandfather Prince Wilhelm it was their favourite song, and I also am very fond of it. Now my friend Baron Schnapp will to you teach it, and it will give me great pleasure to hear it again in the beautiful home of my wife, Princess Phryne, as I so many times have heard it in my own historic *Schloss* far away from here.'

The Prince's face was very solemn while he spoke, and when his little speech was done he lovingly embraced his friend. His broad shoulders shook with emotion and as he turned away he hid his face from the audience. Poor fellow! thought the more sensitive guests; he's recalling the vanished glories of his ancestral home. This must be very trying for him.

But there was no sign of sorrow on the Baron's face. In the ruddy light of the sun that now sank rapidly to the long horizon of the Pacific his cheeks shone like rubies and his bare scalp glimmered with a pink fantastic radiance. He had no difficulty in persuading his audience to sing. They pressed close together and their voices rose in a great chorus that, like a windmill's flapping sails, beat unwieldily on the jewelled air. Men whose trade it was to play heroes, potentates, and clowns; glamorous lovers whose lineaments were known in half the countries of the world; cowboys who for their livelihood and fictitious valour galloped on the windy precipices of the Sierra Nevada; smooth-faced villains and actors of so scoundrelly an air that they would affright the populace of Devil's Isle; players whose living depended upon an appearance of grave or florid benevolence; women of startling beauty, gipsy, vestal, or loose-legged Lais; haughty patricians, proud matronly creatures, professional dowagers under a crown of silver hair – now with intemperate joy they raised their voices and sang as the Baron led them. Some were a little fuddled and flustered, others ripe as a fallen peach, lush as August clover, merrier than birds, free as monkeys; happy as fiddlers in the last hours of a barn-dance, glorious as pipers on New Year's Eve; some had three sheets in the wind, some were prime as mid-May, more mellow than December feasting, and others were like sailors on leave, colts at grass, or nymphs and satyrs before Dionysus' altar. But all united at the Baron's call. He was Silenus and led his motley troop wheresoever he willed.

'*Ist das nicht ein golden Ring?*' he sang, richly and robustly, and tumultuously they answered:

> '*Ja, es ist ein golden Ring!*
> *Golden Ring, schönes Ding,*
> *Eine schöne, eine schöne, eine schöne Schnitzelbank!*'

Hollywood and Los Angeles lay beneath them, veiled in hot mist, and behind them the hills shone dully gold in the last flat waves of sunlight.

The longer the song grew the more complicated it became. The Baron's pointer flitted from picture to picture and voices tripped into laughter, rose and fell again as they followed him over articulative ditch and fence of stubborn consonants –

'Golden Ring, schönes Ding,
Blaue Rose, redliche Dose,
Heiliges Buch, warmes Tuch,
Schmutziges Kind, schnurriges Rind,
Eine schöne, eine schöne, eine schöne Schnitzelbank!'

Apart from his guests, the Prince of Pretzel-Oppenheim lay on his back upon the grass and howled with laughter to the empty sky. Somewhere in the crowd his wife was singing, lustily as the others, the song that had so often stirred the fine rafters – webby with more than spider's craft, loftily imagined – of his storied *Schloss* in – but where was Pretzel-Oppenheim? In Styria, Carinthia, Bohemia, Bavaria, in the Tyrol or the Carpathians, by the Danube or the Rhine? Did wolves bay the moon on its battlements or nightingales sing in lush meadows beneath its walls? Were rawboned highlanders its guard, or did laughing girls patrol its narrow streets and call with silvery challenge to their lovers drinking in cool dark wine-shops? Were battle flags its pride or happy peasants who had never known war? Did fighting songs rally his subjects' hearts or pastoral lays enchant their simple ears? Had his strength lain on stout burghers, honest artisans, or couched more amply on the lusty shoulders of yeomen and roisterous ploughboys? – All or any of these things were equally true, for Pretzel-Oppenheim lay in the good land of Fancy, between the arbitrary mountains of Invention and the whimsical river of Device, and its patents of nobility graced only impostors, by whose grace again its dynasties flourished and its populace grew fat or lean, friendly or hostile, king's men or republicans as circumstances called the cue. And for its exiled aristocrats there were few places better than Hollywood, that was itself but half reality and seldom what it seemed; yet few of them gave in return for hospitality so pretty a gift as a national anthem about a whittling-bench.

Prince Alto got up and stood to attention while his guests

sang with the gathering slowness of valediction the ultimate refrain –

'Eine schöne, eine schöne, eine schöne Schnitzelbank!'

VII

Exhilarated by the party and a large number of cocktails, Juan that evening so far forgot his sentimental loyalty to Lalage as lightly to make love to both Jill and Genevieve. He drove them in his car to a lonely corner in the hills, and then exchanging his driving seat for a middle position embraced them with amiable impartiality. They, believing that half a man was better than no love at all, took his distributed affection in fairly good part. If he kissed Jill too much and too often – for when in the darkness he could remember which was which he liked Jill better – then Genevieve would pluck at his other shoulder like a neglected puppy; and if, feeling sorry for neglecting her, he then gave her a longer embrace than was necessary, Jill would catch his sleeve with impatient reminding fingers. But each seemed, on the whole, satisfied with a moiety of his attention, and neither betrayed an improper jealousy of the other.

After taking them to their homes he returned to his lodging at the dentist's and fell asleep as soon as he got into bed. For some hours his sleep was undisturbed by any distinguishable dream, but then out of the dim and busy chaos of his subconscious brain rose the figure of a girl: neither Genevieve not Jill, but Kuo Kuo. She wore her black concealing garb with the dragon writhing golden on the breast of her tunic, and with her out of the confusion of dreaming came a faint elusive music that seemed partly of her making, for it ran trippingly as she did on close-moving Chinese feet, yet it was not Chinese music for it had the sound of a violin off whose strings leapt a dainty succession of notes, up and down, now climbing to a tiny but inaccessible height, and anon descending to run again with elfin steps on the banks of a sweet-flowing piano-stream. And as the music went so did Kuo Kuo, mocking and elusive, always so near and ever escaping. . . .

A voice broke from some other part of his brain to say that the music was the second variation of the andante movement in the Kreutzer Sonata, and immediately a ready semi-waking tongue of Juan's half-unconsciousness answered, 'Of course; Isadore and that friend of his played it one evening when I visited him.' . . . During this interchange Kuo Kuo vanished and in her place, suave and imposing, stood Dr. Salvator on a fawn-coloured beach that the blue and silver sea was lipping. Around him like white seals lay the nude figures of his disciples, relaxed in wilful thoughtlessness, torpid, motionless, and scarcely human. Some already wore the bewildered expression of seals, and the legs of others had grown together like thick tails. Far away on the very edge of the sea was a lonely figure, too distant to be clearly seen. Clearly though she was different from the others, for her colour was like ivory beneath the moon or pale gold seen faintly in glow-worm light, and she ran with tripping Chinese steps – the music started again – in the shallow edge of the sea. Now she came closer and closer, till suddenly, with the unreason of dreaming, she was so near that Juan could see nothing but a delicately rounded shoulder, and as he had expected her skin was much smoother than the pore-spotted hides of the slug-a-bed white seals; for nature had worked with polishing tools in China when mattock and adze were all the younger world possessed. But though she was so near he could not touch her, for when he reached towards her the violin began to play, and moved by its nimble notes she ran featly round the torpid seals, ever eluding him, and now she carried her tunic like a cloak about her shoulders and the dragon twisted and swam with serpentine activity. . . .

Stirred to wakefulness by this sleepy excitement, Juan was

gratified to think that his dreaming brain had provided him with Kuo Kuo for a companion, however ghostly and intangible, for their brief conversation had whetted his interest and he had looked for her again; but she had left the party early. He fell asleep hoping for new visions, but the rest of the night was empty as a desert. . . .

In the morning he found a letter waiting for him, originally addressed in a confident and half-familiar hand. It had been forwarded from his Great-aunt Rachel's house in Charleston, and her thin writing made a pretty contrast with the rounder script. He opened it and discovered with some surprise that it was from his Aunt Ruth Maitland Motley, whom he remembered visiting his mother at Mallieu and of whom Mrs. Dekker had spoken. She had been puzzled and insulted by his neglect of her since coming to America, but having heard from Lady Motley – to whom Great-aunt Rachel had written – that Juan had been much occupied with travel and sight-seeing (so Lady Motley had phrased it) she was not only ready to forgive him but more than ever eager to see and entertain him.

'Your mother says that you are possibly in Los Angeles,' she wrote, 'and as we are now in Santa Barbara we are practically next door to each other and you can't and you mustn't defer your visit any longer. Everybody is anxious to see you, your grandfather Lowell, who is with us at present, particularly so – but it isn't really fair to distinguish him, for Marcia and Sylvia are constantly talking about you and wondering when they are to see you again – they haven't forgotten their visit to Mallieu Hall some years ago – and I myself would dearly like to have you under my own roof. So come soon and stay as long as you like, for our home is, or should be, yours too. Your grandfather indeed thinks you ought to come into the Bank, where he is sure you would do well. But that is his affair, not mine. All I am concerned about is that you should come to us *now*, and your cousins agree with me in that . . . .'

It was charming of Aunt Ruth to be so kind, thought Juan,

especially as he had left unanswered an earlier invitation – as warm in tone as this one – that she had offered while he was at Motley. At one time he really meant to visit his American relations, whom he had enjoyed seeing at Mallieu – Sylvia and Marcia used to be delightful youngsters – but fate, having drawn him away from the politer paths of society and his habit being to occupy himself with immediate surroundings, he had for long scarcely given them a thought. Now he felt somewhat ashamed of himself, and the generosity of Aunt Ruth's letter inclined him to answer immediately.

But he so disliked writing letters that he kept neither note-paper nor stamps, and the lack of these offered such an obstacle that he decided instead to motor up to Santa Barbara some day soon and reply in person. Some day soon. Not to-day or to-morrow, for there was work to be done at the Tantamount studio to-day, and to-morrow he had promised to take Jill and Genevieve out, and the day after that he was to meet some friends of Isadore Cohen. But soon, quite soon, he would go to Santa Barbara and call on these very pleasant relations. . . .

Mr. Strunk had decided that there were not enough preliminary scenes in *The Deluge*. The flood was a fine catastrophe, but the ascent to the point at which a catastrophe was dramatically proper had not been made sufficiently steep, nor was the character of Noah so largely drawn as to reveal in him the inevitable rescuer of humanity. Mr. Strunk had therefore done a little juggling with Biblical history and prepared a series of scenes in which Noah should talk to God in a burning bush, tell the people of his experience, and to quell their still obstinate unbelief climb a mountain and receive from the hands of God – now present in a thunderstorm – tablets graven with the Decalogue. That these exploits belonged to Moses and not to Noah did not worry Mr. Strunk. 'What's the difference?' he asked. 'They're only names. Anyway folk don't go the movies to learn history, they go to be amused. And I know how to amuse them. I guess we'll have a golden calf too.'

In this way more work was provided for the extras and Juan postponed his visit to Santa Barbara for another week. During this time he tried in vain to discover where Kuo Kuo lived. Nobody seemed to know anything about her, and disappointed by his failure Juan fell back on Jill and Genevieve's company. His relations with them gradually and at first imperceptibly changed. In spite of the scant difference between them and his occasional difficulty in distinguishing one from the other, he definitely discovered that he liked Jill better than Genevieve. Genevieve moreover began to suspect this adverse preference and used all her fascination to retain his favour. When Jill saw this she also started to treat Juan with unusual consideration, and displayed her allurements in the outraged face of Genevieve. Genevieve then found that she disliked Jill, and to conceal her dislike from Juan – whom she knew it would displease – used her friend with exceptional politeness. Jill replied in like manner, and so their conversation was larded with'My dears' and 'My darlings', 'Honeys' and 'Sweethearts,' and they constantly gave each other small gifts of perfume and handkerchiefs. But during these affectionate exchanged Juan noticed that their eyes were hard and glittering, and whenever he was amiable to one the other interrupted and tries to steal his attention.

Excited by their enmity, they both fell hotly in love with him, and so his occasional dalliance with one or the other – for he did not like to leave Genevieve in the cold – acquired a passionate intensity which he had not wanted, but which, when it was there, he could not find it in his heart to discourage.

Phryne Fuller continued to distinguish all three of them with her friendship. She was full of pride and happiness because of the phenomenal success of her party, which had provided Hollywood with gossip for days and bred in her rivals such unquenchable envy that Phryne went about her duties with little songs on her lips and loaded Prince Alto with ever-increasing favours. With a husband who not only gave her an ancient title but also – with the assistance of his chamberlain – entertained her guests with royal assurance, it seemed likely that she could achieve her ambition to become the most important hostess in southern California. The prospect was exciting. She was accounted a great actress, known all over the world and wealthy as befitted such a one; her salary was enormous and her first husband (who died after a year of marriage) had left her a considerable fortune. But so far she had not achieved the social prominence which she felt was her due. Her first husband, though rich, had been uncouth in his ways and disinclined to entertain according to his means. Then had come the period of her widowhood, scrupulously observed to please an exigent public which loved to read of her pious retirement from pleasure. Her second marriage had been brief and unfortunate, and after the divorce her trying battle with corpulence had made her melancholy and unapt for society. But now the horizon was fair, and Phryne felt that it was in her power to achieve social distinction of real magnitude. And taking time by the forelock, she had decided to follow up her reception with a ball in honour of the Prince's approaching birthday.

She met Juan returning with Jill and Genevieve from a trial worship of Mr. Strunk's Golden Calf, and told them all about it.

'It will be next Sunday,' she said, 'and you simply must come. I should never enjoy myself if my heroic rescuers were not there to share my pleasure. Of course I know that this is ridiculously short notice to give, but I've only just discovered that Sunday *is* the Prince's birthday, so I'm inviting people personally – not everybody I want can come, but some of the best-known people have accepted – and I hope that this informality will make it all the nicer and more home-like, which is quite the nicest way to entertain one's friends, don't you think?'

This invitation caused Juan to postpone for another few days his visit to Santa Barbara. He thought again of writing to his aunt, but he so seldom wrote letters that his intention wasted its impetus in continual remands. He had never had a gossiping pen, but once in his first year at Cambridge he had written a long enthusiastic letter to his mother, and in the Christmas vacation found it where she had left it between the leaves of a novel. He re-read it and saw to his dismay that old emotion too often seems to have had a false complexion, and that ardour congealed in ink may leave on the tongue a faint disgust. He had regretted his ebullition of feeling, burnt the pages, and condemned in that one instance the whole practice of letter-writing.

And so Mrs. Motley, Grandfather Lowell, the charming cousins Sylvia and Marcia, and several other relations spending a holiday in Santa Barbara waited in vain to hear from their erratic kinsman . . . But still Juan intended to visit them when he had an opportunity, and indeed looked forward with considerable pleasure to seeing them and sharing in their luxurious enjoyments. In the meantime, however, he was busy worshipping Mr. Strunk's Golden Calf, maintaining his complicated relations with Jill and Genevieve, helping Isadore Cohen to endure the dullness of life, attending practices of Mr. Pumpenstempel's orchestra, and making the acquaintance of Hollywood's *beau monde* under the splendid wing of Princess Phryne.

The ball to celebrate Prince Alto's birthday was not nearly so large as the reception to Dr. Salvator had been, but it began with greater ceremony and finished – though Juan was not there to see the end – with equal exuberance. There was an excellent orchestra and a generous provision of wines, for Phryne ingenuously believed that she could reach more speedily the harbour of her ambition if she left behind her a wake of intoxication, and so her bootlegger had furnished her with all his store. She had abundance of champagne, plenty of sherry, a sufficiency of port, some claret, a dozen bottles of Moselle, a competence of cognac, and a copious supply of whisky, gin, and Bacardi rum. In addition to these Baron Schnapp had prepared a cup of incomparable flavour and astonishing strength.

Juan danced energetically and drank with some heartiness . . . He was not pleased about his relations with Jill, into which he had entered more by accident than design, but which, now they were entered upon, could not easily be left at their present half-way station. Some people, it was true, were contented for long periods with the toys and flimsy scantlings of love; tilting with lips, and similar trifling; but Juan's nature, for good or ill, was more that of Donne, who wrote:

> 'Who ever loves, if he do not propose
> The right true end of love, he's one that goes
> To sea for nothing but to make him sick.'

Now, heated by dancing and invigorated by the Baron's cup, he decided to press forward the affair to its logical conclusion. That this would involve breaking with Genevieve was obvious, for her friendship both for Juan and for Jill was too self-interested to endure such a revelation of his preference; and with natural kindliness Juan could not help regretting her approaching disappointment, though he did not make the mistake of over-estimating its importance, since disappointment is one of the most natural and common occurrences on earth and everybody, as he well knew, must take turns in being its agent and its victim . . . He was dancing with Jill. She danced extremely well. She was undoubtedly pretty and her naïveté was engaging. He remembered her telling him that she had seven hats and liked to eat candy in her bath. A childish, endearing trait. He liked her bright bird-like chattering and a bird-like nestling way she had. To-night she looked better than he had ever seen her before, and all her movements in the dance fitted his exactly.

The night was hot and they went to walk awhile in the

garden. It was very dark and Jill pretended to trip over some obstacle.

'I thought of going down to Agua Caliente for a few days,' said Juan, 'Will you come with me?'

'Just us two?' asked Jill.

'Of course.'

Jill hesitated, and then, despite her naïveté, gasped, 'You mean to get married! Oh, Juan!'

She threw her arms round his neck and clung to him ecstatically. Juan, who had never for a moment contemplated marriage, was startled by this reception of his proposal, but as a hot foment speedily draws irritation out of a physical hurt, so the proximity of Jill, the warmth of her body and the loving way in which she clung to him, soon soothed the shock which his mind had suffered and erased from the surface of his consciousness the prickles of surprise and alarm which so unnatural a suggestion had caused. Indeed, so comfortable was he in Jill's embrace that in a little while the suggestion no longer seemed unnatural, and he began to think 'Why not?' After all marriage in America was no longer a life-contract. It was easy to wed and easy to be unwed. According to Hollywood the marriage service was no more than a means of giving respectability to a liaison. It was not intended to seal with finality the love of a man and a woman, but to dress it for public appearance. Living so much in the public eye the better-known actresses and actors were driven to preserve an apparent continence, and so with the help of the divorce courts they regularised their intrigues, sanctified them with the assistance of the Church, and amid popular acclaim called them marriages. That was the American custom, thought Juan, and living in America he might as well do as others did. Besides, he had never been married before and a new experience was always worth something. . . .

'That is what you mean, isn't it?' said Jill anxiously.

'Yes,' answered Juan, and kissed her. 'But don't say anything about it just yet,' he added, and Jill in a romantic mood consented to secrecy.

After a short time they went back into the house, and when Juan had drunk some of the Baron's cup they danced. Then he drank again to the last ebb of bachelorhood and the prospect of honeymoon. The Prince joined him and they drank to friendship. Baron Schnapp came along, his huge red face jewelled splendidly with sweat, and they toasted his magnificent. cup. Juan felt the reckless gaiety of one who has pledged himself to a hardy and unnecessary undertaking. Eat, drink, and be merry, he thought, for to-morrow we wed. He talked loudly and made jokes at which the others laughed with gratifying enjoyment. The orchestra played lustily, and he saw Genevieve standing for a moment alone. . . . Poor Genevieve. He would dance with her for the last time on this night of hail and farewell.

They danced. Then he danced with Jill again, and as the Prince approached left her once more for Genevieve. Then back to Jill, and this time Mr. Strunk relieving him, once more to Genevieve. The music seemed to grow louder and louder. It filled the air as if with huge yellow bricks slammed one on the other and smacked into place with a great brass trowel. The voices of their fellow-guests like mortar filled the chinks between, and they were surrounded by an impenetrable wall within which forty heterogamous ingeminates excessively gyrated. . . .

'Let's have another drink,' said Juan.

A score of people stood round the bar, noisy and good-humoured, with Baron Schnapp in their midst. He greeted Juan with loud half-German banter and the waggish drinkers, their wits re-stirring, added quips and cracks and sallies that returned again to plague the inventor. It was very hot. Ice chinked in a glass, coldly touched the lip, and promptly melted. Presently it seemed to Juan that nothing could be pleasanter than fresh air, and taking his partner into the garden

– coming from the brilliant light of the ballroom the darkness blinded them – they stumbled over the lawn until they found a seat. With sighs of relief they sat down.

'This is better, isn't it?' said Juan comfortably.

'I'll say it is,' she answered. 'Gee, it was hot in there! But it's a swell dance, isn't it? I never knew anyone could throw a party like Phryne does.'

With lazy ears Juan listened to her artless prattle. He had grown accustomed to her lively shallow repetition of incident and ingenuous comment, and he found it soothing after the noise of the dance. He heard her say, 'I told him he ought to be big-hearted about it,' and though he had no idea to whom she referred he was pleased by her naïve expectation of altruism from the world. She slid from topic to topic, and presently remarked, 'They hadn't got those shades anyway.' Her concern with dress seemed pretty and natural as a bird preening its feathers. Then, inconsequently referring to someone's too recondite small-talk, 'I don't know enough about politics to even begin arguing about them,' she said. And a minute later, 'I just adore white things, like silver fox, and marshmallows, and those big handkerchiefs of yours.'– Idly Juan listened, entertained by her brisk nibbling appetite for life. She talked on, finding everything she had seen or heard a source of interest, until Juan took her hand and asked, 'Where shall we go for our honeymoon – Agua Caliente or Palm Springs?'

There was a little gasp of surprise, and a moment's silence.

'Oh, Juan, do you really mean it?' she said, and with a sudden movement buried her face in his shoulder and clasped her arms about his neck. The agreeable and familiar odour of her hair pleased his nostrils.

'Of course I mean it,' he said. 'I don't go back on my word.'

He drew her more comfortably into his arms, stretched his legs to a position of greater ease, and leaned back into the corner of the seat. A long silence followed and Juan began to feel drowsy.

With an effort he roused himself – one could not fall asleep in the Princess's garden, and there were some people he wanted to dance with – and prepared to return to the ballroom. 'Agua Caliente, Palm Springs, Lake Tahoe – we'll go wherever you like,' he said complacently, and disengaged her arms.

'I don't care where it is so long as I'm with you. Oh, I'm so happy! I never thought you were going to ask me to marry you. I thought –'

'I make up my mind very quickly,' Juan interrupted. Having decided to experiment with marriage he was satisfied with his decision and did not want to discuss motives and trains of thought. And it was time they went back to the party. 'Let's go in and dance, shall we?'

They recrossed the lawn. The darkness was sharply limited by light streaming from the open door, and on the black side of the dividing line, just before stepping into brilliance, Juan suffered himself to be embraced once more. As their lips parted his fiancée stepped backwards into the light, and to his horror he saw that it was not Jill but Genevieve.

VIII

Juan escaped from the party by pleading – not without truth – a sudden faintness. He had sufficiently kept his wits to make Genevieve promise to keep their engagement secret, he had bidden her tell Jill of his indisposition, and then he had fled.

He spent a restless night and the following day was still more unhappy; it was Monday, when there was rarely any work for extras at the Tantamount studio. Juan sat idly at home considering his predicament, and the longer he thought of it the more painful it appeared. He had made himself ridiculous and grievously hurt both Jill and Genevieve. Genevieve was the more obvious sufferer, but when Jill discovered what had happened her pride would be sorely wounded to think that anyone else could be mistaken for her. Both girls plumed themselves on the possession of a distinctive personality, as indeed did everyone else in Hollywood. It was not only the natural desire for individuality that bade them defend their Ego, but the national habit of advertising everything had so popularised this vague and ambiguous virtue of personality that every shop-assistant and dish-washer must claim one, and for an actress it was essential. 'Personality Pays!' said the advertisements, and offered to sell booklets that would teach those lacking it how to acquire one without delay. A personality was as necessary to self-regard as a birth certificate, and a well cultivated one meant assurance of success in a democracy where most things were standardised and merely to say an article was 'different' was to praise it.

Now a personality that could not be remembered in the dark was a poor affair not worthy of the name, and Juan shrank from offering Jill so unpalatable an excuse for his infidelity. She would be angry with him for embracing Genevieve when he was engaged to her, but she would be mortally wounded to think he had been unaware of any difference. That was an intolerable insult. And the same thing held for Genevieve, whose personality had failed to light the dark. Both would be insulted where their pride was tender and high, and to Genevieve he must also admit that he neither wanted nor meant to marry her. . . .

They had spoken the same kind of words in the same way and the same sort of voice. They had sweetly smelt alike – powder, scent, and shampoo – and they had yielded to caresses with the same willing dexterity. Their arms and bodies were cast in the same mould and dressed after the same fashion. Their manners had been acquired at the dictation of similar circumstances, and their attitude to life dominated by the same popular notions. They *were* alike, and Juan felt that his mistake might have been excusable even without the Baron's cup. But to plead justification or even extenuating circumstances was so brutal as to be out of the question. Genevieve and Jill would be less hurt if he pretended his proposals had been wilful deception, for in that case he would be the villain and his villainy, not their lack of individuality, would be to blame.

And yet he could not with equanimity think of making such a confession. How could he phrase an explanation that, resolved into simple meaning, meant that he had played a practical joke whose lack of humour was equalled only by its inhumanity? Nor was the prospect of continuing the deception until they discovered it for themselves any more agreeable, for then he could be disclosed not only as a cold-hearted but also as a singularly maladroit seducer or a would-be bigamist. Seduction, the tawdry scandal of one's ancestors, had gone out with the last of the hansom-cabs, and bigamy (unless for sailors) was the idiot's way to bed. But if he were to save the poor girls' self-esteem he must either confess to fictitious villainy or practise real villainy until it were found out. It was an appalling prospect.

During these dejected musings he was twice interrupted by the telephone as first Jill and then Genevieve called to enquire after his health. He assured them of his convalescence but pleaded to be left alone till he had completely recovered. Both told him how happy they were, and to both, feeling like a traitor, he said how glad he was that they were happy.

He was relieved when evening came, for there was a practice of Mr. Pumpenstempel's orchestra and he would be safer in Pasadena than in his own room, since both Jill and Genevieve might take a notion to visit him in spite of his request for solitude. And in the orchestra he would see men still less happy than himself, whose infelicity might by comparison give him consolation.

Mr. Pumpenstempel's home, usually dark, had all its windows illuminated when he arrived. The entrance to the house was brightly lighted and the door stood open. Juan went in wondering what had happened. He soon discovered.

In the concert hall he found Nikitin talking to a group of strangers. There were ten or a dozen of them, and one who spoke louder than the others and seemed to have authority was a tall and burly man whose original fierceness of aspect was somewhat loosened and made fat by rich living. He had tremendous bushy eyebrows and choleric blue eyes, and he topped Nikitin by half a head. Elsewhere in the hall were thirty or forty other people, guests apparently of less importance, and half the orchestra were clustered like frightened sheep on the platform. The catastrophe which all this obviously intended was so great that Juan's private troubles were driven out of sight, and he stood for some minutes staring at the invaders with feelings comparable to those of Macbeth when the trees of Dunsinane came striding over the fields.

Nikitin, to Juan's surprise, showed no embarrassment as he faced his employer. When he had arrived and found Mr. Pumpenstempel waiting for him he had trembled and felt weak as though his bowels were running out. Half its normal content of blood fled from his brain and he stared with white face at the man whom of all men in the world he least desired to see. But Mr. Pumpenstempel was so busy explaining his unexpected arrival that he paid no attention to Nikitin's quandary.

'We were visiting with friends in Kingston, Jamaica,' he said, 'and then my wife got an idea she'd like to see the Panama Canal. I didn't feel any special urge myself, but as she said, "What's the use of buying a yacht if you don't want to go places?"– That's the hell of a fine yacht I bought. You must come down and see it.– Well, everyone else was willing (we'd quite a party aboard) so we went through the Canal and turned north to have a look at Costa Rica and Nicaragua. I've got some business interests in Central America. Then Miss Comber here thought she'd like to see Mexico City, so we stopped off at Acapulco for a few days and took a trip there. And after that we didn't quite know what to do till old man Bostock –

he's my wife's uncle – said there was mighty good salmon fishing in Vancouver Island, so my wife got a notion she'd like to go fishing and we decided to steam north, though it's a pretty long journey from Acapulco to Vancouver. Then as we were passing here I thought it would be kind of nice to stop in and have a look at the old home. It was just pure luck we arrived on your practice day, but now we are here I guess we might as well have a tune. What d'you say, my dear?'

Mrs. Pumpenstempel emphatically wanted some music, and the other members of the yachting party said how fortunate they were to have an opportunity of hearing so famous an orchestra.

'That all right with you, Nikitin?' asked Mr. Pumpenstempel. 'You got the boys all ready to do their stuff?'

'As soon as they are here they will be ready,' said Nikitin dully. During Mr. Pumpenstempel's explanation he had recovered most of his composure and decided that, failing a miracle, he must philosophically admit defeat. Such luck as he had enjoyed could not last for ever, and he had saved enough money to keep him yet awhile from work. Ach, to be an old man and sit all day in a big chair, he thought. But *che sarà, sarà*. I will have the courage of a fatalist, he decided – and added a swift prayer for miracles.

'That's fine,' said Mr. Pumpenstempel. 'Now suppose we have a bottle of champagne while Mrs. Pumpenstempel telephones some of the neighbours to come in and listen to the concert? It's kind of selfish to keep good music all to ourselves, I guess, and there's a whole lot of folk round here just crazy about – hell, I can't remember those dago names. All your swell composers, I mean.'

Nikitin felt much better for the champagne, and after three glasses he was almost sure that a miracle of some description would occur. Meanwhile in twos and threes the orchestra arrived and Nikitin did his best to keep Mr. Pumpenstempel from looking too closely at them. They appeared more disreputable than ever as, frightened by the unexpected visitors, they gathered in a furtive group at the back of the platform. Their clothes were shabby, they were blear-eyed, unclean, embossed with warts, shambling, lantern-jawed or pot-bellied fellows of whom Nikitin was thoroughly ashamed.– But God was good and he might by a miracle make them play as exquisitely as the original orchestra had done.– Isadore Cohen arrived. He was one of the dozen or so competent performers. Isadore could be relied on to do his best. But following him came the harpist who looked like Herod, his tittering ingle, a piccolo who would better grace a prison hospital, and three second fiddles white as candles, bare-bone wastrels hag-ridden with dope. Ugly though they were they had been profitable to Nikitin, for he paid them scarcely anything and according to the books they drew handsome salaries.– Well, we must take things as they come, he resolved, and meet catastrophe like men.– He swallowed a little more champagne.– But there is no need to despair just yet, he thought, for something unforeseen may still happen.

When Juan appeared Nikitin summoned him in a lordly way and presented him to the Pumpenstempels.

'Mr. Juan Motley, the English violinist. Mr. Motley is a newcomer to the orchestra and we were very lucky to get him.'–

Lucky to have someone I can show at close quarters, he meant, as he saw that Juan's appearance favourably impressed the Pumpenstempels. They had already remarked on the droll look of the other musicians and Nikitin was greatly relieved by their occupation with Juan. They asked in what orchestras he had previously played, and Juan kept the pot boiling with a lavish use of famous names. But while he claimed acquaintance with Sir Henry Wood, Coates, Toscanini, and Stokowski, he was wondering how the devil Nikitin would manage to get himself out of the mess he was in.

'Well, what are we going to have?' asked Mr. Pumpenstempel. The orchestra was all present and a satisfactory number of guests had arrived. 'What are you going to give us, Nikitin?'

'Anything you like,' said Nikitin, 'it is all one to me.'

'You got the boys in pretty good trim, eh? Well, put a name to it, somebody. I guess I got a mighty slick orchestra – they're not exactly handsome but Nikitin tells me they know their onions – so it's up to you to say what you want.'

The members of the yachting party raked their memories for the name of some musical composition, and the guests invited from the neighbourhood replied with a score of different suggestions.

'One at a time,' said Mr. Pumpenstempel good-naturedly. 'Now, who spoke first?'

Miss Comber seized the opportunity. She was a hungry-looking woman with protruding eyes and teeth that took the air, and she had been watching Juan with open admiration.

'I think we ought to have Strauss's *Don Juan* in honour of the orchestra's latest recruit,' she said, and ogled the object of her flattery.

Juan bowed stiffly and Nikitin shrugged his shoulders. 'As you will,' he said, 'everything is the same to me.'

'Atta boy,' said Mr. Pumpenstempel heartily. 'We'll make a start with *Don Juan* then.'

– And finish with it too, thought Juan as he went with Nikitin to the library.

'What are you going to do about it?' he asked. 'We can't play this stuff and you know we can't.'

'Pumpenstempel is ignorant of all music,' said Nikitin impatiently. 'He won't know if you play it or not.'

'But other people will.'

'Perhaps something will happen. The house may go on fire, or there will be an earthquake. You never know. Sometimes they have earthquakes here and one may come to-night.' Nikitin refused to hear any further objections.

The library was in disorder and it took him some time to find *Don Juan*. He puffed and blew as he searched along the shelves and peered into stacks of manuscript. At last he found what he wanted, and loading Juan with a great pile told him to distribute it. Unfortunately among the Strauss music were some horn and other brass parts of *The Flying Dutchman* overture which Juan failed to observe.

The orchestra seated itself with an agonised scraping of chairs. Most of them were in a state of terror and their only comfort was that Nikitin must take the blame for whatever happened. Those who knew how to do it tuned their instruments, and those who did not furtively wiped sweaty hands on their trousers and looked with amazement at the music spread out before them.

Juan sat beside Isadore among the first violins and the little Jew, his eyes large with nervous anticipation, muttered, 'This is going to be pretty dull. It's going to be god-awful dull. Just you see!'

Nearby them a man was hiccupping with consternation, and the flautist who resembled Philip IV of Spain could not keep his teeth from chattering. The harpist who looked like Herod sat black-browed and unmoved by any excitement, but his ingle, alarmed by their prominent position on the right front of the stage, hardly restrained his tears. The leader of the orchestra, a sound musician made poor by a large family, watched with unhid dismay as Nikitin slowly walked to the front of the platform, bowed to polite applause, and turned to confront his men.

Nikitin's eyes were closed and soundlessly he gabbled a prayer for an earthquake. A large and immediate earthquake. But no earthquake came. He groaned, and then straightened his shoulders. If God withheld his miracles he must be a fatalist and take discomfiture like a man. He thought of his money in the bank – full forty thousand dollars – and tapping twice upon his desk raised his arms in a commanding gesture.

The wretched men before him brought their instruments into position, and still wondered if they were really meant to play. With dazed incredulous eyes they watched the impending baton. . . .

The point descended.

Simultaneously the strings – or as many of them as could play – began the opening theme of *Don Juan* and the brasses – the moustached, pot-bellied, pimple-studded, rococo fellows – blared forth the violent introductory chord of the *Flying Dutchman* overture.

Nikitin staggered as though he had been shot and almost fell off his perch. With a few squeaks and expiring grunts the noise before him died, while from behind him there came titters of laughter and Mr. Pumpenstempel's angry voice demanding 'What the hell's the matter?'

Though badly shaken Nikitin ignored this interruption, and leaning forward with an expression of incredible ferocity hissed to the brasses, 'Keep quiet, you fools!' He was too flustered to guess what had happened and thought the mysterious hubbub another of fate's blows.

Then he started again, and while the brasses maintained a puzzled silence – for the music before them clearly demanded action – the others again attacked *Don Juan*. Their music had a dismal sound, for half were out of time and a few among them who could not play at all but imitated the actions of their fellows sometimes allowed an untutored bow to scrape across the gut. Nevertheless a just recognisable statement of the three themes emerged.

But their succeeding contrapuntal interlacement was beyond the power of such a troop, and as Nikitin listened to the scraping he realised that it would not deceive even Mr. Pumpenstempel, and an earthquake could do no more than blot out the memory of this infamy. He heard already the laughter and protests of the audience, but because he could not screw his courage to the point of facing his employer and admitting his fraud he continued to conduct. . . .

In a moment horns should sound. That meant more noise.

Perhaps noise would conceal the awful holes in this tattered pattern of sound. Nikitin glared at the horns and mouthed an injunction to get ready.– These were the fools who had already upset his apple-cart. The brasses, seeing him grimace in their direction, stunned by their initial error and now utterly bewildered, glanced one to the other and muttered, 'Us? God knows what it's all about. But it's us he means!'

Their red cheeks were pale and their moustaches drooped, but obediently they looked to their music and licked their lips in readiness. . . .

Nikitin's baton threatened them, and once more the opening fanfare of the *Flying Dutchman* overture drowned all other instruments with its brazen din.

Nikitin's hands dropped helplessly to his sides. For an instant he thought God's mercy of an earthquake had come, but then he recognised defeat. He listened to the awful note of the Dutchman's trumpeter, blown in the gale's despite to windward as his ghostly vessel heeled in the tempest, and shuddered at its doom. All other instruments were mute, but the indomitable horns continued.

Mr. Pumpenstempel jumped from his seat and roared 'Stop that infernal row!'

The horns quavered into silence, but startled by the apparition of Mr. Pumpenstempel's scarlet face and bright blue eyes Herod's ingle clutched, as if for support, at the strings of his harp and drew from them an irrelevant mocking tinkle and twang that further frightened him into tears.

While he wept Mr. Pumpenstempel strode passionately on to the platform and shook his fist in Nikitin's face. The audience stopped its laughter to listen.

'You call this bunch of tin-gutted saps an orchestra?' he bellowed. 'You're an impostor, sir! A damned humbug, a quack and a rogue! By God, you'll suffer for insulting me and my guests in this way. By God you will! Think you could pull this on me, eh? I'll jail you all, you and your precious orchestra, for conspiracy, fraud, misappropriation of funds, and common swindling!'

Mr Pumpenstempel stamped with rage while the audience left their seats and crowded excitedly below the platform to urge him on. Nikitin sadly shook his head, and the sight of his red beard wagging was too much for the millionaire, who seized it in one hand and clenching the other fist punched Nikitin on the nose. Nikitin yelled with pain and would have fallen had not Mr. Pumpenstempel retained a grip on his beard.

Juan alone among the musicians attempted to interfere as the millionaire prepared to repeat his blow. Quivering with fright the rest sat still, but Juan leapt forward and tried to pull Nikitin away. Mr. Pumpenstempel swung out a mighty backhander that sent his new assailant sprawling. He fell among 'cellos. Now since the first blaring entry of the brasses Juan had been in trouble to keep his laughter out of sight, and he had joined the scrimmage for the relief of action as much as to defend Nikitin, and with a kind of hilarious wigs-on-the-green, free-for-all feeling. As he fell in a huddle of chairs, 'cellists, and music his spirits rose still higher and he looked about for a suitable weapon to express them . . . and found behind him a double bass. He seized it in both hands and swinging its imponderous bulk aloft ran forward to smash it over Mr. Pumpenstempel's head. It thundered like a drum and banged like gunfire as its back burst and swallowed the millionaire's skull in its huge interior. A frantic voice bellowed in its sounding womb, and staggering to and fro, Mr. Pumpenstempel fell over the edge into the arms of his friends.

Now like panic-stricken sheep the orchestra broke its ranks and by the stairs at either side poured off the platform, leaving a wreckage of fluttering manuscript and overset music-stands. Nikitin headed the rout, puffing and blowing and working his elbows. The audience made a half-hearted attempt to stop them, but the musicians with their single impulse of escape were irresistible. Juan, momentarily startled by the havoc he had wrought, recovered his wits in time to join the tail of the stampede.

In the darkness outside he saw before him and on either side black shapes of men who fled blindly from the wrath they had aroused. He could still hear the tumult of anger dominated by Mr. Pumpenstempel's awe-inspiring voice.– The galloping shapes drew farther from him. He was sobbing with laughter so that he could not run, and presently he was all alone. He laughed till his belly hurt him, with the laughter that fills a small boy or a savage before the wild spectacle of farce at freedom. The night was dark and there was no one abroad in the tree-lined streets. The sky was round like a fool's bladder. There was no reason in the stars, and the world's gravity was a ninepin balanced upon ice. Touch it and it rolled. Turn solemnity over a fence to see the legs of lunacy, or catch pretence by the heels and watch mockery leap on to the stage like the devil in an old play. . . .

'Lord, what a precarious thing is sobriety!' thought Juan, and strove to think reasonably of all that had happened.

IX

Not until he was at home and gone to bed did reaction come, and then Juan suddenly realised that he had committed assault upon a millionaire. Turned into every-day language his joke was a criminal offence and there was no good cause for laughter either in that or in Nikitin's fraudulent orchestra. Juan sat up in bed and stared at darkness that was not now the vast and jocular night but darkness man-made and measured by conventional walls. In these surroundings all his troubles returned. He remembered Jill and Genevieve, and with a groan suspected that one reason for his jubilation had been a mind emptied of them after it had borne their burden all day.

Laughter was a shallower and more fleeting thing than he had thought, and common sense, though you blithely kick it through the window, will like a mongrel dog come creeping back through the door. Laughter would neither satisfy Jill nor fob off Genevieve, nor protect him from Mr. Pumpenstempel's action for assault. In their opinion, indeed, it would only aggravate his several offences.

Now like an honest man who, flown with wine, has blithely courted folly and with her for a deceptive hour been happier than ever in his life before, but in the morning wakes to remember the jade with curses and regret because the gay antics that he shared with her seem in that cold grey light but sorry and shameful matters, so Juan recalled his boisterous bit of clowning with groans and misery. . . . It had seemed at the time so apt, so full of the justice of the theatre, to buffet noisy Pumpenstempel with his own bass fiddle and defend poor rascally Nikitin with one of the instruments he had so abused; but now there seemed nothing in it but vulgar brawling in company with, and on the side of, as draggled and shambling a set of wastrels as were to be found in the whole city. Seeing it in this aspect Juan felt no more inclination for mirth than a clown looking at his own face in a mirror, but like a clown wished only to escape from his folly. . . . Happening to a man free of other burdens such a misfortune would have been serious enough, but Juan was already laden with his obligations to Jill and Genevieve and the necessity – if he would save them further insult – of confessing himself a villain. When he stopped thinking of Pumpenstempel he began to think of them, and when he fled from the spectacle of a seducer *manqué*, an innocent bigamist, the destroyer of two poor girls' self-love (and all three wore his appearance), he returned to visions of the millionaire with a writ for assault and battery.

What was the penalty for hitting a millionaire on the head with a bass-fiddle? he wondered. With such a weight of dollars behind the prosecution he might be clapt into prison whatever defence he offered. Not that he had much defence. It would be all very well to say that he had been trying to save Nikitin from Pumpenstempel's dangerous anger, but where was the necessity – except a dramatic propriety which would appeal to no jury – for employing a bass fiddle in such defence? And while the case was proceeding Jill would tell Genevieve that the accused was her fiancé, and Genevieve would indignantly reply that he was hers, and then the story of his perfidy in the garden would emerge, bit by bit, from victims at first incredulous, impatient of each other's fabrications, haughty about the favour they severally stood in – and then doubtful, despairing, weeping and sobbing for pride and trust deceived, till their tears had melted jealously away and emotion fused them into one enemy who ran hot-foot to Pumpenstempel's lawyer with such a story of the prisoner's iniquity as would bank and buttress the case against him with overwhelming proof of his natural depravity.

It was a shocking picture that Juan conjured out of the darkness, and the darkness increased its horror so much that he became convinced of the imperative necessity of flight. Once before he had comforted himself with the reflexion that freedom to come and go as he wished permitted him to escape consequences inevitable to men of a more settled state of life, and now that realisation returned. By guerilla tactics one might still hold one's own with life, and when it was no longer convenient to offer her a bold face, why then, show her a stout pair of heels. Perhaps it was cowardly? But whom would so-called courage benefit? Not Pumpenstempel, unless to gratify him with revenge. Neither Genevieve nor Jill, since he could not marry both of them, nor truthfully explain his conduct to either without brutality compared to which desertion was a fleabite. . . . And if he deserted both they could console each other and even, after some stormy grief, exchange congratulations on escaping a bigamist whose determination had failed to equal his evil desire.

Yes, flight was the only way out of his difficulties. To leave Los Angeles, before the police came to arrest him or his fiancées to marry him – that must be his plan. For a minute Juan wondered if he had best get up and dress and start at once, but various considerations persuaded him that he might safely wait till morning. He lay down, more comfortable now that so much was decided, and considered where he should go. Back East, or into Mexico, or north to San Francisco, perhaps into Canada?

But there was a safer and more comfortable refuge than any of these, that he suddenly remembered with joyful relief. The Motley establishment at Santa Barbara was open to him, and no one would think of looking for a runaway criminal, a Hollywood super and putative bigamist, in the dignified luxurious home of Aunt Ruth Maitland Motley.

Now Juan felt at ease again – or nearly so – and his troubles dwindled when he found that not only could he escape them by so simple and radical a measure as leaving them behind him, but even find in them a reason for exchanging his present condition for one vastly more pleasant. . . . For he discovered, with the abruptness of revelation, that he was tired of consorting with men like Nikitin and all the other scamps and queer fish of the past twelve months, and wanted to live henceforward with people of his own kind. He stretched himself more luxuriously between the sheets and began to contemplate the joys of his new life. . . . He would leave in the early morning, saying good-bye to no one, for it was not safe to linger, since the police might be soon on his track, and there was in any case no one (save Isadore, perhaps) whose acquaintance he wished to seal with a leave-taking or distinguish with regrets for its premature conclusion – the Prince and the Baron were amusing fellows, Nikitin was a good rogue, Phryne a handsome woman; but they represented Hollywood, and Hollywood was the last chapter in the vagabond life that he was going to forsake for ever, and of which he wanted no memories. . . .

Juan pulled his pillow into a more comfortable shape and breathed contentedly. He was going to live an ordered and settled life with the graces of civilisation and the safeguards of discipline. He would probably say yes to his grandfather Lowell's offer to find him a place in the Motley Bank. He would settle down. His cousins were young and pretty, educated, cleverer than poor Jill, mannered to an easy pride, quick-witted perhaps, certainly merry. He was going to Santa Barbara to stay with them in that exquisite country where all kinds of flowers and shrubs grew in obedient gardens, flowers that were natives of every country under the sun and shrubs characteristic of California only in that they grew there more luxuriantly than in their own homes. Whatever was planted flourished. He remembered what he had seen while driving with Jill and Genevieve.

With incredible felicity the coast-line provided a *décor* more romantic than anyone had a right to expect. In it were combined the grandeur of the castled Rhine and the blandness of South Sea islands. Rugged headlands thrust their impetuous rock faces into a sea as mild as milk but infinitely more beautiful – a silky sea all blue and iridescent, covered with tiny lines as though the breeze had a graving-tool in its fingers and wantonly scratched the sapphire surface as it flew hither and thither. And wherever the tide leapt on to a hidden reef dazzling white flowers would burst out of the blue sea. Up they shot like snowy carnations, spread themselves, and died in a flat surge of foam. They looked so robust, these glittering sea-flowers, that it was always a surprise to discover how frail and short-lived they really were. Sometimes the tide was wanton and worried a virtuous promontory by lifting its lace-edged skirt cliff-high, like a ballet-dancer. Every time a wave reached up in this manner it threw off a cloud of spray that glittered in the balmy air high above the walls of the house that often crowned the outraged promontory. For as the new Californians had an eye for the picturesque and money to gratify their desires, many of the more attractive cliffs were topped with houses in the Spanish style of building, all red roof and white walls and arched windows and great wooden doors with iron hinges.

Trees also entered into the romantic conspiracy and grew cunningly about the shore – cypresses and Californian firs that were warped and twisted in their endeavours to escape the annoyance of the wind: no surly breeze, but a humorous company of bluff airs that plagued and tickled them. And the more warped and twisted they grew the more picturesque they looked, till no one could think of these fantastic growths as cousins to the neat domestic Christmas tree. Their branches were knotted and awry, curving like snakes or bent in apparent pain like a witch's back, and their needles grew in great sprouting tufts. Sometimes the branches all stretched in one direction and at one level, so as to make a canopy and a patch of shadow. Such trees were the very picture of pain and fear as they tugged and strained to escape the frolicking wind; but their pain and fear had no more actuality – in that mild climate – than the dragons, twisted and writhing in stranger attitudes than the trees, that Chinese artists saw in a storm-haunted sky and waves' crests rearing long necks to engulf a drowning man. The fierceness of Chinese dragons was a fantastic and airy quality made from the grinning of angry clouds and the hissing of the sinuous sea. Sometimes they guarded treasure. There had been a dragon on Kuo Kuo's tunic that was a treasure-guarding beast. . . .

I should like to have seen her again, thought Juan. She was secret and Chinese, hidden from neck to ankle, from wrist to wrist, in black clothes, and under the silk (he remembered his dream about her) alabaster tinted with yellow wine, so different from the dull white flesh of Salvator's other disciples. . . . But these exotic fancies were not in tune with a settled estate among his own people. Not with Kuo Kuo but with his cousins Sylvia and Marcia would he spend his time. They would pass long days on the shore. They would amuse themselves with simplicity on the rocks – Juan grew sleepy and there was peace in the thought of childish pleasures – on the rocks in the salt air that condoned childishness. They would find seaweed, brown rubbery strips ten feet long like broad tough ribbon, and tapering growths with a hollow bulb at one end, that cut cleanly and tasted villainously if you tried to suck water through. They would catch small crabs in the way he used when he was a boy. First you found a mussel (they grew in navy-blue beds, tighter packed than a pile of plates), and broke it up. Then you tied one of the tougher bits of meat to a string and fished with that, dangling it in a clear and apparently empty pool. Slowly, with infinite caution, a claw appeared from an invisible crevice, touched the bait, drew back – then another claw and snap! the lure was taken. Now you pulled quickly and three times out of five the crab hung on, kicking at the tenuous air and vicious as a snake to find itself on bare rock. . . . You could throw what was left of the mussel into a sea-anemone and watch the soft purple spikes bend over it and pull it in, spike closing after spike, avid for a share, till the green edges of the anemone were folded in like wet velvet and the shred of mussel was hidden somewhere in a smooth and innocent-seeming pincushion. Childishness was proper at the sea-side. . . .

Then he would go back to New York and work comfortably in his grandfather's bank. . . .

But that vision was not so clear, and his brain being three parts asleep would not deal with it. His drowsy thoughts returned to sea-laziness and pictures of waves coming ashore from long Pacific voyaging. They came in smooth and sleek, level-drawn, and then at one point crumbled into foam. The dazzling white rot spread to either side all along the crest, and in a second the whole wave was a boiling front of surf shot with opaque but sunlit green. Broken water surged to shore, moving thickly, like oil paint, like Chinese white, with patines of bottle-green between its creamy ridges. And then the colours coalesce and fade and grow thin, and finally disappear to leave a green translucence among the rocks.

Or a wave would burst on a reef, leaping high with a great white *panache*, and tumble with a roar across the jagged obstacle, and leave grey stone showing once more behind a hundred shining waterfalls. In narrow inlets the water would rise and long seaweed that just previously had stretched all its ribbons seaward would slowly bend and curl backwards, languorously straighten itself and point to shore with a look of easy certainty that this was the best way to lie, and this way, flat and comfortable, it would lie for evermore. But the water would recede and take the seaware with it, drawing it out, caressing it, till it lay again smooth and straight with its fingers reaching for ocean. . . .

X

Juan woke early and got out of bed with the brisk decision of a man whose course of action is both clear to see and pleasant to contemplate. Morning had brought no change of counsel, but rather fortified him in his intentions. While he shaved he thought of the police who might soon be looking for him, and would find him gone, and as he packed he considered the welcome that awaited him in Santa Barbara. His preparations for departure were soon made, and the stript appearance of his room – with all the untidinesses of his occupation now more straitly confined in a suitcase – gave him the satisfaction one has in cleanly striking camp and facing a new day, another hill, a strange champaign; with the added assurance, in his case, that the approaching country would be fitted with all the conveniences of wealth and the circumstances of leisure. His landlady, to whom he paid a month's rent and explained that he had been unexpectedly summoned to New York, was distressed to find him going, and her husband the dentist – a good man with his mouth half-full of breakfast – made equal protestations of regret. When these domestic civilities were over Juan put his luggage into his motor car and drove to an hotel.

He bought a newspaper in the lobby and going into the coffee-room ordered half a cantaloupe, bacon and eggs, and coffee. While he waited for them to be brought he looked through his paper to see if there was any reference to the outrage at Mr. Pumpenstempel's. . . . On the front page there was a column by his old friend Mr. Adelaide, whose repentance had been as brief as the period of his fear, there was a story of municipal mismanagement and fraud in one of the civic departments; there was an account of triple murder in Chicago, committed – so it was alleged – by Red-eye Rod Gehenna's men as a punitive measure on the last of Buck Maloney's gang.– So Red-eye still held his sceptre and ruled as fiercely in Chicago as he had on Egret Island.– On page three there was a picture of a steam-yacht and a paragraph which stated that Mr. Pumpenstempel and a distinguished party had arrived in Los Angeles and would probably stay for a few days before proceeding to Vancouver Island for the salmon fishing. But there was no reference to his private orchestra or the catastrophe which had attended its unexpected performance. . . . On another page a society gossip-writer commented at length and in extravagant terms on the brilliant series of entertainments with which Princess Phryne of Pretzel-Oppenheim was so enriching the season. . . .

There appeared to be no news of criminal proceedings instigated against Nikitin or of the assault committed upon Mr. Pumpenstempel, and Juan ate his cantaloupe at leisure. But when he had finished it and was waiting for bacon and eggs he thought he would look again lest he had missed an obscure and late-inserted paragraph.– Now he glanced at headlines which intimated a fashionable divorce, an aeroplane accident, and a discussion whether Prohibition agents should, in the normal course of their duties, be entitled to arrest expectant mothers. Rapidly he scanned minor news-titles:

Filipino Found Bound, Beaten, Gagged, Slain.
Boy Stealing Bread Killed by Policeman.
Woman's Club Leader Slave of Narcotics.
New Charge in Corruption Probe Bared.
Eagle Tests Speed Plane.
Father Slays Children, Self.
Slain Woman's Kin in Net.
Refusal to Salute Flag Wins Six Months Sentence.
Mexico Holds Red Envoy in Assassin Quiz.
New Charges in Corruption Probe Bared.
Solon Under Fire for Christ Criticism.
Judge Parts 1030 in Month.
Millionaire Faces Big Balm Suit.
Sweeping Prohi Quiz Demanded by Dry Senator –

but all this was everyday stuff of no particular interest, and Juan passed it over without reading more than the headlines. Then, on the point of turning a page, he saw 'Interesting Recruit for School of Thoughtlessness,' and with strange and mixed sensations read the following paragraph:

'Dr. Julius Salvator's well-known colony at Arroyo Beach, where it is a misdemeanour to think even the smallest thought, has just attracted a newcomer in the person of Miss Kuo Kuo, a Chinese visitor to this country. Miss Kuo, an attractive brunette, is the grand-daughter of a mandarin of high rank, and her father was a close friend of Sun Yat Sen. She has travelled widely and is keenly interested in various national and international movements affecting the youth of to-day. After studying phases of Western thought in Los Angeles and San Francisco she was attracted by Dr. Salvator's theories, which have been favourably received by many of our leading citizens, and decided to investigate the results of organised thoughtlessness. "It will be interesting to see if there is any difference," she says. Miss Kuo leaves for Arroyo Beach to-day.'

Juan's bacon and eggs were growing cold before he began to eat them. The details of his dream about Kuo Kuo returned with great clarity, and a lively sensation revived of his disappointment when he failed to trace her after their brief meeting at Princess Phryne's garden party. It was curious that he should discover her whereabouts now when it was too late and his plans for the future were all made. Curious and tantalising. He recalled her enigmatic smile, her attitude, amused and aloof, among all the noisy people in whom there were so few secrecies. And her quest, that might be mockery or dead earnest under a veneer of self-amusement, for a Superior Person. . . .

Clearly she was no convert to Salvator's theories. She was joining his colony for her own purpose, not to become a torpid seal on the beach, but to watch the solemnity with which the disciples embraced their strange ambition. . . . She had contemplated, if she spoke truth, an ideal end to her wanderings, an end of Confucian excellence, and certainly in the past Chinese travellers had journeyed far in search of knowledge, crossing the great deserts of Central Asia, where they were plagued by hot devils and cold, and wind-driven spectres of the sand, until at last they reached the sources of wisdom in Benares and holy Ganges. But on their journey they found interest in demons, and desert tribes, and simple mountain-dwellers, and bewildered peasants. . . . Kuo Kuo had confessed to finding profane amusement by the roadside, and the longer the road the more occasions there would be for such enjoyment. Now, it seemed likely, she had resolved to make a détour, lured from the high road by Salvator's encampment in a nonsensical by-way. . . .

Juan felt restless, as though some new alacrity were invading or rousing in the marrow of his bones. Up his veins crept a tide of happy excitement, small at first, like the silver-tipped waves that follow slack-water and show that flood is making. And this morning feeling of alertness, excitement, and flood-tide was accompanied by a growing disdain of all his rich comfortable plans, so that his previous vision of contentment now seemed uninviting, and the anticipation of ease became a corpulent filling of arm-chairs. The steam of the flesh-pots was too heavy. Fatness clung to the mere vapour, and the rich smell cloyed his nostrils. Better was the salt wind of adventure, a delectable offer of laughter, and more alluring than any domestic prospect was Kuo Kuo herself, lovely as moonlight in a dark dragon-guarded dress, inscrutable as her ancient land, now grave as a pilgrim, now with the mocking-bird's tune on her rose-red lips. . . .

Perhaps, thought Juan it was a little early for him to think of settling down. To settle down was an admirable thing to do, of course, if one chose the proper time. But his resolution had been premature. There was danger in settling down too soon. One had to sacrifice a great deal of freedom in return for a little profit and a great deal of propriety. One had to exchange the high road for a rut in the road from which one could see nothing of the raree-shows, the jugglers and mountebanks who performed in the ditches and wandered down irrelevant lanes. And as for choosing a mode of life for no other reason than that it offered security, that was surely something to be ashamed of. Some green-sickness of the mind must have attacked him before he thought of creeping into the shelter of the Motley family tree, however much gold it grew. To think of entering a bank and joining a complacent domestic circle!

That was not the choice of Purchas his Pilgrims, the record of whose exploits had once heartened him. Such dull intentions had never crossed the minds of John Jourdain, and Andrew Battell who went to Guinea, and Gonzalez who voyaged to Easter Island, and the author of *Cathay and the Way Thither*, between whose leaves, as if for a pledge, he had left an unwanted ring. Their sailing directions had never included instructions to catch the tide which, taken at the flood, cast one high and dry on the beach and left one to call that fortune which was rather a banishing from the high seas.

'I might have done a very foolish and ill-considered thing,' said Juan to himself. 'Good God, I might even have gone into a bank!'

And finishing his coffee he went to pay his bill and ask the way to Arroyo Beach.